MW01105903

His reaction took her totally by surprise. How could he do this to her?

"Any more good news?" The sarcasm rolled off his tongue. "That's not what I'm concerned with."

"Then what?"

"The way he looked at you."

"Don't worry about it. We're adults here."

"Exactly."

"Frank, please. Can't you deal with this?"

He did a double take. "Know what, Sam? No. I can't. And I didn't realize you're so emotionally disconnected." He checked the clock and blew out a deep breath. "As soon as it hits daylight, I think it's best that you go back to your place." He rolled over onto his left side, his back facing her.

"What are you saying, Frank?"

He barely turned his head. "Use your psychic intuition to figure out what I'm saying."

"You're breaking up with me?"

"I think we need to distance ourselves. It's been too hot and heavy these past eight weeks, anyway. You're not the woman I thought I knew."

"How in hell are we supposed to distance ourselves? We work cases together. Every day, if I have to remind you."

"Keep it formal. I'm now Dr. Khaos from you, and you're Detective Wright from me."

"But—"

"No buts. I'm done. We're done." His stomach twisted as he uttered those last two words.

Scorpio obsessed, with a mind as strong as twisted steel, Henry Slater, suave, sophisticated, sexy, intelligent, and wealthy is the perfect man—except to women who tell him what he doesn't want to hear.

Dr. John Trenton is called back to NYC for a case close to his heart, while NYPD Detective Samantha "Sam" Wright and forensic psychiatrist Doctor Frank Khaos, conflicted about their on-again-off-again relationship, take on another case—a serial killer who's orchestrated sixteen murders across the United States over a nine-year period. The seventeenth victim is Sam's best friend, Carrie Baines. When forensic science connects Frank to Slater, Frank is pushed to delve into his past, something he swore never to do. Meanwhile, due to the interstate nature of the crimes, the FBI gets involved, convincing Sam to go undercover. But Slater is clever, and Sam is no match for him. Will her psychic skills and police training be enough to survive this close encounter with a killer, or will she end up as his eighteenth victim? And even if she lives, is her relationship with Frank really over?

KUDOS for *Scorpio*

In *Scorpio* by Ronnie Allen, NYPD Detective Samantha Wright is back, and this time her best friend has been murdered. Dr. Frank Khaos, her on again, off again, lover, thinks she should pass on the case as she is too close emotionally, but Sam refuses, determined to find her friend's killer. In the meantime, a former patient of Dr. John Trenton's is killed, and John comes back to New York to work the case, this time bringing his wife, son, and newborn twins. As Sam and Frank investigate her best friend's murder, they discover that she was the victim of a serial killer—a smart, clever, and cunning man who picks up women in casinos. Someone who doesn't make many mistakes. Sam and her team have their work cut out for them, tracking a killer who seems to be always one step ahead of them. Like Allen's first two books, this one is filled with fascinating characters, an intriguing mystery, some hot sex scenes, and plenty of surprises. I'm betting you won't be able to put it down. ~ *Taylor Jones, The Review Team of Taylor Jones & Regan Murphy*

Scorpio by Ronnie Allen is the third book in Allen's The Sign Behind the Crime series. As such it has some big shoes to fill, but Allen doesn't disappoint. We are reunited with all our favorite characters from the first two books: NYPD Detective, Samantha Wright, forensic psychiatrists John Trenton and Frank Khaos, and Frank's little boy Frankie. As the story opens, Sam's best friend Carrie is playing the slots in a Queens casino, when she is hit on by a serial killer. He charms Carrie, seduces, and kills her, leaving Sam both devastated and determined to bring him to justice. But this killer's smart and Sam may have met her match. When Frank discovers that the lead detective on the case is the brother of the man who killed Frank's wife, he refuses to work with him. Frank and Sam argue, and Frank breaks up with her. Unrelated to Carrie's murder, John

Trenton is called back to New York because one of his former patients was killed, and the cops need John's help. Then Sam's team discovers some disturbing DNA evidence in Carrie's case that turns it on its ear, and John's unique skills are needed on that one as well. As usual, Allen has crafted a tale that is intense, intriguing, sexy, and full of surprises. Scorpio's a page turner that you won't easily put down. ~ *Regan Murphy, The Review Team of Taylor Jones & Regan Murphy*

ACKNOWLEDGEMENTS

Wow! It's the third book in my series two years and four months from the time I was first published in June 2015. What an amazing journey it's been and I couldn't have done it without some very special people who have helped me make *Scorpio* the best it could be before I submitted it. I wholeheartedly want to thank my critique partners and beta readers Sue Pellegrino, Sherry Wilson, Judi Oglio, Jeff Read, and Darlene Corcoran. They spent hours reading, taking notes, discussing plot points and plot holes, all to help a friend. I'm forever grateful.

I also called upon again Ralph Bud Brumley, FBI retired, who helped me create credible scenarios. Any pushing the boundaries of protocol is on me. After all, *Scorpio* is a work of fiction. And again, Butchy Lyon, retired CO at Rikers, assisted me in adding prison details.

And I also called upon again MMA fighter Christopher Lyon for some insider information about the goings-on in the training gym.

My casino security consultant, Tom Toth, gave me valuable information that assisted with major parts of the plot. In regards to the casino, there is one in Queens but *Scorpio*'s casino has a hotel and a buffet. The casino in this book is fictionalized and in no way meant to resemble the real one.

I also want to thank Lauri and Faith at Black Opal Books for seeing my vision, and Jack in the art department for creating my awesome cover.

And, of course, I want to thank my husband, Bob, who totally understood that I had to spend more time in my characters' heads than with him.

SCORPIO

THE SIGN BEHIND THE CRIME
BOOK 3

RONNIE ALLEN

A Black Opal Books Publication

GENRE: PSYCHOLOGICAL SUSPENSE/MYSTERY/THRILLER

This is a work of fiction. Names, places, characters and incidents are either the product of the author's imagination or are used fictitiously, and any resemblance to any actual persons, living or dead, businesses, organizations, events or locales is entirely coincidental. All trademarks, service marks, registered trademarks, and registered service marks are the property of their respective owners and are used herein for identification purposes only. The publisher does not have any control over or assume any responsibility for author or third-party websites or their contents.

SCORPIO ~ The Sign Behind the Crime ~ Book 3
Copyright © 2017 by Ronnie Allen
Cover Design by Jackson Cover Designs
All cover art copyright © 2017
All Rights Reserved
Print ISBN: 978-1-626947-75-7

First Publication: OCTOBER 2017

Published by Black Opal Books **http://www.blackopalbooks.com**

CHAPTER 1

The clanging of hundreds of slot machines—with their glaring lights bombarding her at the threshold of the casino entrance—screeched through her body. She froze.

Finally. Let's make these babies rock.

Carrie Baines gritted her teeth. Her jaw tightened. If someone spoke to her, she couldn't answer. As she wiped her sweaty palms on the sides of her thighs, she felt her tight jeans absorb the moisture. Crap. Her thighs felt damp. The frigid air conditioning didn't do her any favors either.

Come on, girl. Get a grip.

Inhaling deeply, in an attempt to calm the ripples of tension that riveted through her body, proved to be futile. This was not her usual adrenalin rush that made her heart pulsate and nearly jump out of her chest. Today was different. She didn't like it and couldn't figure out why. She'd decided to stand there until the trembling ceased. Not for long, though.

She yanked her VIP Players Card from her cross-body bag and pulled the green beaded lanyard down around her neck. It hung low by her navel and bopped up and away from her body as she strutted around the perimeter of the casino to the Player's Counter in the far right.

She knew she had points on it from her trip here last weekend. Not sure how many, but it would comp her room—which she knew—but she wanted money left over for food. Every penny was worth saving—for the slots.

As she walked, she nodded to the casino staff who knew her. The men and women wearing white shirts and navy blue trousers with sets of master keys hanging from their belts smiled back. They'd better smile at her. She certainly tipped them enough after she cashed out a win or when they brought her the-much-needed drink—scotch and ginger ale on the rocks. She loved this casino in Queens, New York. The machines were all new and when she hit—it was big. Well, sort of big. She'd be happy with any payoff that was bigger than what she had put into the machine. Most of the time, she came home with a few hundred more than she went with. The other times, well, she lost everything and more—too much more. Still, she wasn't concerned. This was her catharsis. The loud noises, excitement, glaring lights got her mind off her problems. Best of all, the casino was a hundred percent smoke-free.

Feeling herself relax, she smiled at the clerk standing behind the counter as she handed over her ID.

"Thank you, Miss Baines." The clerk entered Carrie's numbers into the system. Then she delivered the news with a smile. "You have additional comps for two lunches and two dinners, you lucky woman."

"Oh, thank you so much!" Carrie retrieved her ID and replaced it in her bag as she walked away, thinking that she'd dine at the buffet today.

She was on a mission.

Traversing the narrow lanes between the various machines, Carrie glanced at the top of them just quickly enough to identify them. Five cents. Nope. Quarter. Nope. Dollar. Um, maybe. She looked at the machines on either side of her as she meandered down the green tweed carpet, watching people play. One machine caught her eye— though it wasn't her favorite. For the life of her—every time she'd try to find the three dollar machine that could pay off twenty-one thousand with wild sevens—she couldn't find it. Oh well, she'd play this one, she thought as sat down at a triple diamond dollar machine. One where she could bet on a number of lines, and the amount she wanted to bet per line. She pulled a hundred dollar bill from an envelope that she kept in a secret compartment of her bag and slipped the bill into the money slot. As the machine counted her credits, she put her player's card into the appropriate slot. She looked at the keys, noting her choices as if she was mesmerized. Okay, she'd start off slow. Nine lines, the max, one buck each. That would give her eleven pulls. She sat up tall on the stool in front of the machine, wiggling her tush to make herself comfortable. With her index finger, she set the bet and then tapped the spin key. The tape inside the machine rolled with some unidentifiable music emanating from within, as the bars in front of her landed with diamonds, sevens, and bars in uneven lines—yielding her nothing. She pulled again. Nothing. And again. Nothing.

Come on, Carrie, get your butt off this stool.

Nope. It was as if glue stuck her butt to the seat, forcing her to use her last dollar. She continued to press the repeat-bet key two more times. Nothing. Then she got brave. She upped her bet to two bucks times nine a pull. That would give her three more pulls. She set the bet and pressed play. Nothing. Again, nothing. And nothing. She slapped her thigh. She had just blown a hundred bucks—in less than ten minutes. Oh well. She had lost more in less time. She had the entire weekend left and nineteen more hundred-dollar bills. Plus the ATM if she needed it.

෬෬෬

He watched the curvy brunette with the waist-long ponytail for ten minutes. Looked like Lady Luck wasn't on her side. Grinning, he sat on a stool diagonal to her so he could watch her expressions. She hadn't taken her gaze off the machine to even bother to check to see who was around her. Not a smart move—especially in a casino. At least she had

kept her bag on her lap. She didn't flinch a muscle after losing the Franklin. He assumed she must have money to
spare. His type. As she swirled around in the stool to dis-
mount, his assumption was verified. That was some multi-
gemstone ring with about a thirty-carat amethyst on her left
ring finger. No wedding band? This prospect suddenly became approachable. She got off the stool and turned in his
direction. His gaze caught her oval brown eyes partially
covered with wispy bangs, along with a smile. He gener-
ously reciprocated.

He leaned back on the chair with an elbow on the
backrest not to appear that much interested. As she walked
past him, he shifted his body so he could get a glimpse of
her from the rear. Oh man, those black designer skinny
jeans certainly did her ass justice. Or was that the other way
around? What the fuck? It didn't matter. This woman
spelled hot. He wondered what her occupation was that
she'd have off on a Friday in the middle of winter along
with the desire to spend that day here with a blizzard raging. He figured he'd just follow before he attempted a meet
and greet. Last thing he wanted was for her to be here with
girlfriends to interrupt their rendezvous or a boyfriend. That
would be the worst possible scenario. One that he would
avoid at all costs.

He had time today. His work obligation that brought him
here was complete. This was going to be a relaxing day,
hopefully with a woman whom he'd never see again. Not
just any woman. She had to meet certain criteria. Gorgeous.
Smart. Rich. Free with her body. And most important of
all…

A woman who wouldn't trigger his painful memories.

ꙮꙮꙮ

Carrie walked down the aisle passing the poker tables to
the rear end of the casino. She didn't give the tables a sec-

ond glance. That wasn't her thing. As she walked, she
thought about why. At the tables, she had to think too
much. Winning or losing was her responsibility. Not really—the dealer was in control—but she had to pay attention.
Another reason she never joined table games. Focus and
thinking weren't her strong points when she wanted an escape. She shivered as she let that self-realization register.
With the slots, she could sit back and descend into dream-
land. She only woke up and paid attention when she hit a
bonus. Then she didn't take her gaze off the multiple spins.
Okay, she was off to find the machines with the bonus
wheels. She knew what section they were in, but walking in
a casino, to her, was like walking in a maze. Going four
right turns would never get you back to your starting point.

It felt as if she had walked back and forth a long time.
Too long not to play. She looked down at her trembling
hands. She'd have to compromise until she'd found the
right machines. Sitting on another stool in front of the blaz-
ing sevens slots calmed her for the time being. Okay, five
bars, three across, two diagonal. One buck a line. Good,
she'd be a little frugal this time. Again, she wiggled her
tush in the seat and plucked another hundred from her envelope.

As she slipped the bill into the slot, he sat down on the
stool next to her. His knee touched her thigh when he
swiped his leg around. She felt the tap and looked up. "Oh,
hi!" She studied him just for a split second. "Following
me?"

He shot her a wickedly sexy grin. "To be honest, yeah, I
was."

"Honesty, I like that." She chuckled as she looked him
over a little more thoroughly. His navy blue sports jacket
over a maroon polo and indigo dress slacks fit him real
good. He was big—way over six feet—with muscles that
bulged from the jacket sleeves. He wore tinted squared off
glasses, so she couldn't see his eyes. The lines on his face
under his unshaven skin suited him. His bald head, too.

Carrie smiled as she returned her focus to the machine. She tapped the square to the right—max bet. The wheels spun. To her surprise, she hit. Big whoopee, ten bucks. She frowned.

"Hey, it's better in your pocket."

She didn't turn her head. "Oh, you're still here?"

"Yeah. I'm still here."

She turned toward him, this time smirking.

He extended his hand to shake. "Henry. Henry Slater."

Okay, a gentleman. "Carolyn Baines. Most people call me Carrie." She took his hand, intimidated by his firm grasp.

"Hello, Carolyn Baines. I prefer your real name, if you don't mind. It's more womanly."

"That's so sweet."

Henry smiled. "You like these machines, don't you?"

"You think? I love it!"

He emitted a hearty laugh. "Yeah. I do, too. Don't get here much, though."

"Sorry, to cut the conversation short. I have to get back."

"To where?"

"To my machine!" She turned away, facing the monster head on, erecting an imaginary barrier between herself and the hunk. Yeah, he was some hunk, but no time for a man now.

Go try to get another woman into bed, Henry Slater. I'm done with men like you. Even the one, not like you, who I married.

Carrie pressed the max bet button again. As soon as it yielded nothing, she pressed again immediately—not even giving herself a chance to breathe. The nape of her neck became damp with sweat. She wrung her hands together on her lap. Crap. She just blew another hundred bucks. In twenty minutes this time—no thanks to that intruder. She swiveled around on the stool, her knees bumping into his.

"Looks like you're not a happy camper right now."

She rolled her eyes at him. "So, you're the slot police?"

"No, but I do know when to quit."

"I'm a long way from quitting. Now if you'll excuse me." She got off the stool, but it was crowded in the aisle. She had to body swipe him to get around him. As soon as she passed him, it struck her. That hunk turned her on.

Not now, Carrie. Not now. You have to keep it together, girl. Money's for the taking and I intend to grab it.

Interrupting her thoughts, she felt his hand on her shoulder. She turned around and had to look way up and she wasn't used to having to look that high up, either. His over six feet, was more like six four or five. At five eight, she'd barely hit his shoulders. "What?"

"Mind if I tag along?"

"Yes! I do. You brought me bad luck."

"Really, what about the first hundred?"

"My God! You were sitting close enough. Leave me alone!" She stormed off and pushed through the crowd, earning her dirty looks from the other patrons who then glared at Slater, but said nothing in her defense.

Carrie walked quickly, looking around and up to escape him. His bulky frame couldn't be missed for sure. When she was certain he was out of sight, she turned the corner into another lane. She didn't know how she did it but she had meandered into the aisle with her favorite machine. Too bad, it was taken. She decided to wait. She sat down on a stool opposite the machine, turning her head from side to side looking for her stalker. After a minute, she relaxed when she was confident he had disappeared. The guy at the machine began to rise from the stool. Carrie's excitement readied, but no sooner than she prepared to get up, she felt a tug on her arm. It was him. The behemoth, Henry Slater.

He yanked her down on the stool before she could respond. "How about some lunch?"

She jerked her arm away. "Excuse me! You don't waste any time do you?" She shot him a glare that usually worked on other men she'd tried to dissuade. No luck with this one.

"Come on, you look hungry and maybe some food in

that…uh…toned belly of yours, would change your luck."

"And just how does one look hungry?"

"The desperate look, like you have now, biting your lower lip."

Carrie's eyes widened. "Now you're a shrink?"

"Nope. I'm in the restaurant business. It's my job to know how to draw people in to my venues. And to know when a good meal will make them feel all better."

Carrie laughed. "What a line. Have much success with that?"

Henry slipped his hand into his pocket and pulled out a business card holder. He plucked his card from a slot and handed it to her.

Carrie read the card aloud. "Um, Henry Slater, CEO of Foods Unlimited, supplying the best eateries in casinos in the US." She fingered the black card embossed with gold lettering.

Nice, if it's real.

"So how long have you been Foods Unlimited, Henry?" she asked as she slipped his card into her right jeans pocket.

"I've always been in restaurant management—a frustrated failing chef, I guess. I started the biz about nine years ago. Been real successful. What about you?"

Carrie lowered her eyes before she responded, then her gaze met his. "I'm a hair dresser in a salon in Manhattan. Color. Cuts. The usual."

He laughed, pointing to his shaved head. "Don't count on me to be a customer."

Carrie laughed. "No kidding."

"Come on, how about it? Some lunch?"

"Yeah, okay. I am getting those annoying little hunger pangs. I was thinking about the buffet."

"The buffet it is."

Carrie walked next to Henry to the main aisle around the perimeter of the slot machines. She felt the heat of his strength through his jacket. This was one powerful man. Could she cope with a guy like him? Does she even want

to? She'd hold off on her decision until after lunch. Thank
God, the air conditioning was on high. She was sweating in
the second week of January. The escalator to the buffet was
on the far end of the casino from where they started. Carrie
knew her way, better than most. Their silent walk intimidated her, especially when she caught the sexy smirk plastered on his face. She halted. He abruptly turned toward
her.

"What?"

"Uh, I don't know if this is such a good idea."

"Lunch?"

"Yes."

"What are you paranoid about?"

"Some vibes I'm getting."

"You need to loosen up, little lady. At least you can
come in and admire my work. I designed the buffet."

"Seriously?"

"Sure did. The seven stations, menus for each, seating,
artwork, dinnerware placement, cases, even hired the personnel. The entire architecture. You have nothing to be
afraid of. Everyone in there knows me. Hell. They'd better.
I sign their pay checks."

That's what she needed to hear. Carrie relaxed and continued on their stroll.

At the top of the escalator, she stopped dead at the end-
less line that curled around six lanes and continued to the
rest room about a hundred feet away. A line like this meant
over an hour wait. She liked to eat fast and resume play.
Wasting time was not on her agenda.

"Oh my God! Do you know how long we'll have to wait
here?"

"Come on. I'll show you my magic. Then you'll believe
me and relax." Henry led her to the side entrance, and, before he opened the rope barrier, an employee greeted them.

"Hello again, Mr. Slater. Your usual table is unoccupied." He slipped open the latch on the rope and led them
in.

As they walked to their table opposite the fresh carvings section about fifteen "Hello, Mr. Slaters" came across loud and clear. *Okay, this guy is on the up and up* went through Carrie's brain. He didn't have time to plan this. She needed to relax.

"Do you know what you feel like?"

"Definitely. I know this place well."

They walked to the first plate deck. Carrie grabbed one and took off. She first hit the fresh seafood bar and piled her plate full of peel-and-eat shrimp, then clams on the half shelf. Lastly, she filled the little white ounce cup with cock-tail sauce. Back at their table, Carrie looked up and faced the oil painting on the wall opposite her. A huge maroon, non-descript abstract accosted her gaze. She found the painting unsettling, dark, close to ominous. She scanned the rest of the art—mostly maroon or dark reds in tone, dark blue-red leather upholstery on the seating, the same for napkins and place settings. There were black accents in the art and some other primary colors, but the emphasis was serious. The beige marble tile floor with black veining was stunning and lightened the atmosphere—glistening and immaculate. She contemplated on the painting as she ab-sentmindedly peeled a shrimp and tossed it into her mouth.

Henry returned with his plate filled with sushi, chicken and veggies, a couple of egg rolls from the Asian station. He sat opposite her.

"What's with the faraway look in your eyes?"

She startled as if she hadn't been cognizant that he had sat down. "Oh, The paintings. They're striking. But what's with all the dark maroons?"

"That's simple. I'm a Scorpio and dark maroon is my color." He cocked his head and pointed to his polo.

"Seriously? You decorated your restaurant according to your astro sign?"

"For sure. All of them. It's my signature."

"Interesting. How come?"

"Good energy for me."

"Such as?"

"Aggressive. Relentless until I get what I want. Great organizer. And for your information only, at the moment, highly sexual."

She sat back and flipped her fork onto her plate. "I knew you'd be going there."

"What's wrong with that? You attached?"

"No. I'm recently divorced."

"How recent?"

"A few months. Actually, not officially. We're separated. Not ready to accept another man into my life. What about you?"

"Never been. Have any kids?"

"No. I don't."

Carrie noticed Henry's expression became somber at her answer. He looked away for a moment but she ignored it and downed the shrimp and clams. She refilled her plate a few more times—mostly with salads and grilled steak. So did Henry.

They talked through their lunch, Carrie becoming comfortable with this man. He seemed open with everything, about his life, businesses, even his painful childhood. She, on the other hand, lied her way through. She'd have a hell of a time recalling what she had told him. Her life would never be an open book with all the demons in her closet, especially with someone she'd just met. But then again, who knows if he told the truth, about anything?

She had even kept secrets from her BFF.

Samantha Wright, her very own best friend forever, Sam, had left their profession to join the NYPD. Now she was a detective, of all things.

All during her personal reflections, she felt Henry's gaze on her. He kept a compassionate, non-judgmental expression on his face. Maybe she could deal with a man like him. She deserved to relax after what she'd been through.

Yeah, she deserved it. Getting laid would definitely do her some good.

e⁄ɔe⁄ɔ

The elevator door slid three quarters open on the four-teenth floor and then jolted to a stop, leaving Carrie and Henry to face pitch-blackness in the hall. The jolt caused Carrie to fall against Henry who didn't hesitate to seize the moment and wrap his arms around her. She had to admit, his embrace felt like exactly what she needed right now. He pulled his cell out of his pocket and turned on the flashlight.

"Come on. The storm must have triggered a power out-age. They'll get it back up in a minute. How far down are you?"

"The end. The last room on the left."

The stroll down the hall to Carrie's room caused some anxiety within her that she couldn't control. She had just met this man and she was ready to hook up.

Come on, Carrie, there's still time to chuck this.

Her gut pulled at her, but her heart was yearning—for love, tenderness, the excitement of a man's touch—all of it. The past few months her body raged and couldn't take the neglect anymore.

They made it through the darkness with the flashlight guiding their way. At the door, Carrie fumbled in the front pocket of her bag for her room card. Henry kept the light on her. She flipped the card in her fingers and inserted it into the slot, opening the door. "It worked!"

"The back-up generator." After entering the room and Henry closing the door, the power returned. "See, I told you."

"You sure you want to be in here?"

"Yeah. I've been in my room a few days. Need a change." He walked in, pulled off his blazer and tossed it onto the club chair in the corner.

What she saw amazed and scared her at the same time. This man was cut! Ripped! Every vein bulged from his forearm up through his bicep. A juicehead wouldn't describe him. But steroided up to the gills or not, this man was hot.

He pulled her close and tugged her sweater that clung to her hips up and over her head. He wrapped his arms around her now bare waist.

"You don't waste any time, do you?"

"Nope. Getting too old to waste time."

She nodded in agreement. Reciprocating by pulling up his short-sleeved polo, Carrie felt the ripples in his six - pack as the front of her fingers skimmed his chest lifting the shirt. He helped her along when she couldn't reach any higher.

He grabbed her down on the bed, laying half on her, half on the bed. Henry slipped his hand behind her back and with a twist of his finger, unclasped her bra. He pulled her arms out and tossed it to the floor. He unbuttoned his slacks and pulled them off, with Carrie following suit. All in silence. All with a tempestuous look on his face. She studied him. She felt it was right.

With all their clothing carelessly on the floor, Henry took the lead, and began kissing her neck as he cascaded his hands down her body, up and down, landing on and cupping her breast then squeezing. She moaned, enjoying his touch. She didn't want him to stop. He pushed his body on top of hers and their lips met. They didn't come up for air. This man was consuming her and she was loving it. She wrapped her arms around his neck. He parted from her mouth and ran his lips down the side of her face, kissing her neck. With his left hand, he gently grasped her neck, and his lips sucked on her opposite side. She moaned and then quivered. The emotions that he had sent through her body were ones she hadn't experience in a long time.

He gently pecked her neck. "Did you just come?"

She breathed heavily. "Yes." She smiled.

"That's my favorite part of a woman's body. The neck. I could do wondrous things to yours." He winked at her, then ran two fingers down her breast, past her navel and stopped at her thatch. She separated her legs giving him permission to go further. He slipped two fingers into her, causing her to gasp. She writhed her body, moaning. This man knew how to please a woman in need. After a few minutes of probing with her juices enveloping him, he pulled his fingers out and wiped them on the sheet.

"Why did you do that? I was almost there." Her tone was pleading.

"You're a bad girl."

"How so?"

"You lied to me."

"How?"

"Hair salons in Manhattan don't close in snow storms. The snow melts as soon as it hits the ground because of the underground trains. I live in the city. That won't fly past me. Now you know what you're going to get for lying, you bad little girl?"

"Oh my God! What?"

He rolled her over on her stomach. "A spanking. That's what." He massaged her bottom to warm her up. Then gently, very gently, he swatted her bottom. Not even hard enough to turn her flesh a light shade of rose. More like love pats.

"You can go harder. You know."

"You like this?"

"Y—e—a—h. I love it."

"Okay then." He increased his firmness, giving her heartier full-handed spanks.

"Okay. Okay! Enough!" Carrie wiggled out of his grasp.

He flipped her around. "So now, bad little girl, what do you really do?"

His sizzling smile made her laugh and she had certainly asked for it. "Okay! I'll give in! I'm a teacher. Elementary school. Brooklyn schools don't close very often."

"Oh, man. Why didn't you tell me? I love teachers."

"Carrie caressed his arm. "You do?"

"Yes. They're warm and nurturing. Especially in elementary school. You have to love children. So do I."

"I do love children."

"This may be too forward of me to ask—"

"No, go ahead."

"So how come you don't have any?"

She hesitated. "You may or may not like this, but I decided early on that I didn't want any of my own."

His face reddened. His eyes widened. Carrie saw his expression change but she was too aroused to think in the moment.

"Why not?"

"Many reasons. I don't feel like getting into it right now."

"What if you meet a man you fall in love with? Is that carved in stone?"

"Six—feet—deep."

 espace

As soon as he saw the hostile look on her face, he sat up and straddled her body. As he lay back on his knees, with his groin on her midriff, the rage within him mounted. His anxiety erupted like a volcano. Wild, uncontrollable. Undirected.

You're just like my mother. My fucking bitch mother! That facial expression, looking at me in disgust.

Henry pounced on her, pinning her arms underneath him. She was rigid under his bulk. He grabbed onto her neck with both hands easily fitting around her. Carrie bucked. She wiggled, fighting him, trying to scream, but he deepened his grasp. She kicked up her legs, though wasn't able to bend her knees with his butt holding her down. His thumbs pressed on her trachea. He shook her, bringing her upper body up about ten inches above the bed, then down again, five times in rapid succession.

He pressed harder and felt a whoosh of air expel from

her crushed trachea. She coughed. Her eyes bulged from the lack of oxygen. In less than two minutes, she went limp and her head fell to the side of the pillow.

Henry sat up, perspiration dripping down from his neck over the scorpion tattoo that ran from the nape of his neck down to his waist. He couldn't stop hyperventilating. He couldn't stop himself. His heaving turned to sobbing as he leaned over Carrie's lifeless body.

He slipped her ponytail band out of her thick brown hair, put the band into the top drawer of the night stand, and then ran his fingers through her hair before he lovingly placed her mane over her smooth, once vibrant shoulders. "I didn't want to do this Carrie. I swear I didn't. I didn't plan for this to happen. It's been a year. Damnit! I tried to give you a way out. You didn't take it. So you gave me no choice. You triggered memories. Memories I tried so hard to forget."

Henry did concentrated deep breathing for a solid minute—yeah, he had to keep to his usual—and then he dismounted her. He stumbled into the bathroom, took a shower, sobbing, as the soap and water cleansed away his sweat and smell of sex, even though he didn't get any. After dressing hurriedly, looking around the room to make sure he didn't forget anything, he remembered to remove his card from Carrie's jeans pocket, and then his gaze sighted the thermostat in the air conditioning unit across the floorboard. Smirking, he nodded and fiddled with the dial. He then slipped his hand into his jacket pocket. He pulled out his master key card.

After putting his ear to a door in the room and not hearing any guests, he opened the door connecting Carrie's room to the one next door. He was well aware he was taking a risk. But, hey, it was late afternoon. The chance of anyone being in his or her room in a casino at this time was rare. He sauntered into the room, looked around. Good deal. Housekeeping completed. He put his ear to the connecting door. Again no voices. Henry smiled. This plan never failed him. He entered another room, this one in total disarray. He stood still for a moment with his gaze taking in the bedding that lay half on the bed, half on the floor, the clothes hanging out of the suitcases carelessly tossed in the corners—looked like three women shared this room. Yep, the bras hanging over the chair by the desk confirmed it. Ugh. This mess he couldn't tolerate. He tiptoed to the connecting door. This time he heard people arguing. Okay, his exit plan stopped. An omen? He stopped dead. Thoughts ran rampant.

"When will they stop me?" he whispered. He exited the room through the door to the hallway and disappeared into the stairwell across the hall.

CHAPTER 2

The world was freezing, and mourning. There was a saying that when it rained at a funeral the world was crying, too. Just like today. Sunday—the third Sunday in January—in the secluded back left corner of the largest Jewish cemetery in Nassau County, New York. It wasn't where Detective Samantha Wright wanted to be—in the middle of a raging snowstorm that mimicked her mood. She looked up at the sky—crying, as her tears mixed with the torrents of snow cascading her face and clothing—not being able to stop trembling—and it wasn't just from being cold.

She stood at the gravesite of her BFF, Carolyn Baines, as the gravediggers lowered the coffin, deep, into the ground. The wails of family members and former colleagues didn't compare to Sam's. The cemetery workers ignored her as she fell to her knees on the snow-whitened dirt. She had never lost control like this. She deserved to let loose one time. This wasn't work, where she had to hold it together.

Frank Khaos's arms reached under hers and lifted her up. She turned around and fell into his loving grasp, not at all concerned that the wet snow and graveled up dirt on her black pants suit were getting all over him. She buried her head deep into his bubble jacket. He rubbed her back, held her tightly, but there were no words. Sam didn't expect any.

She was just thankful for being held. She was thankful that Frank was now a part of her life—his son, Frankie, too—for the past two months.

Sam pulled away from Frank, weeping, and shuffled to Carrie's parents. She had known them since she was a kindergartner. She and Carrie had been inseparable since the first day they had met, while they both sat on a bench outside the principal's office waiting for him to reprimand them for arguing with each other. The principal told them to hug and make up and talk about the things they liked. Turned out they liked many of the same things—Sesame Street, dancing, and gymnastics. Moments flashed through her mind—as cheerleaders in junior high school, on the same debate team in college, sitting on the couch in their sorority house rambling on about the cutest boys. Sam gave a silent 'thank you' to God for that day in kindergarten. They had even taught in the same school in the northern section of Brooklyn. Yes, they were definitely best friends forever.

Three female colleagues approached, and they embraced. Their uncontrollable sobbing couldn't be muffled by the wind or snow. Everyone on Long Island could have heard them. The gravediggers finished, leaving the grave covered in mud.

Sam broke away from her friends, blew her runny nose with a tissue then approached the grave. She paused in a silent prayer before she composed herself enough to speak. Finally, she whispered a vow. "I will find out who did this to you Carrie. I promise. Then I'll put the scumbag in his own grave. I promise, Carrie. I will. Even if I have to die trying."

The mourners strolled away from the gravesite to their cars. Carrie's family entered the lead limo. Sam had wanted to get there early so Frank's Ford Explorer was next in line. He opened the passenger door and Sam stumbled into the seat. She bent over, with her hands over her face and rocked.

"I'm so sorry, Carrie. I'm sorry I wasn't there lately for you to help you through whatever got you into this mess. I feel partially to blame. Oh my God, Carrie." Sam looked at Frank. "What made her go there on a school day? There are so many unanswered questions." She inhaled deeply in a weakened attempt to regain her composure. Frank remained silent behind the steering wheel, with his kind and compassionate posture. He was the one man who understood her. He let her find her own way.

Sam fell limp over the center console and Frank held her securely, his arms wrapped around her. "Come on, they're moving. We have to go." He gently moved her back into a sitting position. "Why are you feeling guilty?"

Sam sniffled and looked toward him, absorbing what he had said. "I wasn't there enough for her, Frank. Can you believe it? We haven't spoken in over a month."

He pressed the accelerator and followed the limo. "How come?"

"Last time I called her, Carrie was in a rush. She told me she had an appointment but wouldn't go into details. I knew she was being evasive but I didn't push. I knew she was just getting used to the separation with Charlie, so I wanted to let her have her space. I should have pushed, damn it! I should have pushed."

"Carrie was an adult. She made her own choices. You said you wanted to find out who murdered her? Then you have to get over that guilt thing. Otherwise, Loo won't let you near this case."

She glared at him but said nothing.

"Hey, I'm serious. Emotional involvement? Could throw off your assessment. You know that."

She let out a nasal breath. "Always being the psychiatrist." He hiked his brows. She got his message, putting her hands into a prayer position just under her nose for a moment to compose herself, and nodded. "You're right. Let's get to the precinct now.'

"No. We're going to the house."

"Frank, I can't deal with that now."

"Too bad. You need to pay your respects. Let's find out what they know. If we bring Loo something, you'll stand a better chance. If you recall, you already stormed into Loo's office the day her body was found." Sam glared at him. "So you do remember," he said. "And you remember he gave you a flat 'no?'"

Sam crossed her arms across her chest. "All right already! I get the picture."

"Hey! I'm on your side here. Let's bring him something that'll make him change his mind. Besides, this isn't our precinct's case, and they're not likely to allow you as a rookie to take over."

"Some rookie. I have two major cases under my belt in two months' time."

"Yeah. And I'm sure they'd welcome you to uncover some more low-life cops in their precinct. By the way, they're still trying to get Withers to roll on his wife. He's being too tightlipped. But everyone at Jen's hospital is coming forth. The FBI made four more arrests. I'll tell you, Sam, the FBI is putting their all into this. That part of the Aries case is far from over."

Sam patted Frank's arm. "I'm glad, Frank. You're right. Okay, let's go to Carrie's."

౪ఎఁ

The line of cars in front of Carrie's single-family detached house in the Madison section of Brooklyn double-parked the entire one-way block. In the snow, that was some feat. There was no room left for anyone to pass. No one cared. All the neighbors were in Carrie's house mourning with her family.

Frank pulled in across a neighbor's driveway three houses down and flipped his NYPD ID onto the dash. "We should have stopped to get something."

"I ordered two platters from the deli. They should've been delivered by now."

"I really like this tradition."

"What?"

"The getting together with family and friends after the funeral," Frank said, thoughtfully. "It helps bring comfort to the family."

Sam patted his hand then glanced out the passenger window. She steadied her nerves with a few deep breaths, forcing a sense of calmness, before she opened the door of the Explorer with one strong thrust of her foot. As soon as she opened the door, cold air hit her and frost pillowed from her mouth. How anyone in Brooklyn could say that snow was beautiful was beyond her. It was blackened a minute after it hit the ground. The thought made her smile. She'd take it. A reason to smile. Frank was right. She had to hold up appearances, at least in public, to boost her strength and find out who put her Carrie into the ground. She'd mourn in private.

Sam jumped out, landing on a tire-ridden mound of blackened snow, and passed in front of the SUV to get to the sidewalk. She walked gingerly on the ice-covered ground to get to the "Shiva" house with Frank crunching the snow in his heavy treaded sneakers beside her.

With Frank holding her hand, Sam plodded up the six steps to the front door. There was a sign under the bell. *Do not ring, just enter.* This wasn't Sam's first Shiva visit to a friend. As soon as she opened the door, the warm smells of a Jewish household replaced the frigid air. The hot roasted meats, the tang of pickles, the sweetness of Challah bread, all brought back memories for Sam from when she became a member of the family at their gatherings for Chanukah and Passover. Those Seders were so damn long. She tried to smile as she envisioned herself wiggling in the chair waiting for them to be over.

She felt the same way about today—wanting it to be over and done with. Sam shimmied her way through the crowd, nodding and smiling at people, most of whom she knew.

Carrie's parents sat holding hands on the couch against the far wall. Though only in their sixties, they looked as if they had aged twenty years. Her mother's wrinkles appeared deeper, her eyes reddened from tears, her expression distant. The bags under her eyes darkened from lack of sleep. Her father looked just as worn. Who could blame them? This wasn't the natural order of things. Parents weren't supposed to outlive children. Yet it happened much too often. Sam could attest to that, in her line of work. She never expected it to happen, though, so close to home. She planned to live, eat, and breathe this case until she found who was responsible. She reminded herself about fifty times since the cemetery to embed it into her soul. Needing to compose herself, she decided to wait to approach Carrie's parents until the crowd around them lessened. Not having guts was never her issue—until now when heartbreak immobilized her.

Frank came up to her with a plate of food as she leaned against the edge of the painted brick fireplace that attached to the wall between two windows. He brought her out of her reflection as he held the offering out in front of her.

"I'm not hungry," she responded weakly.

"I beg to differ. You have to eat. You're cranky enough." His stern look shot through her. "Take it."

She forced a smile and accepted the plate. She toyed at the food with a fork before she put a strip of hot corned beef into her mouth. The deep salty flavor made her swoon. Just the right blend of meat and fat woke up the feeling of hunger at the pit of her stomach. Okay, she'd eat first and then get down to business. She ravenously attacked the meat, potato salad and coleslaw still leaning against the fireplace, eavesdropping on a conversation between Carrie's cousins. She even downed a large kasha knish without thinking about it.

The cousins were brainstorming possible reasons for

Carrie's murder. But all they came up with were questions. Carrie's ex was the crux of it. Why did Charlie Baines suddenly walk out after four years? He was their prime suspect, especially since he was nowhere to be found. Was he pissed Carrie wanted to revert to her maiden name of Hersch? Why was their house going into foreclosure? They had just purchased it last year. Anxiety rustled through Sam. She felt weak-kneed. She hadn't known any of this. Not knowing her BFF became more of a reality than she'd like to admit. Why was Carrie at the casino? Her cousins couldn't answer their own questions. Why did Carrie book the hotel for an entire weekend? Wouldn't one day there have been enough? They said the police found eighteen hundred dollars in her wallet. The cousins concluded robbery wasn't the motive. Big whoopee. They probably got that one right.

All right, I need to get to the casino.

Her mind reeled with random thoughts even she couldn't make any analysis of yet. Now was not the time for a formal interview, but she'd bet all of these cousins would be sitting opposite her in an interview room soon. Very soon.

Sam made her way over to Frank, who was talking to Carrie's older brother, Callum. The forty-year old Orthodox Jew—whose *peyous* was long enough to tuck around his ears and slip under the collar of his black suit—leaned against the wall next to the staircase. With a plate in one hand, he used the other to adjust the streamers hanging from the *titzes* under his jacket. He seemed to be uncomfortable, beyond mourning. Sam could imagine why. Despite growing up in a reformed Jewish family, he became Orthodox his senior year in high school, wanting to go to a strictly Jewish University. Now a corporate lawyer, his clientele were the wealthiest of Williamsburg and the diamond district. Coming home seemed to have unsettled him. Even his wife, Bailey, didn't make an appearance because to her, Carrie's family wasn't *Jewish enough*. That's something Sam could not get over. *Family is family*. Callum never did have a firm relationship with Carrie, and it became even more strained when she married outside the religion. Sam doubted if he could or would give any insight into her murder. But she'd sure as hell try to get what she could from him. Her annoyance at him wanted to schedule the interview on a Sabbath, but deep down inside, she knew she would never do that.

Sam stood next to Callum and expressed her condolences.

He merely nodded.

"Come on, Frank. Need to go."

Her gaze tossed him a sense of urgency. He got it. Frank tilted his head toward Callum and put on the bubble jacket that hung over his arm.

Sam skipped down the steps in front of Frank. The snow had tapered off. Sam was happy about that, at least.

"Hey, where are you rushing to?"

"First Manhattan then Queens."

"You're kidding me, right?" Frank jumped into the driver's seat. He waited for Sam to get in. "It's after four. Who's going to be there?"

Sam pushed a key on her phone and put it on speaker.

A voice came through. "Hey, Sam."

"Hi, Nick. We're just leaving Carrie's house. Meet us at the precinct?"

"Now?"

"In about forty. Call Loo, too, please." She disconnected before Nick could respond.

"Taking over, again?"

"Always."

"Your partner isn't going to be thrilled with this."

"Nick's a great guy, Frank. Supportive and he lets me take the lead. You know that."

"Yeah, in the beginning, with the Larcon and then the Withers cases, but he needs his kudos too. Don't shut him out. That's all I'm saying."

Sam registered the thought. She had been working as a detective in Manhattan Midtown-South for eight weeks.

Still, her relationship with her partner, Nick Valatutti, was as strong as a multi-year partnership. They were in sync, so important for the job. "Point taken. I'm going to need his objectivity on this one, too. And yours." She clasped his hand in hers. "Thanks for coming with me, Frank."

"No problem. How could I have let you go it alone?"

"It's not that. You gave up a day of quality time with Frankie. Your son needs you."

He sighed. "I know." Frank pulled away, made it down the block toward the avenue and entered a shoveled road.

"I was watching you and Callum. He seemed to be talking to you much more than he ever did with me."

"Yeah. You're a lot too wild for him. He said you were a bad influence on Carrie."

"What? How so?"

"He wouldn't say. He shut down. He told me he wants nothing to do with this investigation and that he and his parents went through two interviews, and they were cleared. He doesn't even want updates. That's telling. I asked him what the police asked him. He told me to read the police files. I asked him what they told him. Same response. That was it. Very cold. Not emotional. Deep rooted anger, from what I could assess and from what you had told me about him. I didn't push or try to put him on the spot. This wasn't the time or place but I did mention that people can be called in for third interviews. He looked at me as if I was crazy. He's an attorney so I guess he feels he can get around that."

"Fat chance. That SOB. He bullied her as a child, now he's indifferent in her death."

ᥱᡈᥱᡈ

Sam raced through the front door of the Manhattan Midtown-South precinct near Chelsea Park without bothering to stomp her boots on the NYPD welcome mat. She slipped on the sleek tiles and lost her balance with her long strides.

Frank broke her near fall with his hands on her waist. "Calm it, Sam."

She looked up at him and understood his glare. Loo was a man who didn't react well to overly emotional detectives. *Okay, job first.* She stood still, facing Frank, looked around at the beige walls to calm her thoughts, swallowed, inhaled deeply, and then nodded to Frank that she was ready. She released from him and took another glimpse at the walls. For some reason staring at the bland emptiness quieted her brain. She needed that now—mainly to hear and digest what Loo said before she reacted or overreacted.

They walked down the hall to Loo's office, and she knocked on the door.

"Come in." Lieutenant Rojas' voice was strong, but he didn't seem to be annoyed. That was good.

Sam and Frank entered and pulled chairs from the conference table to around Loo's desk.

Her partner, Nick, in his usual detective attire, khaki's and brown jacket, sat opposite Loo's desk. "I'm sorry, Sam, really."

Sam lowered her eyes. "Thanks, Nick. And thanks to the two of you for coming in."

Loo pulled off his black framed glasses, and carefully placed them on the desk, before he spoke. "Detective Wright, I've already said this once, but it seems that you need repetition. You are not getting involved in the Carolyn Baines case."

That was a blow right to her face. Sam jolted. She focused on the man's large round brown eyes to calm herself before she spoke. "But, Lieutenant."

"No buts." He leaned forward in his chair and clasped his hands in front of him.

It's a good thing I cleared my brain. Sam felt a twinge in her abdomen from her Spirit Guide, Dara, and breathed deeply.

If she ever needed Dara, it was today. Right now. *Come on Dara. Let the right words come out of my mouth.* She cleared her throat. "I know the police interviewed Carrie's parents and her brother, Callum."

"Yes. And?"

Sam looked at him eye-to-eye. "Okay Lieutenant, so, what information do you have?"

"What makes you think I have any information that I'd share with you?"

"Lieutenant, even though I've only been here eight weeks, I think I can read you. I know you have all our backs, so if it's personal, you're on it. You were like that with Frank, reopening his wife's murder case when I came onboard. Why would it be different for me?"

Loo compressed his lips, shook his head, darted his eyes between Frank and Nick then, nodded. "It's not." He paused for a moment. "It's the FBI's case. Queens started investigating and they intervened, constructing a task-force at the precinct, but the FBI runs it. They're not going to let you breathe the same air, especially a rookie." Sam hiked a brow. He snorted. "Don't give me that look. Time-wise you're still a rookie. And personal connection or not, knowing you, you'd want the lead. You start opening your mouth, and I'll be fielding complaints all day from FBI headquarters. I'm telling you now that I have no intentions of dealing with that."

"For FBI involvement you're saying this guy has killed before?"

"Yes. Up and down the east coast. Carolyn was his seventeenth victim, over a nine-year period. The first one in New York State, though."

"Who is the lead agent?"

"You know him. Special Agent Brett Case is the lead. He wanted this one. The fact that he has strong homicide investigative experience fell in his favor."

"We were all on very good terms with him on the Withers' case. Can I call him just to touch base and say 'hello'?"

"What part of *no* don't you understand, Detective?"

"Um, how about I call him as a witness? Carrie and I

have been best friends since kindergarten. I can give them information with a professional slant that'll be reliable. I'm actually surprised I wasn't contacted already. And the murder occurred nine days ago." Sam sat back in her chair, looking down at the floor, and then a spark hit her. She looked at Nick and smiled.

Nick folded his arms across his chest. "What's on your mind, Sam? Tell us."

"Okay, you're my partner and not a rookie, so how about you go with me? We talk to Queens and the task-force, and tell them you want the lead?"

Nick let out a humph, then turned his attention to a fleck of lint on his pant leg. "You'd give up the lead?"

"I'd do anything to find the prick who did this to Carrie. Yeah, Nick, I'd give up the lead." She looked pleadingly at him. "Come on, Nick, please. Will you take the lead on this case? You must have seniority over their detectives."

Loo nodded at Nick. "That, he does."

"Okay, Sam. I'll take the lead in your fantasy world of even being allowed near the feds. What makes you think they'll talk to us?"

"You're the lead. You'll figure out something." *Good. Now I'll have time to grieve.*

CHAPTER 3

In the January Florida sun, John Trenton relaxed on a lounge at the Bueno Terrace country club pool and watched his son, Ricky, play in the water with his cousins—Vicki's nephews, Matt and Mark. That infamous Marco Polo game. The repetitions made him cringe. His eyes kept closing, feeling the drowsiness from sleepless nights since the twins were born in November. But he wouldn't have it any other way. He stretched out his arms rotating his right shoulder to loosen up his mobility from the bullet he took rescuing his wife in the Gemini case. Dammit! He felt his face flush—and it wasn't from the sun—at the thought that what the doctors had told him about having a permanent disability might be right. No way in hell would he accept that judgment call. The injury had definitely affected his gym workout and Tae Kwon Do matches at Ricky's school. John so wanted to be at his best for his nine-year-old son. Son. Finally, officially, he could call Ricky his son. His dreams and manifestations for over three years had come true bringing Ricky back to him and Vicki last February. His formal adoption had gone through and now Ricky was a Trenton, down to his original birth certificate.

He closed his eyes for a moment in a "thank you" to God, visualizing Ricky's heartbreaking rescue from the hostage situation three years earlier. John's mind recapitulated the conversation with Vicki's brother Mark—the commander of SWAT and the hostage negotiator, Lieutenant Randy Leigh. They almost didn't let John go in. Even now, relaxing on the lounge, his heartbeat accelerated as he visualized himself taking slow steps, making the five-hundred-yard walk to the trailer take fifteen minutes—with Ricky's birth father holding a rifle on him. John became teary-eyed at the image of Ricky jumping into his arms after the takedown, begging to live with him and Vicki right then. That image imbedded itself permanently into John's soul. Too bad, it took three years to manifest.

He looked over adoringly at his wife holding Alexi in her arms as Zach napped in the stroller. They were beginning to coo and bubble as they tried to communicate. Oh man! He just hoped he still would have the energy to run after them. At forty-six, he wasn't the oldest dad, but he sure as hell wasn't the youngest, either. Most of all, he was never meant to be a stay-at-home dad.

The past eleven months living in Serento, Florida was a far cry from the New York City life he craved. The faster pace, the high voltage energy, the Manhattan skyline, the parties with his colleagues all pierced his thoughts at times. Debriefing Detective Samantha Wright after her first trigger-pull in the Aries case whet his appetite to get back into action. He shook his head, wondering if he'd ever get back.

John stared at his briefcase on the ground reminding him he had papers to grade for the students in his criminal justice class at the community college. One more week and the semester would be over. Then what? He would return to his book, which was coming along, slowly. *Holistic Forensic Psychiatry: Making The Mind Body Connection* was already getting the attention of some New York City publishers.

He also missed his forensic patients at Manhattan Psych. He put it out to the universe to manifest a case for him. But his sabbatical wasn't over—not until the end of February. Unless he could find a damn good reason for cutting it short. However, would they find him medically fit to work within his population—the most psychopathic, criminally insane men in New York City? Then what about Vicki? She hated the city. Two years was more than enough for her. And Ricky? He'd never been in snow, and the winter had been brutal. Duke, neither. John's condo on the Upper East Side wouldn't allow a dog of his size in. Ricky and Vicki would never leave Duke behind and, to be honest with himself, neither would he. He loved that fella. A lot of decisions weighed on him concerning his future and more importantly, the future of his family. He closed his eyes and tried to doze.

Without success.

☙ℰ☙

Ambulance sirens blared, splashing through the muddy snow on the part of the Lower West Side of Manhattan that hadn't been renovated. This neighborhood was dark, even during the day with rundown and abandoned buildings. Seth Rowan swerved the ambulance around garbage strewn on the avenue and wasn't fazed about driving over already crushed garbage pails laying on mounds of snow as they protruded into the street. He hated the section that had been his route for the past fifteen years. He hadn't noticed any change for the better. Still, the gang-infested, crime-ridden, poverty-overtaken neighborhood gave him his livelihood. At least he didn't have to live there. The blowing snow hampered his vision. He knew the address, knew where it was, but he had to check. As he opened the window, he heard bullets riveting out of what he guessed to be an AK-47. Okay, so the Crips gang was at it again. He guessed it was coming from the center courtyard of the tenements—not his concern at the moment.

He pulled onto a mound of snow at the front of the half-way house. For the most part a freebee, it was more like a shelter. That made him grimace. Living conditions here were less than adequate, but it was far better for the male residents than being homeless. Seth shook his head at the realization. He jumped out of the driver's side with his partner exiting the passenger side and the other EMS tech opening the back door and lowering the ramp. The three men pulled down a stretcher, their med bags, and oxygen tank and plodded through the snow up the steps to the porch of the dilapidated Victorian style house. Its wide porch ran the length of the house and around each side. As Seth's partner leaned against the warped wood railing, they both heard the creaking sounds of an eminent collapse, causing his partner to jump away.

The door opened. The three men entered and were directed into the center hall and up a flight of stairs.

Bobby Mitchell lay semi-conscious—alone and moaning—on his twin bed, which was one of ten in the ward style room. Dried blood stained the pillow underneath his head. His gaze stared blankly toward the ceiling.

"Bobby." The driver and the lead technician approached the bed. "I'm Seth Rowan, we're going to take care of you. Can you hear me?" He ignored the stench of urine and feces emanating from the sheets and touched the pillow. "It looks like he could have been hit over the head with a bat."

Bobby groaned, his body taut, his blank gaze still aimed toward the ceiling. Seth took his vitals, afterward giving his partners a concerned look. "How old is he?"

The dorm supervisor checked the paperwork on his clipboard. "Twenty-three."

"What happened?"

"Dunno exactly. A fight. The residents always fight. Not much we could do."

"I'm not talking about that. This was some fight. I want to know what happened to him."

"Yeah, well, I gotta cover my ass, buddy. You wanna know what happened to him, ask him."

"Does he take any meds?"

"None that I know of, but ya never know in here. Most of them have their own street pharmacists."

One of the EMS techs pulled down the faded sheets that covered Bobby up to his neck. His bare torso was black and blue around his abdominal and kidney areas with reddened fists marks from his rib cage up to his neck. On his scrawny frame, the tech saw his ribs protruding. "He took a beat down for sure. Guaranteed fractured ribs." The tech attached an oxygen mask, regulated the intensity, and prepared to start an IV. "His breathing's shallow, Seth."

"Who's his contact on his emergency chart?"

The dorm supervisor smirked at the question. He flipped through the paperwork. "A Doctor John Trenton."

The three EMS techs perked up.

Seth lifted his head from inspecting Bobby's wounds. "The forensic psychiatrist John Trenton? From Manhattan Psych?"

"I guess. Yeah, that's him. The kid works in the kitchen there."

"Hey, Seth, Trenton's been in Florida for almost a year," a tech said.

"Yeah, the kid told me, but Trenton's the only one he talks to." The dorm supervisor scanned the clipboard again. "At least twice a week. Here's his outgoing call list. Trenton's the only one. He's like a dad to this kid. More than what anyone else here got."

"Does he have a PO?"

"Not any more. His probation ended last month."

Seth readied his pen. "Okay, need both numbers."

"Trenton, 917-555-3053. Charlie Smitts, 212-555-1520."

"Hey Seth, let's get him out of here, his BP is falling."

Speeding onto the emergency ramp of Manhattan Borough Hospital, the ambulance stopped in front of the ER. Nurse's aides ran out to assist.

Seth jumped down from the driver's seat. "Make it a straight run to the back. Got a DOA."

&∞∞

Vicki sat next to Ricky at his desk in his homeschooling classroom. It was the perfect room, overlooking the lanai in John's parents' home. She had so much fun decorating it. As much fun as she had decorating her own kindergarten classroom when she taught—dry erase boards, bulletin boards displaying his work, a reading rug in the corner, all in school friendly colors. Even a rocking chair sat over the rug. Ricky helped her pick it all out. She missed teaching, but here in Florida. Never again would she try in the big city. Now on the back burner, she'd hoped to get back to her career when the twins were older. Maybe when they entered nursery school. For now, she was happy being a breast-feeding mommy and working with Ricky to improve his academic levels.

Vicki smiled at her son. This was their time together, when the twins were napping. When they were up, John's parents were the adoring grandparents who never said 'no' to babysitting. She had the perfect life, one that she and John had worked very hard to recreate. Their three-week separation last year truly showed her how much she loved this man. They'd vowed that nothing, nothing in this world, would separate them again. The twins and Ricky completed her life.

"Mom, do we have to do this now?"

"Uh, yes. Why?"

"The Rangers and Flyers game is on."

"Good try. Taping it. Open the book."

He groaned. "But it's so much better seeing it live."

She tossed him a sly grin. "But you could also fast forward through the commercials."

"I could never win with you."

"Well, you know how important school is in this family."

"I hate school."

"I thought you liked learning at home? You always say it."

"Yeah, but when I catch up, you and Dad will want me to go to real school."

"We told you, Ricky, that will happen when you want to."

A distant look overcame the happy one. "Don't count on it. I'll just get myself thrown out again."

Vicki read him, gave him a hug, and held him in her arms. "Maybe not. Let's wait to go there. Okay, darlin'? Right now, you've come a long way in eleven months."

He shimmied loose. "Mom, I'm nine."

"Never get too old for a hug." When Vicki heard John's adoring voice, she looked up toward the doorway and caught John's smile as he leaned against the wall. "Right, babe?" John strolled over, rustled Ricky's long, blond curls, and then pulled over a third grader's size chair to join them at the desk. "What are you two up to?"

Ricky crinkled his nose. "Mom wants to do subtraction with exchange. I hate math."

"How will you ever be able to make sure you get the correct change if you don't know how to subtract?"

"Dad, I never go shopping alone."

"Someday you will."

"When? In seven years, when I'm driving?"

Vickie sighed. "This is Central Florida, John. Can't walk to the corner store."

John let out a breath, put his lips together, and nodded. "Yeah."

"Um, thinking of the city again?" Vicki knew the day was coming that John would approach the topic of returning to New York. She was hoping she could delay it for as long as possible.

"Something came up. Need to talk to you when you're done. No rush. In the meantime, Ricky, you better do the work Mom tells you to do." He shot Ricky his signature look that still gave Vicki a jolt of adrenalin.

His signature look—that intense stare from his azurite-colored eyes that pierced her heart and made her weak-kneed. That same stare he gave her when they first met in the emergency room almost four years ago. She'd never tire of it.

When John got up from the chair, Vicki studied his grim expression. She could have sworn his eyes moistened. He left, meeting her eye-to-eye. The hour she planned to spend with Ricky dragged. Usually, it flew. It wasn't like John to look sad. He was the most positive person she knew, and he always put up a good front. But she knew her husband. And right now something was going on that affected him deeply. If it affected him, it affected her.

ᏬᏙᏬᏙ

John waited for the Google search to pull up real estate properties in Scarsdale. He and Vicki had discussed the possibility of getting the house with the white picket fence and large back yard the night she left him in New York to return home to Florida—and many times since. This memory made him smile—sitting on the couch in his condo, toying with the zipper on her pink jumpsuit as he kissed her neck and décolleté trying to use sexiness to make her change her mind as she rattled off all the reasons she hated the city. Wow! What a jerk he was. But no more. With Vicki, with his precious wife Vicki, and his children, he was a changed man.

John had to admit living in a house grew on him. He liked the space compared to his six-rooms in the city. He had spent his entire life in apartment buildings in Manhattan. The first house he had ever lived in was Vicki's when they made trips here to visit family, but that had been for two weeks, tops. When it became a crime scene at the end of the Gemini case, Vicki didn't want to go near it. Now, eleven months of living in his parents' house more than prepared him for his own. He had four doctor friends living in Scarsdale and knew the area well. He wanted big. So Vicki's family and his could visit at the same time for Christmas. Vicki loved to spend the holidays together. She'd make her fabulous feasts. One thing mandatory, the kitchen had to be the largest area in the house.

The list of homes came up from one of the real estate agencies his friend had used. He wouldn't go on a random selection, not with something that would change his life. No time for renovations, either. So he'd have to compromise, admitting to himself, that was not one of his strong points. He was reading stats on a fourteen room, seven-bedroom Colonial when Vicki walked into the room. She immediately stared at the computer screen.

"What happened and when are we going?

"Uh, that was fast."

She pulled a club chair next to him. "Scarsdale? We talked about that area."

His gaze met hers. "Bobby Mitchell." John swallowed back tears. "He was murdered."

Vicki immediately felt his pain. "Oh my God, John. I'm so sorry, darlin'." She collapsed into his loving arms and let the tears flow. "How? Why? Who called you?"

"He was beaten up at the halfway house. Three days ago. Internal injuries. The doctor from the ER who made the pronouncement called me. It's a Manhattan Midtown-South case. A few minutes later, Lieutenant Rojas called me. Well, honestly, I called him, first. He agreed with me coming back to be the profiler in the investigation. He saw the call records Bobby made to me. You can imagine the rest. Now, more importantly, would you go with me? Babe? Will you? With the kids and Duke? And drive? I don't want Duke in a luggage compartment."

"Don't you remember the vow we made?"

"To never leave each other again?"

"Yes. That one. You have my answer."

"Oh, man! I love you." He took her into his arms and

deposited a long, passionate kiss on her lips. "To be continued later." He winked. "Take a look at this one. We could
rent with the option to buy. It's too spur of the moment to
buy outright."

She scrolled the pictures of each room, then found the
wide, galley style, newly renovated, kitchen. Her eyes
opened wide.

Okay. That's the one.

She still focused on the kitchen. "One thing. How are
you going to cut short your sabbatical?"

"I'll call headquarters and arrange for a medical. I don't
foresee a problem." *I hope.*

CHAPTER 4

When Sam and Nick entered the Queens precinct, a security guard pointed them in the direction of the war room where the multi-agency task-force was meeting on the Carolyn Baines murder case. By the time Nick got through the day before, it was late afternoon, and dusk overtook the city. He had called ahead for an appointment with Special FBI Agent Brett Case, having to jump through hoops from the precinct secretary, then the patrol officer on duty, and stranded on hold until they found out if Case would be in the building. The answer was affirmative.

From the doorway, Sam scanned the ultra-modern, blue-carpeted room with a ten-foot conference table, seating for twelve, with navy upholstered swivel armchairs. Each seat had a laptop in front of it. She wasn't prepared to meet so many people. That threw her off balance—for a split second. Special Agent Case would have been enough to convince the powers that be to permit her and Nick's involvement. Now there were an additional five. At least some were women and she was confident they'd take her side. She hoped Nick could do his magic.

She thanked the universe every day she had a partner like him. He was pivotal in her making the arrests and getting two major cases under her belt—something she'd never forget.

Case smiled as he pointed to two chairs at the end of the table. "Come in, Detectives. We're waiting on you."

A smile? Directed at me? Not a chance, Case.

Sam was glad she chose her beige ultra conservative pants suit to wear—nothing to give Case any reason to make a play for her. She'd sensed his vibes when they first met, chasing down Withers—the guy who was unknowingly taking Withers place—that is. She knew Frank saw it, too. He didn't like it. This meeting was going to be professional and nothing but. After she removed her long beige trench coat and draped it over the back of the chair, she and Nick took their seats and she folded her hands on the table in front of her. She waited.

A mid-forties dark-skinned man wearing a conservative gray sports jacket at the opposite end of the table spoke first. "I'm Lieutenant Hicks. I know both your histories, and your relationship with Agent Case. Even though your excellent reputations precede you, consider this a professional courtesy, nothing more. Lieutenant Rojas and I go back a long way. At first, I wasn't thrilled with a task-force for no reason, but I now understand it, seeing what damage this perp has done. Therefore, my precinct and I will give the FBI our utmost cooperation. As for the both of you being here, I know that you, Detective Wright, and the vic were good friends, so we will use what you tell us as a reliable source. Your involvement will end there."

Sam cringed when she heard him say "vic" instead of Carrie by name. She held her tongue. His last statement made her stomach drop.

"I'll be directing this interview," Agent Case said. "Detective Wright, how long have you known Miss Baines?"

"Since kindergarten." Sam remained focused. She'd only elaborate when he asked the correct questions.

"What can you tell me about her?"

"Referring to?"

"Everything. We need to create a profile to match to the other victims."

Nick shot Agent Case a glare. "Why don't you ask Detective Wright specific questions so we don't go on for hours and waste time?"

Okay, Nick. You're starting your magic.

"Yes. I forgot. This one could ramble. Why would Miss Baines cut work and go to a casino?"

"That's the million dollar question. One I want the answer to, but more importantly why did the perp choose her?"

"Not going there," Lieutenant Hicks retorted, not holding back annoyance.

"Lieutenant, with all due respect, if my partner knows specifics, she'll be able to frame her answers appropriately. Relevancy is crucial. Correct?"

The lieutenant let out an exasperated breath. "All of the murders were in casinos on the east coast. All vics were professional career women."

"Any prominent differences?" Nick asked.

"Unfortunately, none that we've put together, yet," the lieutenant conceded.

"Okay, Detective Wright, what can you tell us about Miss Baines relationship with her husband?" Case asked. "We know it's not him, but—"

Sam cut Agent Case off. "I get it. Carrie and Charlie were separated four months ago. She caught him cheating, first through texts on his phone to another woman, then she followed him to an apartment building. She never confronted him."

"Never confronted him? How can that be?"

"We never had time for a face-to-face meeting, and—"

"Don't buy that for a second, Detective." Case sneered at her. "If you two were that close, you'd be meeting at three a.m. if need be. Girlfriends cry with each other. I think you're wasting our time, altogether."

"I am not!"

"Would she lie to you about the real cause of the divorce?"

"Maybe."

"What else do you know about them?"

"They both had money. She, from family and her career. He was in the computer software business and doing very well during their marriage. They had a house, which I just learned was in foreclosure."

"Just learned?" Lieutenant Hicks leaned forward. "You're shooting wind as far as I'm concerned, Detective."

Sam swallowed and lowered her voice. "Unfortunately, we haven't spoken much in the last few months. Our work schedules. Her cousins said she planned to spend the weekend and that you found eighteen hundred dollars on her. I know she liked going, I do, too, but when we went together, not in over a year though, neither of us brought more than a couple hundred bucks. So that was a surprise to me."

"Our forensic psychiatrist hasn't come on board yet to construct the psychological comparison. Case overload. But we have an idea."

Nick didn't waste a beat. "Which is?"

"Not prepared yet to say. But a victimology analysis will be the key in this investigation."

"I'm tired of hearing that kind of conversation. Why not?" Nick admonished.

Case sucked in his cheeks before he spoke. "As we said, this is the first kill in New York State. The last murder was in New Jersey. A year ago. In that time span, a serial can change MO and target preference. And we don't know why he waited so long between hits. The only common elements were casinos and professional careers. Also, the women were there for the day. Only the day. This time he switched to a woman who was planning to be there for the weekend. That difference struck us as significant."

"The NYPD has a forensic psychiatrist who would be happy to come aboard. You know him."

"Yes, Detective Valatutti. A Doctor Frank Khaos. But I'm afraid this isn't his specialty area. This isn't gang related," Lieutenant Hicks said.

"Neither was the Aries case and he nailed it," Nick retorted.

"I'll think about it. What are your thoughts, Detective Wright? I've listened to your tapes. And I sure hope you do not have one of your recording devices hidden on you."

"I'm no longer carrying it, Lieutenant," Sam said flatly.

"Glad to hear that," Agent Case said as he intervened. "I just want to mention to everyone that Detective Wright has a habit of constructing her hypotheses based on her own theories, not on forensic facts. And since we do not have any forensic facts to date, I'd like to hear what she has to say. Her training and on scene analysis have been very helpful. I'll give her that."

"In addition, I'd like to remind everyone, her hypotheses have been correct." Nick smiled at Agent Case. "So what's in it for us?"

"Nothing," Lieutenant Hicks blurted out, without missing a beat.

"Then, in all honesty, my partner will not do your jobs for you. What other questions do you have before we leave?"

"We'll need a list of Miss Baine's friends. Her parents were too distraught to help us. Her brother, Callum, was less than cooperative. Also a list of where she'd like to go for dinner and any entertainment. We don't know whether the killer followed her to the casino or met her there. We need to know the names of the school colleagues she was friendly with. We already spoke to some and got nowhere."

Nick had that sly look on his face that Sam had learned to appreciate. "Maybe, talking to another friend would open that up."

"What part of no involvement don't you understand, Detective Valatutti?" the lieutenant bellowed.

Nick didn't budge. "I'm just saying. Okay, humor me. What made you conclude it's the same perp and not isolated or a copycat?"

Agent Case tossed his pen on top of the folder. "Okay.

In the past he left a souvenir for the vic."

Nick sat up straight in the chair. "Do I have to pull teeth here?"

"We can't let this leak to the media, Detective."

Nick stared poker-faced at Case. "It won't come from us."

"He didn't leave it with Miss Baines. The token is a dead baby scorpion across their right breast. We named him Skorpios."

Sam perked up. "After the Greek interpretation? Interesting."

"What do you know about it?"

"This one?" Nick said. "Her knowledge of symbolism behind Aries helped us solve the case and nail the killer. I'd say she knows a lot."

"Well, Detective Wright?"

"I have to tell you. I'm a Scorpio, so I know even more about this sign than any others."

The lieutenant let out a frustrated nasal breath. "I'm getting the sense that you're going to refrain from telling us what you think, Detective Wright, unless I allow the two of you to work this case? Am I correct?"

"Correct," said Nick.

"She does realize that she's too emotionally involved to assert herself?"

"I'm the lead. We agreed to that."

Lieutenant Hicks swallowed hard then looked toward two Queens detectives. They both smirked at Sam and Nick. Sam guessed that they were the leads on this case. Already determined and working on it. She didn't know of any lead detectives who'd give up their spot. Couldn't blame them.

It seemed that the lieutenant was struggling for words. "You, Detective Valatutti, assigned yourself the lead? Don't you think I have my own detectives capable?"

"Probably not as senior as me."

"You'd force the issue?"

"Let's just put it this way. We have a resource, Detective Wright, who could solve this case. With a name like you gave it, you just as well might have dumped the files in her lap."

"All right. I have something you need to hear that might change your mind." Hicks then pointed to the female detective.

"I'm Detective Bella Richards, a year under my belt and one of the leads on this case." She nodded to her partner. "We were partnered last year after Doctor Trenton's team was murdered by Barbara Montgomery in the Gemini case. We're still cleaning that one up and found another body. He's Detective—" She looked at her partner. "—Withers, Lex Withers."

Nick looked shocked. "You're the brother of Dingo Withers?"

The detective swallowed hard and lowered his eyes before he spoke. "Yes. My brother murdered Doctor Frank Khaos's wife over two years ago."

                              ❧❧❧

Frank contained his voice not to awaken Frankie. "Now you tell me?" He pivoted himself off Sam and lay back on the bed kicking the blanket off them until it landed in a heap at the foot of the bed. "You never cease to amaze me. Know that? You couldn't let me know at the precinct. Why?" He stared up toward the ceiling. He was just coming back to himself, and the woman he trusted—the woman he began to love, the woman he wanted in his life and Frankie's—just dropped a bomb upon him. How in hell was he supposed to work on a case with the brother of the man who had killed his wife? The sweat on his body evaporated with the coolness in the room—or from anxiety—he didn't know which. Nor did he care.

Sam shivered. Naked, she sat up and tugged the chocolate brown silk jacquard blanket back up to cover them both then rolled onto her side. From under the covers, she cascaded her hand over his forearm. "I thought it was something we needed to discuss in private."

He shrugged her off. "Bullshit."

"I had no idea Lex Withers was in Queens. Last I heard, he was in Brooklyn-South. Why they moved him with his partner was kept quiet."

"So now what, Sam? This is a problem. A major one."

She hesitated. "I didn't expect this either. Nick and I sat stunned."

"But you still accepted the case. You probably didn't even think of the effect on me. Did you, Sam?"

"How can you say that? I most certainly did. Moves like this usually go through the grapevine and fast. What do you think I was stunned about?"

"So now you're going to investigate him, too?"

"What's with the attitude?" she reprimanded. "No, I'm not! I'm involved to find Carrie's killer, nothing more."

"Yeah, right. I know I can't deal with it. How are you?"

"We have to approach this rationally, like professionals."

"Kidding me. Right?" He rolled onto his side facing her. "At the precinct, would have been professional. Not after I fucked you twice." He let his words sink in. "So you actually expect me to breathe the same air as that guy, profiling? No way. They'll have to wait till their profiler can show up. You're on your own on this one, Sam."

She closed her eyes. "I need to solve this case. And I doubt if Lieutenant Hicks would let you slide."

"Maybe he would."

She lowered her eyes. "No, Frank. He accepted our team. That includes you. He has a rep as being unbending."

He scowled. "You volunteered me?"

"Before we found out that Withers was the lead detective from their precinct."

He began to raise his voice then tapered off. "That's

your problem! You jump in before you know all the facts. You should have identified everyone on that task-force—everyone around that table—before you opened your mouth. But, no, you couldn't care less who was there as long as you get what you want. There are other forensic psychiatrists in the city. They wouldn't let me debrief you after you had your first trigger-pull in the Aries case because we were involved. The same would apply for me."

"That won't fly. Withers isn't the person we're investigating. And you're a psychiatrist. So use some of your BJJ training to calm your nerves. Nick didn't ask for introductions, either, and he's the lead. Besides, Lieutenant Hicks and Agent Case did all the talking."

He felt his face fire up. "Brett Case?"

"You knew that. Loo told us. Yes. And he's dealing with it."

"Any more good news?" The sarcasm rolled off his tongue. "That's not what I'm concerned with."

"Then what?"

"The way he looked at you."

"Don't worry about it. We're adults here."

"Exactly."

"Frank, please. Can't you deal with this?"

He did a double take. "Know what, Sam? No. I can't. And I didn't realize you're so emotionally disconnected." He checked the clock and blew out a deep breath. "As soon as it hits daylight, I think it's best that you go back to your place." He rolled over onto his left side, his back facing her.

"What are you saying, Frank?"

He barely turned his head. "Use your psychic intuition to figure out what I'm saying."

"You're breaking up with me?"

"I think we need to distance ourselves. It's been too hot and heavy these past eight weeks, anyway. You're not the woman I thought I knew."

"How in hell are we supposed to distance ourselves? We work cases together. Every day, if I have to remind you."

"Keep it formal. I'm now Dr. Khaos from you, and you're Detective Wright from me."

"But—"

"No buts. I'm done. We're done." His stomach twisted as he uttered those last two words.

CHAPTER 5

Nick and Sam entered the war room in the Queens precinct with Nick having a lot on his mind. Sam had told him about her breakup with Frank on the drive in. On one hand, he understood the conflict. Sam was willing to work a case with the brother of the man who had killed his wife with the additional blow that she put her friend's case above him. On the other, she's the one who solved that case. It would be just as painful for Sam to work on it. Yet, she had the greater motivation. Ah. Who was he to judge? But, the bottom line to him, was that Frank was a major jerk, big time. Guess he couldn't help himself from judging. He'd live with it.

This time the conference room appeared empty, only with Agent Case, Detectives Lex Withers and Bella Richards. The sneers Nick received from both of the detectives pierced his gut. There were no smiles, no pleasantries, no hellos or how are yous. He unbuttoned his sports jacket, sneered back, and sat down in a rolling armchair. Sam took off her beige trench coat. Nick nodded to her. He knew how she operated. Another conservative double-breasted jacketed pants suit. This time, burgundy. He couldn't help but wonder how Sam thought wearing a non-revealing suit would deter any man from making a play for her. Those blue eyes and blonde ponytail with her perfectly refined nose, to boot, were a man magnet. This woman would be hot in a flannel bathrobe with curlers in her hair. Good thing his wife wasn't a mind reader.

Agent Case slid identical folders across the table to the both of them.

Nick stared at the folder before opening it. He tapped it for a few moments with his index finger, composing his thoughts. "Okay. Let's get some things out in the open here before we let our emotions taint the case."

Withers rolled his eyes. He sat with his arms crossed over his chest. "And what may those be, Detective?"

Nick stared back at the man who resembled his brother—a younger version. Bald head, dark skinned and mustache. Bigger build, though. More muscular. His biceps bulged from his jacket. "This has got to be uncomfortable for all of us."

Withers scowled. "Ya think, Valatutti?"

Nick retorted without an iota of sympathy. "I know."

"Okay, let's do get something straight. Especially for you two highbrows from the almighty Manhattan Midtown-South. I've been going through a living hell, too. How do you think I feel having a brother—whom I was close, to by the way—who turned out to be a murdering crooked cop? Uh? How do you think I feel? The DA is up my ass. Know how many times I've been, and my wife's been, brought in for questioning? She's thinkin' of divorce. They even subpoenaed my tax returns and bank records. And had the gall to ask if I had off shore accounts. Can you believe it? It got so bad in Brooklyn—yeah, I actually got death threats— that they moved me to Queens. With Bella. And what the hell did she do? She's gettin' the flack from association. They kept us together to show her loyalty to her partner. So they'd believe I had nothing to do with Dingo's scam. And I didn't. Oh, and let's not forget my advancement in the NYPD. I want to go up to Homicide, too. So before you talk about emotions *tainting* this investigation, think about how my career will be *tainted.* And more importantly than all of this bullshit, my sons are getting bullied in school.

They come home crying, for Christ's sakes, that they're yelled at because their uncle was on the take. They're in third and sixth grade, for Christ's sake."

Nick put his lips together in acknowledgment that he understood Withers's predicament. His own sons were everything to him.

Sam bit her lip and Nick noticed that her complexion had paled. She spoke calmly. "I'm sorry, Detective Withers. I was so wrapped up in our side of the story, I didn't think of the impact upon you. I'm truly sorry."

The five sat quiet for a few moments. Agent Case was the first to speak. "Anything else that needs to be aired?" He looked around at the solemn faces. "Then let's catch this bastard." He gave them a second to open the folders. "Okay, what you have in front of you is far from complete. The first five sheets is a compilation of similar crime scene photos of the each of the other sixteen vics. It's the position they were found in. All the same. On their back, nude, the blanket pulled up to their chin, legs spread apart, arms down at their side. All Caucasian. All long hair, different colors. The common denominator was that they were all educated women with solid careers. Here's where they differ. Nine out of the sixteen were elementary school teachers. Miss Baines makes the tenth teacher. Three women were nurses. One was an MD, a dermatologist. One an interior designer, and two, were accountants. Other commonalities were that all the women had money, were single, either divorced or never married. None had children. That was telling. He took the time to get to know them before he struck—"

Sam interrupted. "That they didn't have children was telling?"

"Actually, all of what I said. He made sure they were available."

"Hold on." Nick put up his palm up facing Agent Case. "So you're saying this guy researched his victims to make sure they weren't attached to family? Serials don't act that way. They don't give a damn. It's much deeper than that."

"We'll get there, Detective."

"Okay, so how did he make sure they were available?" Sam asked.

Case blew out a breath. "We don't know." Sam hitched her brows. He sighed. "Don't know how he met them—"

Sam raised her hand. "Before we go to that, may I say something, please?"

"What, Detective?" Withers asked snidely.

"This could help in the profiling, Detective," Sam responded with the same tone.

"Go ahead," Nick prodded.

"The not having children thing. Did they not have children out of choice or opportunity?"

"We don't know that." Agent Case sat up in his seat. "What are you thinking?"

"I know for a fact that Carrie did not want children. Her reasoning doesn't matter here. Scorpios are known to have a strong parental instinct. I, being one, want children more than anything. So maybe this guy did, too. Did he ask the women if they wanted children and when they said 'no' he snapped? Whether this guy asks the women in bed if they do or not, would be a stretch. It's certainly not a sexy conversation. But something to think about."

"It certainly is. Detective Withers send a blast to the other investigators. Ask them to find out if the vics didn't have children by choice."

Withers nodded. Nick could tell by the look on his face that he liked Sam's hypothesis. He did, too. One thing for sure. His partner knew how to think on her feet.

Case flipped to the next page in his file. "Let's continue. Okay, how do I say this without sounding derogatory to colleagues in the south?" He paused. "Since there was one per state, interest waned rather fast until we caught wind of it, after the sixteenth kill."

Sam and Nick hiked their eyebrows and shot each other suspicious looks.

"Let me explain this, before you two judge. The murders were dealt with by the locals who have smaller departments and less resources. For many, the forensic reports were minimal. Some of the larger cities had more police personnel and better equipped divisions. The forensic investigators decided what data was important and what was not, so the data per event was not consistent. Comparable variables were limited. These departments have to pay for testing and one murder didn't warrant the expenditure. And more importantly, their departments didn't have investigators experienced in serials, thus they couldn't recognize one. This guy is smart. He may have known this—"

Sam flung her pen onto the desk. "How did you get wind of it?"

Agent Case swallowed, as if embarrassed. "He carried out two kills in Jersey. Different casinos. The father of the last vic, before Miss Baines, is an assistant DA. He didn't like the laxness so he reported it to NCAVC who, in turn, entered the data into the VICAP database."

"So he knew about the FBI's National Center for the Analysis of Violent Crimes," Sam said, pursing her lips. "Good for him."

"Very good, and we came in, but it caused a sensitive ripple through the other states and gave us a hell of a lot more work trying to make sense of incomplete reports. But we're working with New Jersey and New York State bureau offices now. When the NYPD entered this case into the database, we got it immediately. He changed his MO with Miss Baines, so we think he'll make another hit—"

"How?" After getting a stare of disapproval from Agent Case and shrugging it off, Sam continued. "How did he change his MO?"

Agent Case sighed. "Can I please just get through this, Detective Wright, before you start your, uh, assessment?" Sam smiled and nodded. "Thank you," he replied curtly before he continued. "The unsub takes the care to drape the hair of the vic over her shoulders. All have been wet, with ammonia. All of the bodies were washed down, except Miss Baines. DNA eliminated in all but hers. So we will get lucky. If he wore a condom, he must have taken it with him." Case paused. "Let me correct myself. He didn't have intercourse with any of them, just a small amount of exploratory sex play. The women were all naked in bed as if they were prepared to have sex, so he may have put on a condom to mislead them. He leaves a scorpling over the nipple of their right breast. Again, not with Miss Baines. All strangled. Red marks from deep pressure around their throats caused petechial hemorrhaging in their eyes as a result. He's strong. Deaths were quick. Those are the commonalities. No clothes left, no fibers, nothing substantial in reports. We assume he had the women undress themselves because their clothing left on the floor had no DNA transfer. We'll see if that remains consistent with Miss Baines. As you can see from the photos, the murders took place in hotel rooms. The adjacent furniture, the club chairs, couches had been checked for DNA transfer in about five of the cases." Sam scowled. Case nodded. "I know, minimal. They came up with a lot of samples. All those people whose DNA was collected, checked out. None were in the room on that day. The vics were all found the day after the murder—in the morning—most from housekeeping personnel. Their murders were calculated to be the night before. In Miss Baines case, she was found around two p.m. the following day. That complicated things further. It was estimated to be about twenty-two hours after death."

"I can see the petechial hemorrhaging," Sam said, touching the tip of her index finger onto the eye area of a photo. "It's obvious with the bulging eyes and black and blues. So how does the timing complicate things?"

"We think she was murdered around four p.m. the previous day. The room was cold. That could slow decomp."

Sam straightened in her chair. "Hold on, cold?" Agent case nodded and Sam frowned. "How cold?"

"The room temp was sixty-five degrees."

"No way. No way in hell would Carrie set it that low. If the room wasn't seventy-four or more, she'd wrap herself in blankets. The killer lowered the temp on the way out to throw us off."

"That's very helpful, Detective. I'll continue. The hotel rooms were in the woman's names. They were secured about an hour to three hours prior to the estimated time of the kill. Except for Miss Baines. She had the hotel room already—"

Sam pounded the folder with a fist. "Okay. I can't help myself. I have to interrupt you, Agent Case. This makes absolutely no sense. If the women got the room, they were at the mercy of the hotel registration desk. How in the world would the killer have jars or cans of ammonia with him? It would have to be a large vessel to hold the amount necessary to clean an adult. And would he carry around a dead scorpion in his pocket? The thought of that nauseates me. So did he leave the woman he had just killed, go to his room to get his supplies, and then return to do the clean up? Leaving the chance wide open for the body to be discovered in the interim? I don't buy that at all. Unless, he was so familiar with the hotels, he knew when housekeeping was done for the day and he scheduled his rendezvous for after that. And even if I bought that, what about friends or relatives of the vics trying to contact them? If they were only there for the day, they would be expected home at some point. But then again, they were single. And another but, they may have lived alone." She shook her head. "Have you looked at all the security footage of the casinos to identify the vics? Maybe they were hanging out with the same man."

"We're doing that now in Jersey, but I have to tell you, casino security systems vary casino to casino, state to state. Some security systems work the tables, others tables and slots. Maybe they have one or two cameras out of forty surveying the floor, and the operator can't possibly know what pick-up is going to be a kill. The operator wouldn't even think of that. So far, there are multiple males that are on both tapes for both days. And there's no photo ID on a player's card, so there's no way of connecting who's who. Our unsub may have driven there, not gone to the player's counter to collect points, nor use a card in the machines. And now some people who are germ phobic even wear gloves when touching a slot machine. We'll use IBIS for the photo identification when the teams put everything together. But for that to come up with a match, our guy has to be in the system. And another thing. If this guy's smart and knows casinos, he might be able to avoid the cameras. Then we'll have nothing."

Sam's gaze fixated on the folder for a moment before she looked at Case. "Smart and knows casinos? Okay, serials who go interstate usually have a job that takes them there. Have they looked at casino employees who have positions that enable them or require them to travel?"

"The lists of thousands are being compiled as we speak. We're doing better than that. We're including regularly assigned employees. Each task-force in each state in which the murders took place is working their own list." Agent Case stared at Detective Withers. "And Detective Withers, who's the lead on New York's task-force, will receive the appropriate list and disseminate orders to others who will interview every last one. To be honest this can take more than several months."

Withers blew out a deep breath. "Okay, so I'm just dealing with New York employees. That would cut the list considerably."

"Not necessarily. If there's interstate travel but a person winds up here, you'll get them, too. You never know who knows someone who knows someone. And the unsub may have made it a point not to do a kill on the day he was assigned there. This guy's not making it easy for us to connect the dots. I have to lay it on the line, Withers. One thing the FBI is known for is thoroughness. We cover everything, down to the minutest detail and take time. With that being said, my ass, our ass, the New York City office's ass, is on the line to make sense of now seventeen murders."

Nick shook his head. *Glad I'm not the task-force lead.*

"What else do you have?" Nick asked flatly.

"DNA and serology reports could take up to two weeks. We're hoping this guy got careless. We *know* he got careless. There was no scent of ammonia on Miss Baines. Now we have to hope he's in CODIS. We marked it urgent so hopefully it'll take a few days at the most."

"Any other difference?" Sam asked.

"For one, the length of time between kills. It was twelve months with Miss Baines. The others were six to ten months apart, max. Sometimes motivations change. Could be for money. These women were rich beyond their salaries. So how much did he know about them? One thing we're certain of was that these were not impulse kills. He made a choice. So we're not looking at a mentally dysfunctional male. Probably not a substance abuser. Probably a man who had a good appearance to lure the women into bed. They weren't prostitutes. Maybe he wanted money from them and they refused. He definitely is taunting law enforcement by leaving a token. He's saying, 'I dare you to catch me.' No, he hasn't sent any messages to law enforcement or through social media."

"So basically, we're looking at a psychopathic personality," Sam said.

"Exactly. Someone you and I could have an intelligent conversation with—that is, until he snaps. And waiting the twelve months can also mean that he did want to stop. We'll only know the answer to that when we ask him."

"Back to the employee thing." Sam paused a moment. "Since Carrie's murder was twelve months from the last kill, wouldn't that lower the numbers? People leave employment all the time. No, that wouldn't matter," she added as if she was talking to herself.

Nick smiled. He's seen her do that, a lot.

"They could have come back to familiar territory," she

continued. "And one more thing. How about delivery people, vendors who supply the casinos? Yes. That goes toward familiar territory. That's what serials do. Um. They might not be stationed there, but I'd also look at companies that supply the casinos."

Nick snickered. Withers closed his eyes and his face flushed as if a bomb had impaled him. "Thanks, Wright. You just multiplied my job by a couple of thousand. I owe ya."

Sam turned the first five pages over and came to Carrie's crime scene picture. She swallowed and wiped a tear from the corner of her eye.

Nick put his hand on her forearm. "You okay?"

She glanced up at him, nodded, and sniffled. "I'm looking at the ligature marks around her neck. There are black and blue finger print marks. Looks like this guy had big hands. Really huge." She picked up a photo from a previous victim. "Carrie's marks are wider and more defined. Could it be he wore gloves when he strangled the other vics? Not winter outdoor gloves, more like latex, like those yellow cleaning gloves."

Agent Case nodded. "Yes. It was determined he did. He seems big enough to control them. So we concluded these were planned at this point. He came prepared to kill. Another reason we're saying he got careless with Miss Baines."

"Hold on. So while in bed with a woman, he stopped to put on a condom and gloves? Did he sedate them?" Case shook his head. "Most women would be suspicious and run, or at least try to," Sam said, putting her index finger over her lips and then raising it into the air to make the point. "Okay so, with the time span of twelve months and not wearing gloves, is it safe to hypothesize that he wanted to stop killing but he couldn't help himself with Carrie because something happened between them?" She looked closer at the strangulation marks. "What are these red bumps on the side of her neck?" She paused, looking at the palms of her hands. "I know! These are callous marks on the balls of his hands. Frank has these. From using weights. Okay we're looking for a big guy, almost as big as Frank judging from the finger size, who's also a gym rat. Make sense?"

☙❧☙

Frank, wearing his Khaos Rules T-shirt, shorts, and ten-ounce boxing gloves, pounded the heavy bag in the back of his Mixed Martial Arts training gym in Harlem, New York. Sweat poured down his face and from his underarms, running down his body. His shirt was saturated. He had been at it over an hour, still concentrating on his form. He knew his heartbeat was at his max but he had no intention of stopping, even feeling like his heart was getting ready to jump out of his chest. He felt his face was hot and red as flaming coals on a barbecue. Grunting and alternating fists, he angled his punches to hit different heights on the bag, pushing full force from his shoulders. When he felt his biceps giving out—the burn too intense—and becoming numb, he bent his arms at the elbows and, with his arms close to his body, he body slammed the bag with his side, alternating from his right side to left. He let himself bounce from the bag about twenty times. When he stopped, he was hyperventilating as he bent over with his hands on his thighs. He picked up the bottle of water that lay by his feet, and guzzled it.

He was glad he was alone on an evening the gym closed at six. He'd be able to get out his aggression, his anger, without one of his gym members seeing their leader and coach so distraught. This was *his time* not to have to keep it together.

Frank hadn't given himself such an arduous session with this bag since Jen was killed. Losing Sam brought up all those memories. Memories of being alone. Memories of not having the emotional and physical closeness. And memories that Frankie wouldn't have a female role model to be a mommy to him. He felt crushed. It hit him that he really did love Sam, now in the present, not just growing to love her. He could kick himself for breaking up with her in such haste.

Frank stood up, closed his eyes before he opened them to get a good look at himself in the full-length mirror that lined the back wall. He didn't like the vision that confronted him. Not only wrecked from his workout, he looked worn and haggard. That repulsed him. He rubbed his hand over his face. That was probably from sleepless nights since he broke up with Sam. He still hadn't told Frankie or his in-laws. Jen's parents loved Sam. Not only because she resembled their daughter physically, but because he'd been happy for the first time since Jen's death. They had definitely seen a mood change in him. And told him so. They didn't need to because he knew he was calmer, less brooding, and he smiled more.

He trudged across the gym, passing the cage. He stopped for a moment and smiled. The vision of himself lying on top of Sam on the matting, holding her tight with her arms above her head, with their fingers interlaced, kissing her, whispering sex talk into her ear while pecking and breathing on her neck, crossed his mind as if a film were playing. He shuddered as he did when her orgasm pulsated through her and he felt her quivers underneath him.

He wanted that again. He craved it.

CHAPTER 6

John Trenton stood by the window in a medical building, staring out at the Manhattan view that he had missed, and craved, for almost a year. Upper Seventies and Lexington. Bumper-to-bumper traffic going downtown. Twenty-plus-story business buildings. His hospital—Manhattan Psych. He inhaled deeply, but the closed window prevented Manhattan pollution from seeping into his lungs. No snow, but it was cold. Cold enough for his bubble jacket over his suit, wool hat and a scarf around his neck. He pulled the scarf off in slow motion, smiling to himself about the battle he almost had with Ricky getting him to put on boots. He figured he let him learn on his own when Duke scampered out into the backyard and Ricky followed in sandals after giving Vicki a flat "No" about the boots. It didn't take three minutes for Ricky to run back into the kitchen, teary-eyed. Socks and boots wouldn't be an issue anymore. John whirled around when the door to the doctor's office opened.

"Sit down, Doctor Trenton," said Dr. Matthew Charles, taking his seat behind his desk and unbuttoning his long white lab coat over his navy suit, pulling it loose from under him. "We have to talk about some issues before I sign these papers."

John didn't sense any warm and fuzzy feelings from this senior citizen. He took off his own coat and hat and tossed them on top of his scarf on the couch behind him. He ran his fingers through his hair before he sat in the armchair opposite the desk. John sat as poker faced as the doctor who was in charge of determining his future. Not only the cutting of his sabbatical short—it was only one month, so that wasn't the issue—but this doctor had the power to determine if John was fit to work within his specialty.

"All right. All your physical tests are fine. Your shoulder mobility will improve, maybe not to a hundred percent, but better than it is now. That's not what concerns me. Have you spoken to anyone in a professional capacity about your risk-taking behavior? There's nothing documented here."

"No."

"Why not?"

"Serento is a very small town. No one there to talk to."

"I don't buy that."

"Seriously, there's no mental health departments in the local hospitals. A patient has to travel at least thirty miles to a separate facility."

After a scowl in response, Dr. Charles opened John's file. "You were seeing a Dr. Burt Landers for a few sessions." The doctor hiked his eyebrows. "I expect you'll be resuming?"

John rolled his eyes. "If it means that you'll sign these papers so that I could continue to work at Manhattan Psych and get back my department head position in forensic psychiatry so I can do what I do best, then yes, I'll continue to see him. For as minimal length of time that I have to."

"Okay. Good. I'm mandating at least ten, one-hour sessions." He looked up at John. Their gaze met.

Wanting a reaction. Like hell. John sat stoic.

"One more thing."

"What's that?"

"No more hostage situations. No negotiating, which, for you, leads to going in unarmed."

"And if the situation warrants it? There are times an intervention is needed, and I'm on site. I'm called by other personnel. I can at least talk a patient down."

"What part of 'no' don't you understand?" Dr. Charles paused. "Okay, if you're in the hospital, I can understand it—talking a patient down, from the outside. You are the department head. Then wait for the armed guards. But no going in for a face-to-face confrontation. Furthermore, Dr. Trenton, and this is non-negotiable. You cannot seek out a hostage situation to become involved in!" John shot him an unappreciative glare. "I see you're not taking this seriously, Doctor! I mean it. Everywhere you go you seem to find yourself in one. Like with that little boy in Florida."

"That little boy is now my son."

Dr. Charles folded his hands on his desk. "All well and good, but if the situation doesn't involve a forensic patient, you'll wait to call in the appropriate personnel. Even if it's just talking in those. Obviously, you didn't learn anything from being shot. This risk-taking behavior is a serious problem. I think you get high on this adrenalin rush. Correct me if I'm wrong." He shot John a long hard look. No response. "I'm mandating that Dr. Landers address this and send in formal evaluations. You have a lot at stake now. You should be thinking about your wife and children."

John blew out a deep breath. He knew Dr. Charles was right.

"If you violate what is going to be documented here, you can be brought up in front of the medical board. And this holds no matter where on this earth you find yourself. Is that clear enough for you?"

"Crystal."

❧❧❧

Sam clenched her fists and pounded the right side of her desk on the first floor of Manhattan Midtown-South precinct. "Damn!" With oblivious intent, she clicked keys on the keyboard to no avail. "Crap! It froze again. Nick—"

Her partner got up from his desk opposite hers, walked behind her, and looked over her shoulder. "What's the matter?"

"Queens sent over some more forensic reports but this—err—stupid machine won't let me open them. All I get is a little X in a box in the upper left of a blank page."

"It didn't freeze. You're in Internet Explorer?" Sam nodded. Nick put his lips together. "We have the latest Adobe." Nick stood behind her. "Try opening in Mozilla. PDF files can be cranky. If that doesn't work, make Chrome the default."

Before Sam could close the program, she heard a commotion in the hallway. She couldn't make out what the voices were saying but it was apparent to her when they came in a few moments later.

Frank grinned ear to ear. "Hey, guys, look who I met in the elevator?"

Sam's eyes popped open. It was John Trenton and Frank Khaos walking next to each other.

Oh my God. He's more handsome in person than through Skype.

With polished John in his pin-striped gray Armani suit, styled longish black hair, and 'rough around the edges' Frank in his usual black T-shirt and skinny jeans, Sam thought of the 1989 movie *Tango and Cash,* with Stallone as Tango, the suited detective, and Russell as Cash, the jean wearing detective. Oh my God! Now it could be *Trenton and Khaos.* She laughed out-loud when she realized the initial consonant sounds of their names were the same, too.

"What's so funny, Detective Wright?" Frank asked curtly.

Nick rolled his eyes and sat back down at his desk.

"Nothing, Dr. Khaos." She hurried over to John and extended her hand to him. "Nice to finally meet you in person, Dr. Trenton." He took her hand and she noticed his grip was as firm as Frank's. She reciprocated. "Visiting?"

"No. I'm back," Trenton added with a smile. "I'm on my way to meet with Lieutenant Rojas about a case that brought me back."

"Yeah? Who?" Frank asked.

"Bobby Mitchell's murder. In a halfway house not far from here." Trenton shook his head. "The kid didn't get a fair shake in life. I want to make sure he gets justice now."

Nick looked up from his desk. "Haven't gotten wind of that one yet."

"That's what I figured. It's been six days since I was notified. I don't have any facts. He doesn't have any family who'd give a damn, either." He looked at his Rolex.

Sam couldn't help but recognize it. He was a man of her ilk.

"I better get into his office. Don't want to be laid out my first day back. I'll catch you guys on my way out."

Sam's gaze followed him as he walked away. She compressed her lips in an effort to suppress her lewd thoughts.

Vicki is sure lucky. A committed hunk and newborns. I could never live with a man like him, though. Not with our clothing bills, alone.

"Hey, Sam. Snap out of it." Frank pulled a chair over to the side of her and Nick's desks. "What do you have so far on the Baine's case?"

Sam jerked around and sat in her chair. "I thought you didn't want to be involved."

Frank wet his lips before putting them together. His cheeks puffed out. "Loo didn't give me a choice. I did try to recuse myself. He told me Jen's killers are done, and what Lex's reactions to you were. Bottom line, he said to me what I say. 'Deal with it.'"

Sam gave him the recap how Carrie's murder changed the profile of the serial killer, that they named him Skorpios, everything she and Nick had been told, down to the minutest details. Nick had opened the new files as Sam talked. He turned the screen so they'd all see it.

Sam scanned the first page. "Crap. No DNA yet. Oooh,

Oh no! They got the warrant for the casino but it hasn't been executed yet. Why in hell not?"

Before waiting for a response from anyone, she dialed Brett Case's number on the phone on the desk with it on speaker.

"Special Agent in Charge Case's office."

"This is Detective Sam Wright. May I please speak with Agent Case?"

"What's this in reference to?"

"A case we're working on."

"He's in the field right now. I can get him your message."

"Okay. Thank you." Sam pushed herself to be respectful. "I wanted to know when we'll be able to view the surveillance footage in the casino."

"That's what he's working on now, Detective. I'll relay that you're waiting for the go-ahead."

"Thank you." Sam heard the disconnect click and looked at the phone, bewildered. "How long does it take him to carry it through?"

"Before the FBI executes a warrant, Sam, they make sure it's right," Nick said. "Yes, it delays the process, and they've been known to wait years in high profile cases. They want nothing bounced. Be patient."

Gritting her teeth, Sam slumped into the chair. "Yeah, right."

Much to everyone's surprise, Case returned her call two minutes later. "Hello, Detective Wright."

Sam understood the cue to be formal. "I'm here with Detective Valatutti and Dr. Khaos. What's going on?"

"I'm actually sitting in the casino with the director of casino security, Louis Handletti and their attorney, David Schwartz. There's going to be a delay."

"Why?"

"They've had experiences in the past where expansive warrants violated the right of others, not the target, and they were sued. They're going to prevent it at all costs."

"This is Detective Valatutti. What do you mean expansive?"

"Mr. Schwartz here, Detective. By expansive, we mean every tape of the entire floors. We're not going to risk it for one person. And, from what I understand, the FBI wants it all, to track employees, as well as patrons."

"This is a serial murder case, Mr. Schwartz," Nick yelled into the phone. "We're not there to create privacy issues."

"Doesn't matter," Schwartz retorted. "This will cause a media circus. Casinos have enough bad blood with the networks. We're not saying it won't happen, Detective, but our legal team will go through the warrant and ask for amendments, and guarantees of indemnities. We must protect our own."

Sam put her index finger up. "Hold on. Hold on. I have an idea."

"You always do, Detective. That's why I called you so promptly. What is your idea?"

Frank gave a smirk of disapproval at the phone. Then he glared at Sam.

She rolled her eyes at Frank before she spoke. "How about if we narrow the search for this warrant while you figure the rest out?"

"Narrow the search, how?" Mr. Handletti's voice sounded suspicious.

"Okay, Miss Baines and I went to the casino together. I know exactly the machines she played. She was consistent and only played in one section. How about you give us the videos for Friday, January eighth, around the specific machines? That will be enough for us to work with for a little bit."

Handletti stuck to his guns. "Still too wide."

"Okay." Sam paused. "She never got there earlier than noon. How about the videos on that day, around specific machines, from noon to four p.m.?"

"If you narrow it to one specific machine, and I mean

one from noon to four," the attorney conceded, "I'll approve it so you can come today to pick up the flash drive."

Sam put her hands up in victory, and mouthed a silent *Yes!* "Thank you! I must ask this, though. Have there been any changes to the machines or their locations? In the last uh, two months?"

"We didn't remove or add new machines, but locations may have been varied," Handletti admitted.

"Okay. Thank you for letting me know this. Will I be allowed to walk around to find the specific machine if it isn't in the remembered location?"

Handletti blew out a deep breath that was audible through the phone. "In that case, yes."

"Since we are being cooperative here, one more thing, please. We'd also like to see the video from Miss Baines floor in the hotel from the elevator to her room, during the same time frame."

"She's good, Agent Case," Handletti said sarcastically. "Okay, I can see that's necessary. Okay, done. And a few more things from me."

"What's that?"

"I will be meeting you at the south entrance from the parking lot and you'll not step foot in the casino without me. You will not stroll to your heart's content. You head straight to the machine, or look for it. I'll note the serial number on it, and have the video chopped to the specifics. Someone in my department will bring the copy to you, and you're outta there. Understood?"

"Oh, so we can't have someone view it with us on site?"

"No. I'm keeping this under the radar until my legal team goes through the FBI paperwork."

"But—"

"Don't push it, Detective. Or I'll rescind. I'm a tough SOB."

"Okay. Thank you."

"When can you be here?"

"In about an hour?"

"I'm in control. Two hours."

Sam closed her eyes. She wanted to slug him. "Yes, sir. South entrance in two hours."

"And a couple of more things, Detective," the attorney chimed in. "Transfer of custody. You will sign papers for receipt and hand over the copy to Agent Case for viewing, since the warrant is in his signature."

Sam gasped.

"No worries, Detective," Case said. "I'll stay here at the casino to take possession. You can't keep the USB device unguarded overnight. In fact, I'll meet you with Mr. Handletti."

"You guys better get outta there, now," grumbled Handletti. He disconnected the call.

Frank put his palm on her forearm. "Hold on, Detective Wright. You don't look happy. We're getting the parts we're interested in. Mind filling me in?"

Sam glanced at Frank's hand, still on her arm. Her blood heated then she pushed him off. "I want to check out the hotel room and have more freedom to look around." Frank glared at her. She shook her head. "No. The room hasn't been used since."

"All right. Soon," Nick said.

"Yeah. But I want to see the footage on site, with an operator who could explain them in specific areas. Who's up for playing the slots?"

Frank scowled. "Not there to play. You heard Handletti—"

"I need to get a feel for what happened to Carrie and that includes the machines we—uh, she—liked." She conjured up the meanest face she could with her nose scrunched and lips pursed. "Whether you like it or not, Dr. Khaos. Hopefully I can persuade that pompous jerk to let me."

Frank bellowed laughter and tapped her nose with his index finger. "That expression doesn't suit you at all, Detective."

"Knock off the hostility. The both of you. If you think

I'm dealing with this teenage garbage, forget it. Last time I'm saying it." Nick closed down the computer and, without looking at them, grabbed his coat off the rack in the corner.

☙☙☙

Sam, Nick, and Frank exited Nick's SUV in the casino parking lot. About a few hundred cars parked sporadically through the three thousand spot area. They snagged a spot not far from the south entrance where Sam saw Agent Case talking on the phone as he stood next to the self-proclaimed SOB, Louis Handletti, who had two guards of his own standing nearby. As soon as she laid eyes on him, Sam intended to knock that guy down a peg or two. Wearing a muted plaid sports jacket—still in good taste—and dark gray dress slacks, this man had the same bravado as another man she mellowed—Carlos Philetano, from the Aries case. Now Frank and Agent Case, in addition to Nick, would see her in action.

Sam approached the casino director, who sported a ponytail, with a smile. "Hello, Mr. Handletti," she said as she extended her hand to shake. "I'm Detective Samantha Wright."

He wet his lips before he took her hand in his. He held on. His gaze scanned her from head to toe and he kept a broad smile plastered on his face. Sam continued to smile. "Welcome to my casino, Detective."

"Thank you. These are my partners—"

He put up palm, facing them, and glanced at their badges hung around their necks. "Just conceal your badges. Come on in." He held the door open for her, but let it go for the men.

Still in the lobby, Sam deepened her appeal. "We really appreciate this, Mr. Handletti."

"Call me Lou."

"Thank you, Lou. I just wanted to tell you this means a

lot to me, personally. All of my cases do. But the victim in this case, Carolyn Baines, was my best friend."

"Really? Oh, man. I'm so sorry."

"Yes, since kindergarten."

"Okay." Handletti's expression turned somber. "Then let's see how I can help you find that scum."

He meant it. His energy field became less tense—less rigid. Good thing she could sense vibes that people sent out. Sam turned briefly to acknowledge her team. The five men looked nothing less than flabbergasted.

"You know what, Detective? Because I like you, I'm going to let you go where you want. On your honor. Since your machine may have indeed been moved. More importantly, coming back here under the circumstances might be difficult. Hey, Ted," Handletti called to one of the guards. "Stay with them, don't interfere, just get the serial number of the machine." He checked his watch. "I just remembered I have a conference call." Sam could tell it was an excuse. He walked off without acknowledging them. The second guard went with him.

Sam tried to remain stoic. Inside, her heart thumped.

The noise level from clanging machines and screaming people reached an abnormal decibel. Sam made her way around the wall-to-wall people, who she assumed were getting ready to blow the rest of their paychecks in the hopes of hitting it big. The noise level was so high she was able to ignore Frank's mumbling as he walked next to her. In all honesty, she didn't need the noise. She was a pro at planned ignoring. With a smile from ear to ear plastered on her face, Sam bolted out in front of him, and making sure she didn't push people out of the way, zig zagged through the casino's center lane and headed to the aisle with the machines that she and Carrie played.

She was never as directionally challenged here as Carrie was, so she always found her machine. She glanced behind her and in between other people to see Frank, Brett Case, and Nick trailing, looking as bewildered as she would be finding her way out of a jungle. Ted remained behind them.

When the men were in sight and focused on her, she continued down the aisle until reaching the spot the Wild Sevens machine used to stand. She pivoted three hundred sixty degrees around. The poker table was to her right. Check. The Wheel of Fortune slots stood to her left. Check. The small VIP section on a raised platform with ten-dollar machines stood behind her. Check. Sam scanned the area, bewildered.

Frank didn't hesitate to show his annoyance. "So?"

"The machines were right there," Sam said pointing right in front of her. "Ted, would you know where they moved them?"

"It's a crap shoot, Detective. Totally random."

"Would they be taken out of this section?"

"Could be."

Agent Case covered his mouth with his hand. "Come on, Ted. You can see why we need the complete tapes."

Ted merely put his hands out. "Walk around a little and see if you can find it. And the configuration may be different, too."

"What do you mean?"

"Was the machine in a grouping that formed a shape or in a line?"

Sam got excited. "Yes!" She ran to the area near a floor to ceiling squared column that a cash machine presently leaned against. "The machine Carrie liked was right here. Two more with different symbols were to the left. On an angle." She walked to another side of the column. "There was a machine here, and three more to the right of that one. And there was a machine on the opposite side."

"Very good, Detective. Those slots were very popular and they *were* moved, but put into a smaller display. Come on."

Ted led the way to the end of the aisle. Sam became very thankful he was with them. She never would have found it. Neither she, nor Carrie ever played there. However, a poker table was to her left. The Wheel of Fortune to her right, and another platform for high rollers took up the space behind her—the same layout.

Ted pointed. "Is that the arrangement?"

Sam hurried to the machine. The Wild Sevens dollar machine stood caddy cornered with four other machines, sides meeting, to form an enclosure. It had four symbols or numbers across depending upon how the spin landed. The player could bet one to three dollars. She sat on the backless stool as Frank and Nick looked at her, appearing to be stunned. Case pursed his lip, as if he was preparing to say something.

"This is definitely the machine. Is it the only machine like this in the casino?"

"No. There are more in the area near the escalator going up to the buffet and hotel. But they wouldn't move the ones in this area over to there. This will be the best you've got, right now, Detective."

"I only played one buck, max." Sam sighed at the memory. "Carrie went all out, three, all the time."

Frank sneered. "That's supposed to make me feel better? You have a problem with this, too?"

"Excuse me? What the hell do you care?"

"So you're playing now?" Frank growled.

"Hey!" Nick admonished. "Keep the personal stuff out of it."

Agent Case reinforced it. "Especially if you want to remain on this case, Detective."

Sam gasped. "No, I'm not playing. Not at all." She spun around in the stool and looked up, scanning the ceiling of the room and along the beams that held the lights. Hundreds of them. The glare was so bright, she needed to squint and even then, she didn't have a clear view. Sam moved a foot away from the stool, looked up and around from the right, left and center. She smirked at Frank and Nick as they stood there—Frank with his fingers in his skinny jeans pockets. "You could help, you know."

Frank scowled again. "What?"

"She's looking for the security cameras." Ted pointed to a box on a column that was a few feet away and to the left of them. "There's one. Hold on." He took out an electronic device and held it up to the camera. "Okay. Got it. Stay here. Give me twenty minutes."

Sam blew out a deep breath. "Sure. Thank you." She walked around the area with her gaze going over every machine. "What will happen if Carrie couldn't find it, either, and played other machines? What will happen if that guy got to her before she played it? Brett, I'm begging you, please get them to work on it fast."

"Believe me, I know that. Sit down. You're getting me nervous walking around."

She plopped on the seat in front of *the favorite machine* and bit her lip.

Frank sent her a glare that could kill. "Don't you dare, Sam."

Her gaze went to Case. His brow hiked. She clasped her hands in her lap and sat straight up tall.

Ted returned sooner than twenty minutes. "Here you go, Agent Case. We got the machine. Don't know if your people are in it. But there was a problem for three minutes on the hotel floor."

"What kind of problem?" Nick asked.

"January eighth we had a blackout, one ten to one fifteen p.m. All systems were down. The backup got lights restored in three minutes, but our security cameras were out for a full five. Sorry about that."

Frank mumbled. "Just our luck."

"Thank you, Ted," Sam said as he walked away.

CHAPTER 7

Getting himself more entangled in his blanket with every move, Frank tossed and turned in bed, not being able to get Sam's hostility out of his mind. Lying on his back, he kicked the blanket to get his arms and legs free, eventually pulling his legs out from under it. Damnit! He didn't need a nighttime workout. His mind—without missing a beat—returned to Sam. When he questioned her, she transformed from ice cubes to icicles. She actually thought he hadn't noticed? Oh, man. He had fallen for her too fast and too heavy. What secrets was she hiding from him? Maybe he should have spoken to her privately, without her partner and Case being there. Would she have become so defensive if he had? And his own attitude left much to be desired, as well. He was giving himself a headache—usually not one of his problems. What he did know was that this woman was no Jen, nor could she replace Jen. He couldn't live with a woman who kept secrets from him. He rolled over onto his side and opened the bottom drawer of his night table. He pulled out his and Jen's wedding picture and stared at his beautiful late wife in her off-white trumpet gown.

Oh, man, Jen. And here I was, thanking you for bringing Sam into our lives. Yeah, she solved the case of your murder and for that, I'll be forever grateful, but to have her replace you in my life—in Frankie's life—in my bed—that was a mistake. How am I going to tell Frankie that we broke up? He was getting used to having her around. He had even slipped once and called her "Mommy." Sam glowed. She loves him. And your parents? They love her, too. And just to keep her around for casual sex? No, Jen, that's not my thing anymore. Getting too old for that. Guess I'll have to be content raising Frankie as a single dad.

He got up out of bed, holding the edges of the frame between his hands, and placed it on the wall in its previous place—the wall opposite his bed so he could stare at it as he silently cried himself to sleep each night.

He got back into bed, lying on his back as a single tear trickled down his cheek.

Frank had no idea how he fell asleep, but he must have. He turned around onto his side when he heard his cell phone ring. He answered on the third ring.

He rubbed his eyes and yawned. "Yeah?"

"Hey, Khaos, still asleep?"

Frank looked at the time on the cell. "Eight o'clock on a Saturday when it's my day off? Yeah, Trenton. Why are you up? This is the middle of night for you, man."

"Not since the twins were born."

Frank laughed. "What's up?"

"Vicki is getting used to the new kitchen and she wants to have a get-together. How about coming up today? Sam told me she wanted to see the babies. And we'd like to have Ricky make a new friend."

Frank hesitated. He sat up and pulled the blanket down to his waist. "We, uh, broke up."

"I sensed something was wrong yesterday, with the formality. What happened?"

"Not exactly sure. But we had different priorities over this case, and I made a snap decision. Thinking about it, it's the right one. I haven't told Frankie yet, though."

"Yeah, well, short-term break-ups are common. Vicki and I broke up for three weeks last year, right at the beginning of her pregnancy that I hadn't known about at the time.

The thing is to make it work so you get back together."

"So you got yourself shot on purpose?"

"Not funny, Khaos. The universe does things in wondrous ways, though. Maybe getting shot showed us that we can't live without each other. I'm not recommending that you or Sam get yourselves shot, by the way."

"Didn't take it that way."

"Well, don't wait for something to happen that will make you regret it. So how about it?"

"I'll call Sam. Speak to you in a bit."

Frank felt the rush of adrenalin pump through his veins at the thought of having to call Sam. Fear, anger, lust, he couldn't put his finger on it. But he pressed the auto-dial. She answered sounding groggier than he did.

"Hello, Frank."

"Good morning."

"It's eight-fifteen, Frank."

"Well aware of the time. John called. He wants us to drive up today to see the twins, and have Frankie and Ricky meet. Vicki is an amazing cook, so I know from experience we have to go hungry. How about it? You busy?"

"You haven't told Frankie yet, have you?"

He lowered his voice. "No. I haven't. Can't you do me a favor, and just go along with it? Until I'm ready to tell him. Please?"

"When will you be ready?"

"Don't know. Are you up for it?"

"I'm going to see the twins," she said flatly. "When do you want to pick me up?"

"It's almost a two hour drive up to Scarsdale. Figure, noon."

"Okay. Good. I'll have time to go baby shopping."

"What do you know about baby clothes?"

Sam's voice lowered. "All my friends have children."

"You sound like you're getting the urge."

"Don't worry, Frank. You're off the hook. I'll be ready at twelve." She disconnected.

Frank stared at the phone. He felt Sam's sadness through the airwaves. One thing for sure, she had that maternal instinct and she'd be a great mom. She had just done a number on him. He went from being definitive about their breakup to indecisive. That was a place he didn't want to be caught in.

Frank heard water dripping from the shower faucet. In a minute, Frankie would be storming into the bedroom. He'd better snap out of this funk. He was right. Frankie stumbled into the bedroom, half-dripping-wet, half-dry, with a towel wrapped around his waist. Frank grabbed it, rubbed him down and rewrapped him with the towel, and then pulled him close and held him in his arms. Frank kissed the top of his son's head.

"Who were you talking to, Dad?"

"Dr. Trenton, and then, Sam."

"Who's Dr. Trenton?"

"He's a forensic psychiatrist, like me. And he just got back from Florida. In fact, you're going to meet him today. He has a son a year older than you and two-month-old twins. We're picking Sam up in a few hours and going to their house. It's quite a drive from here."

"Twins?" Frank saw his son's face light up. "You know, Dad. I sort of want a baby brother or sister."

Frank widened his eyes. "You do?"

"Yeah. I was kind of thinking, Dad."

"Thinking what?"

"When are you going to ask Sam to marry you?"

‿♥‿

Sam sat in the passenger seat with her mouth agape while Frank drove into the circular driveway that led to a multi-car parking area in the rear of the Colonial style home. This house was bigger than any she had ever seen— bigger than any in Brooklyn, that was for sure, where she had been born and raised. Her mind ruminated over her friends' homes—those who had moved out of Brooklyn into suburbia. Nope. None of them compared, either. Sam got out of the Explorer and looked up at the bone, stone, three-story dwelling on two acres.

The back yard looked like a forest to her, but winter had left the massive oaks looking dried out and brown. Snow covered any leaves on the ground, as well as the landscaping in the front yard, but Sam could guess judging from John's taste—when she met him—that the décor would be just as exquisite as the massive structure they were about to enter.

Frank popped the trunk. "Come on, Sam, take some of these packages."

"Oh. Okay, sure." She took the babies' presents out of the trunk.

Frankie carried two boxes for Ricky, and Frank a box of sugar-free chocolate.

Barking, coming from inside the house, caused Frankie to jump back.

"It's okay. His name is Duke and he's your favorite breed—a German Shepherd."

"That's another thing I want, Dad."

Sam chuckled. "What's the first thing you want, sweetheart?"

Frankie stared up at her and bit his lip. "Uh, that's private between me and my dad." He giggled as he hid behind Frank.

Sam cocked her head, stared at Frank, who looked away trying to hide his grin, and when she didn't get a response, she sprinted up the thirteen steps to the front door. She didn't have to ring the bell.

John opened the door holding two-month old Zach on his chest and right shoulder. The infant's face nestled into his father's neck. Sam swooned. John moved aside to let them in, but Sam followed him around.

She patted Zach's back. "Oh my God, he's so beautiful.

He's got all that black hair, like you." She completely ignored Frank and his son.

John laughed. "Come inside. Only have den furniture." He led them into the den off the center hall. "Ricky, come on, Frankie's here."

Sam's gaze took in the massive hexagonal shaped room with a huge bay window furnished with a black leather couch, two love seats, and a couple of recliners that sat on whitewashed bamboo floors. The bright winter sun shone though the undressed windows. She squinted when the glare hit her eyes.

John snuck over to Frank and whispered to him. "You're dead meat."

"Don't I know it. Oh, man, he's adorable. Let me hold him."

After Frank took off his coat and hung it on a rack near the entrance, John handed Zach over to Frank and the baby wiggled to make himself comfortable in the contour of his chest. The baby looked up with his head bobbing.

"Blue eyes, wow." Frank patted the infant's back as he walked over to the couch. "Oh, man, Frankie. You were this size once. Frank supported Zach's head with his palm.

Frankie frowned and sat down next to his dad.

Sam tossed her coat on the couch then looked at Frank. What she saw startled her. "Um, he looks good on you." She sat down on the couch next to him and ran her finger over the baby's cheek. "So soft." Zach bubbled and cooed. "What's the matter, Frankie? You look sad."

"I think I changed my mind. Don't get any ideas, Dad."

Frank curled his lips down.

"What, Frank?"

Before he could answer, Ricky ran in, with Duke scampering in front of him.

Duke ran over to Frank immediately and began sniffing him and the baby. Frankie backed up deep into the cushion, while Ricky crouched next to John on the love seat.

"It's all right, Frankie. Just let him sniff you. He's friendly and he's used to kids."

"Come here, Duke." The dog moved over to Sam. She bent in toward him. He jumped up with his paws on her shoulders and licked her face. Sam laughed. "You're a gorgeous big boy."

"Duke, down!" John reprimanded.

Zach whimpered when he heard his father's raised voice. The whimpering turned to crying and squirming, and then Duke began whimpering, too.

"This, I'm not used to anymore." Frank got up and handed the crying baby over to his father. John laughed. When the baby nestled onto John shoulder, he calmed down.

Vicki rushed in, holding Alexi in her arms. "What's going on?"

"Ooooh, how precious. Hi, Vicki, I'm Sam." She got up and went to greet the woman who resembled herself. Sam couldn't believe it. Vicki stood taller than she did by about two inches. They both had blue eyes—Vicki's were lighter. They both wore their blonde hair in a ponytail—though it was obvious Vicki was a natural blonde, and Sam's was from a bottle—highlighted. She looked at the baby wantonly.

"Hello, darlin'. Want to hold her?"

"Yes!"

Vicki laughed as she handed the baby over to Sam. Sam cradled the infant in her arms with the baby's head in the crook of her arm. She hugged her close. "Oh, my God. If this isn't the most precious." Sam walked with the baby over to the couch and sat down next to Frank.

"I don't know what you two are waiting for, darlins'. The clock is ticking."

"Tell me about it," Sam replied. She looked up at Frank and met a smirk in response.

"Uh, Frankie," Frank fumbled for words. "Why don't you give Ricky the present we got him?"

"Okay, Dad." He picked up one box and went across the room to Ricky. "Here, Ricky, we got this for you."

Sam saw the blond, curly headed boy with the cherub cheeks light up. He was a year older than Frankie—nine—but shorter and slighter in build. She figured that was because Frank was huge. He must have been a big baby. Frankie, too. She involuntarily put her palm over her stomach, imagining—for a moment—how Frank came out of his mother's birth canal. Could she endure that pain? The tearing open of wrapping paper brought her out of her reflection.

"Yes! Dad, I wanted this game! Thanks, Frankie!"

Frank smiled and nodded to John as he rustled his son's shoulder length curls.

"Ricky, why don't you take Frankie up to your room and play the game? You know how to set it up."

"I do, too," Frankie said.

The two boys looked at each other and Ricky sped out of the den with Frankie in hot pursuit.

Vicki watched the boys charge up the stairs before she spoke. "So how did you two meet?" She nuzzled next to her husband on the love seat.

"On the job," Frank replied.

Sam curled her lips down. "It was more than that, Frank. It was my first day in the rank. First day in the precinct. It was weird. I'll tell you. I was sitting on the bench in the hall." The memory made her chuckle. "All messed up from being wet and muddy from a crime scene and he comes over in his tight T shirt and skinny jeans and sits down next to me. I couldn't believe he was a psychiatrist."

"Hey. You didn't look like detective material, either."

She sneered at him. "Well, we just got closer after that. How did you two meet?"

"It wasn't romantic either." Vicki laughed. "It was actually the first night John was in Serento. His father had a fender bender and mine had an indigestion attack so bad, we thought it could have been a heart attack. Thank God, it wasn't. So we met in the ER at the hospital. It was the same night John met Ricky. Over four years ago." She looked adoringly at her husband. "The next day we met at the pool, and *then* it became romantic. Pretty fast."

Their conversation was halted by loud banging, furniture being pushed along bamboo floors, and creaking of bed coils coming from the room above them.

A few minutes later, a combination of laughing, and bellowing, along with bodies smacking on a mat accosted their ears.

John and Frank bolted out of the room and up the stairs to Ricky's room.

꿍꿍꿍

Ricky and Frankie each wore a Karate gi and both boys were plopped down on their backs on a blue workout mat on the floor, sweaty, and looking exhausted.

"What's going on?" John demanded as he and Frank looked at the room in disarray. The bed slid across the room toward the desk, pillows and books had fallen onto the floor.

Ricky sat up. "Dad, I need my pump."

John took the asthma inhaler out of his pocket and handed it to his son. He took two puffs and his breathing eased.

"Frankie, what happened?"

"We started to set up the game, we did, but the game rules in this one were too hard and we couldn't read them. And then Ricky got mad and wouldn't say what he was mad at."

John pulled Ricky into his arms. He let out a deep sigh. "Why'd you get mad?"

"Because I couldn't read the directions, an' I'm a year older than him." Ricky buried his head into his father's chest. "I'll never catch up. I'm stupid."

Frank compressed his lips and nodded to John. John

rubbed his son's back. "No you're not. You're catching up great. You're a very smart guy."

"No, I'm not, Dad."

"Why do you think you're stupid?"

"Frankie!"

"No, Dad. He got over it and then I saw his gi and we started talking about that. And he does Tae Kwon Do, too. And I said I bet my dad could beat up your dad because you do BJJ. But I was just teasing."

"An' I said my dad is a third degree black belt an' he's teaching me an' I go to school for it too, an' I could take him even though he's older than me an' that's when I found out Frankie is younger than me. An' then we had a play match. He's a yellow belt an' I'm still a white belt."

"Yeah, Dad. And I told Ricky he has to talk to you."

"Oh yeah. Why?"

"We got talking about how big we are and Ricky told me he's adopted and that's why he's not going to be as big as John. And you're adopted."

John smiled at the interaction. "Come on, champ. Let's get your room back together. You'll have plenty of time to talk."

When Frankie saw the coast was clear—that John was moving the bed and putting the room back together with Ricky—he whispered to his father, "Dad, he's still sad that his real mom and dad didn't want him and they're in jail. I told him you were adopted when you were ten and he should talk to you about it because, I don't know." Frankie scrunched his nose. "Did you feel the same way, Dad? Were you sad your real mom and dad gave you away?"

Frank hugged his son and closed his eyes for a moment while he held him close. He hadn't thought about that in years, actually since he had met Jen in Iraq. He kissed him on the head. "Yeah, I sure did."

"Why don't you two get washed up and dressed?" John said. "I'm sure dinner should be ready. And Vicki prepared a lot of food."

"I'm starving an' my mom is sure a good cook."

"Yeah, well you beat me. My dad cooks military."

"What's that?" Ricky looked puzzled.

"Everything in one pot."

"What about ya mom? Samantha."

"She's not my mom. My mom was killed when I was five. Sam is Dad's girlfriend."

ຕ⌐ນ

Still holding Alexi on her shoulder, Sam sat on a cushioned bench in front of a bay window that was part of the seating for the table in the hexagonal shaped nook. The previous owners left the white placket wood shades on the window. Sam didn't feel the sun burning through on her back, at least.

The table was set for six. Sam felt the infant's breathing on her neck and a quiver of contentment caroused through her. She always knew she wanted to become a mom, but since she had held Alexi, she didn't realize how much. How eminent the need was. How primitive. She kissed the baby's cheek and kept her lips there, feeling the love and warmth.

"You're blessed, Vicki, three amazing children and a more amazing husband."

"Thanks, Sam. I sure do know that. Things do look promising with that guy of yours."

"No. It doesn't. We broke up last week and he wanted me to come today because he hadn't told Frankie yet. And I wanted to meet you and the twins."

"You broke up? Why?"

"Something stupid. Conflict of interest in a case. And to tell you the truth, I think Frank was looking for an excuse. If his first impulse is to run away instead of talking it through, I couldn't live with that in a relationship. So maybe it was for the best. Oh my God. That smells so good.

"I have to give you a word of advice, darlin'. You need to choose your battles. Not everything has to turn into an argument or breakup for that matter. Sometimes men just blurt out things in a moment of anger. Their inner childishness makes them want their own way. I see that with John. A sophisticated doctor as himself, known throughout the city, and he could still pout like a five-year-old. But I think being a dad changed him. I think he gets it that he isn't a kid anymore."

"I get that, Vicki, but Frank's been a dad for eight years. I think he's not over his wife's murder."

Vicki did a double take. "Murder? How did that happen? John never mentioned that. He just told me that Frank is a widower."

"It was horrific. At first, they thought it was a gang initiation. Retaliation, because Frank rehabs gang members and convinces them to leave the hood. Then when I investigated, I found out it was a cover-up." Sam swallowed hard. "A homicide detective was protecting his wife who ran an embezzlement scam at the hospital Jen worked at. Jen had discovered the imbalances in the invoices." Vicki looked at Sam with her mouth agape. "Yes, Vicki, painful. To make matters worse, the murder took place on Frank's birthday. Plus, Jen was pregnant. Frank had worked with the creep, a lot, too. The case went unsolved for over two years and—"

Sam came to a halt when she heard the troop come down the stairs, plodding into the kitchen.

ଙ୍କଚ

"Still holding her?" Frank smirked. "You do realize you're not taking her home."

"Very funny." Sam kissed Alexi on the cheek.

John slipped Alexi out of Sam's arms. "Come on. When we eat, she's in her rocker."

Vicki plated the twenty-pound turkey that she had taken out of the oven.

Sam inhaled deeply. "Oh my God, Vicki, that smells so good. Let me help you."

"No. You stay right there. Vicki's possessive about her kitchen."

"Thanks, darlin'. It's his mother's recipe but I make it my own. John loves turkey with his mother's stuffing." She placed a large oval black, gray, and yellow platter in the center of the table, piled high with sliced parts of the bird— dark and white meat, thighs, wings, herbed cracker stuffing. Then she placed a rectangular pan with baked yam soufflé, and a bowl with broccoli sautéed with garlic and oil on the table. "Come on y'all, let's dig in. I'm starving."

"Me, too!" The boys' voices trampled each other's.

Vicki placed a gravy boat on the table with her home-made gravy. "It's gluten-free, only the veggies and spices, blended. Oh, and so is the cracker stuffing, Frank."

"Thank you!"

"Why gluten-free, if you don't mind me asking?" Vicki asked as she served her son. "You have John wanting that now, too."

Frank laughed. "Yeah, we did talk about it. Gluten triggers inflammation. So it'll be good for everyone." He tilted his head toward Ricky and noticed him becoming fidgety in his seat. He nudged Sam with his elbow.

Sam understood the message—a need for a distraction— and leaned toward the platter. "Vicki, this smells so good. What did you put in it? No, let me guess."

Frank rolled his eyes. "How would you even know? I'm still waiting for the dinner you promised us."

"Frank, you're a bundle of love today, aren't you?"

He leaned over and gave Sam a kiss on her cheek. "Sure am, princess." He winked at her. "Stop being so serious. Okay, hotshot, so what's in this? I couldn't venture to guess."

"I have a great sense of smell. Okay, garlic for sure, pap-rika, but not the usual one, curry, turmeric, cardamom." She sniffed. "Uh, onions." She dipped the tip of her fork into the gravy on the turkey on her plate and tasted it. "Um, so good. Carrots, mushrooms, and onions definitely. Anything else?"

"Yes, darlin', a couple, but I must say, you did great. Yes, Paprika, but not sweet. This is smoked. Gives a more rustic flavor. I also use nutmeg in the stuffing. That just brings it all together."

"Those two, I wouldn't have guessed."

Vicki served Frank and Sam, and they dug in, ravenously.

Frank took a slug of water from his goblet. "How did you guys get everything set up so fast?"

John blew out a breath of relief. "Thank God we had a real estate agent who was a gift. We ordered new bedroom sets online, sight unseen, and she was here for all the deliveries. On the way up, we stopped at the condo and packed our kitchen stuff, linens. It was a very stressful week. But we love this house."

Frank noticed Ricky sitting with his lips pursed and a faraway look in his eyes and shot John a warning look.

"What's the matter, champ?"

He shook his head. "Nothing."

"You look like Frankie does when he wants to tell me something."

Frankie nudged Ricky's arm with his fist. "Go ahead, ask him."

"I was thinkin', Dr. Frank." Frank smiled. Ricky squirmed in his chair. "Frankie told me you were adopted when you were ten."

"Yes, I was."

"When did they give you away?"

Frank paused before he spoke. "Well, I never knew they did. I never met my birth parents. All I know is that they were young when they had me, too young to be parents. So were yours."

"Mine gave me away when I was five. They're still in jail."

The adults shot each other sympathetic looks.

"I know. Your dad told me."

Ricky glanced up at Frank. "But I still don't know why they did all those bad things to me."

Frank met Ricky's eyes. "You know. There are many different kinds of people in this world. Many do good things. Some do horrible things. Nothing I could say could undo what they did. But now, you have a mom and dad who love you very much, and will never let anyone do anything to hurt you, ever again."

John rustled his son's hair. Ricky pouted. "But it still hurts, why they didn't love me."

Even Frank's shrink mind came to a halt. He'd heard this many times from his hood gym members and they were twice Ricky's age. "Sometimes when moms and dads are young, like yours were when they had you, and mine were, and bad things happened to them, they don't know any better. So they act the same way. I know that's hard to understand, but eventually you will. Now you have a chance at a new life, just like I did," He paused and compressed his lips. "And all the pains will be washed away, if you let them. It took me a long time to understand it, too. Plus, I was impossible. In school I always got into trouble—"

"Me, too!" Ricky interrupted. "I kept getting thrown out. That's why I'm being homeschooled until I catch up."

"So did I. Got suspended all the time. I wouldn't listen to my teachers or anybody."

"Did your new parents homeschool you, too?"

"Nope." Frank gave Vicki and John a serious glance. "That's something you both need to think about. Homeschooling in New York is a lot tougher, more rigid with more standards than in Florida. Much harder to carry through on."

"I know. I did my research. We'll talk about it." John said.

Ricky paled. "I'm not going to regular school!" He bolted out of his chair.

CHAPTER 8

Early in the morning, John entered the war room of the Manhattan Midtown-South precinct where Lex Withers, Bella Richards, and Lieutenant Rojas sat at the conference table. He frowned at the box on the table a courier must have brought in earlier, which had Bobby Mitchell's name written in black permanent marker on the side facing him—Bobby's case files. To him, this was a major red flag. Bobby's case was low on the priority roster. Already shelved. He intended to change that.

John nodded to the team. "Good morning. Thanks, for coming down from Queens. I was surprised to hear you were transferred."

"Yeah. Well, life happens."

Without waiting for a further explanation, nor caring about one, John unbuttoned his sports jacket and continued as he sat down. "So you completed your investigation?"

"Nice to see you too, again, Doc." Withers gave a snide smile. "I see you recovered fully."

"Yes, I did." John rotated his shoulder to limber up. "Almost. I appreciate you taking over the Montgomery case last year. Do you think Bobby's murder is related?"

Withers shrugged. "At first we did. That's why we're on this one. The higher-ups wanted us on it since Montgomery hired some kids to find you. When one of them was killed, Mitchell ratted out the triggerman and IDd him in a lineup.

Thought this was retaliation. But it wasn't. The killer got thirty, took a deal. Then he was unlucky enough to get his lights put out with a shank in a brawl upstate. He didn't have time to orchestrate a hit. Oh, by the way, the woman we found burnt to a crisp that I mentioned to you when you were in the ICU?"

"Sure I remember. What about her? It definitely wasn't Montgomery."

"It was her elderly neighbor in the adjoining apartment. Montgomery offed the hubby, but disposed of his body. We found him in the East River. She hid her weapons in a trunk in their closet. Got rid of those folks just in time. But we handed the feds another case. They took down some pretty big arms dealers."

John shook his head. "Find any other bodies?"

"No, they were all long gone."

"Wait a minute. How long was that guy at Rikers?"

"Montgomery's hit man?" John nodded. Withers shrugged again. "About four months. Spent most of it in the box. No visitors."

"He's allowed out of solitary an hour a day. That's enough. Phone calls?"

"We have a few taped. From his mother. Most of the time she was screaming at him about how stupid he was. He barely could get a word in."

"Mothers protect their sons. Did she visit?"

"No one visited. All his cronies stayed away. He told the DA that his mom is disabled, but he wouldn't get into it."

"I want the tapes of the conversations. He might have slipped something to his mother."

Richards looked eye-to-eye with him. "Doctor Trenton, we know what we're doing."

"With all due respects, Detective Richards, I was called in as an extra pair of eyes to put all of this together."

"Hold on, Doctor Trenton," Lieutenant Rojas said. "As I recall in our initial conversation you called yourself in. I agreed because of your relationship with the vic."

John smirked. "Whatever. And his name is Bobby or Mr. Mitchell." He pointed at the box. "Okay, so what's happening here?"

Richards lifted the cover off the box. She pulled out files. "The tapes are in here, at the bottom. Crime scene photos." She slid the jacket to John. Then she took out two more. "These are forensics and interviews, actually just lists of people we have to interview."

John opened up the first folder. He grimaced seeing Bobby's beaten body. The black and blue marks spread over his entire torso. Bobby looked much thinner than the last time John saw him. "These bruises are from ungloved hands. You had to get a lot of DNA from this."

"I know we did. Final reports haven't come in yet. And to be honest, the poor kid is on a waiting list." Richards looked as pained as John.

John rubbed his temples with his fingers. "Figured that much."

"But we did make three arrests." Richards glanced up at John. "The forensic tests will nail them, but we believe we got them."

John opened the interview folder. "Save me some time. Who are these guys?"

"One lived at the halfway house. Trig Maynor. Had a rap sheet. All misdemeanors, now graduated to A1 felony murder. He worked there, too. In the office, fielding phone calls, accepting rent payments from the residents." John shot Richards a glance. She nodded and continued. "It was city subsidized, but those who worked contributed what they could. He also took messages from disgruntled residents. The place was worn down, but it sure as hell better than being out in the streets."

"I know about the rent. What did Maynor say?"

"Nada," Withers chimed in. "Lawyered up before the cuffs clicked. He's at Rikers with the other two. Did the same thing. All have legal aid. We got them through an eyewitness. But that doesn't matter, now. We have security footage as it happened. Their clothes and fists bloodied from impact. The vic's wallet was found in Maynor's possession. His shoes found in another's, Shel Davisdon. And his shaving stuff in the third's, Wendall Slick. We had enough evidence to indict. But listen to this, their attorneys waived their right to the six days to release or indict, so we carried through the day before yesterday after we obtained a warrant for the security tape."

"Why the hell did they do that?"

"Legal aid attorneys are over worked. Their caseload is too much to handle even for an experienced attorney. They think they're guilty, anyway. Gave the prosecution a present. Because we had time to get the tape we didn't need to wait for the DNA."

"Have their attorneys spoken with them?"

"Couldn't care less. Listen, Doc. We have them. It's a slam-dunk and will never make it to trial. The Manhattan DA is probably putting together a deal, as we speak."

"Okay, so they did it. What I'm interested in is 'why.'"

"And we couldn't give a damn, *why*. Crazy things go down in those halfway houses. The place was in shambles. A motive could be as simple as a robbery. Less has been the cause of a beat down. As long as we send a strong message to the residents that shit like this won't be tolerated, we're good."

John shot his signature look to Withers. "And that's it?"

"Listen, Dr. Trenton," Rojas said. John pursed his lips at the lieutenant's formality but paid attention. "I'm well aware of your reputation to dig deeper until you find something. You're not going to pull the same thing on this team as you did on Carlson's. I'm in charge, and when I say it's over, it's over. I'm not closed to further investigation, by any means. You'll get a shot, but it better be quick. I have a desk piled high of cases to split between you and Dr. Khaos. If you get too emotionally involved, I'm handing this case over to him. And if he gets too emotionally vested in his girlfriend's case, you're getting it. Am I making myself clear?"

"Okay, Lieutenant, I'll go along with that. Lex, you said that two of the men didn't live at the house?" Withers nodded. "What's their story?"

"Don't know, they lawyered up, too."

"Have their attorneys spoken with them?"

Withers frowned. "What planet are you living on, Doc?"

"What?"

"Big bucks attorneys don't make the trek up to Rikers, you expect Legal Aid, to? Don't make me laugh. They'll meet with their clients a few minutes before their court appearance in their holding cells. And they each have different dates so they aren't bused together. Holy crap, you're gone not quite a year and you forget what the system is like here?"

John blew out a deep breath. "I guess I did, but—"

"Don't even think it Dr. Trenton. You're not going up there. There's no evidence the killers are mentally ill. Purely from observation," the lieutenant stated matter-of-factly.

I see I'm getting the same cooperation as I did in the Gemini case. "Okay, I'm not here to battle with you. If the motive is indeed something as simple as robbery, I'm good with it, case closed." He felt the jolt of Max—his spirit guide—enter his crown chakra and travel south. John closed his eyes for a moment. "But, in all honesty, I have a feeling it isn't. And for that reason, I must take this case its full course. For Bobby's sake."

"He's a kid who had a hard life, Doctor. I understand your compassion but—"

"Bobby was an adult who gave me the clues to rescue my wife, Ricky, and the unborn twins, and end the Gemini case, Lieutenant!"

The room went silent. John made sure his signature look pierced the lieutenant's gut.

ဆာင်

Frank set the table for dinner in his kitchen nook as Sam pulled plates from the cabinet. He looked around the space and smiled. He loved the light wood cabinets that Jen had picked out. The brown and beige paisley marble on the countertops and black splash were a perfect match and easy to keep clean. Everything was organized, so even someone not familiar with the layout—like Sam—could figure out what was where in the triangular shape. It was classic. The fridge, dishwasher, and oven were in the standard architectural design—forming a triangle, with cabinets and counters next to them.

He also loved the L shaped design of the kitchen—plenty of counter space so he could spread out.

He hadn't gotten over the grandness of the Trenton's house and he used to think that his—in the Mill Basin section of Brooklyn—was grand. This house was grand. Grand enough for him and Frankie, and even the woman he'd marry. He stared at Sam and mellowed as he compressed his lips thinking about her holding Alexi.

She sure would make a great mom. But is that enough?

Sam caught him staring and cocked her head. "What, Frank?"

He put out his arms out to her. He nodded. "Come here."

She walked into his embrace, wrapped her arms around his waist, as he enveloped her in his arms. She looked up at him. "Frank, it's—"

"We need to talk."

"Um, and you were the one to break it off."

"I know, princess. I'm thinking that was a really dumb move."

"Know what I think?" She didn't wait for a response. "I think you got so comfortable being alone with just Frankie, you'd jump at any reason not to commit. Frank, I can't take that on again, off again. I couldn't take that, again. Period. Been there. I don't need that pain. I'm getting too old to babysit insecure men."

That comment stung. "I'm not insecure. I was hurt when

you chose to accept Carrie's case, when you knew the relationship between Withers and me."

"And that's not insecure? Think again, Dr. Psychiatrist. Besides, Lex Withers is nothing like Dingo. Completely different personalities. Lex is much more welcoming and accepting. Dingo was a closed-minded dick. But no wonder."

"Okay, I'll be forced to work with him so I'll have to get over it. Can we work on us?" Sam bit her lip. "Come on Sam, I really do love you."

She swallowed. "Will you stop judging me?"

"When did I judge you?"

"At the casino. Every time I said something you gave me a condescending look."

Before he could respond, Frankie ran into the kitchen with tears flowing down his cheeks. Frank and Sam looked at him, worried.

"What happened, Frankie?" Frank asked.

"Dad! What did you do?" He sniffled. "What did you two, do?"

"What are you talking about?" Frank demanded. He let go of Sam and knelt down in front of his son.

Frankie whispered. "Dad, Mom's picture is up on the wall opposite your bed." He wailed. "Did you and Sam break up?"

Frank was speechless. He glanced at Sam who stood mouth agape with her hands on her hips.

"You did, *didn't* you?" Frankie bellowed.

Frank lowered his eyes. "But we're going to talk about it."

"Talk about it? Talk about it. If it was up to you, I'll probably never get another mom! I'm never talking to you, again!"

He stormed out of the kitchen and Frank heard him stomping up the stairs.

Frank's mind was blown. He'd put Jen and his wedding picture back up on the wall and had forgotten to take it off before Sam came over. Crap. He was dead meat now. Some way to make up.

"So you really do love me? Uh? And you show that how? By putting back your wedding picture?" Sam let out a deep sigh. "Look, Frank, I know you loved Jen, more than life itself. But you told me you were ready to move on. Jen gave you messages that you *should* move on. You didn't even listen to her!" She turned her back. "I'm leaving." She stormed off into the den and pulled her coat off the couch.

Frank traipsed after her and pulled her arm. "Oh, no, you're not." He yanked open the front door. The blizzard raged, blowing snow at them, covering the ten steps down to the street, forming a slide. Snow covered both their cars—in entirety—in the driveway. Icicles had formed and were hanging from the side view mirrors. Snow mounded up about two feet from snow blowers, blocking the driveway entrance. "Plan on leaving? How, princess?"

"Crap!" Sam stomped her foot, looking out the door. "This won't stop till tomorrow."

Frank shot her a wickedly sexy grin. "Yeah. I know." The smell of the heated leftovers Vicki had sent home with him permeated the space. Hunger pangs hit him. "Come on. Let's eat." He walked to the stair landing and yelled up. "Come on, Frankie. Dinner's ready."

Frankie trod down the stairs into the nook as his dad was placing all of the trays on the table. "So?"

"So what?" Frank asked him.

Frankie pulled out a chair and plopped into it. "So what are you two going to do? You're not kids."

Frank served him turkey, stuffing, broccoli, and sweet potato pie. "Exactly, we're not kids. So I'm not having adult conversation with an eight year old. End it."

"But, Dad—"

Frank frowned and shot him a stern look. "This is a situation that Sam and I have to discuss and work out ourselves. Okay?"

Frankie frowned. "Is Sam going home tonight?"

"I won't let her drive in the blizzard."

"Is she sleeping in the guest room?"

Frank's and Sam's voices trampled each other's. "No."

Frank and Frankie smiled. Frank dug ravenously into his plate. He swooned. "Oh, man, would I love a woman who could cook like this."

"Maybe I can, maybe I can't. I bet Vicki will be happy to give me lessons. She is incredible, isn't she?" A forkful of the sweet potato pie melted in her mouth.

"Yeah, John mentioned to me she's thinking of opening a catering business, but she's not formally trained. I'm not sure how that would work with state licensing laws. But you know? You have a great sense of smell. You probably could learn if you put your mind to it. I'll give you some of Jen's cookbooks and you could practice on us."

"Uh, Dad. Mom used those cookbooks and she still burned everything, and we ended up ordering out. Maybe you should get Sam different ones?"

"I have my own cookbooks, thank you. Haven't used them much—"

Frank grinned. "Start."

ღეღა

As she heard the shower being turned off, Sam pulled down the comforter on Frank's California King bed. She saw herself in the mirror above the dresser opposite it. She fingered her still damp hair from the roots down to the full length, and pulled Frank's black Khaos Rules T-shirt away from her body.

She laughed. She could fit two of herself into it. The short sleeves came down to her elbows, the length came down to above her knees. She turned around when she saw his massive frame, naked, in the mirror. She swallowed the saliva that flowed into her mouth.

She strutted to his dresser, opened a drawer, plucked out

a pair of briefs and tossed it to him, having it land on his already hard length.

"Aw, come on, Sam."

"Uh, prove to me that you deserve it." Her snide smile sent a message even without her words. She needed him, probably as much as he needed her. She'd gone so long without the warmth of a man's body on hers. Since she'd been with Frank, now in his absence, her need intensified. The pulling, the twitching in her sex were constant, especially when she was thinking about him. Which was constant. She'd had to change the batteries in her dildo a few days ago.

"Proof?" He curled his lips down. "Okay." He quickly removed his wedding picture from the wall, entered his walk-in closet, opened a safe with a key, put the picture in, closed the door, and handed Sam the key. "Here. This is the only key. If we break up for good, you give it back to me. Until then, it's yours. How's that, princess, proof enough?"

Sam cocked her head. "The only key? I doubt that."

"Yes. It is. This safe wasn't used. We never needed to get an extra key." He wrapped his arms around her and deposited a peck with his lips on her nose. "I missed you so much, Sam."

"You missed the sex, Frank."

"Hey! You can honestly tell me you didn't?"

She laughed. "No. I cannot."

"Okay, then. Let's see how it goes. But right now—I want to devour you," he said, growling into her neck.

The mere touch of his unshaven cheeks on her skin sent loving energy through her body. She let herself collapse onto him. "Oh, my God, Frank, I think I'm addicted."

"I'll take that, princess. I'll definitely take that." He patted her behind as he led her out of the closet toward the bed. Sam cooed. He lifted the T-shirt up and over her head, dropping it onto the floor. With his index finger, he pushed her on to the bed. "Enough talking."

She welcomed him as he bent down to kiss her. She

spread her arms up, wide to wrap him in her embrace. He rested down on her body. Sam spread her legs and wrapped them around his waist, with bent knees. He adorned her with kisses, around her face and neck as he ran the tips of his fingers up and down her thighs. She writhed underneath him.

"Frank—"

He stopped tickling her. "I feel like getting you good, princess."

"You've already got me. Oh my God, I can't do without your warmth on me."

"We have a lot to talk about, Sam."

"Talk, now?"

"Maybe, not now."

Their lips interlocked. His tongue thrust into her mouth. Their body heat rose. Frank moved his shoulder back to push the blanket off him. It slid down past his waist. He paused then pulled it back up quickly.

"What's the matter?"

"Don't you feel the draft? I think the heater went off. I just heard the grumble of the thermostat."

"Crap. Not with the storm outside."

He jumped out of the bed, shivering, ran into his closet, and pulled out two matching robes. He tossed one to Sam. "Put this on. Stay in bed. I want to check the thermostat. The temp in here went way down, too fast."

"Well, you do have the window open a bit." Sam slipped the purple fleece robe on while she was still in the bed. She rubbed her arms feeling the fluffy material. She sniffed the arm. Frank's scent wasn't on it. One thing with him, he was always on top of the laundry. And he was independent. As she had a moment to think about it, maybe he was the one man that she wouldn't have to baby. She nodded as she re-membered what Vicki told her about John. How he wanted all of her attention, all the time. With Frank, she wouldn't have to give up her career. Even though he wanted her to learn how to cook, he wasn't the type of guy who'd want dinner on the table at a certain time, each night. Yeah, with Frank, she'd have her freedom.

Frank re-entered the room. She startled out of her reflection. "It's okay, Sam. Frankie's room is the warmest up here. He got too hot and lowered the thermostat."

"To what?"

"Sixty-three."

She gasped.

"He's not going to touch it, again."

Slipping out of their robes, they watched the purple masses fall onto the floor.

He plopped back into bed, next to her, and pulled the blanket up to cover their heads. "Come here, let's just warm up. I need to get some sleep."

She cuddled in his arms. Just like in the army, he still fell asleep in less than a minute.

CHAPTER 9

Frank stood chopping an onion and green peppers at the kitchen counter as he waited for the oil to sizzle in the pan on the stove. He had gotten up early, at six, out of habit. Frankie, in PJs, ignored his father and played with a transformer robot at the kitchen table. As Frank sliced mushrooms, he tossed a glance toward Frankie. "Want mushrooms in yours?" Frank watched his son's intent and smiled. It was obvious Frankie hadn't heard him. "Hey! Frankie!"

He didn't look up. "What, Dad?"

"Want mushrooms in your eggs?"

"Yeah. Okay."

"What's with the sulking? You got a snow day. Three day weekend."

"I know. I was thinking about you and Sam all night. I even had a nightmare, but I didn't want to wake you guys up."

"Glad you didn't. You disturbed us enough playing with the thermostat."

"Yeah. Okay. It's the 'if the door is closed, don't come in unless you're bleeding to death, rule, right?" Frankie said in a tone mimicking the one his father would have.

Frank bellowed a laugh.

Sam sauntered into the kitchen. "What's so funny?"

"Nothing."

"At least you didn't empty out my drawer." She glanced down at her sweat pants and T-shirt.

Frank winked at her. "Let's eat." He served the veggie omelets with gluten-free rye bread toast.

"Want to go out and have a snowball fight?" Sam asked as she put a forkful of eggs into her mouth. "Um, this is good."

"It wouldn't have killed you to get up earlier and make us breakfast. Like hell you want to cook like Vicki."

"How about building a snowman?"

"How about at least setting the table? That'll be a good start."

Sam gazed out the kitchen window. "Crap. We'll never get the cars out."

"Sam, how do you get away with that?"

"Get away with what, sweetheart?"

"Not answering my dad's questions."

She laughed. "If I ignore him long enough, he changes the subject."

"I'm going to try that."

"Oh, yeah?" Frank glared at his son. "Don't even think of it." He faced Sam. "Knock it off," he said as he tilted his head toward Frankie.

After a few minutes of silence, devouring their breakfast, the front doorbell rang. Who would come over in this storm? Ah, maybe it was a squirrel. The doorbell rang again. So not a squirrel. Frank thought of Jen's parents. They only lived a couple of blocks away. But at this hour? Nah. Not a chance.

Frankie jumped up and ran to the door. "Who's there?"

"Is Doctor Khaos home?"

Without answering, Frankie ran into the kitchen. "Dad, someone's at the door for you."

He bolted out of the chair. "Who in hell—"

The banging on the door became consistently harder. "Dr. Khaos, open the door."

"Hold on. Who is it?"

"Chet and Dinkins, Brooklyn-South."

Frank opened the door. "Guys, what's going on? Get in here. It's freezing out there."

Sam joined them holding a hot cup of coffee between her hands. "What happened?"

"What makes you think something happened, Detective Wright?"

She gave them a crooked smile. "Why else would you be coming over here in this weather?"

"You have to come with us, Doc," Detective Chet said.

"Why?"

Dinkins looked around the room. "Case related."

"What case?" Sam demanded.

"I'm sorry, Detective." Chet swallowed hard. "That's all we're at liberty to say. We have to go. Now."

"Frankie, get your coat. We'll drop you at grandma and grandpa's. Which precinct?"

"We'll take you to ours, and we'll skype to Queens," Detective Chet said.

"Queens?"

"Yeah, Doc." Chet let out a long sigh. "It's case related. The casino murder."

"Got it. You need me on it."

"No, Doc."

"Wait a minute," Sam said confused. "You mean I'm involved in a case. The casino case is mine."

"That's not it either, Wright."

"Let's get a move on. Doc, you're not going to like this."

≈≈≈

Frank was ushered into the interrogation room in silence. He felt as if ants were riding on his arms. He took off his bubble jacket, tossed it onto the chair in the corner and rubbed his arms vigorously. He had no idea why he was feeling so uneasy. He sat down with his arms crossed over his chest and spotted the flashing green light coming from the camera on the ceiling of the room. He stared at it, knowing it was on and recording. He smirked, staring right into it.

Detective Chet entered holding folders under one arm and a laptop under the other. Lieutenant Rojas followed him.

"Where's Sam?"

"She's in another room."

Frank reacted nervously to the Lieutenant's caustic tone. "Why?" He slumped into the chair. "Why are you here, Loo?"

"The captain called me in." Rojas then sat next to Frank. "This concerns you at the moment." Rojas nodded to Detective Chet that he could continue.

"We received some disturbing forensics back from the Baines case. You were adopted at birth, correct?"

"No. I entered the foster care system at birth. I didn't know they weren't my biological parents and when I was adopted at ten, I found out. Stop the crap. What's going on?"

"The DNA didn't come up with anyone we had in CODIS. But when we extended the search, enough data appeared to confirm familial DNA."

Anxiety rippled through him. Frank felt his body becoming immobile, feeling sick to his stomach. Nausea whirled through him and the acid from his breakfast regurgitated into his throat. He grimaced and swallowed, hard. "Whoa! Hold on a minute. What are you saying?"

"Carolyn Baines murderer, the serial killer, is most likely your brother," Chet said matter-of-factly.

Frank froze in his thoughts. His face heated up as if he'd gone an hour with the heavy bag in his gym. His felt his blood percolating through his veins. He hated this feeling when it wasn't from a workout. "What the hell do you mean?"

He literally saw black—as if his world ended—in death. The blank stares from the others in the room that accosted his gaze confirmed his thoughts.

"Exactly what I said. The serial killer is most likely—"

Frank bolted out of the chair. He grabbed it, wanting to throw it across the room, but he controlled himself. "Where's Sam?"

"So you mean to tell us, you didn't know that you have any siblings?" Loo asked.

Frank's voice couldn't have been louder if he tried. "No! I did not. Where's Sam? This isn't happening. I can't have a brother I don't know." His fisted hand came one inch from slamming the wall before he stopped himself. Frank turned and stared blankly at Loo. "My life was shit until I was adopted and even after that, it took years for me to straighten out. I don't intend to revisit the past."

Lieutenant Rojas exhaled deeply. "Sit down, Frank."

Frank shook his head. No way in hell would he allow himself to be sucked into this game. "Get Sam in here. Now."

Sam pushed the door open and ran into his arms.

He wrapped her tightly as if his life depended upon it. "They think—they think the killer—"

"I know. I heard."

He ran his hand over her long hair and grabbed a fistful, holding it gently on her back. He lowered his chin to the top of her head.

"We'll get through this, Frank."

Frank yanked out a chair and sat down at the conference table. "You better tell me everything you know, and I mean now, Chet."

Sam stood behind him with her hands on his shoulders. He felt the warmth of her comforting touch begin to calm his tense muscles. Frank's right foot involuntarily tapped the floor. "Start talking, Chet."

"What was your birth name, Frank?"

"Francis Hunter."

"What do you know about your birth parents?"

"Not much. They were seventeen. I never saw any pictures, nor would I have wanted to, even when I got older. I had gone through all my paperwork when Theresa and Peter, my adoptive parents, passed on. My bio parent's photos were not in my files. I was born in Brooklyn, October third, and went into foster care the same day. I'm guessing my bio parents didn't even interact with me. I'm going out on a limb here and I'm not sure how I feel about it, but was I the only one who came up?"

Detective Chet swallowed hard. "Not sure, yet."

ော

John traipsed up the ice covered front steps to the halfway house on the Lower West Side of Manhattan. Detectives Withers and Richards trailed after him, the search warrant clutched in Withers's hand.

"Don't know what you intend to accomplish," Withers said.

"Hey, Lex, I'm taking you guys at your word. That you're not opposed to further investigation. You better not put a damper on this." John's signature look met Withers' gaze. "Agreed?"

Withers' nodded and sighed, and shook his head in disbelief. "All right, Trenton. Show us your magic."

John opened the front door. The muddy looking gray paint had peeled off the walls in the narrow hallway, revealing years of careless paint jobs. Soiled hand prints, distinctively male, ran intermittently down the length of the hall. John grimaced at some squirts of blood splatter, at the baseboard, most likely projectiles from the needles of mainlining residents. It surprised him that there was no attempt made to remove the marring evidence that drug use was rampant in here—especially since they received a courtesy call.

He headed down the hall, glancing at nameplates on closed doors. He found the one he wanted. Dorm supervisor, Caleb Minx—the man who John was told was less than cooperative with the EMS techs. That was a bone he'd pick if he had the chance.

Through the frosted glass on the upper third of the door, John saw the man who was in charge of keeping order in this place of disarray. Not a job title he'd want. He knocked but didn't wait for a response. He charged in, accosting the rotund man sitting behind his desk with his feet upon it, and his eyes closed. This place definitely didn't have a laundry room.

John snatched the warrant from Withers's hand and slapped it down on the desk. "Sorry to interrupt your afternoon nap, Mr. Minx."

Withers swiped Minx's feet off the desk onto the floor, taking the couple-of-feet-high stack of folders with him.

"What? Huh?" Minx startled. He nearly slipped off his metal chair. He compressed his lips and sucked in cheeks. "Look what ya just did! Now I gotta go through all this shit."

Withers snickered and got a smile from his partner. "Nah. We'll do it for you."

"Need a drink?" John didn't need a response. The rancid odor emanating from every pore in Minx's body told John that this dorm supervisor had had plenty, regularly. "Take a look at this."

Minx scanned the warrant. "Who the fuck are you? Those two are definitely cops."

"Dr. John Trenton."

Minx stayed still at the sobering moment.

"Got that warrant straight?" John continued.

"Oh yeah? What's your probable cause?"

Withers shook his head. "Ya kidding me, right? A murder was committed here and one of the perps worked in this office, so we have enough probable cause to search whatever we damn well please."

"No, ya don't. You can only search that bum, Maynor's stuff."

"We'll take that to start. We want all of his paperwork, meetings, and conversations with all residents which by law, need to be documented." Richards hiked her eyebrows. "He did document everything, didn't he? Because if we find out he didn't then we'll get an expanded warrant. And your cushy little rent-free housing will go poof. And all those folders you carelessly dropped? We'll look at those, too. No telling which one had Maynor's stuff."

Minx shrugged it off. He rose from his chair. "Search to ya heart's content." As he got to the door, he pointed to the file cabinet. "Maynor's current files are in the third drawer. His room was Three B. His stuff was left in there but no telling what was taken."

John smiled. Minx had to know he gave them a reason to extend their search. He nodded to the man in appreciation.

Minx reciprocated. "The guys know he ain't coming back. By the way, Doc, I'm sorry to hear about the kid. He was doing okay." Minx compressed his lips. "He was really trying to turn it around. And I'm glad the bum is put away."

"Thanks. Before you leave, what made Maynor a bum?"

"Oh, man, don't get me started."

Withers took out his brown book then pulled a pen from his jacket pocket. "Just start. Tell us what you know about him."

Minx closed his eyes and looked away.

"Come on, Mr. Minx. That won't fly." John felt Max's jolt—the wave of energy from his Spirit Guide who's been with him since childhood. That wave traveled from his crown chakra at the top of his head down through the right side of his body to his toes. This time the jolt told him—in no uncertain terms—that he needed to press hard. "Unless you want to come down to the precinct where we'll have privacy. But then again, if any residents see you leave with us, you might be next."

"I get it. Stop with the empty threats. He was a hardass. Thought he was better than everyone else. He was known—uh—rumored—to shake down the guys who came in after curfew. Had them buy him cigs and even the occasional hit. No drugs are allowed in here, but he turned away on that, too, for the right price."

"Yeah, we saw the hallway," John said.

"Yeah, well, the cleaning crew missed some spots."

Withers lost patience. "Just get on with it, Minx."

"He was ornery." Minx frowned. "Never a nice word about anyone. In all honesty, I wondered why he was never silenced, if you know what I mean."

John hiked his brows. "Who were the residents he had the most problems with?"

"We have one hundred twenty men in here who've...how do I say it?...interacted, yeah that's a good word, *interacted* with him. Some with their mouths, more with fists. Mitchell wasn't the only guy who got a beat down."

"How did he get to control the men? Aren't you the supervisor?"

"Only for what goes on in the rooms. Maynor ran the office. Manager. He was here twenty-four-seven. Now I have that privilege."

"So basically you're saying that because Maynor *interacted* with a hundred twenty men, we get to look at their files, too. Right, Minx?" Withers looked more annoyed than pleased.

John snickered. "That's exactly what he means, Detective Withers. All right, Minx. We'll call you when we need you."

"I'm sure you will." Opening the door, he paused for a moment. "I'm really sorry about the kid, Doc." He left the room and closed the door behind him.

Withers pulled gloves from his pocket and tossed a pair to his partner and to John. He put his on before he picked up the files on the floor. Plopping them down on the desk, he grimaced. "What are we looking for, Trenton?"

"I'll know when I see it."

"That's not good enough. See, that's the difference between you shrinks and us cops. We need to know what
we're doing. The simpler the better. We already have what
we want, so why waste our time, not to mention the taxpay-
er's money?"

"Stop the rant."

"Okay. You stop the crap. What did Mitchell tell you
when you spoke to him two times a week that makes you
think this extra work is warranted?"

John shot Withers a long stare. "More like what he
didn't say. I kept asking him how was he getting along in
here, if there were any problems with anyone. All I got as a
response was 'fine.' He was hesitant like he want to tell me
stuff but couldn't. I think he didn't know if the calls were
recorded or not or if the walls had ears. I asked him if he
got receipts for the rent that he paid, and he told me 'no.'
There was a pause in the conversation after that, and he
rushed off the phone, telling me there was a line of guys
waiting to use it. So privacy was the issue. I'm getting the
strong feeling that he did want to tell me something but
again he was held back. He would have come forth if he
could. He told me what he had heard about Barbara Montgomery going after Vicki, but in private. So I'm a hundred
percent sure, he was waiting for privacy here. And someone
stopped him. But I have no idea what."

"Another question for you, Trenton." Withers rubbed his
chin. "If it was so urgent, why didn't he call you from the
hospital? He could have gotten a phone there."

"No out of state calls allowed. Yeah, it sucks."

"No. You still have your cell number?" John nodded.
Withers shrugged. "It's a nine-one-seven area code. That's
New York. I don't buy this for a friggin' minute. I think
you're too damn close to this to know your ass from your
elbow. Not good. We need a sit down with Loo. I mean it."

"Yeah, maybe you're right." John closed his eyes in

contemplation. "But I'm going to turn that around. Starting now."

"As long as we're here, let's get started then. Bella, take the third drawer. Trenton, you and me, will start with these files.

"Why have so many paper files? Why not keep files online?" John shook his head as he opened the first one. "Um, maybe because paper files are easier to alter, because internet files would have an update date? Maybe, possibility. What is all this?" He read the first page. "Prison records? Where did they get this stuff? This guy is out on parole for petty larceny. New admit. Just came from upstate."

Withers threw his pen on the desk. "Damn it, Trenton. What are you rambling about? I can't hear myself think, man."

John looked up, startled. "Oh, sorry, I just think out loud."

"Well, keep your thinking in your brain." Withers returned to his file. He closed it and pushed it aside. Then he took a second and third. On the fourth folder, he stopped. "Hey. This may be something. Okay, listen to this. This guy was here for nine months. He had an appearance before the board, January twentieth. Never made it, because he was discharged January eighteenth. How in hell does one get discharged from a halfway house? That's not terminology they use. No forwarding address and his name on every page is whited out. A name, Stewart Blarey is written in. What kind of creative bookkeeping is this? Okay, our lab guys can find whose name was underneath."

Richards halted. "Hold on. Hold on, guys. All these files have names whited out. Every one of them. What is the freaking purpose in that? And shouldn't Bobby Mitchell's name be on one? Haven't found it. A lot of Ms but no Mitchell. They've had to have government inspections. These would have been caught. Unless they're new since the murder." She flipped through to the back of the file she held in her hand. "Here it is. The state inspectors were here

two months ago. Their next visit is in four months. That's
plenty of time to alter these back to the real identities or
make fresh files."

"They're hiding the identities of the residents." John
took his cellphone out of his pocket. "Why? I think it's time
to call Crime Scene to pack up this room. And schedule
teams to come in tonight to knock on doors."

CHAPTER 10

The traffic coming from Lower Manhattan to Scarsdale had wiped him out. John wasn't used to that traffic, anymore. Loud beeping horns in bumper-to-bumper traffic described how feverishly these commuters wanted to get home. The twenty-four-mile drive through several streets and avenues, and five parkways, took over two hours—every day, both ways—unless he chose to get home at midnight. Then his commute would be cut in half. Living in rural central Florida had changed his lifestyle. He had gotten used to the empty roads without potholes. Yeah, he had to admit he was beginning to miss Florida.

Duke charged toward him and jumped up for hugs with the usual tail wagging. "Hi, boy! You being a good boy with Mommy?" John knelt down and rustled his fur. He still loved Duke's licks and that continued to surprise him, not ever having a dog growing up. John prodded the dog into the foyer and closed the front door behind him.

Ricky ran in soon after. "Dad, when are we going back to Florida? I hate it here."

"That's it? No, hello-Dad-hug? Get over here." John grabbed Ricky into his arms and kissed the top of his head. "Seriously, you don't like it here? Why?"

"I hate the cold, and I miss Grandma and Grandpa, all four of them."

"We'll Facetime them tonight. Okay?"

"Dad, that's not enough. I don't think Mom likes it here either."

"So, I'm being ganged up on. Is that it?" John took off his overcoat and hung it in the closet in the hallway. Next came his sports jacket. "Come on, we'll talk at dinner. And from the smells coming from the kitchen, I can imagine it's almost ready. I'm starving. What about you?"

"Always." Ricky darted off.

John shook his head and laughed. He knew it would an adjustment for them both, and he had hoped their discontentment wouldn't have shown up so fast. Apparently, it was an adjustment for him, too. They were barely back in New York a week. He'd have to deal with this, now. Dinnertime was as good a time as any. He let out a deep sigh, stiffened his posture, and found himself walking into the kitchen involuntarily as he rolled up the sleeves of his dress shirt.

Vicki had pulled a platter of baked wild salmon on top of chopped tomatoes, onions, seasoned with mint, out of the oven, and placed it on the glass trivet at the center of the table. Baked yams caramelized with cinnamon and honey sat on salad plates. She grabbed the bowl with herbed yoghurt out of the fridge.

As she turned toward the table, John embraced her in his arms and deposited a non-demonstrative kiss on her lips. "Hi, babe."

She smiled and her eyes lit up as her gaze met his.

"Let me go wash up. Be back in a bit. Then you, two, can gang up on me."

"What?"

He winked at her and disappeared into the bathroom off the kitchen.

Vicki gave her son a forewarning look. "What did Dad mean by that?"

"I dunno. But I sorta told him that we don't like it here."

"You did what? Why?"

John stood leaning against the doorway with his arms folded over his chest, out of their view.

"Well, we don't. Do you? I mean you said you hate this blankety blank snow, whatever blankety blank means. But it doesn't sound good to me."

John let out a loud laugh. "Ricky, I'm impressed. All of the work Mom is doing with you on taking a breath and speaking in sentences is paying off. Very good."

He smiled and blushed. "Dad, I'm nine. You don't have to tell me something good for everything I do."

John took his seat around the table. "Yeah. I do. Because then when I reprimand you, you'll know I mean it."

"Dad."

John served Ricky a piece of fish as the boy dug into his yam. "Let's eat. I'm hungry. What schoolwork did you do with Mom today?"

Before Ricky could answer, Duke jumped onto Ricky's lap, begging for food, tapping on Ricky's arm with his paw.

"Duke! Down." John stared at the pup until he obeyed. "Lay down," he said, pointing to a wall where Duke was supposed to lay at while they had dinner. The pup retreated. "When did this start?"

Vicki pursed her lips. "Tell your father when it started."

Ricky looked at her with wide, open eyes. He hesitated. "Uh, yesterday, I uh made a sandwich, a bagel with peanut butter an' I had to go to the bathroom an' I left it on the ottoman an' when I came back it was gone an' Duke smelled from peanut butter an' am I in trouble?"

John shot Vicki a concerned look. Okay. Ricky reverted to his old language pattern when he was under stress. Confirmed. This wasn't the first. time. He wasn't going to add to that stress. "No. You're not in trouble. The thing is, people food can make him sick, and we don't want him to beg for food when we have company. So next time, don't leave food out where he can get it. Okay?"

"Dad, he could reach everything. He's taller than me!"

Vicki laughed.

John tried to hide his laugh by taking a forkful of fish. "Um, well, didn't your brother, Commander Mark," he added sarcastically, "police train him? Vick, I don't remember him doing that at all in Florida."

"No. I don't recall that, either. But, then again, we always had him on the lanai when we had dinner. And now that he's had a taste of people food, he'll want it."

"Olay, then it wasn't the training. It was opportunity. I'll call Mark tonight."

"It'll have to be late. We have a community meeting. At the clubhouse. Eight o'clock."

"And I'm just finding out about this now?"

"There was a flyer put into the mailbox. And I knew you were out in the field. Look, it's only for an hour and we'll get to know our neighbors. Before you say anything, Tracey from next door will watch the twins and Ricky. She loves them."

"Yeah, she's cool, Dad."

"And Duke is here. It'll be fine."

"Whoa. Whoa. Whoa. Why do you bombard me with all the details, thinking I'll say 'no?'"

Vicki stopped dead in her tracks. "I didn't think you'd say 'no,' but you like all bases covered."

"Actually, it's a good idea. If you make some new friends, maybe you'll like it better and won't complain about the *blankety blank snow*."

Vicki put her hand over her mouth and gasped. "You heard us?" She paused. "Yes, you did."

John tossed her his wickedly sexy grin. "Yes. I sure did."

ᏒᏍᏒᏍ

Sam and Frank lay intertwined in bed—nude and under the covers—without saying a word. He ran his left hand up and down her right arm as she leaned her body over on him.

His eyes closed as if his mind was a million miles away. She'd let him be. After the bomb that impaled him today that he had one sibling—a serial killer, no less—and possibly another, she could imagine how he'd want to retreat. He opened his eyes and blinked repeatedly as if he was trying to refocus to the present.

He rolled onto his side and pecked her nose with his lips. "So what now, princess?"

"What do you mean?"

"You know what I mean."

She really didn't and he had to have read it in her eyes.

"If this DNA thing is correct, and I have a serial killer in my genes, how can I possibly have another child? As is, I'll be watching everything Frankie does, for life."

"Frankie is a perfectly adjusted little boy, Frank. He doesn't have a mean bone in his body. And tendencies start young."

"I don't care, Sam. I can't risk it. Where does that put you and me? I know damn well you want children. Don't BS me. I mean it."

"Let's wait to jump to that. Let the case be over. We just got back together, Frank. Don't manufacture another wedge to put between us."

"You have no sense of reality. Do you? DNA tests are ninety-nine percent accurate. Science doesn't lie."

"When the time comes, we'll see some doctors. Right now, I don't have any intention of giving up my career. Yes. I melted when I saw the twins. And I'll admit it. I think about how it felt when I held them. I thought about it a lot. But that's not my focus for the immediate future. So can we just be *us* for now?"

"Yeah. We can be *us,* but it's going be on my mind twenty-four-seven. Why they didn't grill me more is beyond me. They wouldn't tell me anything."

"I know. I was there. Remember? Maybe the other person who came up is deceased or in another country. And they weren't even sure there is someone else. Tomorrow let's see if we can view the casino footage. Maybe we can find someone with your likeness."

"That doesn't make me feel any better, Sam."

"Sorry. Okay maybe we find the guy."

He rolled over on top of her and grabbed her in an impassioned embrace. It was her time to comfort him, just like he had comforted her. She put her arms around his neck and didn't want this moment to end. She felt the body heat between them—the energy. They were so in-sync with each other's rhythm. She'd have to make it work. There was no one else in the world for her, other than Frank. From that moment, her mission became to prove to him beyond a shadow of a doubt that she was a million percent present—for him.

☘☘☘

The black van parked behind snow covered pine trees far from the streetlights. So far, that it would not cast a shadow on the road in this Scarsdale residential neighborhood with homes that sat on two acres. Bush borders—some reaching six feet tall—between each property would ensure just the right amount of privacy. The driver of the van held the binoculars, looking out the rolled-down window toward the house. It was the first one at the beginning of the cul-de-sac. It had been empty for months. Now it was rented. They had gotten the blueprints before, the first time they had hit it, last year. A clean get-away. Just like always. They had watched the house this week, and only saw a man and woman with three kids leaving, two newborns, so that would be the home renters' focus now. Definitely. The newborns.

"How long we just gonna sit here, Abby?"

Abby lowered the binoculars and turned her head toward her partner in the back seat. "Calm the shit. We sit as long as it takes. There's a meeting tonight in the clubhouse. Being the newbies, maybe they'll go." She rotated her right shoulder. "Man, this new tat sure hurts. That's what I get for trying a new guy."

"You're sure in a bitchy mood."

"Bitchy mood?" Abby turned around and swiped the young woman across the face with the binoculars. The woman let out a scream, bent over, and covered her face. "Yeah. real bitchy, Selena. Next time, I'll do more than that. Now look at ya. Ya better not get your fucking blood on my seat." She tossed her a dirty rag that was on the floor in front of the passenger seat. "Wipe off ya face. It's only the dirt from the windows." She scanned the edge of the binoculars. "Ugh. Look what ya did. Blood and skin. Just what I needed, bitch. Gimme back the towel."

The second woman in the back seat put her arm around Selena. She dabbed the gash running from the edge of her eyebrow down her cheek to her chin with a tissue. "Abby, you really hurt her."

"Yeah, well, sorry, you piece of shit. Consider it hazing. Ya better not let it stop ya from doing this job. And you, Miss Maternal, back there, you can occupy the kids, if they're home. Seriously, Kit, if your friend fucks up, you're dead meat, too." As she was looking out the window, she saw a man pull out of the driveway. The Mercedes' windows were darkened, so she couldn't see if he was alone, or not. "Here we go."

After the man was out of sight and there was no chance of him seeing them in the rearview mirror, Abby pulled out and rode toward the block with the car lights off. Good thing for them, this house had two entrances. She tossed gloves to the women in the back seat then drove around the back entrance that led to the kitchen door.

✂✄✂

The light was on in a second-floor bedroom facing the

opposite side of the house. Ricky was in his room playing tug-of-war with a thick rope toy with Duke. Ricky was lying on his stomach on the newly installed Berber carpet with his arms extended in front of him holding the rope as Duke pulled him around the room. "Come on, Duke, you have to pull harder. Come on, pull!" Duke growled, dropped the rope, and pounced on Ricky as he rolled over onto his back. The pup's paws were on his shoulders and he licked Ricky until the boy was hysterical laughing. Ricky's laughter permeated the house and the twins crying ensued in an adjoining bedroom.

Tracey came into his room, holding Alexi cradled in her arms. "Ricky, stop it. You woke the babies up."

Duke lay down right next to Ricky and closed his eyes. Ricky's arm was across his body. "So?"

"Your parents aren't going to like this."

"They don't have to know." He winked at his nineteen-year-old redheaded babysitter.

"Where did you learn that?"

He hiked his eyebrows. "Learn what?"

She pursed her lips. "All those very adult expressions."

"Oh, my dad—"

Duke raised his head and cocked it toward the bedroom entrance. He let out a soft whimper, shifted Ricky's arm off him, and darted out of the room, and down the stairs. Ricky saw Duke's fur stand on edge before he chased after the dog, with Tracey trailing, Alexi squirming over her shoulder.

Duke barked viciously before Ricky could process what had happened. Hearing three different screaming voices coming from the kitchen, Ricky ran in, following Duke. The women froze in front of the open china curio. Ricky's gaze darted to each woman. Duke jumped onto the chest of one of the women, pushed her against the perpendicular counter, as another one scrambled out the door to the back yard. The door swung in the wind and snow blew in.

At the same time, Tracey grabbed the phone and dialed

nine-one-one, as she held the crying baby. She ran into the adjoining room to keep Alexi hidden from the draft as she rubbed the infant's back with one hand and held the phone between her ear and neck.

Ricky remembered the self-defense training with his mom after Barbara Montgomery got the better of him in the Gemini case. Never again. And now he had Tae Kwan Do added to his daily activities. He charged the remaining woman—who stood almost two feet taller than him—with his fists, pummeling her stomach and catching her off guard.

Duke's weight pushed the woman he pounced on down onto the tile floor, butt first. The dog then knocked her backward and her head hit the tile. He held her arm firmly in his mouth as his body lay across hers, his intense growling being a warning that she'd better lay still. The blood from her facial wound steadily dripped onto the floor as she screamed in terror.

As the other woman curled down with stomach pain, Ricky palmed her nose, pushing it back, hard and fast. He heard a crack. Blood poured from her nose onto the floor and him. Swiping his leg in between hers, he flipped her to the ground, pushing her around so she lay face down. She was screaming in pain. The two women on the floor continued to scream in panic, unintelligible words in the midst of Duke's growls and Ricky yelling at them to stop. He wiped his bloody right hand on his pajama bottoms. Ricky heard the tires of a vehicle spin in the snow and pull out of the driveway.

He turned his head toward the door for a split second getting a blast of snow and cold air on his face. Shivering, he turned forward and, straddling her back, he tried to grab the woman's arms as she flailed them above her head. He was punched in the face and head even though he tried moving to the side as she fought him. He lifted his body, grabbed one of her arms, and twisted it back. She wailed.

ഔ൦ഔ

John and Vicki raced into the kitchen, and it took a very short time for them to take control.

"Dad!" Ricky yelled as John first slammed the door shut against the pressure of the blowing snow.

John took notice that a woman was lying across a pool of blood then he lifted his son off her. He couldn't help stepping in the red blotches—knowing he contaminated the scene. John held her down with his knee on her back as he grabbed a large bag tie from a drawer. Grabbing both arms, he pulled them behind her, and wrapped both wrists together behind her back.

"Don't you dare move!" John bellowed. "Duke, back off, boy!" He leaned over the other woman on the floor crying like a baby. "You don't move, either! What the hell are you doing in my house?"

Through their sobbing, they couldn't get any words out.

Vicki answered for them, now holding Alexi in her arms. "Bet these darlins' are the ones tonight's meeting was all about."

"I bet you're right, babe."

"What are your names? You, Miss Crocodile tears, I'm talking to you." He pointed to the woman whose arms he had in ties.

"Kit," she said sniffling blood. "Kit Malone."

"And you?" John pointed to the other woman lying on her back.

"Selena. Selena Graves."

"Where did you get that gash?"

Through her sobbing, she caved. "Abby."

"Abby who?"

"Abby Ruthe."

"Where is she?"

"She ran out. Left us."

"I heard her get away in a car, Dad, sounded like a

wheel spinned, like Mom's jeep did in the sand hill."

Two police officers ran in. One of them—a sergeant, by the badge on his blue uniform—approached John. He looked around to assess the scene, then toward the women who lay captive on the floor. "Dr. Trenton, are you and your family all right?"

"No," Ricky said. "They broke inta our house. How didya expect us to be okay?" He wrapped his arms around his dad's waist, with John holding him tightly. John glared at his son, but let the comment go.

The sergeant smiled. "Hold on, son, we just got here. I have to make sure the home owners are free from bodily harm."

From a distance, a second officer studied the injured women on the floor. He called for an ambulance.

The sergeant took out his brown book from his shirt pocket. "I'm Sergeant Day. Who was with you, son?"

To John, his tone was sympathetic.

"Tracey. She's over there, crying with her parents."

Sergeant Day looked in her direction and returned his attention to Ricky. "Can you tell me what happened?"

"Hold off a minute. I want to hear it, too. Let me take care of this." John snatched his cell phone out of his pocket.

"Walk with me over there, son." The sergeant led Ricky to the nook of the kitchen.

John snapped photos of the women on the floor, in every position that he could maneuver around without stepping again on any blood on the floor that came from Selena's head wound or Kit's nose—hard to do with the splatter and now the women's blood evidence was definitely intermingled. His shoes also needed packing in an evidence bag. He took pics of the shoe prints he had made. Intermittently, he glanced at the wounds, but didn't play doctor. It wasn't a deep gash, and he surmised Selena wouldn't even need stitches. And Kit's nose didn't look bad enough to need resetting. He'd definitely ask for a DNA swab of the wounds, though. He snapped photos of the open curio cabinet—

nothing moved, or removed. He took photos of the edges of the closed door that had to be touched when opening the doors as well as the handle. Crime Scene would need his family's prints, too. When John was done, he double-checked and realized he needed to take pics of the entrance to the kitchen. He changed his mind. He'd let the crime scene investigators do that. As long as he took the pictures of the women, that was important to protect Ricky and Duke. He joined the sergeant and his son.

The nine-year-old gave an account of what led up to the chaos in the kitchen, but through his long run-on-sentences way of expressing himself. John knew he was terrified. This was going to be another struggle Ricky didn't need to over-come.

"What can you tell me about the woman who got away?"

"She had long black hair an' she wore all black clothes."

"Was her hair straight or curly?"

"Straight an' she had a black hat on like Mom makes me wear cause it covers my ears."

"Okay. Good. Very Good, son. What kind of clothes was she wearing?"

"Black sweat shirt with a hoodie an' black sweat pants."

"Okay. Very good. You're doing great, son. I want to get this straight. She had on a hat *and* wore a hoodie over it?"

"No. The hoodie was on her back an' her hair came out in front, to here," he said, pointing to the middle of his own chest.

Two EMS techs came in with stretchers—one of which was left in the dining room—and right away attended to the women on the floor. John cringed. They had just further contaminated the crime scene. He'd had to accept it. Their job was to attend the injured, not preserve the scene. That wasn't even part of their training.

"May I untie her?" a tech asked the officer.

"For now. They're both under arrest. I'll issue the Miranda and cuff them in the ambulance."

Kit cried.

"Can I trust you not to fight," the EMS tech asked.

"Yes."

The tech cut the plastic ties and rolled Kit onto her back. As soon as her arms were free, she jolted up and slammed the tech with her fists. The officer grabbed her arms, pulled them behind her back and cuffed her as she shouted obscenities.

From the kitchen, John heard Kit yell, "I think that little brat broke my ribs."

"Yeah, and that vicious dog, broke my back. I'm in agony," Selena screamed.

Unsettling thoughts ran through John's mind. He certainly hoped that neither woman was hurt as badly as they claimed. He didn't need a savvy lawyer to bring up charges that could endanger Duke's life. He intended to prosecute these two to the fullest extent of the law. He looked at the sergeant with a solemn expression.

The sergeant saw Duke lying down by John's side, not making a sound. He glanced over his shoulder toward the women. "You'll have your chance to tell your sides in a while, ladies, and we'll take complete reports in the hospital. We must attend to your, uh, injuries first." He turned toward John, and shook his head. "All right, Dr. Trenton, we'll be talking more."

Ricky stopped the sergeant from leaving. "Hey, aren't you gonna ask me what she looked like?"

The man turned toward him. "You can describe her?"

"Yes. She had a nose ring, an' metal rings on her eyebrows and lips. An' a tattoo on her neck of a lobster, but it was black, not red like a real lobster, an' it was gross." He pointed to his face. "Like it came from…" He pointed to the tip of his right ear lobe. "Here to…" He ran his finger down his neck to underneath his chin. "To here. I almost punched her, that's how I got a good look at her face, but she ran away so I punched the other lady straight into her stomach."

"Can you guess how tall she was?"

Ricky looked around. "Uh, she was taller than Mom."

"I'm five eight," Vicki replied. "Ricky, you did great. We're all very proud of you. You helped get these bad girls arrested and the police have been looking for them a long time."

He wrapped his arms around his mother and looked up teary-eyed. "I want to go back to Florida, now."

John pulled Vicki and his son tightly in his arms and patted Ricky's back. He was without words.

"I mean it, Dad. Where in the world is a kid safe?"

CHAPTER 11

In the war room of the Chelsea precinct, Sam and Frank were prepping to meet Charlie Baines, Carolyn's soon to be ex-husband. Sitting at the conference table, Sam concentrated on a file, barely, looking at Frank out of the corner of her eye, as he fidgeted in his seat and rubbed his temples. She was wearing a dark green three-piece conservative pants suit with a mint green blouse under the jacket and she didn't even mind Frank wearing his tight black T-shirt and blue denim skinny jeans. Not for the jerk they were about to interview.

Outside in an observation room, Lex Withers and Bella Richards watched on the computer screen. Sam had convinced them to let her conduct the interview because of her relationship with Carrie. She knew they had agreed as a test, so she'd think long and hard with her questions to make sure she didn't blurt out anything inappropriate. Yeah. Her concentration and thought processes could make or break her today.

She compressed her lips before she spoke, trying to shake off the arousal that caroused through her body every time she saw Frank dressed like that—which was all the time. She didn't need this distraction—especially for Bella and Lex to observe. "Developing a new habit? Rubbing your temples?"

He ignored her.

She elbowed him in his bicep. "Hey, Frank? You with me?"

He startled. "Yeah. As here as I'll ever be. Look, I'll be okay. Just have to put that DNA crap behind me. Charlie has to know why she went to the casino. I'll push as hard as I can, believe me."

"Okay. I'll believe you." She pressed the call button on the intercom in front of her on the desk. "Detective Valatutti, we're ready for Mr. Baines."

Nick escorted Mr. Baines into the room whom, to Sam—from his lack of making eye contact—looked less than happy to be there. She then glanced up at her partner and smirked. Nick nodded in response. They had learned to read each other well. They'd both apply the pressure. Baines wouldn't stand a chance.

"Hello, Mr. Baines, glad to see you again." She eyed him up and down. "Nice suit, Ralph Lauren?"

He slid into the chair opposite Sam, while Nick sat in the one next to Baines.

Charlie unbuttoned his jacket. "Cut the crap, Sam. The formality doesn't suit you. Why the hell am I here?"

"Same abrupt self, aren't you, Charlie? Why didn't you come back to the states for your wife's funeral? Her parents delayed it a couple of days for you, you know."

He picked at a hangnail at the cuticle of his thumb. "The cops delayed it for the autopsy. Don't BS me." He glanced up at Frank. "So you're the boyfriend?" He let out a guttural laugh as he stared at Frank's bulging biceps and grimaced, focusing on the tattoos covering Frank's arms. Sam tapped on the table with her fingernail, finally getting his attention. Charlie startled. "What are you doing with this tatted mess?"

"Excuse me?" Frank stood up and leaned over the table. His massive frame towered over Charlie's slim, medium build. Charlie leaned back in the chair with his eyes practically popping out of their sockets.

Sam pulled on Frank's arm and he sat down, laughing.

"Why am I here? I was out of the states when my ex was murdered so you and I know I can't be suspect. If I thought I was, I wouldn't be here without my attorney, so do yourselves a favor and clue me in, now."

"As of this point you're not suspect." Sam opened Carolyn's file. "What were you told by the family when you spoke with Carrie's parents about how she died?"

"They're not talking to me, but I sure got blasted by Callum. He hated that we got married in the first place, but he was more pissed that I didn't come back for the funeral, but I believe that was an act. Carrie's parents would spit on me if they saw me. Better, I wasn't there. Callum said that it showed that I had a total disregard for the religion. I burst his bubble real quick by telling him that Carrie didn't either. When he calmed down, he told me she was murdered at the casino. And before you ask, no. He didn't probe me as to why I think she'd be there. Also, that she had eighteen hundred on her. They had checked for prints, only had Carrie's and some bank people because the money was in her wallet. There was no foul play regarding the money and her parents begged for the cash back to go toward the funeral expenses. After checking that her player's card showed two hundred went to the machines and two-K came out of the bank, it was cut and dry. The cops gave in. I don't know anything else."

"Hold on." Frank put his hand up. "What do you mean, 'he didn't probe me about Carrie being at the casino?'"

"He may have known why."

Frank hiked a brow. "Care to explain?"

"No. I don't. Ask Callum."

Maybe this will make him open up. "We haven't told them how she was found. Do you want to know?"

"I have a feeling you're going to tell me whether I want to know or not. So humor me. How was she found?"

Sam looked him straight in the eye. "Your wife was found—naked—in bed—and the only victim without a dead scorpion over her right breast. She had been strangled."

"Oh, man." Charlie collapsed his head into his hands, trembling. "Don't tell her parents that. Please. It'll kill them. How in hell did that happen?"

"We're hoping you could tell us. Let's go back. You two had recently bought a house, less than a year ago. That's not a sign that divorce is eminent." Nick uncrossed his leg and leaned in toward the table, turning his head toward Charlie. "So, Mr. Baines, what prompted it?"

Charlie swallowed hard and let out a deep sigh. "Why don't you ask her?" He pointed to Sam.

"Me? Why?"

"What did my ex-wife tell you, Detective? She told me what she said."

"She told you that she told me that you were cheating on her?"

Frank did a double take. "Uh?"

"I was cheating on her? No way! I loved Carrie. When we bought the house, the thought of a divorce wasn't even in my world."

"She told me you cheated on her. She really believed it."

"She thought I was. She had me followed."

Frank was losing patience. "Where did you go?"

"I was going to a therapist. I didn't know how to deal with Carrie's problem. She wasn't willing to own up to it."

"What problem?" Nick probed.

"You're kidding me, right? You find a woman dead in a casino hotel with eighteen hundred dollars in her wallet, who also takes off work to go to said casino—in a snowstorm, no less—and you can't figure out what her problem was? What kind of cops are you? You should have stayed in fifth grade, Sam."

"How bad was it?" Nick asked.

"Carrie was a gambling addict, full-fledged."

"Yeah, we got that. Tell us about it," Frank said.

"What does this have to do with finding her killer?"

"We're studying victimology, Mr. Baines." Frank gave him a hard look. "The other women this guy killed were also in professional careers and murdered in casinos. You're what we've got. The other kills in other states are also being investigated this way. You need to tell us everything."

Charlie swallowed hard. "She went through her TDA, borrowed almost all of it. In fifteen years, it was over a hundred thou."

"Oh my God! I didn't know that!"

"Guess you didn't know your BFF, Sam." Frank patted her shoulder, offering what comfort he could under the circumstances, and turned back to Charlie. "What else?"

"She went through our savings, maxed out the credit cards."

"Charlie, I'm so sorry. That's why she's been rushing off the phone with me. She didn't want me to sense anything and probe."

"Probably."

Frank paused before speaking. "Did she owe money to anyone, aside from the credit cards?"

"Such as?"

"Mr. Baines, come on." Frank's pretend compassion didn't go past Sam. She turned her eyes away for a moment.

"With such debt, she had to reach out for help," Frank continued. "That goes hand in hand with a gambling addiction."

"Yeah, loan sharks," Charlie whispered.

"Names?" Nick readied to take notes.

"I can't. They'll come after me, too."

Frank leaned back in his chair. "Hate to break it to you, sport, when the sharks find out Carrie is dead and can't pay them, they're coming after you. They have to know who you are."

"Yeah, they do. Carrie and I, we were in bed, and in the middle of, you know, and they broke into the house, smashed the back door window, and charged into the bedroom. The men they had sent charged in. Doubt if it were the loaners themselves. They threatened us both. I didn't know about it and it literally scared the shit out of me. I left the house that night and filed for divorce the next day. Didn't look back."

"When was this?"

"Four months ago."

Frank wet his lips. "Your divorce didn't go through yet which means Carrie's debt is your debt. How much was she in for?"

"Even if they were officially divorced, Carolyn's debt would be his debt," Nick added matter-of-factly.

Charlie smirked. "Fifty-six thousand and I don't have that kind of money to give them. I could sell some of her things, jewelry, but that won't add up to much. Can't you protect me against them?"

"Unfortunately, Mr. Baines, in New York, being a loan shark isn't illegal. What was her vig?"

He stared at Nick. "Her what?"

"The percentage she owed them, interest on top of the usual payment."

"I don't have a clue."

"Did she make any payments?"

"Again, no clue. Wait a minute. I'm no dummy here. If this guy killed before leaving a scorpion—" He paused with a look of disgust on his face. "—on the victim, wouldn't that rule out the loan sharks? I mean, were all those women gambling addicts?"

Sam raised an eyebrow. "That'll be something we have to look at. It'll be hard to find commonalities amongst them, that's for sure. But it adds another dimension to the profile. But, first things first. Can you give us a description of the men? Did they call each other by name?"

"No. No names. It was four months ago, but their faces haunt me every night. Both Hispanic, spoke with accents. In their twenties, at most. They wore short sleeve shirts. Both had tattoos in the crook of their elbows, running from their biceps to their forearm. They just yelled at Carrie something like 'if you don't start payin', your house won't be standin' anymore.'"

Frank perked up. "What did the tatts look like?"

"Weird. Spider webs."

"Gang tatts. Know how many lines there were?"

"Lines?"

"Yeah. In the web?" Frank illustrated on his arm.

"Got it. Both different. What difference does it make?"

"The lines represent time they spent in prison. A way to glorify it. I'll get the book from the precinct. Think you can ID them?"

"Definitely."

"Did they mention who they worked for?"

"No. Guess they knew that Carrie knew."

"Did she tell you how she met them?"

"Yeah." Charlie lowered his eyes and slumped back into the chair. "She just told me that, for once in her life, her big brother was going to help her out."

"Callum?" Sam asked.

Charlie nodded. "He's connected to all kinds of sleaze."

Frank slammed the desk with his fist. "No wonder he said he wants nothing to do with this investigation. He knows it'll come back to bite him in the ass."

"Bring that bastard in here, ASAP," Sam yelled into the intercom on the desk.

"Hold on, Sam," Nick warned. "That's opening up another case altogether. Yeah, that's Carolyn's profile, but our case is the serial. We'll write out a report and hand it over to Organized Crime. At least the bums who busted into your house, Mr. Baines, can be taken off the streets."

"Okay. Frank," Sam said, sighing deeply and registering Nick's input. "Assuming that the women were gambling addicts, what are we looking at personality-wise? What would make them attract this guy?"

"Vulnerable, secretive, lying. In conversation, they wouldn't be truthful. They wouldn't let the guy know their true selves. They'd falsify their occupation. Like him, exactly. Very needy, wanting emotional comfort so they could forget about their problems for a while. Gambling did that for them. The winning was a high. The losing gave them an excuse to be depressed without looking into their own lives. Then, to alleviate the depression, they'd binge gamble again. They'd also use sex to escape. As with gambling, there's no impulse control, no impulse to think before jumping into bed with a man. That's part of a sex addiction, as well. Actually, any addiction. Would Carrie have been the type of woman who'd work off her debt with sex?"

Charlie froze.

Nick took on a serious posture. "Mr. Baines, this could be major."

Charlie swallowed hard and looked down. "There were nights she didn't come home. I left for work in the morning and didn't see her until the following day. I thought she had pulled an all-nighter at the casino, but then—I was putting laundry in the hamper, and I pulled out a pair of her panties. It looked like dried seminal fluid, but I can't imagine her having unprotected sex. Did she have sex before he killed her?"

"No. She didn't," Frank said. "We don't know if she angered him, if they argued about something before they had a chance to have sex. Or if he got carried away. What you can tell us about Carrie's sexual behavior could really help us."

"Oh, man. She was wild. Wilder than me. Like your girlfriend, here."

Frank's eyes widened as he looked at Sam. His lips glued into a sliver. Sam poked him with her elbow.

"Go on," Frank demanded.

"She loved the BDSM clubs, especially, Strident. Come on, Sam, you used to go there with her."

"So that's how you had that outfit when we went to Whiplash? Yeah, that's right. You told me you were going shopping in your closet."

"She dragged you, too?"

"We went for a lead in the Aries case." Frank stared at Sam. "And don't you dare think of it. I'm not doing another club. You couldn't walk in there, anyway. Anyone there hooked on her?"

"With that ass of hers? Plenty. Including me. That's where we met. It was my first.—."

Sam glared at him.

"Okay, my second or third time there. I like to watch. Employer-employee scenes. I never participated. I saw Carrie and I wanted to meet her. I waited till she came out of the scene. She sensed I was a newbie and she led me to a wooden bench at the end of the main room. I didn't see it at first. There were buckets attached to the side of the bench with spanking tools. She pushed me onto the bench and then lay across my lap. She told me to pick what I wanted and to lay it on her. Or if I preferred to use my hand, I should. I freaked out. I looked at my palm, then her ass, then my palm again. She finally broke down and told me the four ways to spank. I was shocked there was even a technique. Oh, man. She gave up and we were talking for about an hour with her still across my lap. A couple who wanted to use the bench interrupted us. So that's it. We started seeing each other and she got me introduced to the culture. Private parties every weekend, swapping."

Frank's eyes widened as he caught Sam's gaze.

She glared at him. "No, I didn't do any of that, as if it's any of your business."

Nick frowned. "Hey!"

Sam snapped out if it fast, and Frank nodded. They had gotten the message. Personal info and conflict did not belong in a case. She couldn't afford to do anything that would cause her removal. Lex and Bella would look for any reason to do just that.

"Mr. Baines, you just gave us an infinite number of additional suspects," Nick said. "Have a number?"

"At the parties? Maybe twelve men."

"Women?"

"Carrie wouldn't do women."

"How many?"

"Same, twelve."

"Any jealous spouse issues?"

Charlie paused.

Nick slid a pad and pen over to him. "Write. Names. Don't forget the sharks."

ひとで

Frank pulled into the driveway by Sam's house. Some remnants of the heavy snow a couple of days ago covered her lawn and left some icy patches in the driveway. Her steps were clear. He looked out the window toward her stoop. "Got some deliveries."

"Yes. I was expecting them." She jumped out of the SUV. A huge smile crossed her face as she eyed her treasures.

Frank came up the steps behind her. She moved over so he could pick up the boxes. He stared at them and grimaced. "What's this? You order from all those shopping channels?"

"Yes. So?" She unlocked the door and went into the living room, unconcerned.

Frank followed her. "What's in there?"

"You could put them on the couch."

He had no intention of letting up. After he placed the boxes on the couch, he lifted each one and shook it. "I asked you a question."

"A couple of bags. A pair of shoes."

"You needed more of those?"

"I see something I like, I get it. It's my stress relief."

"I've seen your closet, Sam. You don't need another bag, much less another pair of shoes."

She abruptly turned and put her palms onto his chest. "Who. Died. And. Left. You. My. Boss?"

He wrapped his arms around her back. "Whoa! Why so defensive? Besides, I'm your stress relief, now. It's more fulfilling, and less expensive."

"Actually, it's free." She teased. "I'm not being defensive. It's just not your business."

"Yeah. Okay. You're right. As long as you're keeping on top of the bills."

At that moment, he saw a haze come over her eyes. And his shrink hat fit snugly onto his head. "You mean to tell me, you're not?" She compressed her lips. "Sam, talk to me."

She tried to pull free of his grip, but she was unsuccessful. "Now, you're causing me more stress. See you tomorrow at the precinct, Frank."

She looked up at him—with what he knew as her saccharine smile. He didn't like it. "Okay, princess, see you tomorrow at work. I was sort of in the mood to play, but things got changed, real fast." He kissed her on the tip of her nose, released her, and headed out the door without saying, goodbye.

CHAPTER 12

John looked in dismay at the manila folders fanned out across the desk in the war room of the Manhattan Midtown-South Precinct, as Withers and Richards carried the same look—grim and frustrated, staring blankly at all of the paperwork that could take over their week. Good thing gray skies hung over the building so John didn't mind being indoors. It hit him that he was beginning to miss the Florida winter sunshine, not believing he had let that thought enter his consciousness. Miss Florida? Not him. No way. But he couldn't prevent smiling at the memory of swimming in the outdoor pool while everyone else in New York was shoveling snow. Another dismal thought hit him. That's what he'd be doing when he got home. Shoveling. His driveway. Crap. Scarsdale got hit harder with the snow than the city. He unbuttoned his navy sports jacket and pulled it away from his frame, making himself comfortable for a long morning.

"First, our lab guys are in the process of uncovering the original names on the files we found," Withers said. "Plus, they found more of the same in the basement. My educated guess? Concealment of some kind of robbery was the motive. Maybe stealing of whatever little assets the residents had. Had to be real petty. "

John raised a fist to his lips and gently tapped, in deep thought, and then shook his head and leaned back in the chair. "No. No. It may have nothing to do with the residents."

"What's going on?" Richards asked. "That look on your face."

"He's in trance-land, again."

"No, I'm not. I'm trying to think back to my conversations with Bobby. Something he said, or didn't say. He rushed off the phone, saying there was a line waiting for it. I don't know, but he was hesitant, like he was starting to tell me something then abruptly changed the subject. I know. I'm repeating myself."

"Yeah you are. But it's like my wife telling her girl-friend something juicy, real quiet like, and I appear at the door and she spots me. All of a sudden her voice becomes loud and she changes the subject to something she knows I wouldn't give a damn about."

"Exactly."

"So what did your son say?" Withers said sarcastically.

"Excuse me?"

Withers peered right into John's eyes. "You heard me. I think to be objective about this case you first need to drop that paternal feeling you have toward him."

"Yeah. You're probably right."

"I know I'm right. Look, the kid had a horrible child-hood and adolescence. Are we positive his death is tied to the halfway house? Or isn't it?"

"We eliminated involvement from the guy in the Mont-gomery case. But I'm not a hundred percent positive," Richards added.

"What about from his childhood?" Withers pressed.

John shook his head. "I was looking for a link between him and a patient I had, but didn't go further with it because it wasn't relevant to do so. To have made a hit on him? No one in his past would have the funds for a hit. No. Seriously doubt it."

"Hold on. Go there." Withers sat up and paid attention. "You want to do this case justice? Talk."

John puffed his cheeks out and exhaled deeply. "I was in a hostage situation at Manhattan Psych right before the Gemini case began. This forensic patient had Bobby and the head of the kitchen held hostage."

"Where is this patient now?"

"All right. This won't violate his rights. He's in a mental health unit in an upstate New York prison. After three years, he was deemed fit to stand trial for five counts of murder."

"What happened?"

"As I said, Bobby Mitchell was one of the hostages. He called out to the patient, 'Hal, is that you?' A few minutes later, he blurted out, interrupting the rescue, 'Who did he want to visit? All his family is dead.' This had happened three years earlier, plenty of time for word to get out into the street. I did talk Hal down. I asked my team to go through all of the files again and re-interview. No family link turned up. My first instinct was that they were cousins, though there was no resemblance. Barbara Montgomery murdered my entire team a few days later, and then I was shot and out of commission. After my wife's rescue, I was still in the ICU at the hospital in Florida. I did speak to Bobby and I asked him how he knew Hal. It was simple. They'd gone to the same Boys Club when they were little. Both of their families were impoverished, so it was free."

"I have to tell you, John," Richards said, "I keep going back to the Montgomery case."

"I'm listening."

"Even though the guy that killed Bobby's friend is also out of the picture, permanently, we investigated that far, but I haven't seen any investigations into his contacts, or prison records."

John rubbed the back of his neck. He needed a moment as a diversion to think. "You both know, better than anyone, that prison takedowns are rarely investigated. They get the guy with the shank, they add another murder to his record. That's it. End of story. Especially if there isn't any family to press for a further investigation."

"Yeah. but Montgomery had lots of contacts. Doubt if he was a solitary," Richards said.

"Bobby told me that the guy who made the hit was the only one there."

"Maybe the only one he saw. Even he stayed out of sight. Did he mention a getaway car?" Richards asked.

Withers glared at her as if this was something she should have known. "The guy got into his own car. Bobby said there was no one else in it, and he got a pic of the plate. That's how we caught him."

She glared back then compressed her lips and shook her head. "Did they discover anyone who took a pic of Bobby taking the pic?"

Withers shot her condescending glare, this time.

"Knock it off, Lex. It's the mom in me. I really do think we could have done more."

"First of all, what mom? You don't have any kids, and second, you've never showed me one iota of a maternal instinct in the year we've been working together, and third, stop trying to impress the doc, here, and fourth—"

John interrupted. "Whoa. Is this case bringing up a sore spot, Bella?"

She stopped dead. "No, uh, I feel bad for the kid. Just because I don't have any, Lex, it doesn't mean I don't have a heart."

"So what do you want to do?" Withers asked.

"Go back into the Montgomery case. Dig into her triggerman's history. Find more people connected. Maybe he was attached to the weapons dealers. Who knows?"

"It's a stretch," Withers said.

"If I recall, Lex, when you were training me, didn't you always tell me to go with my gut? And to follow the trail?"

"Yeah. I have a feeling, I'm going to eat my words on that one." Lex paused and appeared to have frozen. His expression went blank.

John hiked a brow. "Hey, Lex, what's the matter?"

"What if this has nothing to do with the Montgomery case or the halfway house?"

"Go on," John said.

"What if, what if—John, you're not going to like this."

"Come on, say it."

"What if the kid's murder resulted from something that happened at Manhattan Psych?"

"My hospital?"

"Yeah. Could be the reason he didn't call you from there. He worked there and you haven't been there in almost a year. Who took over for you?"

"Dr. Bernard Kessler. He knew the position was interim."

"Yeah. But was he as meticulous as you?"

"Probably no one is as OCD about records as me. What makes you think of that?"

"Going back to the Aries case. I learned a lot and saw all the documentation in my brother's investigation. He set up a red herring, so to speak, with the murder of Khaos's wife being a gang initiation. Only when the rookie, Sam Wright, looked into it, the hospital cover-up came out. So what if someone at Manhattan Psych wanted to cover something up and made a contact with the lowlife Maynor to set up the halfway house? They knew where Bobby lived, so that was a start."

"Yes. Maynor was hated there so he might have wanted to get even," Richards said. "So the items of Bobby's could have been planted."

"But would Maynor be so dumb to commit murder, knowing—uh, he had to know about the surveillance tapes and that he'd be caught?" John paused to collect his thoughts. "Speaking of which, why did he do that, no matter the motive? Um, maybe Maynor was running from something, and he was looking for a way out, so he figured out a way to take him off the radar, permanently. Like, getting busted. Oh, man, if that's the case, and it's a stretch."

"So was the Aries case, but they never had a fall guy."

John nodded. "Okay, let's go over this before I get total-ly confused. One. Maynor may have had a motive for want-ing to be taken off the radar. Correct?" Withers and Rich-ards nodded. "Two. Now we need to look into all his busi-ness affairs and bank accounts. And compare his contacts to any employee or patient, for that matter, at the hospital. Compare names to those on the whited out files, too." Withers and Richards nodded, again. "Three. Look into Montgomery's contacts again. Find a connection if possible to Maynor or his two partners. He may be the leader but the hit could have been brought to him. Four. Interview people at Manhattan Psych who can give info about Bobby's rela-tionships. If they find any, that'll give Lieutenant Rojas a double reason to have me recuse myself. Damn!" John looked at his watch. "All right, we'll look into all of that. Start digging with Maynor's bank accounts. I have to go. I have a meeting in Scarsdale about my break-in."

ຕ໑ຕ໑

John walked up the cobble stone path to the entrance of the newly renovated Tudor style Police Headquarters in the Village of Scarsdale, in Westchester New York.

In a state-of-the-art interrogation room, he sat with his arm around Ricky's shoulders while Vicki sat next to John, rocking the twins' stroller. The conservatively dressed de-tective, Monty Smith, unbuttoned his gray sports jacket and then placed a photo log on the table in front of Ricky.

"Thank you for doing this, Ricky."

"You're welcome, sir."

John hugged his son. This Southern kid had Southern manners.

The detective smiled. "Ricky, I want you to look at each page carefully and see if you recognize the third woman that ran out of the house. Your dad told the officers that her name was Abby Ruthe. Do you remember if the other two women used her name?"

Ricky looked up wide-eyed, as if in awe, at the detective who was bigger than his dad. John hugged him tighter. "Yes. I remember. That name."

"Okay. Very good. Please open the book and look at each picture."

Ricky opened the book, and his eyes widened as he stared at the photos. He looked up at his father.

"What, champ?"

"These are a lot of pictures, Dad," he whispered.

"Yes. Five across and five down. Know how many that is?"

Ricky hesitated. He put a finger on each pic and counted. Detective Smith looked annoyed—John assumed— about the time wasted.

"Yes, twenty-five."

"Okay. Now twenty-five pictures are on each page, so start looking and see if you can identify Abby."

Ricky took a deep breath. He ran his finger starting on the upper left, across the row, then down to the next row as if he was reading. Then the second page. Then the third. Detective Smith looked as if he was losing patience, fast. The man couldn't stop fidgeting, looking at his fingernails. He plucked a pack of gum from his jacket pocket, unwrapped a piece, and popped it into his mouth. John made a long shot guess that he didn't have any children.

On the fourth page, Ricky stopped. He pointed to a woman on the bottom row. "That's her!"

Detective Smith sat up in the chair and paid attention. "You sure?"

"Yes. Those are the nose ring and lip ring. And the same tattoo on her neck. I'm positive," Ricky said, bobbing his head.

"Good job, champ."

"Can I ask a question, please?"

"Sure," Detective Smith said.

"If you have pictures of all these people, how come you haven't put them in jail, already?"

John swallowed to hide his laugh and Vicki covered her mouth, but Detective Smith nearly choked on his gum and, in his laughter, the gum flew out of his mouth and landed in the twins' stroller.

"Oh, man. You're something else, son."

೧೦೧೦

In the interrogation room, next door, Kit Malone with tears flowing, wearing the jailhouse gray garb—a polyester gray T-shirt and elastic around the waist pants—sat at the desk with her head down. John observed her through the one-way mirror as Detective Smith stood next to him with his fingers in his pants pocket. John couldn't help but scan the surroundings—bland, just like in New York. Good. The less busy, the less distraction.

"Dr. Trenton, I don't know what magic you pulled for my captain to allow you to become involved with this case."

John smiled. "Professional courtesy." The detective hiked a brow. John's smile widened. "Yes, after a strong conversation with my captain. Abby Ruthe is also in my specialty age, though my patients reside in hospitals. Do you mind?"

"Actually, I don't. I have enough personnel investigating these robberies. An extra pair of eyes is appreciated."

"Thank you."

"She's no more than nineteen." Detective Smith shook his head. "And they were responsible for over ten home invasions. They had meat for the dogs but yours took them by surprise. Glad it's over. Our residents were petrified. What a mess she made of her life."

"They certainly do. Has she spoken to you?"

"No. She lawyered up immediately, in the ambulance.

Her attorney already spoke to her while your son was looking at the book. I'll go in there when he returns. He went to call his partners. Wanting a deal, I suppose."

"It's not really over. That Abby is still at large. She could get another crew. I want to talk to her, too."

Detective Smith nodded as Kit's attorney entered the interrogation room. She picked up her head, still crying. Her eyes were red, her purple hair straggled and needing a shampoo.

"Okay, let's get this show on the road." Smith opened the interrogation room door.

Detective Smith and John entered.

When Kit saw John, she yelled, "What's he doing here?"

"Who's he?" The attorney looked up at John. "I'm Chuck Cohen, Miss Malone's attorney. And you are?"

"Doctor John Trenton. I'm a forensic psychiatrist." He paused, took his card out of his pocket, and handed it to Cohen before he pulled a chair away from the table. As he sat down he added, "I was brought in as a consultant in this case, and I'm the renter of the home your client invaded." He stared straight into the attorney's eyes.

Cohen swallowed hard. "My client told me you cuffed her hands behind her back with zip ties."

"That I did. To protect my son."

"What do you want? No one was ever hurt in any of these…uh…alleged home invasions. And my client was only identified in one, as was the other woman."

John's intense gaze caused his brows to furrow. "You're representing her, too?"

"No. That would be a conflict of interest. I referred her family to another practice. Speaking of conflict of interest, Dr. Trenton—"

Detective Smith cut him off. "I beg to differ on what you said that no one was hurt." The detective stared at the attorney. "Abigail Ruthe seriously hurt Selena Graves in the car before the said event."

"Yes, Detective Smith, and my client tried to help her. That should count for something."

"Mr. Cohen. Stop. It's only been two days and our investigation is just starting. You've only met with your client for about an hour. Surely you need more time than that to compile your defense."

"Miss Malone's parents want to pay her bail," Cohen said as if he had lemon rind between his teeth.

"We're not at that point, yet." Detective Smith paused. "Miss Malone hasn't been indicted, or brought before any judge. And when I checked this morning, Judge Mace's calendar was booked for at least three more days. We'll call you with the date and time, definitely before seven days has passed since Miss Malone's arrest." Detective Smith stared at Kit. John knew from his tense expression he was going to attempt to intimidate her. "We'll be compiling evidence from the nine other robberies which include photos of the damage done, lists of items stolen, photos of damage to the properties, pictures of the outsides of the houses, tire tracks, identifying the vehicle that made those tracks, and warrants to search their three homes."

"And don't forget fingerprints," John added. "Maybe the crime scene investigators will get lucky and get some prints, uh, just in case a latex glove ripped. Happens all the time. Oh, and yours did, as I recall."

"Stop with the intimidation. The both of you."

Detective Smith put his hands out. "Hey, it's the truth."

"First, my client would have nothing from the robbery in her possession. She never got to her apartment. Besides, nothing was removed from your house, Dr. Trenton."

"My house is now a crime scene. We are living in a hotel with our dog, two-month old twins, and a traumatized nine-year old, not having the comforts of a home. We will also be seeking reimbursement, for the exact damage, the amount I can't tell you, yet."

"How much time can Miss Malone be looking at?"

"Charlie! You have to get me out of this. My parents won't let you let them put me in jail."

Detective Smith snickered but his tone was serious. "You're in jail now, young lady. You mean prison. This time, your parents won't be able to rescue you. You're looking at five to ten years. Medium security. In upstate New York. A good six-hour drive. I'm sure your parents will be thrilled."

Kit's cheeks reddened. Her eyes glazed over as if something possessed her. John prepared for an attack. He saw the turmoil she held inside of herself. The anger. The sizzle. He literally saw her blood boil. The line around her body in her aura turned black. She pushed the seat back from the table. John was surprised her chair wasn't bolted to the floor and that she wasn't handcuffed. She jumped up and lunged across the table onto Detective Smith's chest, just as he and John were standing up.

Smith grabbed her and wrapped his arms around her body with her arms held tight. She fought him with all her might, even with her thin frame, kneeing him in his groin. He grunted. He pulled away from the table and flipped her onto her back down onto the floor with Kit yelling and screaming obscenities. She flailed her arms and as John saw her trying to reach for Smith's gun in his waist holster, John yelled, "Gun," and grabbed her arms back above her head. They both flipped her over and Smith handcuffed her hands behind her back.

Continuing to kick, she screamed, "I'm going to kill you! I'm going to fucking kill you!"

Two officers rushed into the room. The men lifted her to her feet. She didn't stop writhing to get out of their control. As an officer bent down to grasp her ankles, she kicked him in the head. He fell backward, receiving a gash on his forehead. John squatted and wrapped his arms around her legs together close to his body to keep her feet still. The second officer cuffed her ankles with a ten-inch chain connecting to the cuffs.

Smith stood up. It took a few moments for him to catch his breath. Staring at the attorney who sat with his mouth agape, he said, "Make that ten minimum, in max after a psych eval and competency exams to deem her fit to stand trial."

In the midst of Kit's rampant screaming, John, along with the officers, lifted her into a plank position to carry her out of the room.

CHAPTER 13

Having a minute alone in the conference room in the Queens precinct, Sam, wearing latex gloves, gingerly started to pull samples of evidence, one by one—that were tagged, labeled, and inserted into large forensic manila envelopes—out of a white, cardboard box that was filled to capacity with evidence files. The first one made her pause. "Bed sheet, um. The entire thing." She held the envelope, with both hands. "Oh my God, Carrie. This sheet tells all about you. Not the way I want to remember you." She brought the envelope up to her heart and held it there, wanting a solemn moment. No such luck.

Withers and Richards brusquely entered. Still hugging the sheet, Sam looked up at them.

Withers gave her a contemptuous glare. "Still think you're capable of being involved in this case, Wright? 'Cause your behavior yesterday, talking about the clubs and your involvement with them, and now hugging that evidence bag for dear life, makes me seriously doubt it."

She sniffled, closed her eyes for a moment, and swallowed. She looked straight up into Lex's eyes. "Yes, I'm positive. I can. Let's get into this box." She laid the sheet down on the upper left side of the scarred, six-foot wood conference table. She pulled out the next envelope, Carrie's bra. Every item of her clothing packed individually—seven large forensic envelopes—shoes, socks, jeans, sweater, panties, watch. She placed them side by side from left to right across the table. Then her pocketbook. A designer tote. Carrie would freak seeing her three-thousand-dollar bag getting this treatment. Attached to the envelope that protected the bag were smaller envelopes containing individual items she carried with her. Her wallet had been disassembled. Every charge card, medical insurance card, receipt from the hotel was examined and packed separately.

Then came the smaller items from the hotel room—shampoo, conditioner, soap. Next, Carrie's belongings—her own herbal shampoo, conditioner, and styling products—everything packed solo. She read the same note that was on each envelope. *Taken for scent sample, see report.*

Withers dug into a second box that held folders. He found a separate one that read *Scent Analysis.* He flipped open the cover, sat down and, ignoring his partner and Sam, studied the pages in what appeared to Sam to be amazement. Sam went behind him to look over his shoulder—graphs—all kinds of graphs, line graphs, bar graphs, circle graphs stymied her. As Withers turned the pages, he seemed to be getting more confused, as was Sam.

Bella pursed her lips and put her hands on her hips. "Care to share?"

Sam put her hand over his shoulder, Lex handed her the folder, and she moved over to Bella and held it open between them. Sam took a deep grounding breath. "Why do they have to give chemicals unpronounceable names?"

"Yeah, and who can remember how to spell them?" Bella asked.

"Okay, they're comparing the soap, shampoos, and conditioners, but to what?"

Bella pointed with her index finger. "There. They're comparing this stuff to a hair sample. But this says 'Scent Analysis.' Where's the hair sample? The bottom line from all of this is 'no match.' What the hell?"

Sam pulled the last few envelopes from the box. The hair samples were in the bottom one. In the envelope, a glass vial with a glass topper preserved the hair. There were three of them. Three hair samples. Around each bottle was a tape with 'do not open' written on it in a permanent black ink.

Sam took out a vial and brought it up to her nose. No scent. "How can they capture a scent and then be able to study it if we can't open it?"

"A lesson for the two of you. After the sample is studied, it's bottled and preserved. Now that they found 'no match' in their tests, they want any scent contained for court. It's not for you to test the sample. That was done. You go by the report whether it tells us nothing, or not. If you open the bottle, the scent will dissipate when it hits air."

"Okay. Let' go slower, please. So there is a scent on the hair?" Sam asked.

"Yes," Withers answered.

"But if it's not hair products, can the scent have come from the killer? That makes sense to me. Frank's cologne stays on my pillowcase and stuff. Sometimes it spreads to my hair."

"TMI, Sam. It also says here, no commercial products for men or women and it lists every perfume and cologne they tested," Bella said using her finger to scan the list. "Like a hundred of them, and I'm not reading all of them."

"Did they come up with any scents they can identify?"

Bella turned the next few pages. "Yeah, condiments and spices."

"Um. The suspense is killing me. Can't I open just one? I have a great sense of smell." Sam said pleadingly. "Does it say if they're identical samples?"

Bella turned the page in the report, and ran her finger down the page, again. She squinted to read it, even though it was typed. "This is way above my brain capacity. Who do they expect to read, much less understand this stuff?"

"That's why they have their analysts in court. See if there's a summary page. That's usually more user friendly for jurors to understand." Withers sat back and let the two newbies have a go at it.

"Ooh." Sam got excited. "Here, it says a cinnamon base, garlic, cardamom, turmeric, curry, sesame oil, soy sauce, plum sauce, fish sauce, oyster sauce, sambal, rice vinegar, Tamari soy sauce. Those are for cooking Asian food or Thai. Oh come on, Lex. Please let me open one. Carrie had a food scent in her hair. Maybe we can narrow it down. Maybe she went to a restaurant. There's a Thai restaurant at the casino, as well an Asian station in the buffet, but they cook different menus. And if she did, maybe they could tell us who she was with. Maybe the killer had the scent on his hands or on his body. Eww. That wouldn't be so sexy." Lex glared at her. "Oh come on, Lex, can't you call someone? From the smell, I could tell the difference. They're subtle."

"I'll go ask Loo." Shaking his head, he exited the room to go into Lieutenant Hicks' office.

Sam watched the door as it closed behind him. She compressed her lips.

"Don't you dare think it, Sam. You tamper with evidence, you'll screw with the case and when we do catch this guy, he'll get off on a technicality. And you'll lose your job, to boot."

"Calm down, Bella, I know. God forbid, I do anything against protocol." Sam held the envelope with the vials. She peered through the plastic shield to the labels.

"What's the matter?"

Sam pointed to it. "Look at the three vials. Why does this one have a black dot under the words 'do not open'?"

Bella shook her head. "I thought that was a spot from the pen point."

"Let me see that report." Sam scanned the summary, nothing. "Is there a separate folder for the vials?"

Bella dug into the document box. She pulled out the folders with crime scene photos then another with lab photos. "Let's look at these." Bella opened one folder and flipped through it. "On second thought, you better not." She closed the folder and sat down. She looked queasy.

Sam sat down next to her and slid the folder in front of herself. "What's the matter?"

Bella placed her palm on the folder preventing Sam from opening it. "Don't." She gave Sam a serious look. "Autopsy photos. You don't have to see Carrie like this."

Sam closed her eyes for a moment. "Maybe I do. It'll push me harder to find the bastard who did this."

"You can't be working harder on this, Sam."

Before Sam could answer, Withers returned and pulled the document folder box toward him. He lifted the edge of three folders before he took the right one out. He handed Sam the folder that was entitled, 'vial samples.' "Look through this and find what you need." He sat down at the end of the table and crossed his arms over his chest.

Controlling her feeling of exasperation toward him, Sam lay the opened folder between her and Bella, and again saw mathematical equations and graphs that neither of them would venture to understand. She flipped to the report summary. She read line-by-line information that she still couldn't make heads or tails of. Then in the notes at the end of the summary, there it was. "Hold on! Hold on! Here it is! 'The vial with the black dot can be opened for detective investigation, only. Not to be removed from the building.' Okay Lex, I found it. So you just couldn't tell us?"

He kept his gaze focused on Sam. "Nope. In this business, it's learn through doing."

Sam swallowed hard and slowly removed the vial with the black dot out of the envelope. She held it in her palm and blinked back tears, looking at Carrie's three-inch by one-inch hair sample. It was as dark brown in death as it was in life. Sam sniffled. No way in hell would she let Bella and Lex observe her having a meltdown.

"Hey, Wright, pull it together. Tears could hinder the sense of smell. That's the truth."

Guess Lex did see it. She took out a tissue from her bag and blew her nose. She'd let nothing hinder her sense of smell. After a few blows, and she was sure her nasal passages were clear, she put her fingers on the glass topper.

"Just remember, Sam, the more you open it, the odor dissipates. Eventually, the human nose won't detect anything. So choose your steps, carefully."

"Right."

Come on, Sam, commit the smell to memory. Every component of it.

She twisted the glass topper off the vial. The odor hit the air. Bella leaned in for a whiff. Her eyes popped wide. Sam nodded and replaced the topper.

"Okay, it's from food, that's for sure, plus some perspiration. She was either aroused by this guy or fighting for her life. With that body odor, I can't tell if it's Thai or Asian."

"That poor girl."

Sam tried to push off Bella's sentiment. "I picked out the scents in the report, but we need more than that. I'm not a cooking expert."

"Me, neither," Bella chimed in.

"But I sure as heck know who is."

�〜〜

Vicki was in her galley kitchen, pulling a tin of muffins out of the oven. She inhaled deeply as the steam fragrances of cinnamon, nutmeg, and ginger filled the kitchen. She smiled as she looked at the brown tops with snips of grated carrots and plump cranberries showing through. This was her favorite pumpkin carrot muffin recipe, one that she created. The phone on the counter rang.

"Hello."

"Hi, Vicki, it's Sam."

"Oh my goodness! What a coincidence. I'm just taking muffins out of the oven for Frank. Gluten-free. How are ya, darlin'?"

"I'm okay, thanks. We're in the midst of the investigation for Carrie. Uh, you baked for Frank?"

"Yes. He keeps telling John how much he loved them, so I made a batch for John to bring to the precinct tomorrow. What's up?'

ℯↄℯↄ

Sam was glad Vicki couldn't see her reaction through the phone. It wasn't a happy one. She caught Vicki up on the vial with the scent. "Think you could ID what kind of food these spices would be put on?"

"Yes. How would that help?"

"There are six separate restaurants and a buffet with seven stations. If we know where the scent comes from, it would narrow our list of interviewees considerably and give us a focus. There's a choice of two."

"Sure, I'd be happy to help."

"I can't take the vial with the hair sample out of the precinct. How soon can you come down here? And bring every spice jar you have in the house."

"Uh, that's a lot of jars, darlin', and I have to bring Ricky and the twins with me."

"Yes! I'd love to see them. See you as soon as you can." The phone disconnected.

"You look like you have mixed feelings about Vicki."

Sam exhaled a deep breath. "Actually, I love her. She's become a great friend. I didn't expect Frank to go gaga over her muffins, though. He teases me enough that I don't cook."

"Why don't you try?"

"I'm so nervous that I'll burn something."

"Is Vicki that good?"

"Oh, my God. She's professional chef caliber."

A courier opened the door and handed Withers three files and a USB device and then left. Withers looked at the covers and let out a deep sigh. "All right, Sam, why don't you take a break? These files are from the Bobby Mitchell case. Info came in on Trig Maynor's bank accounts. Let Bella and I work on this until Vicki comes."

"But I can—"

"That's an order."

Sam grabbed some folders off the table that she hadn't inspected yet, huffed, and left the room.

ꞈꞈꞈ

Sam strutted over to her temporary desk in the center of the main floor in the precinct. She was getting used to working here but she missed Chelsea. Nick had a doctor's appointment with his wife with a neurologist and the worry of possible Parkinson was on his mind. Lieutenant Rojas had told him to take the week off. He had the time. In fifteen years, maybe he took off ten days, mostly when his kids were sick.

She admired her partner. His devotion to his wife was something she was going to strive for in a relationship. She sighed. Would Frank be as devoted to her? At this point, she didn't know. She plucked her cell from her bag and pressed Frank's number.

"Hey, princess."

She laughed. "Hi. How was Frankie's play?"

"Oh, man. Those kids were so cute. I mean it, Sam. A few of the kids were home, sick, and there were stand-ins. None of them really knew their lines. As much as we practiced with Frankie, he messed up. All of us parents sat in the back of the classroom and tried to hide our laughing. The kids tried so hard. *Frosty the Snowman* will never be the same. But I'll tell you something, princess. Frankie missed you not being there."

There was a prolonged silence.

"Really?"

"Really. He loves you."

Another moment of silence.

But do you love me, Frank?

"I love him, too."

How can I yell at him about wanting Vicki's muffins after this?

"How late are you going to be?"

She told him about the latest developments in Carrie's files and that Vicki was coming to help, with the kids, and muffins for him. The last few words did it.

"Okay, I'll be there in forty and as long as Ricky is coming, I'll bring Frankie."

"I'm sure Lieutenant Hicks will be happy that his precinct will be turning into a nursery. Okay, see you soon." She disconnected.

An hour passed with Sam examining the autopsy photos. The first folder contained five, eight by eleven inch color pictures of the way Carrie was found by the police. Brett Case had explained it accurately during their first meeting—nude, arms down at her side, her hair draped over her shoulder, blanket pulled up to her neck. Another folder held photos of Carrie's neck with the ligature marks quite clear. A scalpel must have been use to remove some layers of skin around the fingerprints.

Carrie, we'll get him. We'll get him for sure. He became careless this time. This prick's luck just ran out.

Her heart tugged in her chest when she opened the next file. Seeing Carrie's stomach cut open caused her to want to puke. She felt the blood drain from her face. Carrie's skin from under her bust line to her pelvic area was cut open and each side was pulled back and held with stainless steel clips. Her organs—all of them—were lying outside of her body in a straight line from her neck down to her groin. It appeared as if chunks of each organ had been pulled off for examination. Their color had faded in death.

Her once beautiful friend had turned into a science experiment.

Hold on a second. They had to examine the content of food in her stomach. That alone could tell us what she ate and where, and if the scent on her hair came from the food she consumed. Damn it, Withers! Enough with testing me, already. Why didn't you show me this folder?

She thumbed through the folder to the summary.

Clams, shrimp, mixed greens, of course salad. Carrie was salad freak. Grilled steak, yam. Nothing ethnic. Nothing sweet. This is a dead end. None of those spices on the hair are used in any of this food preparation and all of the restaurants serve these foods. Maybe not a dead end. So the sample definitely came from the killer. Or from someone who passed by and bumped her from behind.

Sam looked up and heard some voices with oohs and ah's and "how cute," "how precious." Vicki must be here. Sam put her cell in her pocket and walked into the entry of the main floor. A bubble jacket encased Vicki, and Ricky, the same, as he wheeled the twin-stroller. Vicki carried a shopping bag from which the items inside, emitted clicking sounds. Must be her spice jars. There was a snap and lock rectangular canister sitting on top of the awning of the stroller—the dreaded muffins. Sam smirked before Vicki spotted her.

Vicki called loudly, "Hi ya, Sam!"

"Hi! So glad you could come in. Hi, Ricky, how are you doing?"

"I'm good. I've never been in a police station before, not in New York City, anyways."

"Come on, I'll give you the fifty cents tour."

"I don't have any money—to pay for a tour."

Sam laughed. "That's okay. It's just an expression. We're working in the conference room. This way."

Vicki followed Sam as Ricky wheeled the stroller toward the conference room.

Before they entered the room, Vicky whispered, "Uh, do I have to call you Detective Wright, in there?"

Sam smiled, "No, we're informal."

As they entered, Lex and Bella were just putting away Trig Maynor's folders.

Sam made the introductions on the fly—as Vicki and Ricky took off their coats—and she immediately went to unbundle Alexi who was squirming in the stroller. Ever so gently, she pulled down her blanket. Sam smiled from ear to ear, triggering Alexi's giggles.

The infant kicked her legs and Sam swooned, thinking the baby recognized her. Sam unzipped her one-piece snowsuit. She picked up the infant with both hands, moved one to cradle her head, and brought her close onto her chest.

She stood for a moment. It was about time she acknowledged to herself how much she wanted her own.

Sam brought Alexi over to Bella. "Isn't she the most precious?"

Bella didn't change her stoic posture. She pursed her lips. "That's pushing it."

Sam stepped back. *Guess Lex was right.* Bella didn't have one iota of a maternal instinct. Sam responded with a meek smile.

Vicki must have seen the reaction. She jumped past it. "Okay now, what can I help y'all with?"

"This genius here—" Lex pointed to Sam. "—thinks you can duplicate the scent from this vial that's on the hair sample, so then they can narrow down which restaurant of the two would use the combination."

"It should," Sam said. "Because I had the time to look at the autopsy notes and none of the foods in Carrie's stomach would call for the spices mentioned in the report."

"Uh, you looked in someone's stomach?" Ricky crinkled his nose. "How did you do that?"

Sam put on her teacher hat. "Um, sweetheart, we work here on finding the people who do bad things to others. And we have a department called forensics and they do tests on the victims so we can learn what happened to them. We found smells from spices on the person's hair so maybe, just maybe, we can find the restaurant they ate in. Then we

---

can interview all the people in that restaurant."

"Yes, I heard that part when he—" Ricky pointed to Lex, "—told my mom. But how did you see her stomach?"

"Remember when Daddy and I took you to the science museum in Orlando and we watched scientists dissecting a frog?"

"Yes. It was disgusting. I almost threw up. I never want to do that."

"That's okay, but it's sort of the same thing. So let's get all of these jars out now. You can help, you know." Vicki put the bag with the jars on the table, next to another bag containing some bottles of liquids. She began to pull them out one by one. "Okay. These are the standard spices in everyone's cabinets." She glanced toward Sam. "Well, maybe not everyone's." She laughed. Sam smirked. "Don't worry, darling,' you'll learn." Vicki looked at each label before she placed the bottle on the table. "Here we go. Dill…" She placed it on the left. "I'll put them in alphabetical order so we'll find them more easily."

Bella put her hands on her hip and shook her head.

Vicki must have gotten the message. "Sorry, I taught kindergarten for fifteen years."

"Well, can't you hurry it up? We're adults here. Trust me we'll be able to find them. Here, let me give you a hand." Bella put both hands into the bag and came out with bottles of basil leaf, Cajun, caraway seeds, fennel, and cayenne pepper. She put them down on the table, and quickly Vicki rearranged them. Bella pulled out five more—celery seed, chili pepper, chives, cilantro, and cinnamon—and put them in a pile which Vicki then rearranged.

"How much more do you have, Mrs. Trenton?" Lex threw his hands up in the air. "My wife is an excellent cook, and even she doesn't have all this."

"Really, Lex?" Bella looked surprised. "You hardly ever mention your wife."

"Yeah, well. I keep my personal life out of the office," he said, glaring at Sam. "Unlike you and your boyfriend."

He dug into the bag and handed bottles to Ricky. "Here ya go, sport, let your mom do the arranging."

Ricky laughed and handed Vicki the jars—cloves, bottle of pure vanilla extract, coriander and cumin. Bella took out curry, paprika, garlic, ginger, allspice, juniper berries and a bottle of almond extract.

All the while Sam was rocking Alexi who was sleeping, cradled in her arms.

Bella shook her head. "You better tell Frank he better put a move on. Neither one of you are getting any younger."

"I keep telling them the same thing." Vicki finally turned the bag over and the rest of the spice jars rolled onto the table—lemon pepper, marjoram, mustard seed, onion, a bottle of olive oil, orange peel, mint, oregano, oriental seasoning, paprika, black pepper, peppercorns, pumpkin, sesame seeds, star anise, tarragon leaf, thyme and turmeric. From the second bag, she pulled out Hoisin sauce, Soy sauce, Plum sauce, Avocado oil, rice vinegar, fish sauce, Sriracha, chili garlic, oyster sauce, curry paste, miso paste, sambal, and toasted sesame oil.

The three watching her, looked in amazement. "Dang, I didn't think there were that many."

"There's so much more, Detective Richards. Combinations, I never heard of. But I like to make my own blends. Okay, which ones do you know are in there?"

Sam moved Alexi onto her chest with the baby's head on her shoulder, walked to the desk, and handed Vicki the report with the list.

"Okay. This is definitely Asian only."

"You know for sure?" Bella asked.

"Yes." Vicki scanned the table at her selection. She first pulled the bottle of star anise, then coriander seeds and, finally, chilies. She placed them on the table in front of the detectives. "These are essential for Thai cooking and they are not on the list. You cannot do an authentic Thai meal without them and the restaurant would surely know that."

Vicki sighed deeply apparently proud of her conclusion.

"Thank you so much, Vicki! This is awesome."

Frank and Frankie entered the room, with Frankie running to Sam and wrapping his arms around her.

"Sam!"

Frank looked lovingly at Sam then at Alexi in her arms, and then his gaze went to Zach sleeping in the stroller before it finally landed on the muffin canister.

"I heard you did so great today!" Sam told Frankie. "We may have an actor in the making."

Frankie blushed.

Frank picked up the canister of muffins. "Thanks so much, Vicki. These will be gone in a few days."

"Care to share?" Lex asked.

"No way!"

"Don't worry about it, Detective Withers. I made another tray for this office. John appreciates the work you're doing on the Bobby Mitchell case." She picked up another canister from the bottom basket of the stroller.

"So he's big on bribery, uh?"

"Why, no! I always baked for the Brooklyn precinct. I never thought of it as bribery. John knew I needed something to do. I was going nuts."

Frank pointed to Sam. "Here's something you can do, Vicki, teach this one how to cook."

"I'll send my wife, too. She loves that kind of stuff."

"What does she like to cook, Detective?"

"Caribbean, and hot."

"Um, teaching cooking. Something to think about." Vicki looked contemplative.

"Okay, Frank," Sam said. "The bottom line is that the smells from Carrie's hair sample are from an Asian menu. The only Asian restaurant is in the buffet. If the killer didn't have it on his hands, maybe some sauce squirted on her hair. It's worth the trip. Anyone up for the casino buffet, tonight? Don't worry, Handletti said we can go any time since there was nothing we could use on the tape."

CHAPTER 14

John and Detective Smith entered Selena Graves's hospital room in Scarsdale Memorial Hospital. The nineteen-year-old girl lay on her back, with an IV in her left wrist, the right side of her face bandaged from her scalp to her chin. Her complexion—too pale for a dark haired girl—almost matched the light yellow walls. Selena turned her head toward the door when she saw them. Her gaze, as it caught the handcuff on her right wrist attaching her hand to the bed railing, triggered tears. When John approached her bed, the tears turned to sobbing.

John fought back compassion by keeping a formal posture—very unlike him with a teenager. He pulled a tissue from the box on the nightstand and handed it to her. He guessed from Smith's frown and looking out the window at John's gesture, he wouldn't have even done that.

She took it hesitantly and wiped her eyes. "I'm in big trouble, aren't I?"

"I would have to say, yes." Knowing this was going to take a while, John unbuttoned his wool coat, took it off, and tossed it onto the empty bed next to hers. "Has your attorney spoken with you?"

"He came yesterday. He's going to try to arrange bail with my parents."

"Selena, there is no bail yet. You haven't gone before the judge," Smith said.

She turned her head toward the detective. "I don't want to go to j—a—i—l. I never did anything like this before. It was my first time. I was never even arrested before. You've got to believe me. I'm a freshman in college and want to be a doctor, like you—" She turned her head toward John. "Doctor Trenton. I'm so sorry. I didn't mean to mess up my life. Ask my parents, I'm straight As. All the time. I was Valedictorian in high school. I had so many AP classes I'll have my Bachelors in two and a half years, not four. I'm already looking into medical schools. Speak to my guidance counselors, and my teachers. This can't be happening."

Detective Smith shook his head. "Sorry to burst your bubble, but it is. Technically, we shouldn't even be talking to you without your attorney. We just came to see how you're feeling since we can't reach him or your parents. And it's my responsibility to get you before the judge as expediently as possible. When will your parents be coming?"

She lowered her eyes. "They're not."

"Why not?"

"They're leaving on a vacation to Costa Rica, tonight. They're closing on a vacation home and didn't want to postpone it."

John shot a glance toward the detective. Even his stoic expression dissolved. "Who are you staying with?"

She sniffled. "Myself. I'm an adult. And my little brother. He's twelve."

John nodded. "Where is he now?"

"In school." She caught onto what John meant. "He's staying with my grandparents until I'm out. It's the best my attorney could do. No one else is in New York, and they didn't want to pull my brother out of his school."

Detective Smith held his pad and a pen. "What do you mean, 'the best he could do'?"

"They haven't spoken to my parents in years. They don't approve of my parents' life—"

Detective Smith interrupted. "Which is?"

"Never at our house. They switch partners for...ya know...uh, sex."

Smith snickered. "And how do you know about that?"

"They come home, arguing really loud, can't help but wake us up. My dad screams the loudest, at my mom, for enjoying it. Then they run up the stairs to the third level of the house and slam the door. Their regular bedroom is on the second floor. I can take a good guess as to what they're doing." She look up at John. "No, I've never been up there. They keep that room secured with a keypad lock."

The phone rang on her nightstand. Her eyes darted between John and the detective.

"Answer it," Detective Smith said. He handed her the handset.

"Hello. Oh, hi, Mr. Temple." She looked up at the two men. "My attorney."

The husky voice on the other end came through the earpiece. "Who were you talking to?"

Smith reached for the handset and Selena gave it to him. He held it away from his face so that John and Selena could hear the conversation. "Mr. Temple, this is Detective Smith. I'm here with Doctor Trenton. We've been trying to reach you—"

Temple abruptly cut him off. "Yes. I know. I have court appearances for a six-figure case that I'm preparing for and my paralegal has been slower than usual getting the paperwork filed for Miss Graves's case."

"Hear that, Selena? You're not a priority to this legal office." She nodded. "In that case, let us help you out. How about if I record our conversation with Miss Graves and I send it to you?"

"Selena, what do you say?"

"Mr. Temple, I'll do anything not to go to jail."

"I'm assuming, Mr. Temple, that that's your goal, correct?" John added.

"Of course. When I spoke with Miss Graves, I told her that in order to get the best deal possible, she'd have to cooperate. She expressed hesitancy because of fear of retribution from the other girls."

"We're taking care of that, but we need her help in locating the leader, Abigail Ruthe."

"I have to be at the courthouse in ten minutes. Tape the conversation. Selena, tell them what they need to know. Understand?"

She let out a little girl whine. "Yes."

"All good, Detective and Doctor Trenton?"

The men voices ran over each other. "Yes."

The attorney disconnected and Smith put his phone on record.

"With Miss Graves's attorney's permission...what's his first name?"

"Justin."

"Justin Temple, I, Detective Monty Smith, am conducting this interview with Doctor John Trenton and Selena Graves at her hospital bedside in Scarsdale Memorial Hospital on this date of Wednesday, January twenty-seventh, at one-forty-three p.m. I will be asking the questions." John snickered. "Okay," Detective Smith said. "When did you first meet Abigail Ruthe?"

"The day before we broke in."

"That recently?"

"Yes. I told you. I never did anything like this before."

"How?"

"She needed a substitute."

"What happened to the girl that was supposed to take part?"

"I don't know. Abby didn't say. She asked Kit to ask someone who wouldn't get into that much trouble."

"Excuse me? How can that person not get into trouble?"

"If it's their first offense, they won't go to jail if they're caught. That's what Abby told me. She said not to worry about it."

"And now that you were caught, do you think that holds true?" Smith asked.

"Yes. That's what my lawyer will say, too."

"You may be very smart in school, Selena, but you're missing street smarts. Prison time might be mandatory for this. We have no control over what a judge will consider. Dr. Trenton is prosecuting as his son could have been seriously wounded if not fatally, and his dog could have been hurt, as well. You got lucky on those two." Smith's intense stare reinforced the seriousness. "We have some questions that we need serious and honest answer to."

"Okay. I'm so sorry."

"Where did you meet Kit?"

"After class, I went to the donut shop to grab a coffee and bagel. Kit came over to me and slid into the chair opposite me. I didn't know her. She grabbed half my bagel. I was like, 'Hey what are you doing?' I couldn't believe she did that. She said, 'No problem, I have a good job. I'll get ya another.' And she did, she sat back down and we started talking. At first, I just wanted to get up and run out of the store. My friends aren't like her. And I'm on the shy side. My parents had a nanny for me till I was eighteen. I didn't know what to do. She took me by surprise but I didn't want to sound like a nerd, so I stayed."

John couldn't help himself. "You had a nanny till you were eighteen?"

"Hold on, Dr. Trenton. What did you talk about with Miss Malone? We need to hear whatever specific details you can remember. Got it?"

"Yes. She told me she had just moved here from Toronto. She wanted to get away from things and start fresh." She glanced up at the detective and her gaze caught his hiked brows. "No, she didn't tell me from what. I did ask. She told me not to go there. I dropped it. I get intimidated easily. But she looked dazed. Her eyes sort of got glassy, like it was a painful memory. Now that I'm thinking about it, maybe she was running from the law."

"Why would you say that?"

"She was so excited by this, like it was a game. It came

easy for her, so I thought she had done it before. But who am I to say? I didn't even use my own judgement."

"True, now back to my question," John said. "You had a nanny until you were eighteen?"

"Yes, Doctor Trenton. My parents didn't let me breathe. They had to meet every friend before they let them into the house. No boys. With all the sex and partners they have, I'm the only one of my friend's who's still a virgin."

John ignored her response, but it registered. "How long did you talk to her?"

"We met almost every day after my classes. She didn't go to college. I began to like meeting her. I felt like, ya know, liberated, yeah, that's it, liberated, from my parents' hold on me. Like the third time, she started telling me about this group of girls. I guess the first two times was an interview or something like that. Abby was the leader and she screened all of them before they were allowed into her sorority. Yeah, that's what she calls it, a *sorority*. She said they do all these exciting games but no one ever gets hurt. Yeah, right, look at me. Beginner's bad luck."

Detective Smith jumped in fast. "Beginner's bad luck? Planning on doing this again, Selena?"

"Oh, God, Detective! Never!"

"Then I suggest you be more careful with your choice of words for this tape."

"Can't you erase it?"

"Nope."

John stared right into her eyes. "Selena, how could you possibly not know that robbing houses is illegal? I don't buy it."

"I did know it! For once, I wanted to say the hell with my parents and do something that would be a risk. I didn't care about consequences. It was as if I took a knife and stabbed them both in their crummy hearts! They care so much about me? Yeah, right! They couldn't postpone their trip. Yeah, sure they care about me. They let everyone take their place! Even this didn't make them stop and pay attention. They just sent Justin a check for twenty grand and went on their merry way. Maybe I should want to go to jail. Let's see how they'll feel when they have to tell their friends that their only daughter is in prison." Tears ran down her cheeks.

John let out a deep breath. He just got a lesson on parenting, though he knew he didn't need one. He gave her a minute for her breathing to come back to normal. "All right. Okay to answer more questions?"

She nodded.

The detective continued. "Where did you meet with Abby?"

"In the back of a local diner."

"How many women were there?"

"Only us for this particular game, uh, robbery."

"What did she tell you?"

"First, she laid the ground rules. That she was the boss. Unconditionally. What she says goes. No one gives opinions without consequence. I experienced that first hand. We never ask who the others in her crew are. We'll never meet them. Oh, and if we should get interrupted like at your house, Dr. Trenton, she's the first one who gets to run out. We don't dare try to get out first. Then we're on our own. She has no one who'll come to help us."

The detective shot her a quizzical glare. "And you didn't think twice about that?"

"Yeah, stupid, right?"

John merely shook his head. He leaned against the second bed as the detective continued with the questioning.

"How does she choose the houses?"

She got the blueprints. She said she looked them up online, but I think she has someone do that for her."

"What makes you say that?"

"She was on the phone with her source. Real quiet. In the corner. I think it was a guy."

"How do you know it was a man?"

"She said, 'Then I suggest you get your cock out of your hand and do your job.'"

"Do you have any idea where Abby lives?"

"No. No one does. But she hangs out at the Village Diner on the north end. She said she eats there a lot because she hates to cook."

ᏝᎧᏝᎧ

Detective Smith sent out two officers dressed in plain clothes—jeans and fleece sweatshirts—with a photo of Abby Ruthe on their phones to the Village Diner at the northern end of Scarsdale—the opposite end in which Trenton lived. It looked like the traditional diner, trolley car shape, but renovated to fit the upper echelon decor of Scarsdale. Silver and gold exterior, borders around the perimeter—by the roof and dead center—in bright triangular shaped light fixtures. The building sat on over four acres, taking up two. The other two acres held a parking lot. It was so expansive that the officers knew that Abby, if she spotted them, would be able to dart out of one of the five entrances. Five entrances and exits with cash registers and bakery displays at each. The winner of the Best Pastry Chef challenge on a cooking network created the goodies.

Officer Charlotte North couldn't help but stare at the pastry case closest to the entrance they entered from the rear parking lot. Her mouth watered at the sight of seeing the five-layer chocolate peanut butter cake with chocolate fondant frosting and peanut butter cups on top. The seven varieties of cheesecakes didn't look so shabby either, neither did the blondie brownies or any of the twenty or so variety of jumbo cookies.

The young and trim hostess came over to seat her and her partner, but North showed her badge that her fleece sweatshirt concealed and led the girl back to the counter. North's partner, Steve Paulson, let her take the lead.

North pulled out her phone and showed the head shot. "Do you know this girl?"

The twenty-something girl dressed in tight black jeans and a sweater that showed her perfect cleavage, looked up at North and sealed her lips into a sliver.

North saw her gaze travel to her short-cropped military haircut down her bulky frame. The girl didn't speak.

"I asked you a question." North's tough tone intimidated her.

"Yes. That's Abby."

"Is she here now?"

"No."

"When did you see her last?"

"She just left."

"Who was she with?"

"Alone. She's always alone."

"How does she pay?"

"Cash."

"By any chance know where she lives?"

"No."

North licked her lips. "Okay. Does she have any friends here?"

"No."

Her partner shook his head. "What can you tell us about her? Let's start easy for you. What does she order?"

The hostess nodded. "She drinks more coffee than anyone else I know. She can have five glasses, iced, with every meal. Her favorite is a bacon cheeseburger with cheese fries. Can't blame her on that one. Our burgers are the best, around. Then she downs a piece of chocolate cake and, believe me, those pieces are large. I don't see how she does it. She's thin, but in really good shape. Actually, I do know how she does it."

North snickered. "Care to share? I'd like to know that trick, myself."

"Someone said she has that eating disorder. Not the one where you don't eat. The other one. Where you throw up."

North grimaced in disgust. "Bulimia?"

"Yeah."

"How do you know?"

"Women were talking that they saw her throwing up in the toilet before she leaves."

"Women? Customers or employees?" Paulson asked.

"Employees."

"You know, Miss…what's your name?" North spit out.

"Lacy Meadows."

"Lacy Meadows? Sounds like an alias."

"An alias? What's that?"

"A phony name. What's your birth name, uh, Lacy."

"It's my stage name. I'm studying to be an actress."

"Yeah, well, until you reach celebrity status, we need the name your parents gave you."

She sucked her teeth. "Stephanie Samuels."

"Okay, Miss Samuels, we're getting kind of tired of going around in circles with you. So where is this so called employee who saw Miss Ruthe vomit in the bathroom? We mean now," Paulson said.

"I'll be right back. She's working in the Garden Room."

"No. Stay here. Call her to the register," he said impatiently.

Stephanie followed the directions and a few minutes later a petite young woman came to the register. She wore the same outfit that adorned Stephanie's curves. "I'm Callie."

"Callie. What's your last name?"

"Furgerson."

"Thank you. We're looking for someone who knows this woman." Paulson showed her the picture of Abby. "Who might know where she lives?"

"I have no idea." She shot a glance at Stephanie then turned away.

Paulson saw through the blatant lie. "Okay, girls, I think you two need to come down to speak to a detective at our station house. You know something and you just gave it away."

Both of them looked up at Paulson with their jaws dropped.

CHAPTER 15

Thanks to Vicki, the team narrowed down the buffet as the restaurant from which the scent on the hair sample came. Frank led the entourage of Sam, Lex, and Bella—in a line—up the escalator from the casino floor. He wore a waist-length denim jacket that barely covered his belt over a black T-shirt and matching chambray denim skinny jeans. Strobe lights lined the base of the moving stairs and radiated their glaring lights onto the passengers ascending the flight. As he leaned against the railing, Frank felt the heat from the lights on his ankle. He regretted wearing his low top sneakers, even though they were his most comfortable, indoors. Moving his foot away put him into an awkward posture. He moved to stand up in the center of the stairs. His gaze pivoted to all of the people on his left side descending the escalator. People going down looked at him and nodded. Some smiled. Mostly women. He smiled back, more in knowing that Sam had seen. Yeah, it was a childish moment, but he'd seize a chance to tease her. Then he focused his stare in front of him to the people on the floor they reached.

As Frank stepped off the escalator, he walked a few feet and to the side so the others could get off. He stopped and stared at the huge line going in a spiral formation to the buffet entrance. The curve of customers ran around five rows of red ropes, connected with gold stands. The display cases that covered the perimeter of the enclosure to which the ropes led, held decorative jars and huge vases filled with varieties of dry pasta—different sizes and shapes. One wall displayed about fifty bottles of different olive oils, while another displayed the many brands of balsamic vinegars. Patrons examined the showcases as they inched around the spiral lines possibly in the hope of making their hour wait pass more quickly.

Sam didn't hesitate to show her annoyance. "It'll take forever to get in—" She couldn't finish the sentence.

A hotel employee wearing a white shirt and navy dress slacks greeted them. He furrowed his brows as if confused. "Hello, Mr. Slater. I didn't expect to see you so soon. So sorry. I don't believe we have your conference room scheduled for this evening."

Frank's eyes widened. Sam nudged him and shot a glance toward Lex and Bella. The foursome would play along.

"No. I wasn't planning to use it tonight. I just brought my friends for dinner and to play a little."

"Ah. No wonder you're casually dressed. Come this way. It just so happens, your usual table is available."

Frank nodded. He wasn't about ruin this gift. They were onto something and he was getting leery.

As they followed the employee in, a slew of "Hello, Mr. Slaters" accosted Frank. Sam, Lex, and Bella followed without saying a word and observed.

"Wow! Mr. Slater, you're sure known here," Sam whispered to him.

They walked through the busy restaurant. People dining stood around every station—salads, carvings, Italian, seafood, Asian, breads, desserts. The aromas of the fresh food filled the air and Frank realized he was hungrier than he thought. Those filets grilling looked like they'd be perfect for his size appetite. Yes, he'd definitely have a sirloin. And the seafood bar. Oysters were in season. He heard his stomach growl. When was the last time he had eaten?

The employee reached their table. "Here you are, Mr. Slater. Enjoy your dinner with your friends."

"Thank you. I'm starved."

"You always are, sir." The employee smiled. Frank did a double take. "Oh, we have the special that you love. Shall I tell the chef to prepare it?"

"Yes, please."

"And for your friends, of course."

"I really want to sample from the stations, thank you," Sam said.

"I do, too," Bella and Lex said at once.

"Are you sure that will be permissible, Mr. Slater?"

Frank merely nodded, not fully comprehending the off-handed comment.

"Very well, I'll tell the chef. Though, he'll insist on making enough for everyone. I'll send over your favorite hostess." He leaned in toward Frank. "The oyster bar is filled to capacity. Will help you have a nice evening with the lady." He tilted his head toward Sam. Smiling, the employee walked away.

Frank shot Sam a wide grin.

A cocktail server approached dressed in a short, white, frill-hemmed skirt that hit mid-thigh and a white buttoned down the front blouse with buttons opened to reveal silicone girls, carrying a tray of tall glasses of a mixed drink. Her voice pitch was almost out of the range for human ears, and just as giddy. "Hello, Mr. Slater. I brought your usual. Two shots, and the same for your guests." She placed the drinks on the table.

Sam sniffed. "Scotch and ginger ale. Um, I don't drink, so can I please have an unsweet ice tea?"

The server looked confused. "Mr. Slater, would that be okay? For your guests to drink something different than you?"

"Yes, for tonight. She gets sick from alcohol. And to tell you the truth, I'm on antibiotics, so I can't drink tonight, either."

"Oh, that would explain your deeper voice. Sore throat." She walked over and put her hands on his shoulder. "Oh, you poor man. I hope you get better, real soon." She kissed his cheek, and a red lipstick mark remained. "So what would you like, darling?"

"Unsweet ice tea, as well."

"Oh goodie, I'll get four unsweet ice teas. This way everyone follows your rule."

Sam laughed.

"Yes. It's true. Everyone in Mr. Slater's party, must, without exception, drink the same thing he does. All of us must memorize his rules. See, Mr. Slater, I know how to obey the rules." She wiggled her butt as she walked off.

It took all of what Frank could muster not to burst out laughing. He leaned in toward Sam. "I should have you trained so well."

"Not in this lifetime."

Bella wasn't so easily amused. "Um, this Mr. Slater is some winner."

Sam got up and looked around for the fresh vegetable salad bar. She pulled a plate from the utensils deck and walked straight to it. As she was serving herself, the cocktail waitress approached her. Sam looked up and smiled.

"So, darling, are you the flavor of the month or week?"

"You know about Mr. Slater's dating habits?"

She looked around the dining room to make sure no one was watching her. "Believe me, honey, Henry has gone through all the cocktail waitresses, mostly one at a time, but sometimes up to three. And even during playing, we have to call him Mr. Slater, or sir. Don't you have to?"

"Absolutely!"

"And don't you dare slip, even at dinner."

"I don't plan to, heaven forbid! I'm sort of new in the relationship, so tell me, what would he do, if a woman slipped?"

"Oh, my God! I'm not exactly sure, but he'd drag them out, and he'd come back alone. The chef's specialty should be done by now. Oh, one more thing. He loves oysters. It really gets him going. Make sure you bring him an extra big plate." She giggled and left going toward the kitchen.

When Sam returned to the table, Frank, Bella, and Lex had their plates filled. Frank was devouring cold shrimp with cocktail sauce and oysters. As he popped an oyster in his mouth, he winked at her.

Sam wiped his cheek with a napkin. "I see you got your own oysters. That's one of your favorites."

"As it's been suggested, now, twice."

Bella and Lex ignored them, their plated filled from the Asian section.

Before Sam could respond to Frank, a female server approached with a platter of the chef's specialty. Frank's eyes bulged as she placed the twenty-four inch platter in the center of the table. "Enjoy, everyone." She scooted off.

The foursome eyed the lavish platter of lobster tails and filet mignon gently topped with an Alfredo sauce over herbed linguini. Roasted eggplant and zucchini surrounded the perimeter of the platter.

"Guess who's not eating gluten-free, tonight?" Lex teased. "I can. I have a love affair with pasta."

"You'll have to eat some, Mr. Slater." Sam nudged his arm. "Miss Squeaky told me a lot, even your first name, but no woman dare call you Henry, even during sex."

"Is that so?" Frank said as two restaurant employees smiled at him as they passed by. He pulled a lobster tail and filet onto his plate, with the veggies, and scooped some linguini onto his plate as well. He twirled some of the pasta in his fork, salivating from the dripping sauce before he put it into his mouth, groaning. He paused to revel in the moment. After he slowly chewed and swallowed, he admitted what he considered a sin. "I can't remember the last time I ate pasta." He swooned. "This is so good. More than good."

Sam got up and headed for the dim sum, filling two plates, one for her and one for Frank. As she was returning to the table, Miss Squeaky caught up to her. "Oh, I see he

has you trained, too. He loves to be served and pampered."
She winked at Sam before she wiggled off.

Sam's boisterous laugh caught Frank's attention and he
watched her as she almost spilled the pork dumplings. He
had to hand it to her. She made a great save, putting one
plate under the other.

After Sam put the plates down on their table, and before
she sat, she whispered in Frank's ear. "You and Mr. Slater
have some things in common."

He laughed. "Oh yeah?"

"I'll tell you about it later." She gave him a peck on his
cheek then slipped into her chair.

Frank ate with such gusto he surprised himself. "I need
some stretching room." He stood up, removed his jacket,
and put it over the back of the chair as the others continued
to serve themselves. It didn't take long for the platter to be
cleaned.

Their cocktail waitress dropped a serving tray that carried about ten glasses of drinks onto the floor, splattering
the people at the table she was serving with margaritas,
scotch, and bourbon, not to mention cubes of ice and shards
of glass that bounced up. She screamed.

The house music stopped. The silence was jarring. Chefs
at each station came out from behind their counters to get a
better look.

Another employee wearing a navy business suit came
running out of the kitchen. He raced to their table. "You
aren't Mr. Slater, but you sure as hell have a twin! Now
who on earth are you people?"

"Who are you?" Withers yelled with the same intensity.

"Mike Sheffield, the general manager of this establish-
ment. And you are?"

Frank reached into his jeans pocket and pulled out his
NYPD consultant badge. "I'm Dr. Frank Khaos, an NYPD
consultant and a forensic psychiatrist. This is my team."

Frank made the introductions and the trio showed their
badges as Mr. Sheffield stood, staring at Frank's arms.

"Everything is delicious, Mr. Sheffield, and now we need to talk. Where can we go for privacy?" Sam asked. "And we need to speak with our cocktail hostess, as well. And every casino employee who knows Mr. Henry Slater."

എന

Sam and the team followed Mr. Sheffield into his office. It was an ultra-modern space with beige tile floors that had maroon veining. Mr. Sheffield's desk was light brown wood with maroon leather studded trim around its desktop and down the perimeter of each leg. The chair behind his desk, the two club chairs opposite it, and the couch on an adjacent wall were in the same maroon leather. Sam looked around in awe. The paintings were duplicates of the one in the restaurant.

She walked to a long conference table that matched Mr. Sheffield's desk and pulled out a matching swivel chair. She sat down and felt the supple leather with her hands. "I would love to be able to afford this decorator."

"Why don't you ask Mr. Slater?" He shot a snide look to Frank. "He designed it."

The team took seats around the table. To Sam, Lex seemed to be uncomfortable in the luxury. He sucked his cheeks in, looking around the office space while sneering. Bella seemed to like it, making herself comfortable in the seat.

"So is this, Slater guy a designer?" Lex asked.

"First, what is your business with him?"

Sam caught him up on the case—as much as she was allowed to tell by law without violating Slater's rights, which wasn't much—basically just that through the investigation process they got a lead to bring them here. She didn't fill him in on the familial DNA to Frank. That had always been on her mind. She was sure it was on Frank's, too. As a manager, Sheffield had to know about the murder in the hotel. Now it was confirmed. The familial DNA linked the serial killer to Frank, and Mr. Henry Slater was the killer.

"Don't you need a warrant?"

"Not for tonight. We just came to get a feel for the restaurant, and we had no intention of this happening. We weren't planning to do a search or interview." Sam explained. "So, as long as you initiated the conversation, what do you know about Slater?"

Sheffield swallowed hard. "Now I think you should get that warrant."

Lex opened his jacket. He pulled out a tri-folded document from his pocket. "Here. The NYPD is always prepared." Sam smiled. Lex shrugged. "After our meeting this afternoon, one of our detectives put in a call to Judge Martinsson. What can I say? He likes us."

Sheffield skimmed the document. "Slater is the owner of Foods Unlimited. It's a company that designs and supplies the buffet restaurants in casinos along the east coast."

Frank furrowed his brows. "What does that entail, exactly?"

"He chooses the decor, layout, dinnerware, and flatware, selects the food stations, menus, hires and fires the employees, including the chefs, pays our checks."

"He does this all by himself? That's impossible," Frank said.

"I'm sure he has employees in his corporate office, but no one has ever accompanied him, and we've never had any correspondence from anyone but him, nor does anyone else ever answer the phone when any of his managers call. We do have conference calls with him with the managers once a month, and he makes unannounced visits, a lot. He's known to fire employees on the spot if they do anything to irritate him."

Frank raised an index finger into the air. "No. One of your employees made an off-handed comment to me that seemed quite personal about oysters. If Slater was such a hardass, that would be grounds to fire an employee immediately. So you're telling me man-to-man sexual comments are okay with him?"

Sheffield froze. His complexion paled. He wiped sweat from his brow. "Uh, somewhat. He hand selected his employees and managers and we get along. It's been over nine years."

The light bulb went on for Sam. "Mr. Sheffield, the serial murders under investigation started nine years ago. So, please, we need the truth."

"I'm telling you the truth."

"Okay, when I took off my jacket, you knew immediately that I wasn't Slater. What tipped you off?"

"You're kidding me, right?"

"No, I'm not."

"You've never met him?"

Frank frowned. "If we had met him, then we wouldn't be having this conversation."

"Then how in hell did they know to send you in, if you weren't a duplicate for the guy? Your facial features, your build, everything is a match if someone saw you for just a minute. Now that we're talking, I can see the difference. Your attitude, tone of voice, it's more casual. You're probably older than him by a few years, too. Actually, I'm surprised the employee who seated you couldn't tell the difference. Now, you answer my question, before I answer any more of yours."

"Regarding the employee, I can't speak to that. To answer your question, we didn't know." Frank lowered his head. "This was an unexpected fluke."

Sheffield smirked. "That won't fly, Doc." He sat back and crossed his arms across his chest. "I have a PhD in clinical psychology and I'm a practicing therapist when I'm not here, which is most of the time. I'm only in the casino three nights a week. You lucked out."

Frank didn't flinch. "All the more reason for you to help us. You're a reliable witness regarding his profiling. I'm getting that he doesn't have tatts?"

"Not down his arms. But he has a large scorpion on his back, running from the nape of his neck down to his waist."

"How do you know about his back?" Frank asked.

"Uh, I've seen him at the pool." Sheffield had a faraway look in his eyes, and then he looked down. "He's an excellent swimmer."

Sam got a jolt from Dara. Her stomach felt queasy. She went with her gut instinct she had learned to believe in. Sam stared straight into his eyes. "Mr. Sheffield, are you in a sexual relationship with Henry Slater?"

He began to stand up. "This interview is over."

"Sit down, Sheffield. Unless you condone women being killed," Lex blurted out.

Sheffield groaned but sat down.

Frank pointed his index finger at Sheffield. "Look, we don't give a damn about your sexual preference, and you're still alive, but Slater doesn't give a shit about women. All his vics were women. Talk about his sex life. And don't give me the BS that you don't know."

"He's into kink, twosomes, threesomes. He's gone through all the cocktail hostesses."

"So I've been told by our hostess for the evening. Does he go to any clubs?"

Sheffield paused. "Why?"

"It may be where he met his victims."

"He loves Strident. Lower West Side."

The team exchanged looks. Bingo! Sam spoke immediately. "We know it."

Lex sat up straight in the chair. "Did he go there with a female companion?"

"No. Alone. Or with me."

"We'll need you to come down to the precinct to answer some questions, but right now, bring in the cocktail waitress. And when he stays here, does he have the same room? A room reserved for him?"

Sheffield paged the woman before he answered. "No. A different room each time. He just appears at the desk with a suitcase. We're never sold out and he doesn't come during the holiday season."

Sam ruminated over the dates of the murders. She compressed her lips and nodded to herself.

"What, Detective?" Sheffield asked. "What are you thinking?"

"Just going over the dates of the seventeen murders. You're right, none during any holiday."

"How in hell could you recall the dates?"

"She's got a photographic memory," Frank said.

The hostess entered the room in street clothes, tight jeans, and a cowl neck sweater. She held her leather coat over her arm. "I was just leaving, Mr. Sheffield. My shift is over."

"Grab a seat, Summer. These detectives need to speak with you about Mr. Slater."

"Why? What's wrong?" She looked at Frank. "Are you his brother?"

He hesitated. "The jury is still out on that one."

Sheffield glared at Frank. "I'd say the verdict just came in, Doc. Now, I get it. They linked familial DNA to you.

Frank looked up at him with widened eyes.

"Yeah, I've studied it. It must be a hard nut to swallow." Sheffield pulled his card out of his wallet and handed it to Frank. "Here. After you catch him, you'll need to talk to someone. I mean it. And someone you don't know from your department. My door is open."

Frank bit his lip and took the card graciously. "Thanks."

Sam paused a moment. "Summer, what's your last name?"

"Whet. W. H. E. T. Don't laugh. Don't you dare laugh. It's my real surname. My birth name."

"I'm not laughing. What was your relationship with Mr. Slater?" Sam hiked her brows. "In the bedroom?"

She sighed. "We hooked up every time he was here. He could go on for a long time. I've never had a man with his

drive." She looked up at the ceiling as if she was reminisc-
ing.

"Summer, what was his behavior like?"

She snapped back. "What do you mean?"

"Was he gentle, rough, what?"

"Oh, my God. Never, ever, rough. He was the most loving, kind man, who knew how to please a woman. Sometimes, he'd get aggressive when we were playing a scene,
but then I'd expect it. He loved to spank, but he never
bruised me. He liked to handcuff me to the bedposts but it
was always gentle. Why are you asking me this? His only
quirk was that he insisted to be addressed with his surname."

"I'll tell you in a minute. Did you ever play the choking
game?"

She clutched her neck. "Oh, my God. No! Never. Why?"

"Well, you've heard about the murder here, correct?"
Summer nodded. "Mr. Slater is suspect in them," Sam continued. "The woman was strangled."

"No. That is impossible. He liked to be domineering, but
it was in play. You can ask every hostess in this casino. No
one will say he could possibly be a murderer. The very
worst that would happen, is if the women weren't good in
bed, they'd be fired. But no way in hell is this man murderer. And I have proof."

"Which is?" Sam asked.

"He was way too paternal to be a murderer—"

"That doesn't mean anything," Frank interrupted.

Summer shot him an angry glare. "If you'd let me explain."

Frank nodded. "Go ahead."

"He loved children. Once I was serving another table
and the family's three-year-old was having a tantrum. A
really bad one. Kicking and screaming on the floor. Everyone in the section was getting annoyed. But not Mr. Slater.
He just smiled at the parents, who did nothing to try to stop
it, and he got up and knelt by the little boy on the floor. He

just said, 'Hey,' very softly and little boy looked up at him. Mr. Slater just smiled and returned to his chair. He motioned with his index finger for the boy to come to him. And he did. Mr. Slater pulled him up onto his lap and held him close. He took out a toy car from his pocket—"

"A Matchbox car? I used to carry those in my pocket for my son. Go on."

"Yes. I think that's what they're called. I don't have any children. The kid held it and stopped carrying on. Then he put his head on Mr. Slater's shoulder and fell asleep. All Mr. Slater did was to continue eating. No way. No way in hell could this man murder a woman."

The detectives took this in.

Yes! He and I have the same instincts there. I'll use this when we meet up with him. Sam gave herself a mental thumbs up at the thought.

Frank's brows furrowed, as if he was thinking. "Did he ever tell you about his own childhood?"

"No, never. We all knew what he did for a living. I asked him once, teasing, if there's anyone else like him at home and he said 'no.' He's an only child. Guess he doesn't know about you, either."

"All right, Mr. Sheffield. We need a list of all of your personnel who had contact with him. Miss Whet, do you know who he, uh, hooked up with?" Lex couldn't hold back his grin. "We need to talk to everyone." He slid a sheet of paper in front of her on the desk, along with a pen.

"I'll need more than one sheet," she responded meekly.

"By the way," asked Bella. "Did he have any children?"

"He said he didn't. I think it was that stuff he took, the anabolic steroids. That can leave a guy sterile."

"You know about that?" Frank asked.

"Yeah. His veins bulged." She looked up at the ceiling and sighed. "But he was so ripped. So sexy."

Sam let out a deep breath. *Roid rage.*

CHAPTER 16

Detective Smith tapped the rolled warrant in the palm of his hand as John knocked on the door of Abby Ruthe's third floor apartment in a mid-rise building in Tarrytown, about fifteen minutes by car from Scarsdale.

"Those two at the restaurant sure gave up her address, fast," Smith said.

"You know the expression 'no loyalty amongst thieves.' Your investigators will get them to spill plenty."

"I'm sure. How much time do you have open to be able to spend so much time on this case? I'm just curious."

"I'm easing back in. They guaranteed my interim position for a full year. I have a month. But be glad I came. I can give you a lot of insight," Trenton said. No answer resulted from the knock on the door or came from Smith. John knocked harder. Still nothing.

Smith retrieved the key and held it up between his index and middle fingers for John to see. John moved out of his way and Smith unlocked the door.

When they opened it, they both stopped dead. The stench of stale cigarettes filled the air. John's eyes widened and Smith furrowed his brows and shook his head. They had intruded upon the chaotic world of Abby Ruthe. The walls, painted a dark maroon, made the small room seem, as if it was encasing them in a funnel. Her sand-toned wooden furniture had so much junk on the top, there wasn't any surface visible. Tattoo and porn magazines, empty beer bottles, food leftovers on paper plates seemed to be the decor of the moment in tabletop accessories.

Even from a distance, John saw the black fabric couch spotted with cigarette burns. He approached the couch that sat against the wall opposite the apartment entrance. A plywood casket was the makeshift coffee table in front of it. It was about six feet in length and narrow in width, the size for a small, adult woman. Crosses of all sizes engraved into the wood on the front elicited an eerie feel. The latch was unlocked.

"That's unsettling, to say the least," Smith said as he slipped on latex gloves.

John nodded, pulled gloves from his pocket, and put them on as he walked around the room. His gaze led him to the wooden skull above the doorway to the kitchen. Its eyes were round and vacant, John assumed, as a metaphor for Abby's life. He put his hand over his mouth to settle him to comprehend the woman who intended to ruin the peace of his home. Pivoting to each area in the room—the standing lamp with a dark maroon shade, first, he wondered how this allowed any light into the room. It wasn't supposed to, he assumed. Next, he turned to a long table on the wall between the bedroom and kitchen. The oriental style engravings in the black onyx top gave some sense of normalcy, especially since the top was free of junk. Could Abby act *normal* at times—as if there's a standard definition for normal. He walked and stood in front of each end table on either side of the couch. The plain sand colored wood matched the casket. He peered as if trying to penetrate the soul of the furniture. He zoned out in concentration.

"Hey, Doc! You with me?"

He jolted. "Don't call me when I'm focusing. It takes me out of the moment."

Smith waved a dismissive hand. "Whatever you say, Doc."

"I'm damn serious, Smith. You don't know me so I'll tell you. I see things that most mundane people don't."

"Mundane? What the hell does that mean?"

"I'm out of the ordinary, on every level. Let's just leave it at that. You'll see."

John tried to get back into the zone, but the interruption prevented him from feeling the energy in the surrounding air that had become quite thick with Smith so close to him. He wished that Smith would go on his own search.

John bit his lip as he felt toxic energy coming from a black cloth padded club chair on the adjacent wall. His body swayed forward as he saw the gray outline of the aura of the chair. The energy pulled him toward it and, as he stopped in front of it, he put his palm up to Smith, in a signal to stay away. John inhaled and exhaled deeply, activating his diaphragmatic breathing. He blocked out every thought, focusing on the energy of the chair. He saw an outline of a woman's body sitting in it, and the shadowy frame of a woman standing over her. They were unrecognizable but he did see the hand of the woman who was standing, slap the woman who was sitting, across her face. The sitting woman bent over and put her head down to her knees. He saw red droplets—he guessed blood—on the arms of the chair. He saw another woman kneel in front of the woman who was standing. The standing woman had a long paddle in her hand. John psychically heard the screams of a beaten woman. From the glimpse of the woman standing, he recognized her as Abby. Her body was an outline, nothing filled in—a gray cloud—but the scorpion tattoo that Ricky had seen on her neck appeared clearly—in the right spot. His vision evaporated. It was a two-minute vision—the most that his Spirit Guide, Max, ever gave him. In reality, he saw semen stains on the chair as they appeared as a crust-like substance.

"She tortures women in that chair and has sex with men in it, too. I'm guessing she likes kink."

"Gross."

"You like it vanilla?"

"What the hell is that?"

"Seriously?" When John saw that the detective was short in the sex department, he gave up. "Forget it." He looked toward the casket. "Let's look in there."

Smith removed tattoo magazines, and couldn't resist looking at the cover of a magazine under it. On the cover was a twenty-something male-female couple, naked, in the doggie position, with the man cupping the woman's breasts in his hands. "Bodies like these should be illegal."

John looked and titled his head. "Don't kid yourself. They're Photoshopped, plenty. His mind went to his precious Vicki. Even after having twins, her body was perfect. Not one brush stroke needed. He smiled to himself. He needed her bad, right now, and he'd have her, tonight.

After they cleared off the top of the casket, Smith put his fingertip above the latch and opened the top. What they found inside confirmed what John had seen in his vision. Aside from the usual kink of various whips, handcuffs, paddles, ben-wa balls, nipple clips, there were battery-operated dildos—huge ones, much larger than a normal male—and G-spot stimulators. Smith looked shocked but he couldn't help but to lick his lips. Okay, John thought, he has some desires. He might not be as much as a stiff John had originally thought. Maybe he'd fix him up.

"We'll call in a unit. I'm guessing there's an ocean of DNA in here," Smith said as he pulled his cell out of his pocket.

John wandered into the master bedroom with the detective following. It was rather intense with punk rock posters on the wall opposite her bed of her favorite artists, all tattooed and pierced in out of the ordinary places. Smith grimaced but stared at cheek and butt piercings. One guy had a ring inserted into his cheek, from the center of which his gums and decayed teeth showed through.

"Why in hell do people to this to their bodies?"

"We'll get to it. Look over there." John pointed to a file

cabinet on the left side of the bed that acted as the base for a wooden desk, while four boxes were the platform for the other side. John pulled on the handle for the top drawer. It was locked, as well as the other two. He pulled a small pocketknife out of his pants pocket and slipped the blade through the top of the drawer and the cabinet. He slid the knife to the right and the lock unlatched the three drawers. He nodded in satisfaction to Smith. John pulled open the top drawer and saw bills in ripped open envelopes—rent, gas, electric, department stores—just thrown in. The second drawer had file folder style envelopes. The top one was marked 'confidential' in a red block letter stamp. That drew them both in.

Smith snatched it out of the drawer, flipped it over, and unwound the red string. Opening the envelope, he pulled out what appeared to be at first glance, court papers. An examination confirmed it. On the top one, the date was three years earlier. An official name change to Abigail Ruthe from Abigail Ruth Glendale. On the day she turned eighteen. New everything. Social security card. Photocopy of a new driver's license. Three new credit cards—only one was activated.

The documents under these were the liberation papers from her parents, Carl and Mary Glendale, on the exact date.

"This is significant." Smith tilted the papers toward John. "We'll run it under both names and bring in her parents."

John opened the third door. Jewelry, and lots of it. High end jewelry. "Now call in a unit, thorough search."

"Why she didn't fence all his stuff is beyond me. Just goes to show me she isn't all that experienced."

"Or connected," added John. "Maybe that's why she chooses nineteen year olds. Wonder if she has a laptop around here."

Still holding the folder, Smith looked around the bedroom and his gaze again settled on the posters.

John walked toward her double bed. No blanket. Just freshly laundered black sheets and pillow cases—not a speck of dust or a stray hair. He saw a silver piece of something from under her pillow. He walked to the bed and lifted the pillow. He smiled at discovering the fifteen-inch laptop that showed abuse from deep scratches in its surface. John picked up the laptop and the scratches looked deeper when he tilted it. "Knife?"

"Oh, man, there's a lot of rage in this one. And I didn't need to be a shrink to tell that, hey, Doc?"

"I'd have to say, yes."

Smith slipped his phone into his pocket. "Crime Scene will be here within forty. They'll have a field day."

☙❧☙

Frank parked his Ford Explorer in Sam's alley of her Brooklyn home. Frankie jumped out of the passenger seat and opened the rear door. He pulled out Vicki's half-filled canister of muffins. He closed the car door and went to the foot of the steps.

"Dad, what happens if it turns out horrible?"

"Listen to me, however it turns out, you tell Sam that everything is delicious. Worse comes to worse, we'll eat at home." Frank eyed the mail at the top of the stairs. "Guess the mail came late today." He scooped up a bunch of envelopes and thumbed through them.

Oh man, she's got a lot of bills. From those damn home shopping channels.

"Dad, you're looking at Sam's mail? I don't think she'd like that."

Frank stopped dead. "You're right, champ. She wouldn't." He rang the bell.

But it's as sure as hell something we need to talk about.

From the inside, they heard, "Come in."

Frank opened the door and the fragrance of Indian spices

filled the air. He curled his lips down and nodded to Frankie. "Hey, smells good in here, Sam."

They took off their coats, tossed them onto the couch and went into the kitchen. There was a huge salad in the center of the table with a gravy boat filled with dressing. Sam was at the stove, looking at the timer on the electric pressure cooker. He squeezed her around the waist and gave her a non-demonstrative peck on the top of her head.

"What are you making?" Frankie asked.

"It's Vicki's recipe, chicken strips, vegetables, basmati rice, Indian spices and she told me it's fool-proof in the pressure cooker. She loaned it to me. Let's have our salad. The steam is venting." She smiled from ear to ear.

"Sure, princess."

As they were taking their seats she said, "I made the dressing. It's Italian."

"Cool, what's in it?" Frank asked.

"Olive oil, balsamic vinegar, and Italian spices."

"What kind of Italian spices?" Frankie contorted his face.

Sam hesitated. "It was all in one jar and said Italian." She served Frankie and Frank salad, and handed Frank a small ladle for the dressing.

He poured a ladle of the dressing onto his salad. "This looks great, Sam. I'm proud of you." He took a forkful of greens and suddenly nearly choked. He coughed and grabbed his glass of water. He gulped it. "Oh, man, Sam, how much vinegar and pepper did you put in this? Frankie, go easy with the dressing."

"I'm sorry. I measured it, from what Vicki told me, but then I realized I used the wrong sized measuring cups for the balsamic and oil. I reversed them." Frank smirked. "Hey, listen. Vicki told me to expect mistakes."

"Okay, it's a beginner's error. That's okay." Frank got up, dumped his plate of salad into the half-filled garbage pail, rinsed it, and brought it back to the table. "I can do without the dressing." He refilled his plate.

As they were eating the salad, Frankie grimaced. He ran his tongue around his teeth. "Dad, there's something crunchy in here." He picked out a piece of lettuce from his plate. "Eww. What's this black stuff?"

Frank examined the lettuce. "Sam did you rinse the lettuce before you made the salad?"

"Uh, no. Are you supposed to?" Frank glared at her. She blushed. "I thought the grocery store was supposed to."

"Only if it's bagged."

"It was. I'm sorry."

Frank put the bowl of salad aside. "It's okay, don't worry about it."

"The chicken is ready now." Sam went to the pressure cooker, crossing her fingers behind her back. She twisted the cover of the pressure cooker off. The fragrant steam escaped. She pulled a huge bowl from her cupboard and with a serving spoon removed their dinner from the cooker. The rice was perfectly cooked, as were the chicken and veggies. Proudly, she brought the bowl to the table.

"Oh, man, Sam, this looks and smells delicious." Frank took a huge portion and served Frankie. "What did you put in here?"

She looked at Frank's plate. "Oh, curry, turmeric, garlic, cardamom, cinnamon, cumin, nutmeg. And chopped onion and carrots."

Frankie took a tiny forkful and put it in his mouth. He paused, probably waiting for the taste to settle in. Then he took a large forkful. "This is delicious, Sam. No kidding."

"Yes, it is, princess. Don't count on leftovers."

"Sam, those are the kinds of spices Vicki had at the precinct. Do you have the same ones?"

"Not that many, sweetheart, only these. Because I love Indian food. So Vicki told me which ones to buy."

"Where are all the pans you used to cook all this stuff?"

"It's only one, Frankie. Everything goes into the pot at once and it cooks together."

"Wow! Dad, this would be easier than the one pot you use!"

Frank paused with a thought. "Uh, Sam…" He paused again. "The garbage pail was filled but I didn't see any chicken packaging, or onion skin, or carrot ends." After he gave her a hard stare, he grinned. "Uh, when Vicki lent you the cooker did she by any chance put the food in there, with it?" He bellowed a laugh.

"Oh my God, Frank! You couldn't let me get away with it, could you? Crap!" She flung her fork down onto her plate and crossed her arms across her chest.

Frank laughed. He couldn't stop. Finally, he got it out. "You're busted. But who cares, I'm starved." He dug in.

Sam started to laugh, too. "I'm sorry, Frank. We were so busy interviewing the people from the casino. All of the women had nothing but kind words to say about Slater."

He put his hand up to stop her. "It's okay, really. How did you get this from Vicki?"

"She wanted to come down today and go to the children's store on the avenue. The outfit we got Ricky was too big. I was judging on Frankie's size. Anyway, you could have let me get away with it."

His eyes shot toward Frankie. "Nope. Not with me. No lying tolerated."

"As long as we're being honest, you gonna tell Sam that you looked at her mail, Dad?"

"You did what?"

"I didn't open the envelopes."

"You better not, Dr. Khaos."

Frankie's head turned toward his dad, then to Sam. He was grinning. "Don't worry Sam, I got your back."

"Oh yeah?"

"Yes, Dad. I love Sam."

Frank looked at his son in compassion. He had meant what he said.

Sam reached over and hugged him. She became teary-eyed. "I love you, too, Frankie."

"Dad, do you love Sam?"

"Yes. I do."

"Sam, do you love my Dad?"

"Uh, yes."

Frankie sat back in his chair and crossed his arms across his chest. "Okay, then it's decided. You, two are getting married."

"Hold on, champ."

"Frankie, it's January," Sam explained. "We just met in November. That's two short months."

"Seesh. How long does it take two adults to find out that they love each other? If you guys wait much longer, you'll be too old to give me a baby brother or sister."

CHAPTER 17

John entered the lobby of the Manhattan Midtown-South precinct. He walked down the narrow hall, passing the bench that stood against the wall hosting a handcuffed suspect. Two police officers stood with their right hands on their weapons, ready to launch forward if necessary to keep him still. It was an eerie silence. Coercion must have been the reason. From the looks of this haggard, but large built man, it had to take more than a warning.

Detective Withers opened his office door and signaled with bent fingers to the man. A police officer helped him stand with his arm under the man's bicep. He took his time while smirking at Withers. The officer hurried the man into Withers' office, with John following. Withers slammed the door shut.

"Sit down, Mr. Karrot." Withers tried to conceal his laugh with a yawn. "You're just in time to join the party, Doc." Karrot hiked his brows. Withers shrugged. "This is Dr. John Trenton. The kid your cousin whacked was his patient."

Karrot started singing, "So cry me a river…"

"Stop being a wiseass."

"Why the fuck am I here?"

John stared at the rotund man whose body was covered with curly black hair. His full beard came down about six inches past his chin and his straggly hair was at his midback. He was huge, at least five inches taller than John's six-feet-two, and about eighty pounds heavier. A flabbier heavier. "We're interviewing all contacts of Trig Maynor."

"Yeah, well, I haven't had contact with him in two years."

"Really. Then how come he called your number six times the week before he was arrested?" Withers pushed a file folder with a phone number highlighted in yellow, in front of him. "That's your number, isn't it?"

"My phone was stolen. Or I lost it. Who cares?"

John scratched his cheek. "It's interesting that he'd continuously talk to a person he didn't mean to call. Don't you think?"

"What can I say? He was a friendly kind of guy." Karrot sat back into the chair and even with being cuffed, interlocked his fingers behind his head. "I'm not sayin' nothin.'"

"Okay, but before you make that decision, please look at this." Withers slid another folder toward him.

"What's this crap?"

"Open it. You can read, can't you, Karrot?"

"It's Mr. Karrot from you, pig. Yeah, I can read."

Withers sucked in his cheeks. "Okay, Mr. Karrot, how do you explain these cash deposits into your one and only bank account?" He pointed to a deposit of nine thousand dollars. And a second of seven thousand dollars three days after the first.

"Holly crap? You mean someone gave me cash? Woo hoo! Now I can take that trip I wanted."

"You mean you have no knowledge of this money?" John asked.

"No, I don't. The bank made a mistake."

"That's great, Mr. Karrot." Withers pulled out a form from a folder. "We need you to sign this affidavit that you do not own this money." He handed Karrot the paper with a pen. Karrot took the form, fiddled with the pen between his fingers, paused as if he was thinking, and then, awkwardly signed it. "Thank you Mr. Karrot." Withers picked up the phone handset that was on his desk. "Gloria, please let the team know we have the affidavit so they can now proceed." He hung up.

"Hey, proceed with what?"

"I wouldn't worry about it, Mr. Karrot," John said. "If monies are deposited into an account wrongly, the federal banking commission can legally withdraw it."

Karrot's cheeks flushed. "You're shittin' me."

"Nope. It's the law. Now before Detective Withers faxes that paper, would you like to say something? Because, in all honesty, we do have proof that money came from Maynor, straight to you."

"Hey, Doc, what are ya giving him info, for?"

"Guess I'm a good guy. You see, Mr. Karrot, I was very close to Bobby Mitchell, and I really want to find out why Maynor and his two cronies decided to beat him to death. I'm so determined that my team," John said, pointing to Withers, "would nail anyone as an accessory, even if they're remotely connected. You know, the guilt-by-association kind of thing."

"I knew nothing about that. I swear. You can't do that!"

Withers intervened. "Yeah. I can and I don't buy that you don't know about the money for a second. Now, this is a simple question. How did Maynor get so much money? He was living at a halfway house."

"I don't know. Seriously, Detective, I don't."

"Okay, then. What did you do, that earned you all that money in two payments from Maynor?" Withers leaned forward in his chair. "Now think carefully because each scenario carries different prison terms."

"I didn't have him do anythin'. And I didn't do anythin', either. I think I want a lawyer cause I ain't goin' to prison for no body."

"Good decision. And we do have a right to hold you for forty-eight hours. It's after six, the courts are closed. You'll be our guest tonight in a holding cell, and you'll be allowed to make a call for legal aid, tomorrow morning." Withers closed the folders.

"Hey, hold on, Detective. You can't keep me here."

"Why not?"

"My mama. She lives with me. She has Alzheimer's. She's seventy-six. Doesn't know which end is up. She wanders out of the apartment."

"So who's watching her now?" John acknowledged, his serious tone.

"I hire a baby sitter. That's what she needs. A nineteen year old neighbor watches her for seven bucks an hour." He checked his watch. "And she expected me to be home by now. She's got college tonight. I'm serious, Doc. My mama is the most important person in my life."

John compressed his lips. "Would the sitter leave her alone?"

"No. Never. She's a good girl."

"All right. Here's what we'll do," John said. "We'll have two officers escort you home. If what you're telling us is the truth, about your mother, they'll let you stay." Karrot squirmed in his seat. "Can the sitter come early in the morning?"

"Yeah. She stays with her all day, while I'm at work."

Withers flipped open the file. "Yeah, you're a school janitor. Correct?"

"Yeah."

"Says here, you *were* a school janitor. Interesting, you left your job a day after Maynor made the first deposit. Were you thinking it would be a long-term arrangement? Continuous money flow, so you wouldn't have to work?"

"You knew all that, so what are you fucking with me for?"

"We know all about you. What we need you for is to connect the dots. Unless you want to go down with Maynor." Withers put his pen down. "Want to know what else we know?"

"What do you know?"

"Your mama passed on last year. From pneumonia."

John snorted. "You mean to tell me, Detective, that he's been lying to us? That doesn't bode well for you, Mr. Karrot."

"Oh, yeah? How so?" Karrot demanded.

Withers leaned in closer to Mr. Karrot, as if he was telling him something confidential. "Ever hear of 'credibility' or being a 'reliable witness'? And I'll give you a tip. A cop, like me, never asks a question he doesn't already know the answer to. So you've been lying through this entire interview."

"I want my lawyer, now."

"Good decision." Withers pressed a button on the intercom. "Get an officer in here to escort Mr. Karrot to his accommodations for the evening. And before you ask on what grounds, you're a material witness with financial connections, notice, I said connections, as in more than one, to a suspect in a murder investigation. Does that do it for you, Mr. Karrot?"

An officer entered the room and grabbed Karrot by his arm, but he shrugged it off. He kicked the chair from under him with all his might not realizing it was bolted to the floor. He yelped in pain as his ankle twisted. The look of anguish stayed on his face as the officer pulled him out, limping. Withers chuckled. "You know what they say about Karma, right, Doc?"

☙❧☙

At the same time, in the adjoining office at the precinct, Sam, Frank, and Bella sat around a conference table for six. "Listen, Frank, we need you to go in. You can pass for Slater. Just don't take off your jacket."

"What part of 'no' don't you understand, Sam? One night was more than enough. It would be better if Bella and Lex go in and speak to the owner. Who is he?"

"It's a she. Madame Lilly. She's a dominatrix. And the difference from Whiplash, is that here, she doesn't have an observation room, so you're in the same room as the people doing the scene. If she sees you're squeamish, she pulls you out and bans you from the club. No weaklings allowed."

Frank threw his hands up and out. "Well, that eliminates me. So how did Charlie make it in?"

"She's a new owner, less than six months. And Frank, you can deal with it. I know first-hand."

"Yeah, in private. And I'd have to go like I did, last time. Practically naked. I couldn't get away with it. But, Bella."

"No way will I get dressed like that. Or should I say undressed."

"You know, Bella. It'll probably do you some good. Release your inhibitions, find your inner woman."

She scowled at Sam. "I like my internal woman, just fine, thank you."

The trio looked toward the door as it opened. John entered with Lex. "What's going on?" John asked as he pulled a chair from another table over.

Sam let out a deep sigh before she caught him up on the conversation with Charlie Baines and Mike Sheffield. "And since Slater goes there, maybe that's where he originally saw Carrie. I'm trying to convince Frank to go speak with the owner. One of the women we interviewed from the casino told us Strident is one of his favorite hangouts and the hostess we spoke with, Summer Whet, told me that too, when the girls came in for extended interviews. It had to be where he met Carrie. I don't believe in coincidences. He probably followed her and deliberately sought her out at the casino. So he looks for women who are free with their bodies. If we can find out that Carrie and Slater were there at the same time, then that's golden."

"Oh, wait a minute." Frank sneered. "How do you know about the new owner? Been there lately?"

Sam pursed her lips at Frank. "I was there once, when she first took over the place."

"Hold on. Back up," John said, ignoring Sam's and Frank's bantering. "What do you mean, follow? Care to be specific?"

"I haven't a clue." Sam sighed. "Did he follow her home? Did he watch her go to school, so he knew that she was a teacher or a professional woman, like his other victims? Did he follow her that Friday from her house to the casino? What made him choose Carrie at the casino rather than one of the other hundreds of women there? Was it a fluke, or planned? I don't know, but it's sure the best thing we've got so far."

"If the owner—"

"Madame Lilly," Sam said.

John hiked a brow. "Oh boy. If Madame Lilly knows Slater, she could give us some very relevant info. I'd recommend it, Frank. Pretend you're Slater. See the kind of reception you get and from whom."

"Frank, we spoke with the owner of Whiplash. It didn't turn out so bad. And he even offered you a job."

John laughed. "A job?"

"As a dom."

"Okay. I can see it."

"Knock it off, pal. And if I recall correctly—" Frank winked at Sam. "—it gave us the beginning to a real good night, too."

"That's a little TMI, Frank. No, we were interrupted to go to the double homicide scene, of Valerie and Mrs. Larcon. That was the Aries case, John." She turned back toward Frank. "So you didn't recall correctly. I know! How about you going with him, John?"

"Uh, no. Not my thing at all. Don't do the inflicting pain part."

"Maybe you'll be able to teach Vicki something new," Frank said.

"Hell no. There's a fine line between playing a scene

and, with an out of control man, it leads to abuse." Sam did a double take. John shook his head. "I'm not out of control but Vicki was already in an abusive marriage when she had just gotten out of college. She'd be terrified. The guy did eleven months and thirty days for spousal abuse and was forced to promise to stay out of Florida."

"I had no idea, sorry," Sam said.

"Thanks. It was short-lived, only three months, but it left her scarred. Please, don't tell her I mentioned it."

"No problem," they all said in unison.

There was a minute of silence before John broke it. "Okay, so who's the next possibility?"

"Not me," Withers blurted out. "My wife would kill me. Even if it's for the job, there are boundaries I shall not pass."

Running out of options, everyone just stared.

At Frank.

ℰ୬ℰ୬

Darkness overtook the Upper West Side in Manhattan as the lights through apartment building windows replaced the daylight. This upscale neighborhood had mid-rise apartments built in the 1960s and renovated to the hilt.

On the twenty-sixth floor, Henry Slater stepped out of his walk-in shower dripping onto the dark maroon bath mat that lay on the tiles at the base of his sink cabinet. He grabbed an extra-large towel from the rack over the adjoining tub and wrapped it around his body encasing his shoulders to his waist. He spun it off, and ran the towel over his bald head, then to his torso swiping it slowly over his pecs and six-pack.

When he got to his groin, he slowed and moved the towel in circular motions down his length. He paused then rubbed up and down until he became hard. He groaned. He shook his body to come back to the present then inspected the one-thousand-thread-count white towel before he re-placed it onto the rack.

He looked around the room. The floor to ceiling maroon titling with beige veining on the walls and floors was be-coming too much for him to bear. It was symbolic. He felt weighted down by what his life had become. Weighted down by all the dark colors. The hell with him being a Scorpio. The best thing about his sign was the sexual prow-ess it afforded him. Too bad, he hadn't had a good fuck in a long time. Crap. It had actually just been a week. And he'd already become bored with Summer. She was too easy. Yeah. She was his sub, but this twit over did it. *Give me a bit of a challenge*, he thought. Yeah, he was dying to get laid. He'd have to look for a new woman, fast.

Tile floors in the opposite pattern, beige tiling with ma-roon veining would more to his liking. He decided to re-decorate. It would be the fifth time he redecorated this apartment in Manhattan. Neighbors on the lower floors al-ways complained about the construction noise, but the owner always approved the renovations. Had to. He himself owned the building. Plus, the superintendent wouldn't care. Slater appointed him as a figurehead-owner in case he had to skip town.

Slater looked in the mirror at his six-feet-four frame. He flexed his biceps, his pecs. Yeah, he confirmed it. He was an Adonis, every woman's dream. If he could only find a woman, with whom he could have a solid relationship, not a one-night hook up when he was in town, whatever town that was. A woman he didn't wind up killing. He was get-ting tired of it. Bored, actually. The last time, he started to become aroused then the bitch ruined it. So what was the purpose? Maybe he'd have to step up his game. Get a little more into torture—well, he'd prefer to call it, titillation—for him, not the woman—instead of a relatively quick strangulation. He'd thought the last one would do some-thing for him, Carrie. She was the hottest he'd done and the sweetest—especially the auburn highlights in her dark

brown hair. He'd thought she was the woman of his dreams
until she brought up his painful memories. Oh well, it was
her fault. What kind of teacher takes off from school to go
to a casino? And what a disgrace she was not to want to
have children. He paused in his thoughts. No. Torture was
not for him. He hated the site of blood. Yeah. That was his
anal nature. One woman had the gall to call him 'Mr. Crazy
Clean.' He'd worked hard to become that man. That self-
made man who was a money magnet. He couldn't accomplish that if he wasn't anal. So be it.

He checked out the lighting fixtures that ran around the
perimeter of the rectangular mirror. All of the thirty-watt
iridescent teardrop bulbs were working. He couldn't, rather
wouldn't, accept any one of them, out. He nodded. Yes.
He'd definitely remodel. All nine rooms.

No. Just seven. He'd leave the two nurseries intact, for
just in case he'd find that one woman, again, who'd he let
live, like he did those four other times. Those rooms were
perfect. One for a boy. One for a girl. Yeah, another woman
he'd let live. Yeah. He'd be a great dad. He'd been thinking
about fatherhood again, a lot, lately. He was forty and not
getting any younger. He certainly made enough money to
support more children and give them the best of everything.
The best education. The best nannies. The best clothing.
Not like him, who grew up with crap, low-life parents who
wouldn't know what it was like to love their children. They
had him after they were released from prison—the third
time, all from petty larceny gas station robberies. He shook
his head. They should have been left to rot in prison.

Some people would let their past determine their future.
Not him. The day Henry Slater came into being—the day
he changed his name from Benjamin Hunter on his eighteenth birthday—he made up his mind to do something with
himself. He had to. In a dream, he had an epiphany. God
gave him a gift. His size and his intelligence. Hyperventilating, he put his hands on the edge of his sink.

In another nighttime dream, something about the restaurant business drew him in. He closed his eyes, recalling that recurring dream that became his worst nightmare.

It was summer and he was sixteen, roaming the streets in his neighborhood. The sign in the Italian restaurant window read "Help Wanted." Yeah, I want help, too. Opening the door, he went to the back where the entrance to the kitchen opened to a massive area with industrial cooking stoves, ovens, refrigerators. Everything. He was amazed. It was spotless. Wow. The female owner approached him and yelled at him that he just came in. He grimaced. Getting yelled at was not his thing. His mother's screaming at him pierced his gut as he stood and stared at the woman. 'Get the fuck away from me. You shouldn't have been born you disgusting piece of shit. You're wasting my life! You know that?'

He cringed, breathing deeply. His mother's voice came through clearly, even in the dream.

Yeah, being yelled at brought out the worst in him.

The early-forties woman had a full-length tomato-sauce-stained apron covering her white blouse and jeans with her cropped hair covered by a net. He just smiled. Looking up at his huge size, even at sixteen, she became intimidated. She backed off. A wall blocked her. Something pushed him to her. Something made him do it. He felt the force of an unknown entity. He saw his mother in her place.

The vision was clear—his disgusting, neglectful mother who never made him a meal or read him a bedtime story, or went up to school to meet with his teachers, who pretended he didn't exist, and locked him in the closet…just because.

His hands involuntarily wrapped themselves around her neck. With his body, he pinned her against the wall. After a minute of fighting, her gasping, her body went limp. The image of his mother disappeared. The restaurant owner lay on the floor.

He cringed at the memory, gritting his teeth as he tried to hold back tears. Why was he thinking of that, now? It was a damn dream!

He knew why.

Two words.

His brothers.

He'd had heard from someone in the neighborhood in which he grew up—Bensonhurst, Brooklyn—when he went back to do some reflection on his past—many years later—and with an MBA on his wall—that he had two brothers, both older. His parent moved to Bensonhurst when he was five so the neighbors there didn't know anything of their past. Not even about their prison records. They were no longer there. In a fluke, having dinner at a restaurant, he met some people who after conversation connected him to the family named Hunter. It was from them he learned about his brothers.

He cursed his parents for not placing him for adoption as they did them. They had denied giving him a chance at a normal life. He had no idea who his brothers were, nor did he ever try to find them. He had just found out about them nine years ago.

The same time the tormenting nightmares returned.

Right before his killing spree.

Revenge. Revenge. Revenge.

On his damn mother.

He walked into his bedroom, lifted the maroon comforter off the bed so he could slip under it. Restless, he kicked off the blanket. He lay on his back staring up at his reflection in the mirror that covered the entire ceiling. Oh man, he'd sure make a special prize to that one woman. The next time, he'd go for a blonde. A blonde with a pony-tail, Grecian nose, with her own natural boobs, and blue eyes.

He turned onto his side. "Okay, baby doll. Looks like you and me are alone, again, tonight." He embraced the nude, life-like full-body doll that lay next to him. "Oh, man, your skin is so smooth." He ran the tip of his index finger around the face of the rubber doll.

CHAPTER 18

Soft music played in the background and sandalwood scented candles burned in lanterns on Sam's dresser and night tables, giving off the perfect amount of light. Romantic was the word for the mood. She had learned which scent Frank responded to amorously. One that didn't make him choke. Frankincense and sage were "no-no's." After dinner at their favorite Italian restaurant, he brought her home first then he needed to drop Frankie off at his grandparent's house. She had time to change her bedding to the set he loved. Satin, light blue. He had told her he loved that one because it made her eye color pop. And the feel of the seven-hundred-thread-count sheets was heavenly.

She did everything to please him. But was it enough? After Frankie told them they were getting married, she had begun to think about it, a lot. Obsessed was more like it. She obsessively loved sex with him. She couldn't imagine herself with any other man. Did he love her enough? Would he want another child at forty-four? And with the familial DNA match hanging over his head, would he want to? She decided she'd be willing to adopt. She'd do anything to hold a newborn close to her heart whom she could call her own. Would Frank?

She sat down on the sand and blue comforter waiting for the bell to ring. Her heart fluttered and her throat became dry in anticipation. Frank still did that to her. Was it her lust for him? Or was it nervousness that he'd still want to break up? She wouldn't know for sure until he was in her arms. The bell didn't ring. Instead, she heard his heavy footsteps ascending the stairs.

She jumped up off the bed and into his arms at the doorway. He pulled her up and her legs wrapped around his waist as she wound her arms around his neck. There was no hesitation. Their lips interlocked. It seemed like forever since they've had the time for intimacy. Apparently, Frank had needed it as much as she did. He tossed her down on her back on the bed and then yanked off his T-shirt, skinny jeans, and briefs as she removed her clothing. He helped her along, pulling her jeans off, feverishly. Neither cared— where on the floor—their clothing landed. Not the most romantic or sensual way, but she planned to make up for it.

Sam lay underneath him, her favorite place, panting, as her body heat intermingled with his. Talking about sex, as they did in the precinct earlier, always made her hot. She'd been aroused since then. She knew that it did with him, as well. Frank held her arms above her head and their fingers intertwined as he nuzzled his head in her neck. His scratchy five o'clock shadow stimulated every cell on her body, no matter what he'd touch. She knew that in a few minutes he'd make her leave her body in total abandon. She arched her neck and he devoured every inch of it with his moist lips, sucking and nipping at her skin. She couldn't stop moaning. He sent erotic sensations through her entire body. Frank certainly knew how to pleasure every part of her. He was ravenous. She moaned then short gasps escaped her throat.

His lips cascaded down her breasts and he suckled on her nipple. His tongue swirling around the tip, made her swoon. She tightened her fingers around his and she arched her back. She opened herself up to him. She wanted him to go lower toward her sex. He unclasped one hand and rubbed her belly before his fingers tiptoed down past her thatch. Her body quivered under his touch and she moaned, loud moans. Her skin fired up. Every hair stood on edge. He tickled her there then stopped. He tapped her with his middle finger right above her clit. She was almost at the apex and she knew he knew it. Just another minute or two. Her vaginal cavity twitched. Her mound swelled, begging for stimulation. He had to notice it. The moist engorged skin. The slipperiness. She screamed his name. She was yearning for the release but he wouldn't give it to her. All he did was smile with closed lips.

Sam looked up at him with pleading in her eyes. He was teasing her, holding back her orgasm. But she knew her man and she wasn't rushing him. He hated to be rushed in bed. They had all night and didn't have to be at the precinct until ten a.m. She decided to give it back to him, but good. She could tease even better than he could.

Sam sat up and pushed him down with her palm, flat on his back. He went willingly. She got on top of him, straddling him. Her wetness teased his stomach. She felt him tighten his stomach muscles, underneath her. He groaned. She slid down over his groin. She felt his hard length rub against her. His groin pulsated and with his hands on her butt, he moved her in circular motions. She was wetter. He was hard and warm. She knew he wanted to slip into her. She waved her index finger at him. He was being naughty wanting it so fast. She raised her right leg off him, and slid her body down onto the bed and stayed on her stomach. He groaned in disappointment. Too bad, Frank. She moved to lay perpendicular to him. Her left arm lay across his stomach, her breasts next to his navel.

She lowered her face toward his length, inhaling the musky scent from her own liquid, deeply, and then swirled her tongue over his head. Her saliva increased in her mouth. Her throat was no longer dry. He let out a low grunt, then a long groan. She slowly let her tongue travel up and down his shaft and then around it before she encased the head with her mouth. She sucked hard as Frank arched his back and pumped his butt up and down, his signal to her to suck harder. As she drew him into her mouth, as far back as he could go, she felt his head as it rubbed the center groove in the roof of her mouth. She gasped. She was giving herself an orgasm at the same time she was giving Frank one. Her moans of ecstasy came out muffled. Saliva dribbled from the corners of her mouth. Sam grabbed his balls into her hand and massaged, and then with her fingernails gently scratched the underside. Frank was losing himself. He was moaning, grunting, and with a man his size she was pushed up and down with him.

He ran the tip of his fingers around her butt cheeks, tickling her. She bolted in surprise. He let his fingers roam the small of her back. She wiggled her bottom, in pleasure. Tingling sensations swirled through her. He put his hand in between her legs and nudged them apart. With palms facing upward, Frank slipped his fingers into her sheath and his palm rested on her lower butt. Electricity overpowered her. Frank removed his fingers from her canal and spanked her right cheek. She screamed with pleasure. He smacked her left cheek, harder. He stimulated her mound with already wet fingers and more juices dripped onto his hand. He spanked her, again, alternating cheeks as they were both climaxing. They didn't hold back the sounds. Both their bodies quivered. At the moment his cum squirted, he pushed her head back and slipped his shaft out from her mouth. His head fell back onto the pillow. She continued to rub and pumped him with her hand, her fingers sliding over the tip, extending the intensity of his climax. He pounded the bed with his fists and grunted as she continued to rub him. He gritted his teeth, his facial muscles tightened, but she could tell he didn't want her to stop. His body went limp from exhaustion.

Content from her own release, she ran her fingers through her hair to push it over her forehead and away from her face. She was flushed and panting as she shimmied up on the bed and collapsed her head onto his chest.

CSCS

For a couple of minutes, they lay still. Frank, still breathing heavily, ran his fingers over Sam's arm. The aroma of her sex spread to her body. He stared toward the ceiling before he spoke.

"Okay, Sam. Spill it. To what do I owe the pleasure?"

"You mean that literally?"

"Yeah. Literally. You worked hard tonight. Instead of me doing all the work."

She gently slapped his arm. "That's not true. I work hard all of the time. And you actually think I'd use sex because I have a hidden agenda? That's disappointing, Frank."

"The answer is 'no,'" Frank said.

Sam pouted. "You don't know what I'm going to ask you, yet."

"Yeah, I do. And we don't know nearly enough for me to go under at Strident. And be confident that I'll get out of there, alive."

"Crap, Frank. You know me too well, too soon. But I didn't use the sex." He hiked his brows. "I was going to ask you, anyway." She sighed. "Nothing will happen. We got out unscathed from Whiplash."

"It's a different setup here. You said so, yourself."

"Okay, we'll Google it and find out as much as we can about it."

"That won't help. There are no pics of the inside of the clubs, nor of the owners, online, anymore."

"You're a third degree black belt in Jiu Jitsu, Frank. I think you, of all people, know how to protect yourself. So what are you afraid of?"

There was a long pause. "Okay, princess. Want to know what I'm afraid of? I'm afraid of running face-to-face with my brother. So forget it. It's not happening. And in all honesty, I think you should have known better than to ask. And, now, you're trying to manipulate me. I'm not having it, Sam." He sat up and turned his back to her, with his legs off the bed.

She sat up and put her hands on his shoulders. "I'm not trying to manipulate you. It's the best lead we've got. Okay, so I'll go in. If he is there, I'll friendly up to him. At least now, we know what he looks like. Unfortunately, there's no security footage inside the club, so without convincing the madame to tell us the dates Slater and Carrie were there, we have nothing."

"Don't know how that would work, either. You went there as a customer. And now as a cop? Doubt if the madame would trust you."

"I could speak with her first. I'll even show her a pic of you. Say we're investigating some sort of fraud. I'll tell her that I can't tell her much."

"You know what? You can't do anything until you run this by the team. And, I mean the full task-force. You certainly can't go in without backup. Shoot an email tonight asking for a meetup." *I'll let them tell her she's crazy. She'll have to listen to Brett Case.*

"Okay. You're right. I do need to run it by the team."

Frank lay back down. "Right now, princess, all I know is that I want more of you." He sat up, grabbed her down onto the bed, and growled into her stomach. She laughed, uncontrollably.

He moved up to meet her eye-to-eye. His lips connected to hers and they weren't coming up for air. Their heads moved in-sync with each other, with both of them letting out moans and groans.

The phone on her nightstand rang. Twice. She turned her head toward it, but couldn't see the caller ID. Her arm slipped out from under him and she answered on the fourth ring.

Her voice sounded groggy. "Hello."

"Whose car is in the driveway?" the stern voice asked.

"Daddy? Oh, God, I have company."

Frank mouthed, "Crap."

"How long have you been seeing him?"

"Two months."

"Two months, uh? Have you met his family?"

Frank rolled his eyes. He knew what was coming.

"Yes, Daddy, I have."

"Then get yourselves together and come down. Level the playing field."

Frank groaned. He knew Sam's parents were both MDs. Her father was a neurological surgeon and her mother was a pediatrician. They were also very conservative. He'd have an uphill battle, especially if they saw his tatted arms. His tough attitude wouldn't do him any favors, either.

"You're in the house?"

"We'll wait in the living room."

"Give us some time to clean up."

Her father hung up. When she heard the click, she just stared at the handset. "Frank, I'm sorry."

"No problem, Sam. It was about to happen soon. Don't worry, I'll grab the shower in the second bedroom." He pecked her on the tip of the nose. "Take your time. Let me go down on my own. I can handle them."

"You sure?"

"Very." He got up off her, grabbed his clothes off the floor, and dashed out of the bedroom and down the hallway.

Sam got up and went into the adjoining bathroom.

Frank was used to showers in the military. Two-minutes max. He used Sam's Lavender bath gel to make sure the scent of sex was off him. He dried, hastily, threw on his jeans, and a sweatshirt over his T. At least for now, his arms were covered. Sam's parents were up in their late sixties. No need to give them strokes.

He walked down the stairs taking his time. In all of his times over here, he only saw a couple of photos of her parents from family affairs. None current.

He reached the base of the stairs and saw her parents on the couch as they stared up at him. Way up. They leaned back into the cushion, probably in an attempt to give them more room to see his stature. "Hello, Drs. Wright." He extended his hand to her father for a handshake, first. "I'm Frank Khaos."

Her father seemed hesitant. But he shook Frank's hand, staring at their size difference. Frank noticed he had a firm grip. The man with a full head of gray hair and a moustache looked as if he was repressing a smile. "George Wright."

Frank then warmly shook her mother's hand. He was gentle with her. He sat down on the love seat adjacent to the couch. "It's nice to meet you, both."

"It's Marilyn."

"So you work with my daughter?"

"It's our daughter, darling," her mother corrected.

Frank smiled. Interesting that her father didn't address Sam by name. *Cut it out, Frank. Now's not the time for profiling.* "Yes. I work with many of the detectives throughout the city."

"What do you do?" her father asked.

Um, Sam never told them about me? That's telling. "Sam never mentioned me to you?"

"We keep asking her if she's seeing someone, but she's very evasive." Her mother folded her hands on her lap. "She abhors us getting into her private affairs. I think it's because we were so overprotective of her, growing up, being an only child. So what do you do with the detectives?"

"I'm a forensic psychiatrist."

Frank could have sworn he saw Sam's father's hair stand on edge.

"You're an MD?"

"Yes. I am. Why?"

George smirked. "You just don't look the type."

Frank grinned. "What type do I look like?"

"More like a…"

Frank figured now was a good time to get down and dirty. He pushed up the sleeves of his sweatshirt to his elbows. "More like a what?"

Her father looked feint. His complexion paled.

"Dr. Wright, you okay?" Frank got up and sat next to him to the couch. He grabbed his arm to check his pulse.

Dr. Wright pulled his arm away. "I'm fine."

"You two better get used to me. I'm not as intimidating as I look."

"Oh, yes, you are!" Marilyn said.

"You look like a fighter who belongs in a ring."

"That I am, sir. I'm a Mixed Martial Arts fighter and we compete in a cage. It's an eight sided ring. I should say, I was. Now I rehab New York City gang members in my training gym in Harlem."

"Gang members? Isn't that too dangerous? I mean, I can't have our daughter involved with that." Marilyn shook her head. "No, this is too much. We insisted she stay in teaching, with all that's going on now. But she just blocked us out."

"We couldn't do much," George admitted. "But I will tell you that we don't sleep so peacefully anymore."

Frank smiled at Sam's parents, understanding their sentiments. It was dangerous on the streets. "Sam doesn't have any contact with my gym guys. No worries."

"How in the world did *you* ever get into medicine?" her mother asked.

"Well, I was enlisted eight years and did four tours in Iraq. Army. Special Forces. I was a medic. I decided when I got out I wanted to become a doctor. I went to college and med school and worked in trauma. Then forensics caught my interest."

"And gangs?" Sam's mother was still in disbelief.

Frank compressed his lips, contemplating how to tell them. "I had a rough early childhood. I actually could have been drawn into a gang. That's a conversation for another time. I've been in martial arts for years. When my adoptive parents passed on, they left me enough money to open and maintain a gym. It's my way of giving back."

Her father nodded. "So, how serious are you with our daughter?"

Frank wet his lips. "Well, if my eight year old son had anything to do with it, we'd be married, already."

"You're divorced?"

"No, widowed. I met my wife Jen in Iraq. She was my nurse. Sam solved the case of her murder. It was a cold case. Over two years."

Marilyn looked at him teary-eyed. "Oh, my God, Frank. We're so sorry."

Frank saw them both mellow. George compressed his lips and looked away. Marilyn wiped a tear from the corner of her eye. That was a good sign.

CHAPTER 19

Detective Monty Smith entered the interrogation room where Carl Glendale—Abby Ruthe's father—paced nervously back and forth with his head down. As Smith looked up at the man, he saw beads of perspiration on this distraught dad's brow. He looked at the man in a professionally tailored dark blue suit who'd lost his daughter three years ago.

The detective compressed his lips, in a moment of empathy. He stopped chewing his gum and tossed it into the pail next to the door. Glendale turned toward him with his back leaning against the wall.

Smith spoke as he removed his jacket. "Thank you for coming in, Mr. Glendale. Have a seat, sir."

Glendale sat. "What's this in reference to? I got a call at work from a sergeant asking me to come in. All he told me was that it's about my daughter." He lowered his voice. "Is she—"

"No. She's all right as far as we know."

"Thank God." He put his hands up to his forehead, elbows on the table and leaned forward in the chair. He blew out a breath. After a moment, he straightened and removed his jacket, hanging it on the back of the chair next to him.

"When was the last time you saw your daughter?"

"I last saw Abby...uh...three years ago when the judge signed her emancipation papers. For three years, I've been waiting for a call, like this one, or worse. I was hoping I'd hear from Abby. Wanting to make amends. Hoping she'd grown up. What's going on?"

"You don't live in this area…"

"No. In Yonkers."

"Have you heard about the home invasions throughout Westchester?"

"Yes. I saw it through the social media. You don't think Abby?"

"We know she is. That's how we found you. We got a warrant to search her apartment. We found some of the stolen jewelry and the court documents." Glendale looked confused. "Two women with her in the last heist were caught and they gave her up."

"Oh my God! Was anyone hurt? She didn't kill anyone, did she?"

"She did hurt one of the women. She seems to have a violent streak. Kill anyone? What makes you say that?"

℘℘℘

The office receptionist opened the door. "Dr. Trenton is here."

"Show him in, please."

John walked in and stopped dead. He stared at the well-built man with a short military haircut, oval shaped dark brown eyes, olive complexion. He was looking at a double for Frank Khaos. They even had the same facial lines. He knew about the familial DNA linking Frank to the serial killer but another sibling? This was too unsettling and it threw him off guard. He couldn't stop staring with furrowed brows.

"Dr. Trenton, you okay?"

John snapped back. "Yes. Hello, Mr. Glendale. I'm sorry. You resemble someone on my team, a forensic psychiatrist."

"Well, they do say everyone had a double."

"We were just talking about Abby and if she could become violent enough to kill," Smith said.

"Could she, Mr. Glendale?"

"I told Detective Smith I haven't seen her in three years."

"Okay, when she did live with you, how did she treat her friends?"

"She was a loner, but when she did have girls over at the house, we never had to break up any fights, if that's what you mean."

John paused in contemplation. "Did you have any pets?"

"No. My late wife was allergic."

"I'm sorry. When did she pass away?"

"A year before Abby wanted the emancipation. It was ovarian cancer. Abby became uncontrollable. Started failing in school, cutting, then she quit altogether. She only had one more year to go to graduate."

"Does she have any siblings?"

"Yes. Two brothers. My sons are fifteen and eleven."

"How are they doing?"

"Very well, actually. Very much into swimming. They're big for their age. I'm six-three. They're doing very well in school, As and Bs. Nothing like Abby. She didn't get along with them at all. Pretty much ignored them."

"Did she have any tattoos or piercings?" John asked.

"No. I hate those things. I never would have allowed it. Does she have them now?"

Detective Smith opened a folder and pushed a photo of Abby on the table in front of Mr. Glendale.

"That is my Abby. What the hell is that tattoo on her neck?"

"A Scorpion," John said.

He grimaced. "Oh my God. That's disgusting."

"Tattoos are usually symbolic. Have any idea what that could mean?"

"Only that she's a Scorpio. What else would it mean?"

"We'll get into that when we fully profile the case. What do you do?"

"I'm a corporate attorney. My firm has offices in Manhattan and Yonkers." He slipped his card out of his wallet. "I'm a senior partner."

"Mr. Glendale, do you have any siblings?"

"No. I'm an only child. What's that got to do with anything?"

"Something I was thinking about. When I first saw you. The resemblance is uncanny. But you're smaller build. What are you? About one-ninety?"

Glendale put his hands out. "What?" His brows furrowed in confusion. "No, I'm two-ten."

John didn't let up. "Where were you raised?"

"In New Jersey. Why?"

"Were you born there?"

"No. I was born in Brooklyn. My adoptive parents live in Jersey."

"Adoptive?"

"Yes. I was adopted at birth."

☙☙☙

Frank and Sam sat around the conference table in the war room at the Queens precinct with Lieutenant Hicks, Detectives Withers and Richards, and Brett Case.

"Okay, Detective Wright, why did you call this meeting? My department has enough to investigate in the Baines case without adding more, at the moment."

"We got a major lead, Lieutenant."

"Which is?"

Sam caught him up on their experiences at the casino buffet, and the interviews of the personnel who knew Henry Slater. "So now I'd like to go in, to Strident, to see if I can attract Slater."

"I see a lot of faults in your thinking, Detective." Loo leaned forward in his chair. "First, we have no idea if Slater would return. Second, we can't send in a team to help you out if he does latch onto you, and you can't take him on, alone. He's as big as Frank."

Bella sucked in her cheeks. "Oh, I'm sure she's taken on Dr. Khaos, alone, plenty of times."

Sam became livid. "Bella! That's totally out of line!"

"Whoa! I'm teasing, honey. Everyone knows you two are a couple. You've both made it clear."

Frank shot her a look that could kill. "Listen, Bella, whether we show it or not, it's not for anyone to comment on. So, watch yourself. The point is, that I agree with you, Loo. Sam cannot go in alone. And I'm not going for reasons I made clear to her and should be obvious. Actually, I don't want her going there at all."

"And Bella and I aren't going in, either," Withers added.

Agent Case stared at Frank.

"Don't you think of it, Case. I can see it in your eyes. You want to go in, fine. Go with another woman from your office."

"That would be a no-go. There are enough people working this case, already. I couldn't pull anyone else. You want us to forget your...uh...relationship? Then you forget it and act professional. And trust her. Sam would be great to go in. She's familiar with the territory, and she knows the madame. We'll talk to her first. So what are you worried about?"

"I'm worried about her reputation. If it gets out that a cop frequented a club like this, well it could affect her in the department."

Sam shook her head. "What a cop does on his or her time, is exactly that, personal, and has nothing to do with the job. Our union saw to that. Nothing illegal happened. They check IDs, thoroughly. No alcohol. No drugs. Not even sex. Frank, I'll be fine. And if Slater is there, he wouldn't make a grab for me or any woman. He follows them. A team could be waiting on the outside. When he leaves, they could grab him."

"Another flaw, Detective. We need to know the day of the week he goes there, or it'll all be for naught." The Loo hiked his brows, waiting for an answer.

"He goes Wednesday night, around eleven-thirty. One of the female servers I interviewed told me. Oh, and the fourth Wednesday of the month. He never waivers from that. So, Lieutenant, it's a no brainer. And the only thing I need to confer is with Charlie Baines, to see what day of the week he met Carrie, there." Sam sat still, blew out a deep breath, and crossed her arms across her chest. She pursed her lips. "So?"

Frank shook his head. Before he could say something, he got a text.

How soon can you and Sam get up to Scarsdale? Like ASAP.

"Are we done here?"

Lieutenant Hicks blew out a breath. "Yes. Give me a day or two to think about it, Detective. We have enough time to ensure we don't make a mistake. What's the rush, Frank?"

"Dr. Trenton wants me and Sam to head up to Scarsdale, like now."

He got looks of curiosity.

"He didn't say why."

"Okay, go."

ⲉⲟⲉⲟ

Frank and Sam entered the Scarsdale precinct. The shiny white tile floors attracted his attention. "Nice place to work."

John must have heard them in the hall. He opened the door and exited the room he was in. "Glad you came up." He led them to a small lounge. "Come into this room with me, first."

"What's going on, John?"

John licked his lips. I'll tell you everything. Come on."

Frank noticed his stalling and solemn expression, but didn't push it, yet.

They entered a room with two beige faux leather couches that were perpendicular to each other on a brown-tiled floor. Club chairs were in the corners of the room. John sat on one of the couches and motioned for Frank and Sam to sit on the other. They took off their coats and tossed them onto a chair.

Frank leaned forward and clasped his hands between his thighs. "Spill it."

"Remember you told me that when you asked if they only found one DNA match, they didn't answer you?"

"Yeah, when we were at the precinct. They wouldn't give me anything else. Why?"

"I found out there was another DNA match while you were on your drive up here. It's two generations down, so not a sibling of yours, but a niece. That's why it took longer to confirm."

"You're kidding me?" Frank clutched Sam's hand. "Who?"

"No, I'm not kidding. It was DNA found at one of the previous home invasions, the ninth. It was that of the young woman who ran out of my house who Ricky IDd. Abby Ruthe."

Frank put his palm up at John. "Tell me straight. Why did you call us up here?"

"Because we have her father here." John paused. "Your brother."

Frank bolted off the couch and headed toward the door. "I'm not meeting him."

Sam tugged on his hand.

He jerked it away. "Knock it off, Sam. I'm not putting myself through that."

"Frank, sit down," Sam insisted. "We need you and him to go back into your backgrounds. We can solve both cases."

"Then you go back with him. I'm not dealing with any crazies from my family's past."

"Frank, he's not crazy," John said. "He's a corporate attorney. There are also two boys, your nephews, who have socially acceptable behavior. They're fifteen and eleven."

"Don't shut out your family." Sam's eyes were pleading. "Frankie would love to have cousins. Come on, Frank."

He exhaled deeply. "How old is he?"

"A year older than you. He's torn by this, too. Don't dwell in your self-pity party." John stood firm. "We didn't tell him about the serial killer DNA match, yet. This information about his daughter's involvement is killing him. He's alone, Frank, a widower."

Frank mellowed. "From what?"

"Ovarian cancer."

Sam put her hand on his forearm. "What do you say, Frank?"

"Was he adopted at birth, or did they keep him?"

"He was adopted a day after birth and he told us his birth name was Carlton Hunter."

Frank's mind whirled. After forty-four years, he discovered that he had not one brother, but two? And his sibling was a widower, as well. How was he supposed to deal with this? He was so devastated by his early childhood that he didn't straighten out for years after his adoption. How could they expect him to go back into his past? He sat for a few minutes, leaning back against the couch with his eyes closed. He always told his gym guys they had to come to terms with their past and move on. Yeah, right. It was harder to do, than say. Oh, man, he might as well meet his successful brother before he had to take down the killer in the family. "Okay, let's do this."

The walk down the hall took forever. Frank felt like he was going to his own execution, except for the fact that Sam was tightly clutching his hand. John opened the door and moved aside to let Frank and Sam enter. Carl stood immediately when Frank approached him.

The two men stared at each other—a foot apart—speechless. Frank looked at the man only an inch shorter than him but about sixty pounds lighter. He followed Carl's gaze down his tatted arms. Carl grimaced. Frank was itching for a fight. "Got a problem?"

Carl smirked and sat down. "Yes, I have a problem. Abby should be your daughter, not mine."

"Okay. Good. You're as thrilled about this as I am. What now?" Frank said with a sneer at John before he took a seat.

Detective Smith shoved a picture of Abby in front of Frank.

Frank picked up the photo, looking at her tats and piercings. "I know what you mean. Okay, Scorpion." He glared at John. "You're not relating both cases, are you?"

Mr. Glendale's gaze darted to each of the men. "Both cases?"

Frank look up at John and the Detective. John nodded, giving him the okay to tell. "Hate to break it to you, sport. We have a brother. A suspected serial killer."

"Suspected serial—"

"Not actually suspected, confirmed, but it's the innocent-until-proven-guilty, thing."

"Who the hell are you? What the hell are you?"

"Didn't they tell you anything?"

"No, Dr. Khaos, we didn't," Smith said.

"Doctor?"

"Yeah. I'm a forensic psychiatrist and a NYPD profiler." Frank pointed with his thumb to Sam. "This is Detective Samantha Wright. Her best friend was killed by the guy. All we got is his name, Henry Slater. Ring a bell?"

"No. Not at all. So how did we come up? What's the relation?"

"They got DNA off Carolyn Baines's body, Sam's friend." Frank paused. "Slater wasn't in the system so they extended the search and came up with familial DNA. Mine, and now I just learned about Abby. We had gone to the casino where the murder had occurred and everyone thought I was Slater. So there's no doubt. The DNA tests were accurate."

"So why do you need me?"

"We need the both of you," John said. "Both your birth names were Hunter. Frank knows nothing but that they were young, and his adoptive parents have passed on, so what do you know about your birth parents?"

"Not much. Believe it or not, I had such a wonderful life with my parents, I had no idea that I was adopted. They were of the opinion not to tell. I found out five years ago, when I was going through their wills and they were older, so it was time to make me executor and put me on the deed to the house and bank accounts even though I'm an only child. They knew they could trust me. They were in their early eighties. I was going through their safety deposit box in the bank when I saw the adoption papers. I literally freaked out. I had a meltdown right there. I was pissed they had held this from me. Then, as I thought about it, I became relieved. It was a closed adoption. My birth parents were sixteen."

"That, I knew. They were a year older with me."

"The agency that handled it was The Andrews Agency in downtown Brooklyn. I never inquired. I approached my parents later and they told me my mom couldn't conceive. What did you know?"

"I was adopted at ten. I spent the early years in foster care. When I was adopted they had new birth certificates done. In the system, the paper trails disintegrated so I don't know my history of where I was. Are your parents alive?"

"My dad passed on last year and my mom is in a nursing home for Alzheimer's patients. She's eighty-nine."

"Glad you had a great life."

"Thanks. Yours must have been rough. In foster care all those years."

"Sure was, and I had the antisocial behavior to prove it."

"So what turned you around?"

"Love, for one, martial arts, but I think the military really did it for me. Did four tours in Iraq, Special Forces."

"This is getting too coincidental." Carl fidgeted in the seat. "Way out of my comfort zone. I was in Iraq for two tours, infantry. When were you in?"

"Enlisted, Eighty-nine to ninety-seven."

"A year earlier. My battalion chief was a Marcus Willtower, if I remember correctly."

"Marcus Willtower?" Sam shrieked. "He's DEA now."

Carl sat stunned. "You know him?"

"Yeah. We got reunited in our last case. I patched him up a few times back then."

Carl pointed to Frank. "You—You were a medic. I carried him to you."

Frank smacked his forehead. "Oh, man. Yeah, you sure did. We met in Iraq and we didn't see any similarities? How is that possible?"

"Uh, I think being covered up with blood and in uniform, with bombs going off around you, gave you other things to think about, no?" Sam said, bewildered.

"So now what?" Frank asked.

Detective Smith nodded. "Now that you two have come to terms with this, how about solving these cases?"

Frank and Carl nodded.

"What do you need me to do?" Carl asked.

"For one—" John made a list in his mind. "—we start with the Andrews Agency. Find out if they handled both adoptions, even though yours, Frank, was ten years later. That is, if they're still in existence." He turned toward Sam and the detective. "Which one of you can get the warrant faster?"

"Murder usurps robbery," Sam answered. "We're attached at the hip with Judge Martinsson since the Aries case, so we'll get it." She paused and skirted her gaze between Frank and Carl. "For a positive effect on the agency, I think it would be beneficial for both of you to go when we execute the warrant."

"Done," Frank said.

Carl nodded. "Sure."

"Find out—" John paused. "—if there was a third sibling for whom they handled an adoption. Or, if there was a sibling the family wouldn't place."

"What are you getting at, Dr. Trenton?" Detective Smith asked.

John stared at Frank. "Okay, for one, these two turned out fine and successful and their sons have socially acceptable behavior. If the third sibling was kept with his bio parents, it would explain that the psychopathic behavior, in this case, was environmental, not genetic."

"Oh, yeah? I know what you're getting at, John. Knock it off," Frank challenged. Then his gaze shot to Sam before looking John in the eyes. "What about Abby? My niece. How would you classify her?"

"Definitely not a psychopath. Delinquent. Yes. I'll need to talk to her first. I would say she's still grieving about her mother. What do you think, Mr. Glendale? Were Abby and her mother close?"

"Too close. Attached, still from the womb would put it mildly. And Abby looks just like her mom. I was so angry when Mary passed on that I neglected Abby and spent all my time with the boys. I think what she's doing is to get even with me."

"That could do it." John crossed his legs. "Did you and Mary fight a lot?"

Carl's eyes widened. "Yes, we did. Threatened divorce, too. I didn't want to because of the children. Since they had acting out behaviors, I thought they'd become worse."

Frank leaned forward and rested his arms on the table. "Let me ask you something. You said the boys are doing well, so what acting out?"

"Very minor stuff with school. Not doing homework. That was the biggie. They'd miss schoolwork during the periods Mary and I fought. But both boys excelled on tests so that gets them their high grades."

Frank was startled. "Sounds like me. I did the same thing. Wow. Fight about what?"

"Mary always wanted more romance. I'd come home from court exhausted. After the diagnosis and going through chemo, her urges stopped. It was more peaceful in the house, but then the kids were ignored, again. Her cancer was fast growing."

Frank raised his index finger to make a point. "Okay, listen to me. I know this from my gang kids. Parents who stay together because of the kid's issues have more problems all around."

"Well, you listen to this." Carl covered his mouth with his hand before he spoke. "Abby, in her infinite wisdom, blamed me for Mary's cancer."

John held in a smile. Frank noticed. He knew about John's position on the mind-body connection. Frank agreed with it. "John, why don't you explain it?"

"Explain, what?"

"Why did Abby blame you?" John asked.

"This is what she told me, verbatim. 'You're not giving mommy enough sex, and she's so mad that she's dying inside. And she got ovarian cancer because that's the sex center.' I'm living with this guilt every day."

"Okay. First, Abby is right. But there are tons of women who want more romance in a marriage and don't come down with ovarian cancer. It is a mind-body connection. Mary is the one who wanted out of the marriage?" Carl nodded. "Well, the universe brings things to us to solve problems," John informed him. "It's a tough nut to swallow. I'm interested in Abby. Has she always been intuitive?"

"Always. Since she was a toddler. I'd say she's truly psychic. She saw things that no one else saw."

"Such as?"

"Accidents, in her dreams. She'd wake up hysterical, crying. Sure enough, the next day we'd find out there was an accident, the very least in the same vicinity. But she couldn't recognize any of the people."

"Um, I can relate. Okay, we'll bring her in." John turned his attention to the detective. "Get as many units out that you need."

Detective Smith grabbed up the papers from the desk, as Frank and Carl got up to leave. They gave each other military bear hugs. Sam and John headed out the door. Frank caught up with them after Carl left through another exit.

John walked up next to Frank. "I meant what I said. This could be environmental."

Frank stopped dead. "And I meant what I said when I told you to stop. I am not having another child." He realized what he said and too loudly. He turned around to look at Sam who pushed past them and ran out of the front door.

CHAPTER 20

Two officers escorted a cleaned up Mr. Karrot into the interrogation room where John and Withers sat around a table waiting for him. Withers smirked. "Good to see you're awake."

"Why the hell am I in these rags for? I haven't been arrested."

Withers looked up at the man in the short-sleeved gray button down shirt and elastic-around-the-waist matching pants. His stomach bulged over the waistband. "Sorry about that, Karrot." He laughed. "Can't help laughing. I get a kick out of saying your name. Seriously, it's the only clean clothes we have around here. Hope you enjoyed your shower and breakfast."

"Yeah. Just like the Hilton."

An officer shoved him into a seat.

"Your attorney met with you this morning, correct?"

"Yeah. A real doll. She was kinda cute, but I don't know how much she knows. Just outta law school a month."

"That's fine," John affirmed. "She may be motivated to help you more, to prove to the DA she's good."

Karrot rolled his eyes. "So what do you want from me?"

"We're further along than when we spoke to you last night. Seems that you and Maynor had a business together, that was quite profitable."

"What business?"

"Your attorney did advise you to answer our questions. Correct?" Karrot nodded. "Good," John said. "Very good. We found documents at his place and our computer guys verified it. Ever hear of the dark web?"

"Dark web? What the hell is that?"

"Well, ya see, Mr. Karrot," Withers said. "It's hard to find. They keep it underground. Can't Google it. But New York City has the best crime lab in the county, and the FBI has a cybercrime unit. They did a little digging. It seems that you and Maynor ran a pirating site, actually several. It also seems that the two of you bought the eBook version of novels by first time authors, and featured them on various video sites for download. Your innocent victims had to log in and to download it, for ninety-nine cents, they had to give their payment details. It wasn't the eBooks you both wanted to sell, it was the credit cards. Maynor used the cards to buy major items, the jerk. We found a brand new couch in his apartment, then, his paperwork led us to a shiny refrigerator in yours. Bingo. And the large cash deposits? Those, uh, corresponded to cash advances on the cards. We're still investigating. But I make you a bet, that Bobby Mitchell overheard a conversation between Maynor and you, or another partner, and he was murdered to cover that up. And we'll probably find more than the eBooks. How am I doing?"

Karrot's complexion paled. He began sweating and swiped his wet palms on his thighs. "I had nothing to do with the murder, Detective, I swear. I don't even know who that Mitchell guy is."

"And you know what else we know?"

"I don't give a shit. So entertain me."

"This will sure be entertaining. When we were in Maynor's office at the halfway house, we saw all the names of the residents covered with that Whiteout shit. And in their place, were strange names. That struck us as real funny. But doing the due diligence that we New York City detectives are known for, we discovered—now listen carefully, this is major—that the names were of the author's whose work you two dimwits pirated. Maybe it was his creative bookkeeping to keep track of what he did but there was a perfect one-to-one match. And that, Mr. Karrot, gave us a solid connection. Questions?"

Karrot slumped into the seat. "I told that prick not to keep records there. What a fucking moron."

"Our sentiments, exactly. Good. Glad you understand me. Well, right now, you're being arrested for copyright infringement, credit card fraud, and we'll see what the FCC has to add. And there will be a full FBI investigation."

"I want a deal."

"Too early for that." Withers depressed a button on the intercom.

Two officers came in, handcuffed him, and read Karrot his rights as they escorted him out.

John let out a deep breath and slouched back in the chair. He sat back in a solemn moment. Then he glanced up at Withers and put his hand on Withers's arm. "Thanks, Lex."

"We have some more investigation to do for a done deal, but I bet this was it."

"Me, too."

"Glad you now have closure, John, and I'm glad the kid got his justice."

℅℀℅

In her kitchen, Sam unpacked boxes from a home-shopping channel as Vicki looked on in approval. She was holding Zach in her arms, and Ricky entertained Alexi in her stroller. The baby cooed and bubbled. A twenty-one piece set of mauve-colored enamel cookware lay on the kitchen table.

"Sam, this set is unbelievable. You'll love it. I'm so glad they still had it in stock. It's every piece you'll use and to-tally non-stick." Vicki picked up a fourteen-inch-in-diameter, three-inch-deep frying pan. "Especially this one. Did the stoneware come yet?"

"Yes, yesterday." Sam walked to her cabinet, opened the door, and showed Vicki the nine-piece set in a pink, yellow, and white floral design."

"Great, darlin'. That rectangular roaster, you'll use a lot. The size is perfect, for lasagna to roasting a chicken. I love mine. It's black, white and yellow, to match John's Manhattan condo. He admired mine the first night I cooked dinner for him. I bought it for him for Chanukah. What do you want to cook for Frank, tonight?"

"He wanted fish. And I have to do it, right, Vicki, especially after the slow cooker fiasco."

"Uh, that was a pressure cooker."

Sam looked bewildered for a moment. "Okay, I get it. Major question. How do I decide what spices to use on what? I bought one of every one at the market. About fifty bottles. I wanted to be prepared."

Vicki laughed. "You certainly will be. Just remember they only stay fully fragrant for about six months after you open the bottle. Be prepared to cook incessantly or you'll be wasting a lot of money. Okay, you have a great sense of smell, so that's exactly what you have to do. Smell them. What kind of fish did you buy?"

"Salmon steaks."

"Okay, salmon can go great with sweet or savory. Cinnamon, turmeric, curry, cumin, paprika, will go with sweet. The Italian spices, oregano, basil, thyme, rosemary, dill, garlic, onion, or cilantro, will go with savory. Those are the main ones. And you can combine. John loves garlic and onions with everything. How did you want to prepare it?"

"Okay, I bought this cookbook..." She pulled it off the counter and turned to a page she had marked. "This says 'poached.'"

"Poached is a little more than steamed. The fish is in the water and you can put in any seasonings you want. It'll flavor the fish."

"And there's a yoghurt dill and mint dressing. I think I can manage this one. I bought everything."

"Okay, just make sure you bought plain regular yoghurt, not Greek. That's too tarty for dill and mint."

"Oops. Need to make another trip to the store."

"It's a learning process, darlin'. And you'll get it. Cookbooks are great. Every recipe was tested. Vary anything you want, just not in baking. That's a science. I have to run. I'm meeting John to make a visit to his uncle. He hasn't seen the twins yet or met Ricky."

"That should be fun!"

"Yes. He's a judge in criminal court and he and John are close."

Vicki bundled up the twins. Ricky put on his coat and wheeled the stroller to the door. Vicki and Sam hugged.

"Thanks so much, Vicki."

"My pleasure."

Sam helped Vicki down the front steps holding up the front of the stroller. Vicki opened her car door and loaded the twins into their car seats. Ricky hopped in.

Biting her lip, Sam stood and watched as Vicki pulled out of the driveway and drove down the block. She felt devastated after Frank responded to John that way. Just yesterday. Why in hell she was cooking for him tonight was beyond her. She knew why. She deeply loved the man. And his son. She'd love to call Frankie her son. Maybe after they caught Slater, Frank would be more open. Maybe he would want to adopt. She knew he felt positive about adoption. He'd been adopted.

She'd propose to Frank. Yes. That's what she'd do. When the time was right.

Hopefully in this decade.

⁂

Frank sat behind his desk in his office at the gym. He

wore his Khaos Rules T-shirt, a little baggier this time, squishy workout pants, and white, low-top sneakers. He was thinking about the dinner Sam had made for him and Ricky, tonight.]

She didn't mention the major faux-pas he made in Scarsdale yesterday. He knew that it kept him up all last night. How stupid could he have been? The salmon dinner was not bad. It was actually pretty good, no, better than good. Sam prepared the fish to perfection. She was trying. Sam would really be the perfect partner for him, and a perfect mom for Frankie. She'd certainly understand his work schedule.

He'd thought about her constantly—how much he craved her, how much he loved her. He was truly worried about her going to Strident tonight with Brett Case. Yes. He'd propose to her. When the time was right.

Hopefully in this decade.

He was shuffling files on his desk when one of the trainers opened the door.

"Got company, Frank." He moved aside to let Carl and his sons enter.

A huge smiled crossed Frank's face as he stood and looked at his nephews. He paused for a moment. Wow. He actually had family. He came out from behind his desk and gave his brother a military bear hug, shoulders tapping, Frank's left arm bent at the elbows, Carl's right arm bent, as their fists connected.

The two boys looked up in awe at Frank.

Carl smiled. "Yeah, your uncle is pretty big, isn't he?"

The fifteen-year-old responded, first. "I'll say."

"Andrew, Cameron, say hello to your Uncle Frank."

Frank shook both their hands. "Hi, guys. Want a tour?"

The boys looked at each other and didn't have to answer. Frank saw them both light up. Their smiles reached ear to ear.

Frank opened the door. "Come on. Ever been in a gym?"

The little guy, Cameron, couldn't contain himself. "Uh,

no! Dad takes Andy but said I have to wait a few years." He smirked. "I dunno why."

Frank laughed as they walked down the main hall. "'Cause you're still growing. But this kind of a gym you can go to. Your cousin Frankie goes to a gym like this, with me, in Brooklyn. It's much smaller but has some of the same equipment." He stopped at a wall of photos. "See all these guys in white pants and jacket tops? Those are called gis. They're all pretty famous in the field of Mixed Martial Arts. Some in Jiu Jitsu, some Muay Thai."

The boys looked confused.

"Never heard of those?"

They both shook their heads. "We've seen the gis, but we don't know those two things you said."

"They're different kinds of fighting. And there's competitions for each of them. I'll tell you all about it, later." He led them into the main section of the room, which housed the cage in the center, and MMA equipment around the perimeter against the walls. About twelve men were working out in various sections—all wearing the Khaos Rules T-shirts and shorts.

The boys stopped dead at the entrance. They stared with their eyes practically popping out from their sockets.

Carl didn't react that much differently. "Quite impressive, Frank."

"How come everyone's wearing the same thing?" Andrew asked.

"It's the gear of the gym. In here, everyone's equal. And so are you." Frank stopped at the cubbies. He tossed a small T to Andrew and an extra small to Cameron. He handed a large to Carl. Then the shorts, cups, and socks. The more the boys piled up, the bigger their smiles. "And put everything in the lockers, even your cells."

"Uh, why the cells?"

"No cells allowed on the floor, bro."

"Frank, I'm expecting a call back from a judge. He doesn't appreciate playing phone-tag."

"My gym. My rules. Besides, the reception in here sucks. I planned it that way. So, uh, deal with it."

Carl sneered at him then grinned. Frank could tell his brother wanted to rebut, but guessed he was holding back because of the boys. "Okay, boss. Just this time." Carl cocked his head toward his sons.

"Go change in the locker room and meet me in the back of the gym." Frank pointed toward the hanging ropes.

A few minutes later, the trio was standing in front of Frank with their mouths agape as their gaze scanned the surroundings. He walked over to the shelves in a cubby and pulled out a ball used for dodge ball. He quickly tossed it to Cameron, who didn't know what hit him as the ball bounced off his chest.

"Hey, Uncle Frank! You didn't warn me."

"Warn you? You expect someone who wants to start a fight to warn you? Uh uh. Go get it and toss it to one of us, fast. Don't think about it. Don't make eye contact. Go."

Cameron hesitated.

"What's the matter?"

"Uh, nothing."

"Then, go. Go. Go. Go."

Cameron ran to pick up the ball that had rolled to the left of the cage. About ten yards. Frank could tell the kid wasn't in the best condition. Though slim, he'd become winded. "You have to get him into the gym, Carl, even for cardio."

"I see that. Cam, you okay?"

"Yes, Dad."

"Toss it."

Cameron tossed the ball to his brother. Then it went to Carl. To Frank. To Andrew. To Carl. They spent over fifteen minutes with the ball. Frank saw his nephews fatigued. Sweat poured. He went over to the cooler against the wall, and pulled out four bottles of water.

"Drink. And you listen. The three of you need to be in better shape." He looked at his brother. "Even you, big guy."

The boys laughed at their dad.

"Hey, not funny. Don't you have Phys Ed in school?"

"I'm taking swimming," Andrew said.

"I was taking swimming until I got kicked off the team."

"Cameron, Why did you get kicked off?"

"I couldn't swim the laps they wanted."

"Why not?"

"Because Dad has us studying so much, we aren't allowed to go to all the practices."

"Okay, bro, we have to talk. Are you ready to try the ropes?"

"Yes!"

CHAPTER 21

The night arrived—lieutenant approved—the fourth
Wednesday of January. Sam, over-prepared, dressed
in her black bustier and floral lace black stockings,
sat on a small couch—opposite the doorway, the perfect
spot—in a meet and greet lounge at Strident. Another room
that was different from Whiplash, the club she went to with
Frank for the Aries case. This time she wore her hair
down—flowing down her back—instead of in a pony-tail.
The mesh patch covered her tush, secured tightly. There
was no need for Brett Case to see that part of her in the
flesh—literally. This was the first room people checked
when they entered the club.

Wall-to-wall people—of all adult ages, nationalities,
physical conditions, and in all stages of undress—
consumed the rather large space. Sectionals and couches
formed groups where people convened depending upon the
activity they wanted to play. Those who wanted metal re-
straints sat in the red area, where all the furnishings were
red and the walls behind the seating area matched in color.
Others who wanted rope bondage sat in the blue area in
front of the blue wall. Those who wanted racking sat in the
green sections. Sam sat on the seafoam-blue section for
women who wanted to be a sub and play a spanking scene
with a man. Other areas were for same sex games. Male—
yellow. Female—pink. People of the opposite gender

wouldn't approach someone in these areas. It was the code of ethics. Respect. The first thing someone would see when they entered the room was the striped walls then it was easy to find your section. The regulars knew exactly where to go. She hoped Slater would.

Sam sat seductively with her right leg over her left thigh as her black stiletto heels accentuated her sensuality with toned calf muscles peeking through her stockings. She looked around for Slater—and Brett Case. Her partner was already ten minutes late. When she had gotten there, Madame Lilly was in a scene. Sam didn't feel like watching it, nor did she want to interrupt her. It was a woman-woman scene, not what Slater would choose. She stood up, looking around the room. She looked higher up and no one around Slater's height appeared in the group. As her gaze scanned the sections, one by one, she spotted Brett Case entering. He wore black leather leggings, showed a bare chest with a black bow tie around his neck. He was built, that's for sure. She had never cared for overly muscular men, until she'd met Frank. Now she was a fan of muscle magazines and even watched wrestling on TV. She still grimaced at their violence toward each other, but she became aroused so quickly, she shocked herself.

She was surprised she didn't have the same turned on feeling when she saw Brett Case in the flesh. She nodded, consumed by her thoughts. Her feelings for Frank were deeper than the skin.

He stood, scanning the room—his gaze did a quick pass over her—then landed on the yellow section.

Sam watched him approach her with a broad smile. She forced one, in return.

"Hi, babe. You're looking mighty fine, tonight, uh…"

"It's Princess," she retorted with a tone that she hoped would send him the message that she wasn't available. He had heard Frank call her Princess, many times. She stared right at him. His bright blue round eyes sparkled in the glaring lights around them. He had gone tanning for the occasion and was quite the handsome man. Why wasn't he in a relationship? Or did he keep it to himself? He never mentioned any girlfriends or dates. Or wife. He'd certainly be a good catch for a woman. Maybe she'd fix him up.

"Um, Princess." He sat down next to her. "That's cute, and childish."

She glared at him. "Yeah, well. I've had it since I was born. What's your name for the evening, dud?"

He laughed. "Butch is as good as any. Any sign of him?"

"Nope. But that doesn't mean he isn't here. He usually gets here…" Sam checked her watch. "Um, in fifteen minutes. Be patient."

"Does the madame know you want to see her?"

"Nope. I like surprises." She stood with her right leg bent at the knee and rested it on the couch as she stretched her body tall, hands on waist, and looked around the room. She deliberately positioned her butt to be toward Case's face. She could just imagine his reaction. She wanted it so, if Slater did show up, he would have to use his charm to get her. The cocktail waitresses at the casino had told her he was big on charm and charisma. She wanted to see that part of him, to tell Frank.

She understood why he didn't want to come, but she was pissed at the same time. Tonight he was in the gym bonding with his brother and nephews. That was good, at least. Okay, she'd let go of her anger.

Brett tapped her butt with four fingers. "Sit down. I'm tired of staring at your ass."

She spun around, not comprehending his tone. Okay, so not every man had to want to squeeze it. She wiggled back down on the couch. "Don't like it?"

"I'm getting bored sitting here and it's a waste of tax payer's money. Lieutenant Hicks insisted I go with you. Let's make this a worthwhile visit." He got up, swaggered through the room, and stood in the middle the yellow section.

Why would he go there? Sam followed him. She stood at the border of the section, actually over the line.

"You're not allowed in here, girlfriend," a boyish look-ing guy in his thirties told her. He smiled with a wink.

She giggled and stepped back. But she planned to ob-serve Brett.

He sat on the couch next to the young guy. "I'm Butch." He extended his hand to shake.

"Cal," the younger man said, reciprocating. "This is your first time here, isn't it?"

Brett laughed. "It's that obvious?"

"Totally. You're out of your element. I see it in your eyes. So what brings you here?"

Sam sat on a nearby club chair. She couldn't hear them, but it was a good thing she could lip read. A skill she picked up when she was teaching. She just had to know what her students, who sat in the back of the room, were whispering.

"Actually, I'm meeting up with a friend."

Cal nodded. "What's his tag?"

"Not exactly sure. But he has a scorpion tat on his back. A huge one."

"Ah, that's, Stinger."

Sam perked up, but she wasn't about to blow her cover, yet. She noticed men getting up and leaving the section, not looking back. That was telling.

Why is Brett oblivious to what was happening around him? Either that or he wasn't used to being in a place like this. At any rate, he sure didn't do his homework. No, can't be. He has always been prepared.

"You know him?" Brett asked.

"Everyone does. Swings both. Don't you know?"

"No. Don't know much about him. We met casually at the casino and he told me this club is great if you want to get into the scene. We planned a meet-up so he could show me around."

"Bad move, Brett. You're telling too much," Sam whispered with her hand over her mouth.

"That's cool. Wait a minute, man. He played you. Sure it was for tonight?"

"Yeah. The fourth Wednesday of the month."

"Well, he was here last week. Told us he'd be away for a few weeks. His biz has him traveling, a lot. Guess you're on your own."

"Guess I am. Thanks for the heads up."

"Gotta go. My partner is here. Nice talking to ya, Butch." He got up and hugged the man.

When they walked away, Brett went over to Sam. He hand signaled to her to get up and follow him. He led her over to a couch next to the back wall. "He's not coming tonight."

"Don't kid yourself. Something is very wrong."

"Why?"

"Let me educate you. Obviously you didn't see the other guys get up and leave when you opened your mouth." She gave him a stern disciplinary glare. "One, people don't tell strangers about someone else, not in a club. Two, people keep their backgrounds quiet. No one would know what business Slater is in or anything about it. And you shouldn't have said where you met him. You broke the code of confidentiality. Someone certainly wouldn't tell you with whom he plays. He gave you too much information. And his tag probably isn't Stinger, either. I'll make you a bet. He smelled cop. And why did you go into that section, anyway?"

Brett compressed his lips. "Okay, since Slater didn't have consummate sex with any of his victims, and he does play sub and dom, I got the thought that he may swing both ways. That was confirmed. I felt I might get more honesty from a man. So why did he talk to me at all? He should have left immediately, the others did."

"Good question. We'll investigate this Cal. Let's go find the madame."

They left the lounge and walked down a long hall.

Madame Lily was closing her office door. She turned to see Sam and Brett. This woman was tall and in six-inch platform stilettos stood over six feet. Her long red hair cascaded down her back to her waist. That was a lot of hair. And it was her own, if Sam remembered correctly. But her boobs weren't. She had covered them completely, too. She wore a black leather vest with leather skinny jeans. Even with hiding the cleavage, for a woman in her upper fifties, she looked damn good.

Madame Lily smirked and put her hands on her waist. "What do you want, cop? Last time you were here, I got suspicious. You were always looking around, wanting to find someone, or avoid someone.

"Didn't come in an official capacity then. Where can we talk, in private?"

The madame frowned and tilted her head toward her office door. She unlocked it and entered with Sam and Brett following her. Lily went behind her desk and pointed to the couch.

Sam looked around the high style room, all sex-red. Ugh, she had enough red in the Aries case to last a lifetime. So much so, she donated all of her red clothing to charities. There were all sorts of spanking tools, ropes, balls, hanging from a rack on the wall opposite the desk and above the couch. Even electronic toys. This was probably where lessons were taught to newbies.

"Stop looking around and tell me what you want. I have to get into a scene."

Sam turned away from Brett before she put her fingers into the cup of her bustier. She lifted her right breast, took out a miniature phone from underneath, wiggled the *girl* back into the cup, and turned the phone toward her. "Know this guy? Rather, a guy who looks like him?"

"Excuse me? You kept your phone. And you damn well know the rules here!"

"Sorry. We're investigating a murder case."

"I'll let that slide. I don't want to be slapped with a warrant. Why him?"

"He's a suspect."

"If that's who I think it is, no way. He's the sweetest man. No woman has ever complained that he's too rough. And he's powerful. If he wanted to do damage, he could."

"What would you do if a man did get carried away?" Brett asked.

"He'd be thrown out, never to return. I'm on top of things."

"Okay, so he's good at following the rules. What can you tell us about him?" Brett asked. "Have a name?"

"Nothing. This is a private club. Everyone uses aliases. All cash, so there's no credit card trail. The same as every other club. You should know that, uh, Princess."

Sam uncrossed her leg and leaned in toward the desk. "So what's his alias?"

"I prefer not to mention it," the madame said, sitting back in her chair.

"Let me repeat, ma'am. This is an FBI investigation." Brett removed his ID from his right boot and slid it on the desk, to her. The madame looked startled. "It's a serial murder case," he continued. "And we have pretty positive evidence that this guy's look-alike is our guy. We will get a warrant to interview everyone, which you just admitted you wanted to avoid. And that will certainly be an intrusion. So help us out. We need every detail you've noticed. Every quirk."

The madame swallowed hard. "Okay. His tag name is Adonis. He knows he is one. One thing that made him different from the other men is that he liked to get phone numbers from the women. He was so kind in after care, in consoling them, that most of the women gave it to him. A few complained to me. They didn't want the relationship carried to the outside. Most men didn't want it either. But I think he wanted a relationship. He wanted to find the perfect partner. When I approached him and told him the concerns of the women, he just merely shrugged and kissed the top of my head. He walked away, unconcerned. I yelled after him, but it didn't make a dent. I told him the next complaint, he's out. I haven't seen him since."

"When did you tell him this, exactly? About him being out?"

"Last week, actually," she replied.

"Isn't he usually here the fourth Wednesday of the month?" Madame Lily nodded. Sam blew out a breath, relieved her information was correct.

Sam showed her a pic of Carrie. "Recognize her?"

"Yes. Why?"

Case jumped in to respond. "She's his first victim in the city. We think he meets women some place, and follows them. He selects highly educated women, and his kills are at casinos along the east coast. The first, in the casino in Queens. If you know her, this would be that *some place*."

The madame slumped back in her cushioned chair and let out a deep sigh. "Okay, this is that place, as you said, Agent Case. I have owned this club over fifteen years, pretty silently, so when I took over six months ago, everyone thought I was a new owner. I have never had a public complaint or a health violation, and they investigate our kind of club vigorously."

"What are you saying?" Sam asked.

"Here's what I'm saying, Detective. If you have to get a warrant, it will be public record. If I tell you what I know, I want full immunity from anything you find. And I want that in writing. The people in my club are my utmost concern, and I don't want any killer—no matter how much money they bring in—to destroy what I had so feverishly developed from the ground up. Can you guarantee that?"

Brett began to speak. The madame cut him off.

"And one more thing. I do not want the federal government to start an initiative to propose more regulations and screenings for these clubs. We have enough, already."

"What did you mean by 'no matter how much money they bring in'?" Brett asked.

"Women loved to have scenes with him. He's booked up for months. However, that woman never had a scene with him, and she's not on any future appointment lists."

Sam and Brett exchanged inquisitive stares.

"You have future dates that he'll be here?"

"Yes. But I wouldn't count on it. He had three women scheduled for tonight. They were pissed he didn't show. And it's not like him to be a no-show."

"He has appointments booked for months?" The madame nodded. Sam couldn't believe it. "For what?"

"He's an expert on the rope. We call it a *rigger*. Creates the most amazing designs I've ever seen. Magazine quality but he refuses to let us photograph him. It's against the rules, anyway. Though, the women would love it."

Sam salivated and had to take a quick swallow. "Restrictive tying?"

"That depended upon the woman. He actually has an interview checklist for the first time he meets with a woman."

Brett concealed his chuckle sucking in his cheeks. Sam sneered at him, knowing what he was doing. It took him a moment to compose himself. "He interviews the woman?"

"It's for safety, Agent. He asks for likes and dislikes, any health issues that can come on from stress, experience, how restrictive the woman would allow him to go, or not. Things of that nature. He'd never just meet a woman and get right to the scene. That's why he was so trusted."

"Okay, he didn't show, tonight." Sam bit her lip. "He must know we're onto him. He'll run. Crap."

"Thank you, Madame. We appreciate your honesty and assistance." Brett seemed to have meant it. "I'll have something drawn up. Can you come to the Queens precinct tomorrow afternoon? We'll need your records of his past appointments, who he played with, and anyone else with even the most remote connection to him."

Lily cocked her head. "But one thing. Records of that

nature aren't kept. For confidentiality. Once the appointment is met, the paper trail is shredded. What I give you is from memory. And at my age, that might not be so reliable." She hiked a brow and shot them a sly glare. "Understand?"

"We'll take what we can get," Brett said as he and Sam stood.

Sam replaced the phone inside her bustier as Brett did the same with his ID into his boot. They opened the door and left the office, walking straight down the hall to the exit.

ॐ

Loud house music blocked out the voice of the woman yelling at him as she pinned him with his back against the black wall. Her breasts leaned flush against his torso. The red-haired twenty-something woman who wore a black skimpy bikini top and G-string bottom stood there with her hands on her waist, not in her submissive stance. She then abruptly backed away, still keeping her hands in place on her hips. He'd have to punish her but good tonight, even though it was his fault he was late. A phone conference with one of his Georgia casino managers took longer than he had planned. Business always came first. He smiled at her rant, but his full-face black mask hid his playful expression. He opened his arms wide, which was her signal to come into his embrace. She followed her master's directives and rested her head on his pecs against his tight black jersey long-sleeved top, with her arms going around his waist. As he kissed the top of her head, reassuring her that it would be all right, he raised his head and noticed a couple strolling down the hall. There was no hand holding, not even talking.

It hit him hard. That stunning blonde was exactly the kind of woman he had imagined for himself. He had to see her face. Disengaging the embrace, he gently pushed the redhead to the side. He raised his finger in a signal for her to stay put. His gaze followed the couple. Focusing on the knockout's derriere, he became hard. Feeling himself becoming engorged was not something he had done so spontaneously, recently. He followed about ten feet behind them, then ducked into another hallway where another woman—a brunette, this time—accosted him. He wrapped her in his arms, and pushed her back against the wall, pretending to be amorous. As the couple exited into the night, the blonde, barely turned her head. He spotted her nose— the perfect Grecian nose.

That woman was his.

He had to find her.

Just like he found Carrie.

☙☙☙

Coming straight from the gym with his brother and nephews, Frank pulled into the driveway of Sam's house and drove toward the garage. He beat her home. For the first time, he felt content. He was adjusting to the fact that he had family, a brother and nephews. He couldn't wait to tell Jen's parents and Frankie. His little guy would be so happy to have cousins. The energy from his workout with Carl was still riveting through him. So in tune with his body, he felt the blood running through his arteries. He put his hands into a fist and pumped his biceps. He was still pumped-up for Sam. She'd lust over him tonight, that was for sure. And coming home from the club, in her usual state of arousal, he'd lust over her. He sat behind the wheel, smiling. He shut the engine, and after a few moments, he realized he was getting cold.

He got out of the car, jogged to the front of the driveway, and vaulted up the stoop confronted with boxes.

More boxes from those at home shopping channels.

On closer inspection, there were two from Manhattan department stores.

Damn it, Sam. This has to stop. Carrie had a gambling addiction, but I'll tell you, princess, you're not far behind.

Sam drove into the driveway. She flashed her brights onto him, and Frank squinted shielding his eyes with his hand. She shut off the engine and got out of the car.

She had to see the boxes, and then Frank's sour expression. "Oops."

She wrapped her arms around his waist. He definitely knew it was to avoid his wrath. He pushed her arms away and picked up the boxes. He lifted them to be in front of her eyes. "Again? More?"

She ignored him, bolted up the stairs, unlocked the door, ran into the living room, and up the thirteen steps to the bedroom. He dropped the boxes on the couch—so carelessly, one fell onto the carpet. He left it and chased after her.

Reaching her bed, Frank looked down at her with a wide grin. All Sam could do was laugh. "What's so funny?"

"It's just not your business," Sam said, and then she removed her outer clothing. Still in the bustier, she plopped down on the bed.

"You're going to get it, now." He pulled off his bubble jacket, tossed it to the ground. "Tell me what happened tonight, and then, then we talk about you and those damn boxes." He tore off his sweatshirt, slipped out of his jeans, and lay down on top her, covering her entire body. She moaned in contentment. He grabbed Sam's arms and held them above her head. As he pecked her neck with moist kisses, he whispered in her ear. "Tell me about club and Slater. I'm dying to ask you how Brett reacted to you, but I really don't give a shit."

"Oh, Frank."

He rolled off her onto his side, resting his left arm across her stomach.

"You don't give a shit?"

"Nope." With two fingers, he untied the lace bow at the

bust-line of her outfit. He pulled the laces open as if it was a shoe—but more slowly, with one string coming out of the holes one-by-one. With the metal tip, he tickled her breast as he swirled the tip all round it. Sam giggled. "I guess Slater was a no-show, right?" He then did the same thing with the other lace.

"How did you know?"

"I'm pretty sure you or Brett would have texted me and at the very least, I would have gotten a call from you. So what did happen?"

"Not much in the club. The madame, though, was very cooperative. We spent a long time in her office. She's coming in tomorrow with the schedules. Get this, Slater had appointments set up and he missed three tonight."

"Slater takes appointments?"

"Um, um."

"For what?"

She smiled coyly. "Bondage, with ropes."

"Ah, that's something we haven't tried, yet."

She gave him a seductive smile. "No. We haven't."

"We will. I wonder if Carrie had appointments with him."

"Madame said she didn't. Carrie may not have seen him at the club. It's huge. Could be though that he saw her. Now Brett was dumb enough to talk too much, but even if Carrie knew Slater from the club, she wouldn't have told him her real name, or what she did for a living. I know that for a fact. Even Charlie didn't know her real name until they began dating." Sam paused in reflection. "I've been thinking about this, Frank. Slater changed his MO with Carrie. He didn't wash her body down. He also waited a year since his last kill. What if the relationship with Carrie was supposed to be a good one, but she said something that triggered him? All of the women at the casino loved sex with him. They didn't say anything to get him nuts. And no woman was ever hurt."

"Okay. So we're looking for a trigger word." He used

both hands to pull down the cups on Sam's bustier and bring the garment down past her waist. Her phone popped out and fell to the carpet. He laughed. "And now *my* triggers are staring me right in my face." Frank nuzzled his face between her boobs and kissed her with his lips going from her neck to her belly button, following his hands lowering the outfit past her pelvis.

"Ohhh. What about the boxes?"

"To hell with the boxes, for tonight. I love you, Princess."

CHAPTER 22

At ten a.m., after a pleasure filled night, Sam and Frank joined the Skorpios task-force—Brett Case, Bella Richards, Lex Withers, Lieutenant Hicks, who sat around the conference table in the war room of the Queens precinct.

Lieutenant Hicks accosted her as soon as she made herself comfortable in her seat. "Where is your report from the club, Detective Wright?"

"I emailed it to you this morning, sir."

"Save us the time to read it, Wright," Withers demanded.

"Bottom line, Slater wasn't there. Agent Case called in units to be on the lookout at casinos up and down the east coast." She pulled copies of her report from her tote. "Here, I took the liberty of bringing in copies for everyone," she said as she distributed them.

They read the two-page single-spaced document in silence.

"Very thorough, as usual, Detective."

"Thank you, Lieutenant."

"He hasn't gone north, yet," Agent Case added. "There are under-covers in place in the casinos, twenty-four seven. If there's a spotting, we'll be contacted ASAP."

"I want to go in," Sam replied without missing a beat. Case glared at her. "Okay, jurisdiction, I get it. If he goes to back to Queens. Madame Lily told us he has schedules. Only last night he wasn't there. Maybe he has schedules for the casinos, too. Oooh! For the previous murders, were there clubs in the same vicinities as the casinos? And did the victims frequent them? Has that been his MO for the past nine years?"

Lex groaned. "Valid point, Sam. Definitely worth the correlation. I owe ya, again."

Brett nodded. "Very, good. That could help us a lot with the victimology profiling. I'll send requests to the out-of-state teams."

"So, if he does in fact return to Queens, it's settled that I go in, correct?"

"Like hell you will!" Frank responded the loudest anyone had ever heard him speak. "We have enough to grab him without a set up. This guy's way too big for you. And in an angry state, the only thing that will stop him is a bullet. And I'd prefer it wasn't yours."

The lieutenant put up a hand to stop him. "Knock it off, Dr. Khaos. It's not your call. She may have to go in. He only goes after Caucasian women, so that eliminates Bella."

"Then let Agent Case get a woman from his office."

"Frank, we have enough people on this case already. I told you that. If we need a decoy, it's Sam. End of story. Believe me, she can handle herself."

"Then I go with her as her tail."

Case blew out a nasal breath. "Frank, be realistic. If he sees you, he'll be thinking he's seeing double. Right away, he'll know it's a set up. He'll go into hiding, immediately. We can't endanger civilians if it's at the casino or in any other public place. Not what we want." He pursed his lips as if he had an idea. "The manager you met at the casino, Mike Sheffield, he'll work with us—uh—we'll convince him to work with us. We'll have him put in a call to Slater that something is wrong, maybe the refrigeration system, and he has to come in to deal with the servicemen. That they're complaining the warranty isn't paid for, or something like that."

"That would work," Sam said. "To the CEO of a restaurant, the refrigeration is the most important thing."

"Let's do it. Put in a call to Sheffield," Frank said. "Worse come to worse, I'll go, confront him. I can take him."

"You'll do no such thing, Khaos." Hicks glared at him. "Calm it down." The lieutenant paused. "Or I'll remove you from this case and have Trenton take over."

Frank swallowed hard, but he did take it down a notch. "Okay, hear me out, please. If we get him to come to the casino, why don't you just arrest him, right there and then? I still don't get it. The FBI is skilled in non-violent takedowns."

Case looked as if he was fuming. "Okay, I'll explain more fully. One, it's not as simple as an arrest. We need more information. Finding his primary residence is of utmost importance, especially with a serial killer. The information we can attain can put all of the murders to rest. If we just bring him in, he'll clam up. I know you're concerned, Frank, and you're asking, 'Why Sam?' Here's why. She's familiar with the casino. She knows where Carrie would go. And more importantly, she's as maternal as Slater is paternal. Sam is the perfect one to do this. Now relax."

Frank got up and went toward the window. Looking out, he mumbled, "I'll try."

Case opened a file. "I'll dial, but you talk to him, Frank. He's also a therapist, so he'll get it."

Frank turned around. "Hold on. I got it." He pulled out a card from his wallet. The others stared at him. "What? He offered me therapy for the DNA thing." He handed the card to Brett and took his seat.

Brett dialed with the phone on speaker. Sheffield answered on the second ring.

"Hello, Sheffield, here."

"Mike, it's Frank Khaos. I'm sitting here with my team. We're on speaker."

"Sure, what's going on?"

"Are you alone?"

"I'm not, actually."

"Make yourself alone, right now."

"What do you need?"

"Privacy."

"Hold on a minute. I'll tell my employee to leave. All right, Dylan, we'll talk about this later."

The sound of feet shuffling spread on the carpet and then a door slammed.

"Now's not a good time for that, Dr. Khaos."

Frank compressed his lips and the team exchanged glances. "When's a good time to talk?" Frank mouthed to the team. "He's not alone."

They nodded in the affirmative.

"Not until tomorrow. Got to run. Meetings all night."

"No can do," Frank insisted. "This is an urgent case. We need to talk with you now."

"I'm under no obligation to talk to you."

"What happened to 'call me if you need me'?"

"That pertained to you. The familial DNA thing."

"What did you find yourself involved in, Sheffield?"

The phone disconnected with a click. The team looked at each other as if an epiphany hit.

Sam got a jolt in her stomach from Dara, though she didn't need her. "I just got a creepy feeling that Slater was with him. Those footsteps sounded heavy."

"Me, too," Brett said. "And I'm not psychic."

"Go on, Brett," Frank said.

"At the strip club Madam Lily seemed pretty open to talk to us. Except for one thing. She said she didn't have real names, and I'm guessing that included phone numbers, too. But, I don't buy that for a millisecond. What if she knew Slater and Sheffield played together? And she knew that and called Sheffield? Maybe not to warn him. That would make her an accessory. But to make sure there were no repercussions to her and her club. That was her utmost priority."

"We could be onto something there." Sam's breath hitched. "Remember when I came out and asked Sheffield if he and Slater were in a sexual relationship? He damn near froze until we told him we couldn't care about that. What if, and it's a stretch, what if Sheffield was in on it? What if he cleared the way for Slater to have free rein? Set up the meets, maybe tagged women Slater would want." Sam smacked the desk with her palm. "Oh, no! Remember I said at our initial meeting that something was strange? I didn't know how Slater would have ammonia to clean the bodies, especially if Slater didn't have a room. It could be that Sheffield kept all of the supplies in his office and Slater would have access. That's something else to check. Lex, please get warrants to search Sheffield's office and all of the managers in all of the casinos in which murders took place. Maybe Slater had other managers on his bankroll, too. And if Sheffield and Slater are connected, I bet Sheffield told him the night we were there." Sam paused. "Yes! That could be the reason Slater skipped the club. He's laying low."

"Sam, that's a big what if, with capitals. And that doesn't give us probable cause," Withers added. "But we could find out how many casinos Sheffield works in, if he travels. And coordinate the dates. We may have that information already." He pulled out the third folder from a pile. Our lab guys put together these charts. Okay, Slater stays three to five days in all the casinos, work related. None of the seventeen murders took place on any of the workdays." He paused. "Hold on. He did have a room on the day Miss Baines was murdered. Another change in his MO. And there was no Mike Sheffield on any of the employee rosters for any other casinos."

"That doesn't mean he didn't accompany Slater." Sam paused a moment. "Ugh. He could have used aliases. We need to check dates that Sheffield wasn't at work. If he took vacations."

"And what are we basing this on, Sam?"

"Nothing. We can be totally on the wrong track. We need to bring in Sheffield for questioning. As soon as possible. If he is involved and heard from the madame, he might skip."

"Give me a minute." On his smartphone, Withers Googled the casino's main phone number. He dialed on the desk phone. A receptionist answered. "Yes, please connect me to Mike Sheffield's office...Yes, his secretary would be fine. I just have to change an appointment with him...Yes, I'll hold...Hello...Yes, I'd like to speak to Mr. Sheffield, please...Oh, he left for the day?" The team exchanged dubious looks. "Earlier than expected?...This is Leroy Johnson...A business associate gave me his number...Who? Henry Slater...Just missed *them?* Oh, crap. Okay, please leave a note for Mike that I called. I'll catch up with them at home. Thank you." He disconnected. "Well, I'll be. Okay, Sam, we now have probable cause."

Frank punched the folder in front of him, deliberately and fast. "Sheffield wrote his address down in our interview with him. Get a unit out to his apartment."

"Okay, let our officers take care of this," Lieutenant Hicks said.

ⱷↄⱸↄ

It was noon and cloudy when Abby turned the corner onto the block of her apartment building which stood between two mid-high buildings in a middle-income neighborhood. The sight of police cars parked at the front entrance shot a jolt of anxiety through her. Shit. They must have found her apartment. Crap, how did they do that? Damn, she knew how. The two dimwits that she used in her last heist ratted her out. Had to be. She'd get Selena and Kit but good, in time. Even if they were in jail, her connections on the inside would do whatever she wanted.

She couldn't drive down the block because police cars

were stopping everyone for searches. And she couldn't back up, either. Cars were behind her. This was no good. Residing in a lowlife prison for years was not on her bucket list. Even though she'd block the street, she only thought of one option. Run. She put the Accord in park, shut the engine, bolted out of the car, tossing her tote over her shoulder. She ran down the block she had just driven down, leaving cars beeping their horns. Another not good. The cops would find plenty of evidence in her car. Screwed wasn't a strong enough word.

She thanked God that she was at least wearing sneakers. She was actually happy she was in track and field before she dropped out of High School. Ugh, school. That thought always nauseated her. Running always allowed her to think. Usually, it would be to plot more heists. She did her best planning during a run. Too bad the last one got all fucked up. That said a lot about her planning. Shit. This time, she thought of her past. What the heck was she thinking of that for?

Abby made it two blocks. It was a one-way street with cars going in the opposite direction. Police cars couldn't go up the street. There'd be no room for them to pass. There wasn't time for them to block it off. She felt free, but where would she go? Thinking about the last heist, the realization hit. Even with Selena and Kit busted, they didn't know about her apartment. Who did? Wait a minute. Wait a fucking minute. They knew about the restaurant they always met in. And the cunt waitresses who used to be in her crew probably told the cops her address. Had to be. She'd be sending that Stephanie Samuels and Callie Furgerson venomous thoughts tonight. Lesson learned. From now on, no one was allowed out of her crew. If they want out, they have to disappear—permanently. She'd had never resorted to murder, or even that much violence, until the last heist. Maybe she was more on edge than usual. Maybe because she had two newbies whom she didn't know if she could trust.

Surprise. Surprise. She couldn't.

Okay, she had to revisit her plans. But, nah, murder for some reason didn't sit well with her. Actually, the thought of taking someone's life terrified her.

She loved the thrill of robbing houses—the thrill of violating someone's property—those who had happy homes. Unlike hers, since her mom died. But she couldn't blame the death of her mom. She did blame her domineering dad who worked more than spent time with her. He doted on her brothers, but her? He probably hated all women since Mom died. He always walked around more pissed than grieving. Plus, she was a constant reminder of her mom. The two of them could pass for sisters. Well, that was pushing it. But, close enough.

She was about a half a mile away now. Abby slowed down and jogged in place. She was always in oblivion when she ran. Looking around grounded her. Okay, she was near the park entrance. She's been here often enough. Without scaling over the five-foot-high stone barricade and running through the massive field to the other side—especially since she couldn't see what awaited her there because of the sloping terrain—she continued to run around the perimeter of the park to a corner where there were stores she frequented. Another not good. She'd be recognized in a millisecond. Abby continued around to the opposite side of the park where there was a yellow taxi stand. She opened the door to the first one in line and jumped in the back seat.

"Yonkers. Colonial Heights."

"Yes, ma'am."

Yonkers. Yonkers? Why the hell would she think of going there? That's where she used to live—before she dumped her dad and dumbass brothers. She had absolutely no intention of going to her house. She wouldn't give the successful Carl Glendale the satisfaction. At the disowning hearing, he did nothing but denigrate her. *'Yeah sure, you could make it on your own. I give you less than a year to come crawling back.'* Well, it had been three years, and she still had no intention of crawling back. She figured she'd stay at a local motel. The cops wouldn't look for her so close to where she was raised. She hadn't stepped foot in Yonkers since the emancipation. Hopefully, there would be new store owners and she wouldn't be recognized. A thought hit her. She'd have to remove her nose and lip piercings. 'Low key' would be her new profile.

The drive was eighteen minutes. Before arriving at the avenue, she pulled out the piercings as inconspicuously as possible by slouching down in the seat and pulling her hood over her head. She pretended to be dozing.

The cabbie startled her. "Miss, what intersection?"

She pretended to waken and she looked out the window. "About ten blocks down. Hurry up. I'm exhausted."

He laughed. "Why is a young person like you so exhausted for?"

"Just worked a double shift and my boss is a dick."

The cabbie said nothing, just smirked.

She'd walk to the motel when she got out of the cab. He pulled over to the curb. Abby looked at the meter. Thirty-five bucks. Shit. These cabs sure knew how to rob you. Ah what the fuck? She'd do what she had to. Thank God, she carried enough cash on her from hocking some jewelry from a past heist. She liked to hold onto stuff for six months at least so the property wasn't so hot. She pulled a fifty out of her wallet and handed it to the cabbie. She exited the cab without saying 'thank you.' The less she spoke, the less he'd remember her. Yep. She had all her bases covered.

Abby waited until the cabbie pulled away from the curb. She crossed the street and walked the two blocks to the shabby motel. After scanning the lobby for anything suspicious, even though she had no idea what that would be, she approached the desk and asked for a room. They had one. She paid for three days in advance. That would give her time to think. She had enough cash on her to buy food, and to go shopping for a change of clothes.

In her room, she plopped down on the bed. She took out her cell phone and checked her email. As there was a knock on the door, a thought hit her. She had location services on.

She didn't respond to the knock. She snuck to the wall in the far corner of the room—the one with the door attaching to the adjoining room. She tugged on the doorknob. Locked tight.

"Open the door, Miss Ruthe. It's the police."

"Fuck off."

"It's over, Miss Ruthe. We have the key."

"Then fucking use it, douche bags."

Three patrol officers opened the door with guns drawn and pointed at her.

Abby froze.

ভৈভৈ

John Trenton and Detective Monty Smith peered through the one-way mirror. Abby paced back and forth the length of the interrogation room. John glanced up at the clock. Three p.m. She focused on a one-inch-in-diameter patch of peeling paint on the wall opposite to where she stood. Almost in a trance, she strolled over to the wall and with her fingernail on her index finger picked at the piece of plaster. A larger piece fell to the floor, and she watched as in slow motion as the plaster dropped to in front of her toe. She laughed, and then continued to pick at the wall. The original one-inch spot spread to about four inches. Abby turned her head from side to side and into different angles to admire her work.

"Something a four-year old would do." John reached for the doorknob. "Her intent is telling. She's fairly behind in emotional maturity. Bringing in her dad?"

"No, Doc. She's emancipated. Legally he doesn't have to be involved. She's the one who initiated it. And she's over twenty-one, anyway. I just don't get these kids. They have a warm home, siblings, and one parent. And that's not good enough for them. Ready to go in and talk to Miss Ruthe?"

"Sure."

They opened the door and entered.

Abby looked up at them with a smirk. "I'm not talking to either of you. Get lost."

"Don't even want an introduction?" Smith asked.

"Get—the—fuck—lost."

"No can do," John interjected as he took off his coat and sat at the conference table. "Come on, Abby, sit down." She stared blankly at him. "I'm Doctor John Trenton."

She turned toward him. "I'm not sick. I don't need a doctor. It's hot as hell in here." She took off her sweatshirt, and sat down.

John's gaze went from the scorpion tat on her neck down to the tats on her arms. "I'm a forensic psychiatrist. I work with the New York City Police Department."

"Then what the fuck are you doing up here?"

"The headquarters' captain permitted it. Besides, it was my house you and you friends were caught busting in to."

"So? Victims aren't allowed in interrogations."

John curled his lips in approval. "You know that, how?"

"I study things."

"You could be putting your knowledge to better use, though. You're wanted in ten home invasions in Westchester. How long did you think you could keep going in the same area?"

She shrugged. "I guess it's time to move then, isn't it?"

"You'll be moving, all right, to an upstate prison," Smith said matter-of-factly. "Do you want to call your dad? We've been speaking with him. I had to let you know that."

"No! Don't you dare bring that scumbag in here. If I never see him again, it'll be too soon."

John moved back in his seat. "Why so hostile?"

"Don't you dare go there, shrink. I've been to plenty since my mom died. You all do shit."

"Well, at a time in your life like this, family can be very important to have around."

"I don't need any family. I have my girls. They're my family."

John uncrossed his legs and sat up in a more professional posture. "Your girls?"

She nodded with a smug look on her face. "Yeah, my crew. No matter where the fuck you put me, they'll be there to break me out." Abby slumped into the chair. "And that Kit and Selena, you better protect them, real good."

Detective Smith leaned forward in his seat. "Care to explain that?"

Abby must have read his intent. "No. I want a lawyer."

John shot Smith a glance. "Okay. Who do you want to call?"

"Just get me a damn phonebook."

CHAPTER 23

As they walked down the corridor, Frank's cell rang. "Hey, John. By the way, Lieutenant Hicks threatened to remove me from the Baines case if I became overzealous. Not something I'd want."

"Oh, yeah?" John chuckled. "Rojas told me the same thing if I had gotten too involved in the Mitchell case. Glad he didn't have to do it. We're pretty much done. Where are you headed to now?"

"Going through the case files with the team. Why?"

"Want to make a pit stop in Scarsdale?"

Frank moaned. "Not really. Why?"

"Abby Ruthe was picked up. She's being less than cooperative. I'll tell you, she's tough, street tough, talks about her girls."

"As in gang?"

"Exactly. I think she'd relate better to you, than to me and Monty Smith. And definitely better than to her dad. She doesn't want to see him, at all. She's got some deep rooted anger. Doesn't make sense. He seems like a together guy."

"He is. The boys are pampered, not as strong as they should be for their age, and he works a lot. But join the club on that one."

"So how about it? She'll be in a holding cell tonight and can't call a lawyer till tomorrow. I have no qualms about interrupting her beauty sleep. And you and Sam can stay at our house tonight. Frankie covered?"

"Yep. At his grandparents. I'll ask Sam. We should be good. Always have a change of clothes in the trunk. We'll be out of here in about an hour."

∽∾∽

Abby ravenously ate the burger, fries, and soda that John had brought her. Based on what the waitress told the cops, Abby could eat with a bottomless pit. John even remembered the five-layer chocolate cake. Too bad, she'd have to hold it all down. At about five-five, she was maybe a hundred thirty, tops. Most women would balloon up with that much food, unless they had bulimia.

John had a feeling she wouldn't want to regurgitate in front of him. He sat opposite her with his right leg on his left thigh. He leaned back in his seat in a relaxed posture. "How are you feeling Abby? You downed quite a bit of food. Always eat like that?"

"Yeah. So? I burn it off."

"How?"

"I run. Ran about four miles today. And I haven't eaten anything. Usually I can run eight."

"This is the first time you're eating today?" John checked his watch. "At six o'clock? That's not good for you."

"Stop the fucking lecture. You sound like my bastard father."

"I'm not lecturing. I just made a statement. Ever had your blood glucose level checked?"

"No." She sent him a glare of death. "I'm not interested in listening to any of your statements. Why can't you just get out of her and leave me alone?"

"Nah, I'll hang out here. I'm waiting for someone."

"Yeah. Who?"

"A colleague."

"I get it. Don't expect me to talk to anyone else. Not happening." She swallowed hard and put her hand up to her throat. "I need to go to the ladies room."

"Feeling that you overate a little?"

"Yeah, I do that, sometimes. The food gets stuck. I gotta get outta here, unless you want me to shit in my pants or throw up on the floor."

"We know you're bulimic."

"What the fuck is that?"

"Eat and then throw up."

"Yeah, my mom did it. Another reason my dad hates me. Call someone, please."

John sat back and pressed the intercom on the phone on the desk. No need to make the girl suffer and you couldn't stop bulimic behavior on the spot. She'd need some intense counseling for that to happen. "Miss Ruthe needs to use the rest room, like now." He turned back to Abby. "Did your dad ever take your mom, or you, to a doctor?"

"She refused." Abby grabbed her throat." I can't talk." She gagged.

It was as though ten minutes passed when a female officer strolled in. John looked at his watch and hiked his brow.

She ignored him. "Come on, Miss Ruthe."

"Give her privacy in the ladies room, please."

The officer smirked. Abby got up, holding her stomach, and, at the door, leaned over and purged in the hallway—her vomit, splashing on the officer's shoes and uniform.

John looked away.

∽∾∽

Anger stewed within Sam from Frank's off-handed comment to John when he didn't think she'd heard. '*I'm not having another child*' kept reverberating in her brain and sent chills through her body whenever she recalled the words. She sat with her hands folded in her lap in the passenger seat of Frank's Explorer on the drive up to Scarsdale. Should she confront him or not? Frank was going through his own personal hell right now. How could she impinge her feelings on him when he couldn't think straight? No, now was not the time. She loved the man with all her heart. That meant respect. She looked toward him as he kept his gaze straight on the traffic ahead. She reached over and put her palm on his forearm. He glanced over and smiled. Taking his left hand off the steering wheel, he patted her hand with his.

Frank understood her. He got the message that Sam was giving him space. They were so in-sync with each other—not only in the bedroom. Their unspoken language didn't need an interpreter.

"I'm sorry, Sam."

"About?"

"Come on. You know what about."

"I certainly do. Did you mean it?"

Frank compressed his lips. "I don't know what I mean right now, Sam. Every time I think of the possibility of bringing a psychopath into the world, I cringe. To knowingly do something that can be harmful...well, that's just not me."

"John said his behavior could have had environmental causes."

"We can't know for sure until there's a CAT scan and PET of Slater's brain. Then we'll see if there's frontal lobe damage."

"Um, would you want to go through those tests to eliminate you?"

"Me? I don't have damage. You mean genetic testing. For sure, insurance wouldn't cover it just on a whim. When we get to that point, a genetic or fertility specialist could make a referral, but I'm guessing on that one, too. And results are inconclusive anyway."

Surprised, a shot of adrenaline rushed through her. "Are we going to get to that point?"

"Yeah. Eventually."

"In this decade?"

"Come on, Sam. Let's wrap this crap up first." Sam pouted and he shook his head. "But I am thinking about it, a lot."

"Oh, yeah? And what might those thoughts be?"

He hesitated. "If push comes to shove, uh, would you be willing to adopt? A newborn? Or a toddler?"

"Yes, Frank. Yes," Sam responded teary-eyed.

∽∾∽

Frank and Sam held hands as they walked down the hall to the visitors lounge in the Scarsdale headquarters to where John told them to meet him. Frank opened the door for Sam to go in first. They saw John at a desk with an open file in front of him and detective Monty Smith seated in a chair next to the desk.

"Don't you ever rest, Trenton? And you even shaved?" Frank teased.

"I rest plenty. Right now, this young woman is in trouble, so no rest."

"And I thought he was bad," Sam said, pointing a finger toward Frank.

"Knock it off, Sam. What's going on?"

They sat on the couch and John spun around in the chair to face them. "Abby is disgruntled, angry at her mom for dying, angry at her dad for ignoring her."

"Hold on, that's the usual teenage crap."

"She's an adult."

"Big deal, twenty-one. Does she know right from wrong?"

"That's what I want you to decide on when you talk to her."

"You deal with the same age group as me. So why me?"

"Number one, my patients are diagnosed with schizophrenia and psychosis. She's far from that. Two, most importantly, she's your niece. Make a dent in her to see if she has any signs of remorse. Convince her to want to see her dad and brothers."

"Let me get this straight. You want me to convince her to want to do something I wouldn't want to do? I wasn't so thrilled to meet my brother, if you recall, and I definitely don't want to meet my birth parents."

Sam nudged him. "But you're glad you did, aren't you? You came home so excited you had a family."

Frank shot her a hard stare. "But I sure as hell know that I don't want to meet Slater, and my parents are out of the equation. I'm not interested in either of their stories. When we get him, I'm done."

"Actually, you're not," John stated matter-of-factly.

"Excuse me?"

"You're the profiler on this case. Did you forget that?"

Frank slumped into the couch, and slid his hands over his unshaven cheeks. "With all the shit that's going on, I guess I did."

"If we bring him into custody, you're going to conduct the interview—"

"Yes. I know. Got it."

"If it gets too crazy for you to handle, and it can under the circumstances, Lieutenant Hicks will bring me in, and I'm happy to do it. Just be honest with us, Frank. This is a rough one. Maybe, in this case, they'll let you recuse yourself."

"Thanks, John. I appreciate it. Let's go meet Abby."

"Okay." Smith leaned in. "She did ask for a lawyer, but you're family."

"Got it. Another reason you want me to talk to her."

Smith picked up the phone on the desk. "Please bring Miss Ruthe into the conference room."

ↁↁↁ

Abby could hardly keep her eyes open as two female guards escorted her into the interview room where Frank was waiting. She blinked repeatedly after laying her gaze on him.

"Hi, Abby. Sorry if I woke you but this was the time I could come up to see you." He studied the tats on her forearms that the short-sleeved top didn't cover.

Still staring at him, she slid into the seat opposite him. "I asked for an attorney, so I'm not speaking to anyone."

"We're not talking about your case."

"Bullshit. Who are you?"

"Take a look at me. Haven't a clue?"

She looked down at her hands on her lap.

"Don't bullshit me," he continued. "What are you thinking?"

She looked up, startled, he guessed, by his language. "You resemble my dad, you're bigger, but I don't know how. He doesn't have a brother, and there's no cousin I know who looks like him."

"Well, I didn't think I had a brother either, or two nephews and a niece."

"Uh?"

Frank unzipped his sweatshirt jacket and slid his arms out. Abby's eyes bugged out when she looked at his tats. "I'm working on a case for the NYPD. They found out I have a brother, and a niece who were in the system for crimes they had committed. The niece is you and that led us to your dad. So I was reunited with one of my brothers. My second brother who's wanted by the police is still out there." Frank remained silent for it to sink in.

Abby swallowed hard. "My dad always told me he's an only child. That's why he wanted us to have siblings."

"He didn't know, either."

"How can that be?"

"Well, our biological parents placed us for adoption at birth. Your grandparents adopted your dad immediately. I wasn't so lucky until I was ten."

"Grandma and Grandpa never told us anything."

"No, they didn't. Your dad found out before your grandpa died and he was going through the family papers."

"Where were you until you were ten?"

"In foster homes. Then I was finally adopted. I'll tell you, I was a pain in the ass kid. I was constantly in trouble."

"What did your brother who's wanted by the police do?"

"Some pretty gruesome stuff. He murdered seventeen women." He paused watching for its effect on Abby.

She looked at him with her mouth agape.

Frank took a wild guess that this was the first time Abby ever had a speechless moment. "He strangled them. In bed, pretending to want sex."

"No shit! I can't believe you told me that!"

"I'm totally honest, all the time. Deal with it. You mean to tell me you've never had sex?"

"That's none of your fucking business! My dad would never have said that."

"What would he have said?"

"Not that way. He made everything seem like, uh, you know, sugarcoated. Even when my mom got sick. It wasn't until close to the end that we found out. I'm pissed at him for not telling us. We had no time to prepare ourselves. We have feelings, too."

"I understand that."

"What do you do with the NYPD? And what's your name, anyway?"

"I'm Frank Khaos. I work in the capacity that Dr. Trenton does. I'm a forensic psychiatrist."

"You work with kids?"

"Yes, and young adults who've made some poor decisions."

"Yeah, like me."

He nodded. "We can't talk about your case until you have an attorney, and I'd be happy to talk to you about everything then, and I will, but we can talk about your emancipation. That okay?"

"Yeah."

"Why did you want it?"

"You met my dad, right?" Frank nodded. "And you can't tell?" she asked.

"He seems like a hard working guy to me. He and your brothers worked out with me in my gym."

Her eyes lit up. "You have a gym?"

"Yes, a Mixed Martial Arts gym in Harlem."

She nearly jumped up out of her seat. "No shit! I love MMA! I was trying for years to get my dad to pay for lessons for Muay Thai. He said it's not for a refined young lady. Now, not in a million years, could I pass as refined? The only thing he'd let me take is track and field. Oh, my God! Can I go with you? I know how to use everything, the heavy bag, the rope climbing, all the moves. I do mock amateur fights in my gym in a cage. Please, please?"

೧൭೧

John, Smith, and Sam observed through the one-way mirror in the adjoining room. Sam was happy her man made a dent in Abby. She'd hadn't seen him in a one-on-one spontaneous interview. It confirmed to her what a great dad he was.

"Carl was right," John confirmed. "Abby is a better fit to be Frank's daughter than he is."

"Well, you can't change that, John, but maybe Frank can show him how to loosen up and get his daughter back," Sam said.

Smith shook his head. "Don't forget that she has a long list of felonies on her, mandating jail time. And I doubt if a judge would even grant her bail. She has enough money to run."

ো৵৵

Frank bellowed laughter. "Well, I now know what would make you wake up in the morning and have a purpose. How are you learning all this?"

"I pay for it on my own. It's damn expensive, as you know."

"Yes. It is. So, you're telling me that you wanted the emancipation because your dad wouldn't let you have Muay Thai lessons? That's an extreme reaction, isn't it?"

"It wasn't only that. He was so restrictive on what I could do. I was almost eighteen and he drilled me on everything. I had no privacy. He wanted me to ask permission to go out at night. He blew up if I pulled an all-nighter. I never came back pregnant. I never had to get an abortion. I never came home drugged or drunk. Seesh. Then he got real pissed. I stole condoms from his dresser drawer. I don't know why he got his balls in an uproar for. He never used them, with my mom anyway. I told him I wanted out and I wanted to be on my own. He told me that he'd do one better. I could divorce my parents. One of his friend's sons did it. He's the one who told me about emancipation. I don't think he thought I'd take him seriously. I called his bluff on everything. He should have known. So he wanted it as much as me."

Frank's expression must have showed shock to Abby.

"That, my dork of a father didn't tell you, did he?"

"No, he didn't, but I sure as hell will speak to him. Hold on a second. When we study MMA we learn balance and how to respect our mind and body, correct?" She sniffled and nodded. "So where does the bulimia come in? That's definitely contrary to bodily respect."

"I've tried to stop. But I can't. I've been doing it since I was about three. I watched my mom put her fingers down her throat then I'd do it." Frank widened his eyes. "Sick, right? And she kept the secret from my dad. Now, I can't stop, no matter how many meditations I do."

"Would you be willing to go into treatment?"

"Yes. Can that be instead of jail?"

"Can't talk about that."

"When am I getting the fuck out of here?"

"That I can't answer."

She folded her arms across her chest. "Then I'm done."

Frank began to rise from the chair. "Okay, bye, Abby." He got up and turned toward the door.

"No! Wait!"

"Yes?"

"You're my uncle, right?" He nodded. "Can you get me released to your custody?"

Detective Smith and John entered the room. "Sorry, Miss Ruthe, it doesn't work that way. Unless your attorney can pull a miracle out of a bag."

"What if I return everything? What if I tell you everything? My partners, my sources, my, uh, fences. I'm sick with bulimia. Can't you use that as an excuse?"

Smith put his hand up to stop her. "Miss Ruthe, we have to take one step at a time. Please stop talking. You don't want any of your rights compromised. You'll tell your attorney everything, and I'll do what I can to make sure you're afforded that time. Okay?"

Holding back tears, Abby merely nodded.

Smith pressed the intercom obviously saddened by this young woman. "Please come in and escort Miss Ruthe back to her cell."

The three men left the room, all with solemn expressions.

CHAPTER 24

Mike Sheffield sat with his hands folded in his lap and his stagnant gaze forward in a black wood straight-back armless chair in front of a wall mirror—with his back to the mirror—in the bedroom of his multi-million dollar condo on the Upper West Side of Manhattan. The building, erected in the early 1960s stood twenty-six stories. Sheffield's apartment took up part of the twenty-fourth floor.

His dominant—Henry Slater—stood in front of him. "Good boy. Don't move." There wasn't any action or verbal response. Henry turned his back and took a few steps toward Mike's dresser that Henry designed in an extra-long dark cherry wood. Its expanse took up eight feet of the adjacent wall. Henry pulled open the center drawer that ran from the top to the bottom of the dresser. Lying there were the ropes he wanted. He pulled out a twenty-five foot silk rope like the one he used for tying women at Strident. He ran it over the palm of his hand, and then brought it over to Mike who still kept his eyes forward. Henry slid the rope over Mike's cheek. "Like that Mike? Nice and soft on your skin, right?"

"Yes, sir."

Henry let out a vulgar laugh. "Well, not tonight." He dragged the rope across the back of the chair before he grasped it in one hand with his fist clenching it. Going to the dresser drawer, he pulled out a one-hundred-foot long, one-inch in diameter hemp rope and put the silk rope back into its place. He stood with his legs straddled over Mike holding the rope in both hands. Slater grasped the thick rubber ball at one end of the rope in his left palm as he let the rope hang loose with his right. He twirled the rope in front of Sheffield's face—as one would do playing jump rope—but with a smaller radius.

Sheffield knew what to do. Stay still, quiet, and let his dominant control him. That had been his role for the past nine years—in complete trust. Slater smiled at the stillness. Sheffield didn't react.

Both men were bare-chested and wore black skimpy briefs. Slater looked up at the full-length mirror on the wall behind the chair. Man-oh-man, does Mike need to get into the gym. His back muscles sure needed more development and he needed a waxing. Then again, he was a smaller built man than he was. Slater pursed his lips. Yeah, Mike was at least a hundred pounds less than him and a good foot shorter. He had a plan for tonight. He'd keep it a surprise. Sheffield loved surprises, but Slater saw the guy getting a little nervous in the quiet. Beads of perspiration formed on his forehead.

"What's the matter?"

"Nothing, sir."

Slater moved the rope he held in between his hands to the front of Mike's neck, then millimeter by millimeter drove it up his neck and over his squared chin, up to his once broken nose, and paused when the rope reached his blue eyes. Slater held it there. For a moment, Mike closed his eyes. After a kick in his stomach from Slater's knee, he got the reprimand and opened his eyes. The rope still lay across them. Slater then moved the rope up to Mike's full head of straight blond hair, and across the top of his head and around down to his neck, then shoulders. Slater brought the rubber ball side to the center of Mike's chest. Mike knew what to do. With his right hand, he reached up and grabbed onto the ball to keep it centered and right above his breastbone.

"Good boy." Slater looked to his right, to the California King bed. "Nice. I like those dark maroon sheets and blanket."

"Thank you, sir. I knew you did, sir. I am the good boy."

"Yes you are," Slater said. "Now you're going to tell me everything I ask for." He brought the rope over Mike's arms and around to his back. Slater didn't walk around him. He checked in the mirror to make the placement of the two layers lay close together pinning Mike to the back of the chair.

"Yes, sir."

"I know there's a lot you wanted to tell me on the way over here and I, like the good master I am, made you wait."

"Yes, sir."

When the rope made it to Mike's chest again, Slater twisted it around the ball in Mike's hand and brought the rope down. Mike propped his body up. Slater ran the rope under Mike's right thigh, adjusting the rope to fit snugly in his groin area. "What were you talking about to that guy on the phone? Who's Frank Khaos?" He jerked the rope hard in an upward movement. Mike grunted in pain. With his free hand, he clutched the edge of the chair. His knuckles turned white. Slater chuckled. "What the hell is familial DNA?"

"When someone the police is looking for isn't in the system, they expand the DNA search to family."

"I don't have any family."

"They're onto you, sir."

He tugged harder on the rope. "Who?"

"The police."

"How? I'm not in the system, as you said. They couldn't have even found my apartment."

"They sent a guy with a team to the casino, sir. I thought he was you. And so did everyone else."

"What?"

"Whether or not you want to believe it, you have a brother, sir. Frank Khaos."

Slater lost it. His brother found *him*? He literally felt his muscles expand. Taking less than thirty seconds, he pulled the rope around Mike's left shoulder, down to the center ball, wrapped the rope around it, then slid the rope down and under Mike's left leg, positioning it tightly in his groin area and up in the back. He pulled up hard—as if he was pulling up a hundred seventy pound weight in the gym.

Mike screamed in pain and then quickly lowered it to whimpers. He tried to stifle the noise. Mike grimaced compressing his lips with tears running down his cheeks from the corners of his eyes.

"Good boy. You keep in the scene."

Hyperventilating, Mike could hardly get the words out. "He's a shrink. You need to disappear, Henry. It's just a matter of time."

Slater moved the rope across Mike's body.

"We'll both go to prison for life, Henry, or worse."

"Nah, do you know how long it'll take them to find your other aliases? No way. They'll have to spend another decade tracking me. Relax."

While Slater walked behind him, still holding up the rope over Mike's left shoulder, he pulled a small patch out of his brief and removed the plastic binding. Adhering the sticky side to Mike's back, he slid the rope to the other side and then to front, encasing his submissive's neck. He put his palm on the man's shoulder until he felt the muscle relax from the sedative. He hated to use it, and usually didn't. He wanted his victims to feel the experience. But, Mike? Now, that guy was special to him. For nine years, they played together. For nine years, Mike gave him his complete abandon. "Yeah, well. I'll take care of it now, so you'll have nothing to worry about." Mike didn't seem to understand. He closed his eyes, almost dozing. A moment later, he actually fell asleep—damn him. Slater heard the snores. He pulled tightly on the rope, hard, harder, until there was a pop in Mike's trachea, strangling him. "Good boy. You stayed in the scene." Mike's head fell down limp over his neck.

Slater looked down at his friend he'd just murdered. He blew out a deep breath. "Ah, what the fuck? He knew the risk."

Slater sat down on the edge of the bed. He stared at the bold maroon and silver striped wallpaper that covered two walls. The wall behind the bed was a pearl gray paper. He decorated it for Mike—actually the entire apartment. He frowned that he wouldn't be visiting here anymore. He slipped into his jeans that lay folded neatly on the bed, pulled his sweater over his head, grabbed his jacket and holding it in his hand approached the door. He briefly turned toward his dead friend and smiled deviously. He closed the bedroom door.

෧෨෧

The night Sam and Frank planned to spend with the Trenton's was cut short by a two-minute phone call. They met outside the apartment building on the Upper West Side.

Brett Case led the entourage of Frank, Sam, Lex, and Bella down the hallway on the twenty-fourth floor of the luxury apartment complex. The walls were faux painted with golds, silvers and a splash of black interspersed within the spiral pattern. The marble floor matched, not only in color but also in design. Sam stared at the wall design mesmerized as the colors flowed around each apartment doorway and met on the opposite wall seamlessly.

Case stared at her. "Are you with me, Detective?"

She jolted. "Definitely. This is really nice."

"I couldn't live in it. Too closed in. Like a rabbit hole in Iraq." Frank squirmed. "At least he gave me his real address."

"True. Too bad he's dead," Sam said.

Frank paused for a moment. "Maybe he knew the end was near."

Two, male, uniformed officers met them at the doorway. Case showed his badge. "Well, are you just going to stand there? What have you got?"

One of the officers flipped opened his brown book. Sam frowned. She would have had the entire report memorized and ready to shoot out. Waiting impatiently, she shifted her body onto her right leg. Frank placed a hand on her shoulder. It was the signal to calm it down. Not her strong point. She just wanted to get in there and do her own assessment. It was the only one she trusted. Case seemed to be a stickler for the rules, and she didn't need a reprimand from the FBI on her record.

She decided to try. "Can I just go in there, already? Crime Scene isn't here yet, are they?"

"No," the officer replied.

"Sam, not until we get the report." Case stared at the officer. "Now."

The officer read off his notes. "Vic had no shirt on, just black briefs, not even that revealing, tied up in his bedroom with rope, some red marks near his groin area possibly friction from the rope but none on his torso, strangled with the rope, sedative patch on his right shoulder, I don't know the drug, don't know the kind of rope either, never saw that before so I don't know the material or the pattern, nothing in the bedroom or any other room is disturbed. There are creases on the bedspread as if someone sat on the bed. We didn't touch anything or search in any drawers. Scene is exactly the way we came upon it, sir. It's minimal, Agent Case. We did block off a path for entry, so stay within the tapes, please."

"Thank you, officer," Sam said as he moved out of the way so they could pass through the apartment door. Pulling booties out of her pocket and slipping them over her sneakers, she stood in a small hallway that led into a living room. The officer was correct. Nothing was touched or moved out

of place. Actually, she couldn't tell. The place was so immaculate not one speck of dust left an outline around the
assorted glass knick-knacks on the coffee or end tables. She
wanted his cleaning lady. Sam did walk within the tape.
Preserving a crime scene was a priority, especially to her.
She was fanatical. Working as a detective, her appreciation
for forensics grew by the day.

She entered the bedroom where Sheffield was still un-
touched. There'd be a tsunami of evidence in here—DNA,
trace and visible, once Crime Scene hit it. She slipped
gloves out of her pocket and tugged them on. She stared at
the man already showing a grayish pallor. Frank and the
team came up behind her wearing booties and gloves, as
well.

Sam looked up at her colleagues. Bella seemed to have
turned a little green. "Hey, Bella, this is totally not your
scene, is it?"

"Good guess, Wright. But I can handle it."

Sam walked around Sheffield's body. She didn't want to
touch the rope, but she could tell it was hemp. There were
some short frays of threads throughout the material in its
natural beige color. "This one's close to a hundred feet."
Her gaze traveled the rope to follow the direction the killer
took in creating it. "Okay, I've only observed rope tying
once, not my thing, and I'm a bit claustrophobic so I
wouldn't tolerate it too well. We all assume Slater did this,
correct?" All of them nodded. "These two were partners a
long time, so Slater wouldn't have to be gentle. Madame
Lily told us that women loved tying scenes with him. He'd
use a silk rope on them. I did watch videos—"

"Why?" Frank asked.

"I wanted to see if I'd be interested in trying it. The videos online are educational, not sexual. The silk rope is very
soft and pliable and is supposed to feel sensual on the body.
The goal is not to make the pattern too tight. There are hundreds of patterns. There's nothing saying that a particular
pattern has one way of making it. Slater is a master at this.

Madame Lilly called him a *rigger*. He probably creates his own designs.

Lex approached the dresser. The center drawer was ajar. With the tip of his index finger, he opened the drawer. He lifted another rope.

Sam recognized it. "Now that one is silk. And about the standard twenty-five feet."

Frank smiled as he ran his gloved finger under the rope while it was still hanging on Lex's index finger. "This does feel nice, Sam," he said with a wink.

"Maybe, Frank, but you need to know what you're doing. An untrained person could do real damage, even cause death. If you want to learn come back in a couple of years."

He responded without missing a beat. "Okay, forget the rope play."

"You two finished, uh, playing?" Brett didn't look pleased. "Sam what can you tell us about this guy?"

"You know what? Like in the Aries case, let me start with the sign. That'll give me the clues to his reasoning." She walked over to the bed. She noticed a crease in the blanket. "This is what the officer noted. I bet Slater sat down on here after he killed Sheffield. If he was in briefs, too, there would be DNA." She headed to the doorway and turned to face the interior of the room. "First, he's the perfect master. Criminal Scorpios like to have total control. They dominate. He'd never be a submissive. There are so many myths but the bottom line is that they'll destroy anyone who gets in their way. Male Scorpios are large and think they are God's gift to women. In one myth, a giant scorpion was sent by Apollo to kill Orion, whom his twin, Artemis loved. Apollo was fearful of his sister's virginity being taken away. Little did he know." Sam chuckled. "In another myth, Artemis herself sent the scorpion because Orion chased after other women. The theme? He's a definite womanizer. That goes along with what Madame Lily told us. Slater likes to collect phone numbers. Scorpio murderers will murder on a whim, once they make that decision. They're intelligent, organized, and business minded. Along with that, he's a narcissist. He thinks he's the best at everything. All of which we know Slater is, and highly sexual. His tag name, Adonis, proves it. Scorpios are very maternal like me, and paternal. Summer confirmed that. Just like Brett wants to use that characteristic. Their color is dark maroon. No surprise there. A couple of major things. One, if the personality suits it, like in a criminal, they blame others, so if Sheffield was his counterpart, he'd feel that Sheffield knew they were going to get caught. Slater would take his partner's death lightly. It's the he-knew-the-risk kind of thing. Two, Scorpions, the arachnids I'm talking about now, when cornered will sting themselves to death, rather than be captured. So when we meet up with Slater, count on him taking himself down, instead of letting us bring him in."

"Oh, man. Sam, that last point is the most important." Frank ran his tongue over his lips. "So his termination at the scene would be difficult. Crap. I do have questions for him, but I want him gone. If I don't have to meet him face-to-face, I'm good with that."

Case shot Frank a hard look. "Frank, Sam just reinforced why we can't make an arrest at the casino. If this, in fact, is the persona we're up against, his wanting to end it himself will do nothing but cause chaos. The FBI wants him brought into custody. Away from the public." Brett paused. "The families of the women he killed want justice and closure. Questions need to be answered."

"Justice could be his death, too."

"Frank, forget it. One thing that's in my files is that they need to find his residence when he was in the states in which the murders happened. We discussed this. And more information just came in. Nothing was in his name. A case isn't complete until we find that. There may be clues to other murders and the vics may not have been found. We may be looking at a lot more than we have. We'll take years if we have to."

"He's a master at lying, too, so don't ever expect the truth as to where he lived," Sam interjected. "Or an honest answer to anything, for that matter."

"Another reason why it's mandatory we find his residence here in New York, and we'll work backward from there. Information accumulated at a residence doesn't lie."

Frank walked around to Sheffield's back. "Hold on. This sedative patch tells me a lot."

Lex looked him in the eye. "Okay, shrink, what?"

Frank sneered. "He didn't sedate any of his other victims. I think this shows some remorse. He wanted to make Sheffield more comfortable so he wouldn't feel the pain. Our lab guys will be able to tell when he put the patch on in relation to the strangulation and the rope tying. These patches are time released, work like a tranquilizer. He may have some drug or pharma connections. These aren't over the counter. When the person feels more stressed, they release more of the drug. That would be telling. And Sheffield had to feel the patch going on. It would feel cold or damp at the very least. And he let him do it? That's a crazy kind of trust, even for a submissive."

"Okay then, Frank, are you saying that he didn't want to have to do it?" Sam furrowed her brows in thought. "I'm saying that because he waited a year before killing Carrie. Can a serial change? I know, Brett, I know. You told us that already, but I'm still not convinced. Can they not want to kill anymore? Can they exert self-control? He did have positive sexual relationships that didn't end in murder. I have so many questions for this guy."

"Tell me about it," Frank added. "To answer your question, yes, they can change. And they can want to stop. Something significant in their life can initiate that. But this kill is a cover-up. He did this knowing exactly what the intent was behind it. I hate to say this. I really hate it. But the only way to know for sure if he wanted to stop is through a one-on-one interview." Frank sighed. "Yeah, you're right, Brett."

"Hold on. Let's get back to their relationship," Sam said. "Submissives can make their own decisions as to right and wrong and how far they will go. They can put a stop to the scene. A slave is a different story. Um, wait a minute. Sheffield may have known he'd be facing life in prison or worse as an accessory. If he let Slater kill him, like suicide by cop, that would prove Sheffield did help Slater with the other kills. Lex, we must find the aliases."

Lex smirked. "We're jumping way ahead of ourselves. What now? Aside from hitting the interstate files again."

"We'll get Crime Scene up here, now, but Sam, Frank, I need you to think very carefully on this one." They gave Brett their full attention. "At any point during the time you were at the casino, did you two come across to anyone as a couple? Or straight colleagues?"

Frank took it in, swallowed. "Sheffield guessed we are a couple."

"And the cocktail waitress, that Summer Whet, she knew we are. As Slater's flavor of the month or week, as she put it. I don't know who else she told, but when we interviewed the others, no one said anything."

"Listen to me, the both of you, and listen carefully. I'm getting very close to pulling you both off this case. And *not* letting you go in, Sam. I'm sure Sheffield told Slater who you both are, not only you, Frank. If he'd kill someone he was in a relationship with for nine years without thinking twice, he wouldn't think twice about hurting you, Sam. Or worse. And, if and when I do make that determination, I expect you to adhere to my decision. Clear?"

Frank smiled as if he was glad to hear that, and Sam rushed past him to exit the apartment.

He forgets that I'm a Scorpio, too. In no way will I break my promise to Carrie.

CHAPTER 25

Sam and Frank, both nude, snuggled in her bed when they returned from Mike Sheffield's apartment. Under the covers, she held him tightly with her arms wrapping around his neck and their faces lying cheek to cheek. She felt his five O'clock shadow.

"What's the matter, princess?"

"Nothing. I just want to be held."

"Don't bullshit me," he said as he slid her arms off his neck and laid her body down on the bed. "Come on, tell me."

She wiggled in Frank's hold. "Slater. He's getting to me."

"Oh, yeah? You're not usually squeamish."

"No. I'm okay, really. Don't worry about it. I'm just drained."

He placed his palm ever so gently on her cheek and turned her face toward him. "How's he getting to you? Think I'm going to turn into him?"

"Oh my God! No, Frank. Why in the world would you say that?"

"Familial trait."

"No. Forget about that. Now. You're nothing like him. Carl doesn't have any of those traits. I'm taken aback you let that cross your mind."

"Then, what is it?"

She sighed. "I don't understand him. He obviously knows right from wrong. He stopped himself from killing for a year. Now he's killing for cover-ups. He's not sticking to the serial profile. It's frustrating me because I can't categorize him. It's my control thing. Is he doing this deliberately? Think he wants us to stop him?"

"I don't know about the last question. That's what makes it difficult to set up definitive criteria on any of them. If we profile other serial killers, we get the same thing. Look back at Barbara Montgomery, from the Gemini case. John told me she killed to get revenge for her life, for the abuse in her life, but then as they got close to her capture, she did the same thing that Slater is doing. She killed to cover her tracks. Did it take her out of the serial profile? No. Both of them are extremely intelligent. If I'd had to guess, they're both in the higher end of the IQ scale. That's why I'm torn about what I want in his capture and I know it's not up to me. He'd make a great study for future police work."

She paused in contemplation. "Seriously, Frank, do you want him for police work or to clarify your background?"

His silence made the air stand still. "Very good question, princess. Who knows if we'll ever get to confront him. I'll have to think about your question, long and hard."

"Well, as long as we're talking about it, think it out now." He grimaced. "No, I'm being serious," she said. He fell back onto the bed. "Frank, will knowing more about your past help you move on with your life? Or change the direction you're going? Uh, with us?"

"Sam, stop."

"No. I'm not going to stop. Once you were adopted at ten, you moved on. You never once thought about your origins. You repressed it, totally."

He turned onto the side. "You of all people know, that when things are going along too comfortably, the universe gives you a jolt of something to shake things up."

"You were going along too comfortably? Speak for yourself, Frank."

"Come here." He pulled her into his arms and leaned his face in for a long kiss.

She put her hand up on his shoulder. "No, Frank, just when we're talking about something, you want to get intimate. I love you, Frank, with all my heart, but I need that *us*. And I'm so afraid that the more you find out about Slater, the less we will be *us*."

"There you go again, Sam, the issue is about me, and you make it about you. Think about that." He turned away from her.

"I'm sorry, Frank, really." She placed her hand on his shoulder. "But tell me, how is knowing more about Slater going to help you? What do you want out of it, aside from torturing yourself?"

"Honestly?" She nodded. "Maybe once and for all, I can find out about why my parents gave me up," he said. "Excuse me for not being politically correct. But, yeah. That's what it felt like. Like I was disposed of. Now that I found out I have a family, it triggered my thinking about it. Obsessively. And never did I ever want to meet them. Why now? After forty-four years? I feel like I've been living a lie. My entire life, where I came from is a lie. I need to know my heritage, my family history, for Frankie's sake. And get this one, Sam, just when I found out about the DNA thing, Frankie comes home from school with an assignment to write up his family tree. No way in hell, am I letting him put on it that his uncle is a serial killer. I'm never letting him find out, either."

"I'm so sorry." She wrapped her arms around his torso as he stared up at the ceiling. "Listen, a lot of people who are adopted want to know their family history. Mostly for illnesses and tendencies toward that, blood types, organ transplants, but knowing that with Slater doesn't make sense. Why do you say you're living a lie?"

"I had no idea where I came from. I didn't even know that my first foster family wasn't mine."

"Um, ever think that Theresa and Peter are sending you a message?"

"My adoptive parents?"

"Yep. You told me Theresa's psychic and had the abilities I have, and a lot more. That's why you understand me so well and my analysis of AriellaRose in the Aries case."

"What are they sending me a message about?"

"Maybe telling you it's time to come to terms with your past. It's time to investigate. Have you ever prayed to them?"

He closed his eyes and compressed his lips. "Constantly, after Jen was killed."

"Did she answer? Did you visualize her?"

"Yeah. I did. I never told anyone, though. The night of the day Jen was killed, I was inconsolable. I felt Theresa's arms around me, holding me, just like she did whenever I had a melt-down. I was too old to call it a tantrum. Same thing. Wow, haven't thought about them in a while. Oh, wow."

"Well, why don't you ask them for guidance in this case? What you should do."

"Maybe, I will, princess. Maybe, I will." He patted her arms with his palm.

"What now?"

"We'll find him," Frank said. "That I'm confident of. Tomorrow we have to go into the office. Case and Withers have a plan. Apparently, you and I weren't privy to it. Can guess why."

She rested her head on his chest.

"Right now, princess, I need to catch some shut-eye. You should, too. Tomorrow will be a long day."

❧❧❧

Brett Case sat around the conference table in the war

room in the Queens Precinct with the rest of the team—Lex Withers, Bella Richards, who wore business attire—as they waited for Sam and Frank to join them. Folders spread across the conference table took up most of it.

"All right, I'm going to tell them—"

Sam and Frank entered the room and voices went silent. Bella sneered at her, Sam assumed, for coming in so casual, with a button-down-the-front denim shirt and jeans. "Um, Sam, you're becoming as casual as your guy, here."

Sam ignored the comment. "Okay, Case, what's going on? You made a plan without us?" she said in attack mode.

"Yes. The both of you are too emotionally invested. Now sit down and listen. As much as I don't like it, we do need the both of you, contrary to what I would have preferred and what I told you last night at Sheffield's apartment. This morning, orders came down from the top. Yes, even I have superiors. Slater has been spotted at the casino, a little while ago. We have a unit there, but they've been instructed not to engage him for the reasons we've discussed."

"What was he doing?" Frank put his hands out. "It would have made sense for him to run."

"He's playing the slots. Casual, like nothing is wrong."

Frank pounded his mouth with his fist. Then he lifted a finger into the air. "I bet he's planning something."

"We wait until we catch him in an act." Sam shot him a startled look. Brett understood. "No. Not in a murder, but something related, which we'll know when we see it. And as I also told all of you last night, we need more information from him."

Sam nodded. "Goes along with what we discussed, Frank. Remorse. Maybe he wants to end the killing. He wants us to stop him."

"No, he's too conniving for that. If he wants us to confront him, he's got a motive. He wants to win." Frank paused. "Or he wants something from us."

"I want to get there, anyway. Summer Whet could give

us some information. I want to know if she gave Slater a heads up, even though we made her promise to avoid him and she agreed."

"Sam, first, go to the ladies room, and give the officer out there who'll accompany you, your bra."

"Why?"

Brett ignored her. "And Frank, take off your T-shirt and give it to the same officer."

"Why, Case?" Frank yelled.

"Sam, how do you feel about being a decoy?"

"No way in hell are you putting her in danger, Case. No fucking way!"

"Frank!" Sam admonished. "I want to do it. I promised Carrie that I'd find her killer if it takes my dying breath. I'm not backing down. Frank, I mean it."

"You'll both be wearing mics, tiny clear ovals, for you, Sam, in a seam inside your bra, and one in the seam in the nape of your T-shirt, Frank. Go take care of that, then come back in here. Now. We'll hear you, but you won't be able to hear us. He'd notice an earwig. I'll tell you how we'll communicate when you come back."

They both left the room. Frank came back in less than a minute, shirtless and agitated. Bella and Lex stared at him, wide-eyed. He didn't react. "Case, you're not putting Sam in danger, I mean it."

"Hold on, hotshot. We'll have UCs throughout the area. When she comes back in, I'll tell her what we need."

"I don't care how many undercovers are in the facility. He's slick, huge, and he can carry her out."

"We're not going after him in a public place. As I said, we can't afford any civilian injuries, or worse. Sam can handle it. She did great with Jesus Parvos two months ago, right in her own home, alone. She's smart and can think on her feet. She's proven to us that she's capable, Khaos. I'm not telling her yet, but I can see her having a great future with the Bureau."

Frank's eyes widened at his last word.

Sam came back in with a sweatshirt on as Case finished talking. "What Bureau?"

"Not talking about that now. Sit down. This is what we need. What do you think about being on the make for a new boyfriend?"

"Excuse me?"

"There'll be loads of other women there so how good are your pick-up skills?"

"Slow down, Brett. I want to call Summer and the other women to find out what they told him, if anything. He may already know me and want to go right for the kill." She pulled the file on the desk to in front of her and opened the file to the list of interviewees. Sam dialed Summer's number from the phone on the desk and kept it on speaker. Summer answered on the third ring. "Hi, Summer, this is Sam Wright."

"Oh, hi. Catch him, yet?"

"No, but we're close. I'm just calling to find out if you had any contact with Henry Slater after our interview."

"No, Detective, not at all. I left New York that night. I didn't even go back to my apartment."

"How come so fast?"

"I called my parents and told them. They live in Philadelphia, and my dad is an attorney. He's not thrilled with my occupational choice and he used this as an excuse to get me away. He demanded that I come down immediately and I brought the other girls with me. One thing that's great about my dad, is that he's protective with my friends, too."

"Very good. If you hear from him, please call me."

"Yes, I will."

"One more thing. Did he ever do rope play with you?"

Summer giggled. "All the time."

"All right, where?"

"He used rope all over my body."

The team shot each other glances and hid their laughter from bellowing out. Bella rolled her eyes.

"No, I meant in which location?"

"Oh! At the club, or my apartment."

"Did he ever invite you to his apartment?"

"No. Never. I did ask him because I was nosey and he didn't appreciate it."

"So what did he do?"

"A spanking, but his feel so good."

Sam squirmed in her seat and glanced up at Frank. He snickered. She shuddered. "What does he do for rope play?"

"He does different ones. Never the same ones, twice. Why?"

"Just trying to create a profile on him. Why do you think he does different ones all of the time?"

"That's easy. He says it's because he wants the element of surprise so the woman doesn't know what to expect. He doesn't want us to become too comfortable, or bored."

"What a guy," Lex murmured.

Bella gently smacked his forearm.

"Um, okay, thanks, Summer. I'll call you again if I need to. Bye." Sam disconnected. "There's a fifty-fifty chance, Slater doesn't know about me. So, Brett, what else?"

"A lot."

Sam's breath hitched then she involuntarily swallowed.

"For one, the New York office wants him brought in alive. We knew that much. You're to get as much information as you can about him, through conversation. We need to find his apartment as I've said before. His business arrangement, partners, where he works. We haven't found any address on him. His business, Foods Unlimited, is registered to a Steven Blackman, an LLC registered in Delaware. What a shock. The residence for Blackman is in Miami. It's probably another alias, don't know yet. If you have to go to his apartment, you go. Give him nothing to become suspicious. Be descriptive of what you see in the rooms, furniture placement. But don't say, 'oh look at the couch on the far left wall,' or something like that. He'll know something is up if you do. You have to be convincing, Sam."

"Hold on!" Frank scowled. "If Slater never took the other women to his apartment, why would he take Sam?"

Case, for the first time, to Sam, looked concerned. "Okay, Sam, here's where you really have to make a connection with him. More than on a sexual level, which none of those other women did."

"Got it. What do I tell him I do?"

"You're not trained enough to lie convincingly. At least not to someone as astute as Slater. You have to tell him you're a cop."

Frank exploded, pounded the desk with his fist, and flew out of his chair. "Oh no, she's not!"

"Frank!" Sam yelled. "Calm down."

Brett rose from his chair and went face to face with Frank. "Are you looking to be handcuffed and taken out of here, Dr. Khaos?"

Frank paused. He mellowed. "No, Agent."

"Then sit down." Frank sat and looked straight at him, as Case sat down and continued. "Slater is smart, Sam. If you're armed, he'll find it, so you can't go with a weapon. Understood?" Sam nodded. "It's risky, as any undercover sting. Our goal is to not have anyone get hurt, on either side. Take your time. No rushing."

An officer entered holding Frank's T-shirt and Sam's denim button-down-the-front shirt and bra. She handed the items to them.

"Go outside in the hall and change quickly. We have a lot to go over."

Sam and Frank left the room, returning in less than five minutes, Frank with a frown on his face.

"We'll all be in a van in the parking lot, ready to follow if you leave with him. Eyes will be on you in the casino. We have our cameras in each of the security cams, so ours will be a duplicate of theirs. Any problems whatsoever inside, we'll be on him in five seconds or less." Sam hiked a brow. "Yes, that fast. So relax. Now to the outside, we have fifty vehicles in our surveillance team. You'll never recognize them. We'll have you surrounded. All you have to do is distract Slater with conversation so he doesn't think of the possibility of him being followed. Make him laugh. The UCs in the casino will be your protection and surround you as well. The four of us," he said with his gaze going to Frank, then Lex, then Bella, "and I, cannot step foot into the casino, just in case anyone there did speak to him. Questions?"

"Yeah. I have a question. Why do I have a mic, if I'm going to be in a van?"

"For just in case you come face-to-face with him, Frank. We plan in advance."

"Not exactly sure how I feel about that one."

"To be honest, Khaos, the Bureau doesn't give a rat's ass how you feel. If I say you go, you go."

Sam raised her hand. "I have questions. How will we communicate?"

Brett pressed a button on the intercom. Sam felt the jolt of an electrical current under her left breast. She literally jumped up out of the seat.

"You're kidding me, Brett, right?"

Case pressed the intercom. "Take it down a notch, Agents."

"Three notches," she yelled into the intercom. "What the hell was that, Brett?"

"We can hear you. If you're on the right track and we can use the info you said, you'll get one gentle buzz." She felt the buzz and it wasn't strong enough to cause a physical reaction. "If we need more info, you'll get two." She felt two. "If we're taking action, you'll feel three. This way we're in constant communication. Okay? What else?"

"What happens if he wants me to go to a room in the hotel?"

"He may not, knowing Sheffield can't be a backup. If he does, we take him down right there. Anything else?"

"So you want me to become friendly with him?"

"Yes."

"How friendly?"

"Let me put it to you this way, Detective. As an undercover, if need be, you go as intimate as he demands. If he gets suspicious of you, your life will be in danger. But there's no other way to accomplish what my agency dictated. Our UCs will make contact with you in the casino. They will walk past you and brush against you. There will be different ones in case Slater observes you. He'll get leery if he sees the same people trailing you. And they're not only men, so don't get comfortable. Detective, your other cases made you an asset. This case will determine the rest of your career." He stared at Sam firmly, then pulled his wallet out of his pocket and removed money from it, handing the bills to Sam. "Here, four hundred dollars to play with." She took it without saying a word.

Yeah right, intimate. Not if I have anything to do with it.

Brett flipped on the button on the mic in his jacket lapel. "Agents, did you hear Detective Wright's voice? Any adjustment needed?"

"No, sir," came the voice through the intercom on the table. "We'll be able to tell the distance he's from the mic. The closer he is, the higher the range monitor will go."

"You better make sure, that range monitor stays low, Sam."

She glared at Frank. *Maybe making you jealous is exactly what you need.*

౬౧౬౧

Sam's eyes opened wide as she entered the casino mid-afternoon. The flashing lights and clanging machines sent shrills though her. Anxious about meeting Slater face-to-face—if he was still on the premises—she tried to calm herself through deep breathing. Calming thoughts didn't work. Her gaze darted all around her and she couldn't focus. The last thing she needed to do was convey to Slater that she was nervous. She consciously had to stop herself. She stood still. But the mission distracted her. If only Brett had told her in advance they were going back to the casino today, she would have worn green and purple. Those colors calmed and protected her and they were the good luck in gambling colors—her green and purple gemstone jewelry. It was Friday, not Thursday—Goddess Fortuna's day. The Goddess of Gambling had always given her good luck on Thursdays. She scanned her body for any spec of green and purple. Guess nervousness did overtake her because it took her time to zoom in on the green and purple flowers on her cross-body bag. Then it hit her. She smiled. Yes! She *was* wearing her sugilite and moldavite 14K pendant—purple base, green stones on top. She'd be protected. Okay, so she'll still be lucky today, and safe, she thought.

All right, Dara, I haven't called on you the past week, but please lead me in the right direction when I meet Slater. Please let my words flow, just right.

She stood in place after her thought language conversation with Dara. Usually she felt an affirmative jolt in her stomach area. Today there was none. Could it be Dara was upset with her for the lack of communication, lately? She'd have to deal with it.

Sam knew the way to the machines she liked to play. The aisles hadn't filled with people yet, still early for the late gamblers and too late for the early ones. She walked around nonchalantly, not specifically looking for Slater. She'd let the UCs do that. So far, none of the agents made contact with her. Walking down an aisle that led to her favorite machine—where it was newly positioned—four across, diamonds—Sam noticed two Asian men, each one sitting on a stool opposite each other. As she passed between them, one of the men turned his legs toward the center of the aisle and brushed his knee against her knee. He looked down the aisle behind her without any acknowledgement. Okay, she'd met two agents.

Sam walked more confidently around the bend and the

up the parallel aisle to her machine. Yes! It was unoccupied. One to three dollars, with four rows across and with max bet, could pay out twenty-one thousand dollars. With one buck, the max payout was seventy-five hundred. Carrie had always played max, but Sam played one. Today, she'd have the fed's money. A thought hit. If she won, would she have to turn the payout over to Brett? She frowned. What the heck? It was fun to play—especially if the money wasn't hers. And that was a first. Sam pulled a hundred out of her wallet and put it into the slot. The machine calculated her credits. One hundred. *Now let the games begin.* Sam settled in the stool, almost forgetting why she was there.

She pressed max bet becoming mesmerized as the tape turned. Oh yeah, she sure needed a slot fix. Her first spin yielded nothing, with a variety of mismatched symbols. The next spin, four, red sevens accosted her gaze. Oh my God! She jumped off the stool and yelled, "Yes, a jackpot. I love you, machine!"

People surrounded her, as the machine calculated her win. Three-hundred-fifty bucks. Men and women smiled and then departed.

All of them. Except Henry Slater, who bellowed out laughter.

CHAPTER 26

As the crowd dispersed, Sam quickly pressed "cash out" before she'd realized that the man they wanted was right behind her. She slipped the ticket into the front pocket of her cross-body bag and snapped it shut. The three-dollar diamond machine right next to the *hot one* became vacant and she slid onto the stool, now looking around to assess her surroundings. Her gaze hit him. Right in his chest.

Sam had to look way up. "Oh hi!"

"Hi, yourself," was his sexy deep-voiced reply. "I know you."

Her stomach sank. How could her cover be broken, already? *Stay calm, Sam.* "Really?"

"Yeah, I do, gorgeous." He sat down on the stool of the winning machine, lifting his body to pull out the sides of his navy-blue sports jacket.

"Please do tell." She had to admit, his charm *was* overpowering. This man looked just like Frank—a few years younger judging from his facial lines, or lack thereof—but his persona was the opposite—polished. And so was his energy. Slater's energy field shouted 'dangerous' not safe and protective like Frank's.

He took the liberty of leaning over toward her and grabbing a hold of her ponytail, bending his nose to it and inhaling while closing his eyes, and then, ever so gently let it slide through his grasp, taking the ponytail band in his fingers leaving her hair flow down her back. "Nice. I like your hair down." He held the band between his fingers so she could take it. When she did, their fingertips touched.

Chills went through her, though she did not recognize them as arousal or fear. Leave it to her to be so sensitive to energy. She'd rely on that for her safety today. Knowing his dominant nature, Sam held back. Ordinarily, if a man did that to her, she'd smack his hand or give some wiseass rebuttal, at the very least. But, with Slater, she had to play nice. She giggled. "Thank you. So how do you know me?"

"You were at Strident, Wednesday night."

Crap. Madame Lily ratted me out. Better not lie on that one.

"Yes. I was. I didn't see you."

"No, you wouldn't have. I stood in a corner involved with someone as you walked by, and out the exit with some dude. Plus, I wore a mask. Your boyfriend?"

"No. He was someone I was showing the ropes to."

"So, you're in the culture."

"Somewhat."

He curled his lips in approval. "I like what you just did."

"What was that?"

"You cashed out your win and put the ticket away. I know women who'd use it immediately and blow the entire amount. That irks me."

"Me, too," she lied. "Better in my pocket. By the way, what's your name?"

He extended his hand to her to shake. "Henry. Henry Slater."

"Samantha Wright." She reciprocated with her hand. He held it gently and didn't react with any recognition. "Most people call me, Sam."

"I'd prefer Samantha, if you don't mind. More feminine. And I love feminine."

She smiled warmly. *Ugh, this guy is overkill. Oh God, Sam, poor choice of words.*

"So tell me, Samantha. The casino's pretty empty. What brings you here on a Friday afternoon?"

"It's my day off and Friday is my good luck in gambling day. It worked."

He bellowed a laugh. "If you say so."

"What about you?"

"My day off, too…well, any day can be a play day. I work from home most of the time. Came to see some friends. They're out on vacation."

Sam frowned. *Enough with the small talk, I've got to get a move on.*

Henry looked over her head and a huge smile crossed his face.

"What?" Sam turned around and noticed a young couple with a newborn girl in a carrier dressed in a pink onesie with lace around the collar area, coming up the aisle. She waited for them to walk up next to her. "Oh, my God! Isn't she the most precious?"

"She sure is," Henry said as he put a hand on Sam's shoulder. "Don't you think it'll be too noisy in here for her?" he said, addressing the parents.

Yes! Summer was right!

"You're probably right," the young dad answered as he pulled a little cap out of the diaper bag hanging on the handles of the stroller and slipped it on the newborn's head, covering her ears.

Sam bent down toward the carrier. "Ooh, how old is she?"

"Three weeks," the proud daddy responded.

"Ooh, she's so beautiful, oh, and I got a smile. Hi, sweetie," she said, and then she looked up at Henry who had a smile from ear to ear on his face. She'd use that, but good. "I want one so bad," she whined. "Enjoy her," she said as the couple went on their way.

"Thanks, ma'am."

Sam sat on the stool and sighed. "Oh, my God. That made my day."

"Really want one that bad, uh? So do I."

"You do, Henry? So you're not the type of man who'll run when a woman mentions children?" she asked snidely.

"Hell, no."

"Glad you understand. My clock is ticking. I'm thirty-seven and all of my friends have children. One just had twins."

"Twins? Oh, man, that's hard."

"Here, I'll show you." She pulled out her smartphone from the front pocket of her bag, and with her finger, skimmed through the top of her photos. She showed him a pic. "Here. I'm holding Alexi. She's two months here. She's John and Vicki's."

"You look like you'd be a great mom, Samantha." He paused as if he was deciding to tell her something or not. Sam waited and gave him space. "You know, I've been waiting a long time for a woman who could be a partner. Hell, I'm forty. The women I've been meeting lately are all sluts. Sex has been cool, but none I'd consider a life partner." She sighed in agreement. Henry shook his head. "Seriously, not a maternal instinct amongst them. And to me, that's the most important thing."

"And you sound like you've got a strong paternal instinct."

"I sure do. What do you think the most important trait a man should show in a relationship?"

"Want the list?"

He laughed. "Yes, Samantha, I want the list." He sat comfortably on the stool with his hands folded between his legs and gave her his full attention. "Well?"

"Oh, you're serious."

"Yes, damn serious."

"Okay, these will probably scare you off."

"Try me."

She exhaled deeply. "Loyalty; honesty, I'd never lie so I wouldn't want a man to; uh, intense; being able to have an intelligent conversation; bright; successful in his career;

secure. I don't want to babysit an insecure man. Oh, and sexy, I gotta have sexy, very often."

"So far, I'm not running scared."

"I'm glad. What do you want in a woman?"

"Pretty much the same things. But having children in a must. Married first and a kid nine months later."

"You sound like you have it all planned."

"Yes, I do. Feel like taking a ride?"

"To where?"

"My apartment. I want to show you how much I have it all planned."

Sam studied him, in amazement. "Seriously?" He nodded. "Where do you live?"

"The Upper West Side."

Oh my God! This is a gift.

"You know what? I usually don't go with a man I've just met, but I feel good vibes from you, Henry."

"You'll never get anything but good vibes from me, Samantha. Oh, man, I love the sound your name makes as it flows off my tongue."

Sam looked at him with her mouth agape.

"That's pushing it, uh?" he asked.

"I would have to say 'yes.'"

"Okay, I'll tone it down, but I have to tell you, I never met a Samantha. And it feels real good. So, how about it? It's only twenty miles but it'll take about an hour."

"Sure. Believe me, I know what traffic in the city is like. How about I follow you in my car?" She felt two buzzes. That was a no go.

"No, come in mine. I'll bring you back. I want to talk and get to know you."

Sam felt one buzz. Her directive to do what he suggested. "Okay, sounds good. You'll bring me back here later?"

"Sure thing."

Henry looked up at the sign hanging from the ceiling and then guided her with his hand on her lower back in the right direction. They walked through the casino toward the car parking lot. Patrons were beginning to pile in from the buses that arrived every half hour. Sam hid her urge to scrutinize everyone to assess if they were agents or not by looking up and smiling at Henry. Her attempt would have been futile, knowing the FBI set up everyone or anyone—any age and any culture—to be their watch. No one looked twice at her. That wasn't a sign, either. *Okay Sam, forget about the agents. Can't get Henry suspicious.* Henry was non-demonstrative and stayed next to her. Reaching the exit to the parking lot, he held the door open for her.

The young couple with the newborn exited after them. Henry smiled.

"You were right, sir, it was way too noisy. Next time she stays with Grandma."

 e/ɔe/ɔ

The blue and white carpet-cleaning van parked in the first lane, in the first spot of the parking lot closest to the entrance, wouldn't attract any attention. There were plenty of carpets to take care of in the casino. The inside was different, though. The surveillance technology—video and audio—had been up and running before Sam and Slater had made contact and, with Sam's mic, they didn't miss a word of their conversation.

Case, Frank, Lex, and Bella, along with two FBI technicians, wore headphones to block out extraneous noise. They watched a screen in front of them—a map laying out the aisles in the parking lot.

Right now, Sam and Slater were walking down aisle seven. The young couple with the baby was two aisles over but parallel.

"She's good, Frank," Case said as he adjusted the camera to the outdoor lights. "We still don't have an ID on which is his car. That isn't a surprise. Our foot-teams checked out over three hundred plates since we spotted him.

None were registered to him. And before you ask, none were registered to anyone with the surname Hunter or a Steven Blackman."

"He's certainly has all his bases covered," Frank said.

They watched the young mom adjusted the baby carrier in its brackets in the rear of their Altima as the dad got into the driver's seat. He coughed heartily, twice.

"Okay, they're doing a hand-off. Next," Case said into the mic.

"That guy's an agent?" Bella said astonished.

"Yes. Detective. We use every human silhouette imaginable."

"Was the baby a plant, too?" Frank asked snidely.

Agent Case smiled. "Yes, the most important one. I was testing the paternal instinct scenario that Summer elaborated on, and I knew Sam would go gaga over the baby." He hiked a brow at Frank. "What are you waiting for?"

"Don't be a smartass. What about you?"

Agent Case kept his gaze on the screen. "I've got four kids at home and my wife's expecting our fifth in June."

"Wow," Frank said. "I never would have guessed."

"That's nice." Bella said. "How do you know which is *next*? We don't know his car."

Her inquisitiveness didn't seem to irritate Case. Frank appreciated that.

"There's over three thousand spots here. We continue with hand-offs until we find them."

Bella leaned in toward the screen. "And then what?"

"We either continue with hand-off surveillance or use floating-box in the entire trip to his residence."

"Excuse me?"

"Okay, we don't just tail. We *surround* them. Every car around them will contain agents. Just watch, Detective Richards." She looked stunned. Case had to explain. "Listen, Slater is so high up on the wanted scale, I was appointed fifty vehicles for our surveillance team. I think I mentioned that. We have cars already stationed along the usual route just waiting for instructions. But knowing Slater he could take a different one."

"Ah, now I get it." Frank nodded. "We used hand-offs chasing down Withers, or the guy we thought was Withers, when he drove from Manhattan to Atlantic Beach in the Aries case."

"Exactly, Frank. But with him, we didn't have a hostage situation." Frank felt like he was getting sick. He swallowed gastric juices that came up. Case looked at him. "Look, for her own safety, we're treating Sam like she's a hostage."

Frank wet his lips before compressing them. His Sam better make it back to him

Mom, wrap your arms around Sam when you have to, just as you did with me. She'll know it's you.

Slater and Sam walked three aisles to the right, and up another three. They reached his car, a 2010 Mercedes sedan. The driver in an old black pick-up truck with a smashed right fender parked opposite him used his camera to zoom into his rear plate.

Oklahoma came onto Case's screen, with the number. "Okay, good, that driver in the pick-up was responsible for keeping an eye out for him."

The truck then pulled out of the spot and down the aisle to the south exit of the lot. Case sent a relay to the fifty cars on the team. Slater drove down his aisle and turned right. Guessing which direction he would go, Case notified a another vehicle—a Hummer—that would take the advance and pull out in front of Slater's vehicle which he did by cutting Slater off right before the parking lot exit. Slater returned his appreciation with the middle finger salute. Through the mic, they heard Sam laugh. In bumper-to-bumper traffic, Slater drove out of the lot via Woodhaven Boulevard and headed south toward Aqueduct Road. His luck, he caught every red light. But it was the FBI's luck. At every light, different vehicles joined the surveillance team. When Slater moved into the center lane, the Hummer moved with him and agents surrounded him on every side.

"Okay, he's heading to the Nassau Expressway," dictated a technician.

The Hummer would stay in front of Slater until he was handed-off. The Hummer moved into the left turning lane.

Slater did the same. "Damn. I can't lose this guy."

"Well, you're not the only one going into Manhattan, especially at this hour," Sam said.

"Yeah. You'd think I'd be used to it."

Slater turned left at the first cross street and stayed on Aqueducts Road. An FBI vehicle—a Dodge Charger—got behind him after Slater made the left, tailgating. As they got to Lefferts Boulevard, another vehicle—a Jeep—joined the tail, as the vehicle right behind Slater eased into traffic and continued straight. The heavy street traffic made it easier for the FBI vehicles to take position. Aggression and intimidation ruled the approach, coercing civilian cars to let them in. Beeping horns, rolling down windows and cursing had to be somewhat fun for them. Eventually, every car around Slater contained multiple agents. They knew when to allow their colleagues in and how to keep civilians out of their circle. Slater turned left onto Lefferts Boulevard. The Hummer stayed in place and both he, and Slater attempted to turn right onto the Nassau Expressway ramp.

Case sent a signal to the Hummer. The driver pushed the button on his dash—the stall switch. He simulated a breakdown right before the merge onto Nassau Expressway.

"What the hell happened?" Slater yelled as he pounded the steering wheel with his fist, stepping on the break, hard. "Hummers aren't supposed to stall."

Even though they were going slow enough, Sam jolted in her seat. She looked behind her at the piled up traffic, compressed her lips, and pretended a sneeze.

She came through on the camera. "Okay, good, Sam knows something's up." Case sent her a buzz in affirmation.

"Actually, I'm lucky I'm with you, Samantha," Slater said.

"Have a tendency to get a little high-strung?"

"That's putting it mildly."

Sam patted his arm. "Ooh. Then I'll have to be on good behavior."

The driver ran the ignition a few times. No start. Horns coming from behind them were loud enough to bust an eardrum.

"That's good, but I have the same question as Slater. What the hell happened?" asked Frank.

"See up ahead?" Case pointed to the map on his screen with the layout of the FBI vehicles. "I only saw three of our vehicles in place in each quadrant. We're waiting for the fourth, so the driver stalled to give us a chance to play catch-up. With this bumper-to-bumper traffic at rush hour, anything can happen. There he is."

"Who?"

"That motorcycle." Case gave the signal to un-stall. "Okay, let's get a roll on," he said to the van driver. "We'll never catch up to him so he won't see us again."

The van driver drove up the aisle and out of the lot.

The driver of the Hummer turned the ignition on, continued, and Slater and the traffic behind him eased onto the merge to the Nassau Expressway. They crawled by the inch. The driver of the Hummer forced his way over two lanes to the left as the motorcycle replaced him in front of Slater. The motorcycle exited to the Bronx with Slater following.

The motorcycle took exit nine on the left as a UPS truck took its place in front of Slater. They continued to exit ten on the left, and merged onto the Grand Central Parkway toward LaGuardia Airport, staying left to stay on Grand Central.

Slater moved into the center lane, giving an agent in a van the chance to stay next to him on the right. As they approached their exit, Slater moved back into the right lane in front of the van but, quickly, a Ford Taurus got in front of him. The van lagged back and followed. Slater took exit forty-six toward Manhattan Randall's Island. The van continued straight.

When they entered onto the RFK Bridge, the FBI vehicles backed away, as four new ones slipped into their places surrounding Slater. He even let them in. Slater took FDR South, exit fourteen to Ninety-Sixth Street and continued to West Ninety-Seventh Street transverse. As he turned left onto Columbus Avenue, four new vehicles surrounded him. On West Eighty-Seventh Street, he pulled into the garage of twenty-six story building—Mike Sheffield's building.

৩৩৩

Henry pulled into the underground parking garage. Each reserved space had the apartment number written on the ground.

So far so good, went through Sam's mind. She was alive and well and the FBI had her back. Henry drove up and around three aisles before he pulled into the spot for the Penthouse.

"Penthouse? Seriously?"

"Yep. Only the best. I've busted my ass to accomplish the best. I settle for nothing less. Now you stay right there." He exited the car, ran around the back to open the door for her.

"Thank you, sir," she said as she exited the car.

He smiled. "You'll be calling me, sir, a lot. Glad you're used to it. It means I don't have to train you."

They both laughed. Next to the spot, the elevator door opened as soon as Henry pressed the button. They both entered and the glass-enclosed cylinder took them straight up to the Penthouse.

Sam leaned in close into Henry. Her claustrophobia reared its head. Recognizing it, he wrapped her in his arms.

"Um, nice." He rubbed her arms as he held her close. "It'll only take thirty seconds."

Sam closed her eyes the entire trip up that seemed to take forever. He hugged her tightly and as she buried her head into his chest, he rubbed her back.

The elevator opened and they entered the living room of his apartment.

CHAPTER 27

O h my God, Henry, I hope that wasn't the only way up. That was intense."

"No it wasn't, baby. Come on, calm down. There's an exit to the hallway next to the dining room."

Sam glanced up as if to God and mouthed a silent 'thank you.' Her gaze took in the massive living room. She stood for a moment at the entrance before Henry gently prodded her in with his palm on her lower back.

"Henry, this is beyond amazing. This is such a huge space. I always thought Manhattan apartments were compact."

"Not when they're renovated like this building. It's three apartments combined. Actually, it's the entire floor. Come on."

He took her hand in his as she continued to look all around her. "The wallpaper, the lighting fixtures. How in the world did you create those hanging lamps? It's looks like everything's in mid-air."

Henry smiled at her complements.

Give it all you got, Sam. You can have him eating out of your hand.

"Who is your decorator? I want her!"

"You've already got *him*. It's what I do. I just redid seven of the nine rooms, actually."

"You know? I never asked what you did. That's usually

the first thing people ask of each other when they meet."

"We were just so enamored with each other." He winked at her. Sam laughed. "No seriously, I would have asked, too, but I guess our chemistry overpowered us."

Bullshit with a capital B. You already know. Sam smiled. "Awe. Anyway, that must have been some project."

"It wasn't that bad. I kept the floors and the wall faux art." He pointed to the cream and burgundy swirl patterned wall. "I just switched out the furnishings. It was too dark before. All deep burgundies. I'm feeling lighter in my life now. I wanted a lighter environment. I just didn't get to the bathrooms yet. Replacing walls of tiles is a longer project."

"Well the white leather sure brightens things up." They walked through the living room into a narrow hallway. "Where to now?"

"I want to show you how prepared I am to have a family. To the end of the hall." Side by side, they walked down a hallway too narrow to hold a piece of furniture or a piece of framed wall art without bumping into it.

Two closed doors to the right confronted her. "This one first, for your viewing pleasure." He opened the door.

The sight that confronted Sam brought warmth to her heart. She stayed at the entrance, staring into the room with amazement across her face. It was genuine.

"Take off your shoes."

Leaning against him, she did without any hesitation as Henry took off his moccasins. Sam tiptoed onto the light pink short-textured carpet. Its softness surrounded her feet and she melted into it. "Wow," came out of her mouth so faint she was certain it wouldn't be picked up by the mic. Sam was wrong. One buzz confirmed it. She became teary-eyed as she looked around the room, at the whitewashed wood crib with the matching changing table to the right, and caddy-cornered rocking chair. She turned and put her palm on Henry's chest. "Henry, this is stunning." She slid her feet though the softness to the crib. The bedding was pink and brown—brown polka dots on a pink background.

She picked up the matching Teddy Bear in the corner and with one hand held it to her heart. "Oh my God." Sam fingered the silk butterfly mobile that hung over the crib. "Love these pastel colors. Henry, I wouldn't want to change a thing."

"Go sit down on the rocking chair with the Teddy."

Still clutching the Teddy to her heart, she focused her gaze on the soft pastel butterfly design on the cushion. She sniffled. Sitting, she rocked gently looking around the room. The wall opposite the crib was decorated with wallpaper matching the crib bedding.

"This is where you'll be nursing," he said with pride.

Sam sighed. *Why did he have to be a killer? Sam, knock off the nostalgia. You're on the job.*

"Ready to see the next room?"

"Yes!"

He extended his hand to her and helped her get up. "Come on." He slid the Teddy bear from her grasp and placed it in the corner of the crib. It fell over, and, frowning, he repositioned it.

How's that for obsessive-compulsive?

The next room was just a few steps away. He opened the door, and the color baby blue hit her gaze—the same softness on the rug. She shuffled her feet deliberately to feel the texture, giggling like a little girl. When she reached the crib, she placed her palms on the whitewashed finish. She stared up at Henry in amazement. "One of each. That's okay by me. Oh gosh. Blue and brown plaid. The Teddy bear. The mobile. And the opposite wall matches perfectly. How in the world did you accomplish that?"

"Easy. The wallpaper is hand-painted. But I will tell you, I went through hundreds of fabrics to find the identical match."

"That was easy?"

"It's easy because I knew what I wanted. One thing about me is that I plan, incessantly." He shot her a hard stare. "Nothing is spontaneous with me."

Um, that's major. Oh my God! He does know me. He might as well have just come out with it.

She felt Dara's confirmation jolt in her stomach.

"So when I see it, and it's what I envisioned, I want it immediately. Like with you. I knew I wanted you the minute I saw you at Strident, Samantha. I knew I'd find you, eventually, because it's right. It's meant to be."

"Um, nice philosophy."

"Come on." He took her by the hand and they strolled out of the room down the hall.

Entering the living room, she walked over to a freestanding couch in the center of the room and sat down. "Oh my God. Is this pebbled leather? I have bags with this."

He hiked an eyebrow. "I'm impressed."

"Things like this I know. Much to the chagrin of my wallet."

"Spend too much?"

Reel it in, Sam. Don't want him going off the deep end.

"Not beyond what I can."

"What do you do, anyway? I haven't asked you."

Definitely need to be truthful now. He already knows. She let it come out matter-of-factly. "I'm a cop."

He slipped to the other end of the couch. "You're a cop?"

"Yes."

He was flabbergasted. At least he pretended to be. "In what division? Are you armed?"

"Calm down, Henry. No, I'm not armed. Off duty and no guns allowed in the casino. It's locked in my car."

"What level are you? Or do they call it rank?"

"We call it rank. I'm a detective."

"Oh, man, I wouldn't have taken you for a cop, much less a detective. So have an interesting case you're working on?" He slid back close to her and wrapped his arm around her shoulder.

"Yes, actually. But we're not allowed to talk about them, legalities, and it's the innocent-until-proven-guilty thing."

"You know. When you're pregnant, that's going to be a dangerous job."

"Yes." She sighed. "I do think about that, a lot."

"Well, with me, you won't have to worry about it."

"What do you mean?"

"In all honesty, I fell for you already, and when you're carrying our baby, you won't be working at all. For life."

"Uh, you made that decision, quick. I thought nothing is spontaneous with you."

"There's nothing spontaneous about it. I've been thinking about you since I saw you. I always had it in my mind that when I meet my life partner, and we have children, I want her to be a stay-at-home mom. I made sure that I'd make plenty of money to support my family. The only responsibility you'd have is taking care of the children and keeping me happy, and in turn, I'd keep you more than very happy." He paused for a moment. Sam didn't know what to think. "You'd never do laundry, or house cleaning, or even cooking."

"That last one got me. So you'd do everything?"

"I love to cook and I hire help for everything else. Want a snack?"

"Sure. I could go for something."

"Stay put." He patted her hand as he got up from the couch. He walked across the fifteen-foot space into the kitchen.

"When he was out of sight, Sam put her palm over her mouth and coughed. Then she whispered, "Guys?" She felt the affirmative buzz. Okay, they were still with her. Her mind wandered in Henry's absence.

I have to be in touch with Frank, fast. He's obviously recognizing a difference in himself, changing the furniture, but he can't be stupid enough for him to think the authorities would let that slide because he says he's a 'new man.' I have to be real careful with this one. I'm positive he knows who I am. Something absolutely does not make sense. Remember, Sam, he's a master of 'the lie.'

Sam picked up the remote from the whitewashed wood coffee table. The apartment was definitely childproof. No glass in sight and the tables all had rounded edges. Sam put the TV on and flipped to her favorite at home shopping channel. She watched the special of the day, smiled, and took out her phone to order just as Henry returned with a large platter of cheese, crackers, and grapes placed in a fancy floral arrangement.

"Here you go, Samantha, some nourishment for that amazing bod." He placed the platter on the table as he looked at the TV. Abruptly turning, he removed her phone from her grip.

She tried to distract him. "Henry, this is amazing! You just put this together?"

"Yep." He sliced a piece of Brie, put it on top of a butter cracker, topped it with a grape and brought it up to her mouth. "Open."

She graciously accepted. "Thank you."

"Now, tell me, what's all this about?"

She struggled to chew and swallow before she answered. "What about?"

"This? You order a lot?"

"What I can afford."

He prepared another cracker with cheese and a grape, and brought it to her mouth. "Open." She did. "Now just listen. Okay, here's the way it's going to work. From now on—" He slipped the phone into his pants pocket. "—you're going to ask permission before you buy anything."

Sam gulped, almost choking on the snack, and felt the buzz.

"Yes, sir."

"Okay. Good, but call me Daddy. We're going to live in the lifestyle and you're going to be my—"

"You want me to be your slave?"

"I hate the word *slave*, but you're going to be my submissive. How else will we teach our children to obey me unconditionally?"

Now this is getting weird. She felt a buzz. "Um, I see your point."

"Glad you do. There are certain things I'm intolerant of."

"Such as?"

"Lying, stealing, disobedience, being disrespectful. And all of that would go for you, too."

Sam stared at him, wide-eyed.

"Well, I think I have to reinforce it. Come on."

"To where?"

"You're having a time out." He took her hand in his and led her down the hall. He opened the door to the little girl's room.

"Where am I having my time out?"

He walked her to the crib. "When you're a bad little girl, you're having a time out in the cribbie."

Sam started to giggle and it turned into full blow laughter. She couldn't control herself. He reached down and slipped off her socks as she leaned on him. He pulled on the lever and lowered the front railing of the crib then he lifted her across his forearms.

Sam kicked her legs in delight before he put her down on the mattress.

"Oh my God, I can't fit in here."

"You're in it already and it's a great mattress, lie on your back and bend your knees."

"This is comfortable. How long am I staying in here?"

"We're not done yet, baby." He leaned over and his fingers touched the buttons on her jeans.

She put her palm on his hand. "What are you doing?"

"Whatever I want, Detective," he said, delivering the words in an ominous tone as he shot her a sinister glare. "Move your hand, and put your arms above you and hold onto the railing."

"Henry—" He glared at her. She felt two buzzes. She grabbed onto the crib railing behind her. "—uh, Daddy—"

"Hush, baby. You don't obey, do you?" He shimmied

her jeans down past her bottom and frowned. "Why would a woman with such a toned body wear a full brief?"

"It's more comfortable."

"From now on you wear a thong or none at all." He pulled down her jeans and slipped her feet out of them. From the drawer in the table on the side of the crib, he grabbed a blue mattress pad. "Lift your butt." She did and he slid the pad under her.

"Oh, my God, Daddy," she said, not controlling her laughter.

"Hey, baby, don't get me mad, now. I mean it. You know what I can do when I get mad. Don't you?" She hesitated. "Sure you do. I believe you witnessed it first-hand. With your friend—Carrie."

"What do you want, Henry?" Sam felt three buzzes.

"Ssh, we have time for that. No worries. Right now, no talking." He slipped off her briefs and put them onto the changing table. "Oh, man, you are exquisite." Smiling, he separated her bent legs. He stared at her vaginal area and wet his lips.

"What, Daddy?"

"Um, I'm thinking about what I'm going to do to you. Hush. Be quiet. Relax."

As he moved his hand to her pelvis, Sam closed her legs.

He gently patted her thigh. "Don't. Open. Now," he said with a voice that intimidated her into obeying. With his index finger, he gently touched her all around the labia folds. Sam let out a guttural sound and compressed her lips to hold it back. "Oh, man, you're nice." He tapped her clit with his index finger and watched her pelvis twitch. "Oh, man, baby, I can sure please you, but punishment, first."

"What kind of punishment?"

"Hush. You think you can put one over on me?"

"What?"

"Don't lie to me, Detective," he said as he stimulated her mound with two fingers. She remained dry. He snickered, but stopped. "You're on the job, right?"

Sam bit her lip and then swallowed.

"Yeah, and I bet you're wired somewhere. No, don't tell me. Let them hear everything. Let your fucking shrink boyfriend hear everything I'm going to do to you."

Sam released her arms from the railing and sat up.

Immediately, he pushed her back down and held her shoulders firmly against the mattress. "Hey, nothing bad. You're staying alive as long as I get what I want."

She looked him eye-to-eye without intimidation. "And what do you want?"

"I said, no rush." He rolled her over onto her side. Sam let go of the railing. He smacked her behind, once.

"Oh!"

"I'll tell you when I'm ready. Right now, this is what your punishment is going to be." He rolled her onto her back. "Grab onto the railing behind you." She did. With two fingers, he rubbed her clit hard and moved them up and down to her opening. He paused, encircling it as Sam held her breath. Still dry.

From his frown, Sam knew he was pissed. She continued to restrict her breathing, holding back.

"You're in conflict, Detective. Are you so devoted to that shrink that you won't allow yourself pleasure by another man? After all, I was told we look alike. He was even mistaken for me, right?" He swatted her vaginal area with his closed fingers. Sam gasped. "Now, I'm upping the ante." He raised her left leg and placed her heel on the railing of the crib against the wall then lifted her right leg and placed it over the lowered railing. The crook of her knee fit just right. "If you move your legs, I cuff them. Got it?"

"Yes, Daddy."

"And if you dare fight me, even with all the training you have, I can easily do to you what I did to your friend. And my friend. I'm assuming your people found Mike Sheffield's body by now."

"Yes."

She felt three buzzes again. Teams were assembling or

had been assembled but she didn't know where they were. She'd have to trust an unknown with her life. Police training one-oh-one—trust your team with your life. Right now, self-doubt riddled through her.

"I'm going to pleasure you until you let loose and show me the orgasm of a lifetime. And then there'll be more fun." He pulled a finger vibrator out of the drawer of the changing table and slipped it on his middle finger.

Sam recognized it as one she had.

Oh no.

"It's brand new, battery and all. You see, Detective, I had our entire date planned." He waved his fingers in front of her eyes. She closed her eyes and turned her face away. He tapped her cheek. "Open your eyes. It's more wondrous to keep them open during sex. I'll educate you in case you didn't know. Relax, Detective. The worst that will happen to you in the next couple of hours are mind-blowing orgasms. What could possibly be wrong with that? And for some reason, I'm getting the feeling that you're not a cold potato in bed, in spite of you being bone-dry now. Am I right? Ssh, don't say a word." As soon his vibrating fingers touched her thatch, Sam's pelvis twitched. "There ya go, stop holding back. Breathe."

He slid his fingers over her now swollen mound and held them there. He pressed hard. Her thighs trembled.

"Ohhh!"

Oh my God. At least when I do it, I can lift my fingers if it gets too intense, too soon.

Sam raised her body up from the mattress. She tried to wiggle out of his control.

"Hey, Detective. Now, you're getting me pissed." He pushed her stomach down and leaned his left arm on top of her, immobilizing any movement. With his right hand, he pressed harder on her clit and rubbed down to her opening. He put two vibrating fingers inside of her, reaching her G-spot, massaging it with his fingers then brought them up to her mound, again. He repeated this. Fast. Steady. And hard.

Sam's wetness surrounded his fingers and dripped onto
the pad. She moaned, load moans, quivers went through
her. As much as she tried, she couldn't withhold it. Much
sooner than usual, she trembled in release, feeling her heart
palpitating out of her chest and sensations running through
her entire body.

"Good girl. Don't you dare move a muscle." He slipped
the vibrator off his finger, wrapped in a towel paper and
tossed it into a pail. He disappeared into the adjoining bathroom.

Sam couldn't move if she'd want to. Her body continued
to tremble from the aggressive release.

She heard running water in the sink. He returned wiping
his hands in a pink towel with a lace border. Henry plucked
a baby wipe from a package on the changing table. Without
saying a word, he cleansed Sam's vaginal area. He then
took an adult diaper out of the drawer.

"Henry."

"Hush. You're my baby doll." He removed her legs
from the railing and placed her feet flat on the mattress. He
slipped the diaper under her butt, and fastened the sides.
"Now you can sit up. We have a lot to do."

Sam's phone rang in his pocket. He pulled it out and
looked at the caller ID. "Daddy?"

Her breathing normalized. "Crap. Yes. My father. De-
cline it, please," she said, pleading.

"Answer it."

Sam took the phone and sat up. "Hi, Daddy?" Henry
pressed speakerphone. She opened her mouth agape and her
stomach sank.

"Hi, princess, where are you?"

"I'm in the city with a friend. Can I call you later?"

"Sure, but I wanted to tell you I stopped by your house
and brought three boxes into the living room. I didn't want
them to take a walk."

"Boxes from where?" Henry said in a demanding tone.

"Who are you?"

"Henry Slater, your future son-in-law, Mr. Wright."

"It's Dr. Wright. And what do you mean, future—"

"Just what I said, I'm going to marry your daughter. Boxes from where?"

Dr. Wright snapped. "She orders from TV."

"You sound annoyed."

"Yes. You're a genius. Sam, who is this guy?"

"Henry's wonderful, Daddy."

"What about that psychiatrist, Khaos? Thought he was wonderful."

"Daddy, Frank's on again, off again. He doesn't want to commit. I can't babysit him, anymore."

"Dr. Wright, let me alleviate your concern. First, any man who doesn't want to marry your daughter and cherish her is a douche bag. With me, I'll take away all those credit cards, pay them all off, and she'll have to get my permission to buy anything. And we'll have the babies she so dearly wants, and I'm guessing the grandbabies you want. You do want grandchildren, don't you?"

"Yes, of course, more than anything else."

"With me you'll have them. Samantha will have a life of bliss."

"Mr. Slater, what planet are you living on? My daughter doesn't ask permission for anything. Nor, would she let a man run her life."

She felt two buzzes. She'd better make this right. "Oh, Daddy, with Henry, I'll learn. He knows what's best."

"I don't understand this game, Princess, but I'm not playing. Call me when you get home." Dr. Wright disconnected.

"He's intrusive, isn't he?"

Sam looked up at him exasperated. "Tell me about it. They've been helicopter parents my entire life."

"Okay, I think you learned your lesson. Time out is over."

"Thank you, Daddy."

He lifted her out of the crib and carried her out of the

bedroom across his arms as Sam rested her head on his shoulder. Being drained, she couldn't help it. They walked down the hall and into his master bedroom.

Sam's gaze scanned the elegant bedroom with the round king sized bed catty-cornered between two windows. The fabric in the cream and burgundy panel shades matched the bedspread, with cream being the dominant color.

As he laid her down on the bed, her phone rang, again. "Oh, man, Samantha!" He pulled it out of his pocket.

"Then why don't we shut it off?"

He chuckled. "I want to hear your calls. Who's this? Colonel? Facetime?" He turned the phone toward her.

"It's Frankie."

"Answer it."

"Hi, Frankie, what's the matter?" Sam got off the bed and held the phone high as she walked to the doorway. She didn't want Frankie to see her bare legs.

"I can't reach my dad." He became more teary-eyed as he spoke. "I'm in trouble again, Sam."

"What happened?"

Henry snatched the phone from her grip. "Hey, bud, what happened?"

Frankie shook his head as if trying to settle himself. "Who are you? You look just like my dad."

"I sure do, don't I?"

"Are you, Uncle Carl?"

"No. Who's Uncle Carl?"

"My dad just met his brother Carl and he didn't know he had any brothers. And I have three cousins now, two boys, Cameron and Andrew, and a girl, Abby."

"Well, a family reunion. What do you know about that, hey, Samantha? Well, Frankie, I'm your Uncle Henry. This is going to be easier than I thought. So tell me, why are you in trouble?"

Sam's mind reeled. *What does he want?*

"I failed two tests in school."

"How?"

"I didn't study because I wanted Dad and Sam to study with me, and they were busy."

"What grade are you in?"

"Second."

"Well. Frankie, you have very smart genes in you. Your dad's a doctor, and your Uncle Carl, what does he do?"

"He's a lawyer."

"And I'm an MBA."

Sam wide-eyed stared at him.

"What's that?"

"An advanced business degree so I can make a lot of money, so what I'm saying is, it's about time you did your schoolwork on your own, don't you think?"

"No. What are you doing with Sam?"

"Well, Sam and I are going to get married."

Frankie blew. "Oh no, you're not! Sam's marrying my dad and she's going to be my mom! You let Sam leave, now!"

"Whoa! Hold on, bud. Your dad seems to be lagging in that department. I love Sam more than he does. I'll give her the babies she wants."

He broke down crying. "No! You're not! We love Sam! My dad will give her babies." Frankie dropped the phone and ran off yelling, "Grandpa!"

Henry smirked and disconnected the call.

"Why did you have to upset him like that?"

"Because, Samantha, it's life's lessons. Can't pamper kids. Now, sit down." She sat on the bed and Henry sat next to her. He placed his hand on her bare thigh. "Okay, kiddo, if you don't know that I was setting you up from the beginning, you don't deserve to be a detective." Sam sighed deeply. "Yeah, you never had a cover." Sam felt four buzzes. Teams were close.

"Who told you?"

"Want the list?" She nodded. "Well, I'm not telling you. You actually thought my employees weren't going to be loyal to me? But don't worry, Samantha, I'm not going to hurt you. But, hell, if I don't get what I want, you and I are getting on a helicopter, right from my roof and we're going to Switzerland. And we'll live a happy life together. I promise you."

"What do you want?"

He picked up her phone. "Who's the lead detective on my case?"

"Lex Withers."

"Number?"

"It's 212-555-1600."

He dialed.

"Withers."

"Hello, Detective Withers. This is Henry Slater. I heard you've been looking for me."

"No shit."

"Now. Now. Be nice."

"What do you want, Slater?"

"I want to see my family."

Sam looked startled.

"Yeah, Samantha, it's not about you. It was never about you. I want my brothers, Frank and Carl, and my nephews, Frankie, Cameron, and Andrew, and my niece, Abby, here in my apartment, in two hours."

"Don't think I can do that, Slater. We can't risk putting civilians in danger, especially the kids."

"Do you want Detective Wright back, safe and sound?"

"Of course."

"And you want me to turn myself in, correct? You have to want that. So families can get the closure they need. Across the United States, I might add."

≈≈≈

In the van parked outside the building, the conversation with Withers came through the mic. Frank was busting. The conversation Slater had with Frankie left Frank fuming. He wanted his hands around the guy's neck, not in a family reunion. And the way Sam responded so lovey-dovey, though she was protecting her life, gave him a much needed dose of reality. He wasn't planning on letting her go. He was proud of Frankie for standing up to Slater. Frank needed to do the same.

"I'll call you back. Give me a few." Withers disconnected. "Agent Case, you got that?"

"Got it loud and clear. Give in to his demands. We need a lot of information from him. I'll instruct Frank on what the bureau needs. Tell him about Abby."

Frank glared at Case. "I'm not putting the kids in harm's way. Withers was right."

"Give us some credit, Frank. Every unit in Manhattan will be on the premises. Manhattan North obtained the warrants, for arrest and the vehicle confiscation, as well as search of the apartment. We're sealing off the rooftop heliport. He has nowhere to go. Manhattan North ESU has been assembling from the time Sam found out the location. They're right outside the building now, front and back, and in the hall outside the apartment, and in the garage. They removed his vehicle." Frank listened while pounding his fists on his thighs. Case got Withers on the phone. "Start setting it up."

Sam's phone rang. Slater answered. "Okay, Withers, what have you got?"

"We'll meet your demands and allow your niece and nephews in the apartment if you allow the Emergency Service Unit to do a sweep."

"For explosives and weapons?"

"Yes."

"Listen, Withers, I have neither. This is a multi-million dollar building, and I own it. Destruction is not my style. Celebrities live here."

Frank tossed a gaze of astonishment toward Case.

"We do a sweep or no go. And they stay inside during your meeting."

"I only want family in here."

Frank interrupted the call. "Slater, Frank Khaos. Listen to me. Whatever shit you went through in your life; I wasn't far behind, man. We do need to talk, but the kids can't be in danger."

"Well, if it isn't my big brother, Frank. What is it, by about four years? Don't worry, they will not be in danger. I give you my word."

"I want to speak to Sam. Now."

"Frank?"

"How are you?"

"I'm fine. Listen, Henry shows too much affection to children to hurt them. If I can convince him to let the team come in, will it be a go?"

"Yes," Withers said.

"Henry, come on, what are you afraid of?"

"What am I afraid of? I'll tell you what I'm afraid of, Samantha. They'll take me out before I have the meeting. I must have my meeting—"

"No, they won't, Slater," Withers interrupted. "As long as you don't pose an immediate threat." He spoke into another line. "Guys, you got that?"

"Yes, Detective. This is Sergeant Crane, Mr. Slater. I'm heading the ESU team assigned to this. We only take out those who pose a threat. And when we're in there we must confirm Detective Wright's safety."

"I'm not a threat, believe me. I've been waiting for this for nine years. Nine angry years." Slater paused, as if needing time to mellow his temper. "Yeah, okay, they can come in. I know I won't get this chance again. But you're not removing Samantha from the premises until I release her, after our meeting. I'm not having a gun fight over this. Or I can take care of her, now."

"Don't you dare hurt a hair on Sam's head, Slater!" Frank yelled.

"Well, aren't you a picky one, big brother who can't commit? I'm in charge here, remember that."

"Okay, done," Withers said. "The teams are going out now to collect everyone. Just one thing. Abby is in a Scarsdale jail awaiting indictment."

"For what?"

"She orchestrated ten home invasions."

"How old is she?"

"Twenty-one."

"Get her brought down with an escort."

"We'll try."

"Do it. Two hours, Withers." Slater hung up.

CHAPTER 28

"Okay, baby," Henry said as he returned his full attention to Sam who sat on the bed next to him. "This has been a long time coming. I'll finally meet my family." He compressed his lips. "Things could have turned out so differently."

Sam gently put her palm on his forearm. "Yes. It could have. May I ask you something, please?"

"You can ask, but I don't know if I'll answer."

"What did you mean when you said that you've been waiting for this for nine years?"

"That question I'll answer at our family reunion. Okay, baby, here's what we're going to do while we wait. Stand up."

Sam stood. Henry slowly unbuttoned her denim shirt. When he opened it, his eyes widened as he gazed at her breasts, and then at her pendant. He lifted it into the palm of his hand. "Wow, Samantha, this is spectacular. And so are those," he said, gliding his index finger over her bra. "These are perfect, and yours," he said, practically salivating. He bent down and kissed her bosom over her bra as he slid her shirt down her arms and let it fall to the carpet. The sucking sounds he made, as well as Sam's moans came through the mic.

Frank got up and punched the wall of the van. Case pulled him back down into his seat.

Slater put his arms around Sam's back and as his fingers slowly skimmed her skin, he detached the clasps on her bra, and removed it sliding her arms out of it. He stood grinning with his gaze traveling her body from head to toe. He licked his lips. "Wow, baby, you look so cute in a diaper."

That mic better work a few feet away.

Sam giggled as she responded. "Thank you, Daddy. Now, what are you going to do to me?"

He patted her behind. "Hush, it's not for you to ask."

She pretended to enjoy it and moaned. *His touch isn't as good as Frank's.*

Henry opened the top drawer of the night table next to the bed. He pulled out two ropes. "Ever do rope-play?"

Her eyes widened. "No. I'm a little claustrophobic as you saw in the elevator."

"I did indeed see that and you didn't look like you were fooling. Okay. Noted and taken into consideration. I'll go simply. Here, feel it."

"Silk?"

"Yes, a hundred percent. Extend your arms out."

She followed his directions. She reminded herself that she knew enough martial arts from the academy and with the additional training Frank gave her, she could protect herself if he went near her neck. She visualized the movements in her mind—knee him high, narrow in between his arms, and elbow hard into his jugular, if her arms were free.

Slater doubled the rope and brought it around her back and to her front sliding it on her skin. "Feel it? Nice and soft?"

"Yes," she whispered.

He slipped the ends on her left side through the loop then pulled the loop to her mid-chest. He lifted each top rope so it went above her breast and positioned the one underneath. He tucked the pendant under the rope so it lay against her skin. "There, one above and one underneath. Makes you more perky, but then again you're perky to begin with," he said with a wink. Henry twisted the rope on her mid-section, laid it vertically, brought the opposite ends around her and back, twisted them, and then brought it to in front of her. "Here, hold this in a fist, with one hand above the other." She did it. He ran three fingers under the rope. "See? Not tight."

"No, I'm good, Daddy."

"Now lay down on the bed." She sat down and he lifted her, positioning her body into the center. "Comfy?" She nodded. He picked up the longer silk rope. "Bend at the knees and keep your feet flat on the bed. After she did, he repositioned her legs by spreading her feet to about twelve inches apart. He doubled the rope, wrapped her feet once and pulled the ends through the loop, which sat, centered between her feet. He let one end fall and he wrapped her right leg around and around with the rope until he got to the top of her thigh. Then he did the same with the other rope. He brought the two ropes together and intertwining them, he wrapped her hands the height of her connecting fists. He then made a big bow with the remaining rope, and tucked it in so she couldn't get at it with her teeth. "Comfortable?"

"Yes. How long will I be like this?"

"I honestly don't know." He lay down on the bed next to her with his arm resting on the top of her bent knees. "Relax, just go with it. I want to see some deep breathing."

She inhaled and exhaled several times but anxiety was setting in. She felt cold.

"Come on, Samantha, relax. Let your legs and arms fall into the rope. You don't have to tighten your muscles." He poked her thigh with his index finger. "When you relax and breathe into it, you'll get that feeling of euphoria, your subspace. That's the goal, to get to your subspace. The feeling of complete abandon, as if you're floating. You're safe. Feeling cold?" She nodded and swallowed. He pulled the soft stuffed blanket over her to just below her neck. "I have some things to prepare for our reunion, so I'll be back in a bit. Stay put." He got up and pulled out a large pair of shears from the night table drawer.

Sam's eyes widened.

"Don't worry. It's a safety precaution."

"What kind of precautions?"

"You'll see. Relax." He patted her feet and walked to the door. "Relax, you'll be fine. Ordinarily, I wouldn't leave you but I have some papers to prepare."

☙ ❧ ☙

Henry walked into his office two rooms over from his bedroom. The room was furnished with a sand wood colored desk that protruded from an immense wall unit that covered the longest wall in the room, over sixteen feet. Business and marketing textbooks filled the shelves. He pulled open a double-door cabinet beneath one of the bookshelves and took out a thick manila envelope. His gaze focused on it.

The Last Will and Testament of Henry Slater

Henry took the envelope and brought it over to his desk. He inhaled and exhaled deeply, giving himself the courage to open it. He pulled the document out of the envelope and opened it to the third page. After each note he jotted down, he nodded then he smiled after writing more notes, continuing to the fourth and fifth pages. He scanned the rest of the fifty-page document, pausing periodically to note that everything was correct. After flipping the pen that he held onto the desk, he then went over to a file cabinet, and pulled out seventeen stacks of hundred dollar bills. At his closet, he pulled out a suitcase and deposited the stacks, and placed the will on top of them. From the middle drawer in his desk, he pulled out seventeen black folders tightly packed with handwritten notes and placed them into the suitcase on top of the rest.

He brought the suitcase into his dining room and put it into a corner, out of sight. Then he went into his kitchen, pulled out a platter of deli with assorted breads from the

fridge, and brought it to the seating-for-fifteen whitewashed
wood dining room table. From the matching curio, he took
out cream Lennox plates with matching utensils and napkins, and arranged the plates to the right of the platter with
utensils folded within the napkins on top of them.

There was a knock at the door.

Not in any hurry, Henry walked to the front door. There
was another knock. He looked through the peephole. There
was a five-man ESU unit in full gear with Tasers, guns, a
few rifles, and shields waiting to accost him. They stood in
the at ease stance. "Remember our deal?"

"This is Sergeant Crane. Yes, Mr. Slater. Open the door,
please."

Henry opened the door and the team entered, standing in
the front hall as they looked around. "Nice, uh?"

The sergeant smirked. "Sure is."

"Before you jump to conclusions, it's from hard earned
money and legal business deals. I just made better career
choices than all of you did. Go ahead. Look around. On
second thought, this just hit me. Don't you need a warrant?"

"You gave us permission," the sergeant replied as he
plucked the warrant out of his vest. "Here you go. Nothing
is spontaneous with us, either."

Smiling, Henry took it. "Ah, so our Samantha *was*
wired."

"You stay right here. Where's Detective Wright?"

"She's in the bedroom resting. As per our agreement,
she stays."

Crane nodded and Henry could tell he was seething. His
jaw was so tight the man wouldn't be able to talk soon. The
sergeant raced to the bedroom door with another officer
who had a hand held electrical detection device in his hand.
He scanned the perimeter of the whitewashed wood door
frame for wiring. A laser confirmed that a body was on the
bed. The officer nodded that is was clear.

"Detective Wright, this is Sergeant Crane. Are you okay?"

"Yes, I am. Just go along with Henry."

The body was stationary. "Sergeant, I'm not getting any movement."

"I want proof her answer isn't recorded and that she's alive."

"Ask her whatever you'd like," Henry said from a distance.

"Detective, what breed of dog do you have?"

Sam laughed. Her head moved upward. "I don't have a dog, Sergeant, but Frankie wants one, a German shepherd."

"There's movement, Sarg."

"Good enough for you?"

"Where are you having your meeting?"

"In the dining room."

The unit dispersed to cover each room with bomb detection equipment. In five minutes, they returned.

"I told you, there are no bombs in here."

"Just take it easy, sir, and let us do our jobs, okay?" Sergeant Crane said.

"Sarg, you have to go see the two rooms back there."

"Oh, yeah?"

"Go look, we have him." Four men stood around Henry in the at ease position.

Henry shrugged. "Whatever you say, Sergeant." He stood leaning against the door frame between the living room and the dining room with his fingers in his slack's pockets. When none of the officers looked in his direction, his fingertips moved ever so slightly in his pocket.

The doorbell rang.

"Okay, Mr. Slater, go sit in the dining room and we'll bring in your family."

"No. It's my residence. I open the door."

An officer ran a body scan over him. "He's clear."

∽∾∽

The door opened and Frank came face to face with his brother—the serial killer. He didn't know what to look at first, their identical physicality, or around the guy to find Sam. It took him a moment to ground himself. He blew out a few short breaths before he took a step. This was going to be harder than he anticipated. Carl stood next to Frank with the same amazed look on his face with the boys standing behind their dads.

"Come on in. It's about time we met. Don't you think?"

As the boys scrambled in after their dads, they looked around the room as words of amazement came from them. Their voices trampled over each other's with 'wow', 'how cool.'

Frank stood in front of Henry. The initial shock wore off. "Where's Sam?"

"She's in the bedroom. You can talk to her though the door, but don't you dare open it. It'll get ugly, believe me."

Crane intervened. "What do you mean 'it'll get ugly'?"

"If he gets aggressive, I'll get aggressive, then you guys will get aggressive, plus, in front of the kids that doesn't fly with me. And I have a lot to say. I'm sure the FBI and my brothers want a lot of questions answered."

Frank raced to the door. "Sam?"

"Frank?"

"It'll be over soon. You okay?"

"I'm feeling a little restricted."

Frank was about to grab Slater by his collar. He felt two buzzes. Crap, he forgot about the mic. Damn, Case was quick. He'd better play nice. He'd be booted out of the department if Slater could get out of this on a technicality that Frank himself initiated. "What does she mean?"

"I'm teaching her to get used to bondage. She'll be fine. It's loose. Come on, let's go inside." The ESU stayed outside the room as Henry led them into the dining room where the boys were already eating deli sandwiches. Henry must have read the worry on Frank's face. "Stop worrying. Nothing's drugged. Frank, sit next to Frankie, and Carl, next to your boys." The men took their seats. Henry glared at Carl. "Now, where's Abby?"

"They're bringing her down."

"Are you representing her?"

"No."

"Have a friend who is?"

"No."

"Why the hell not?"

"She's emancipated."

Henry sat back in his chair and a solemn expression crossed his face. At first, Frank felt his concern was genuine. "How in the world could you let that happen?"

"She was a very difficult teenager and she demanded it. I thought she'd come running back, but I was wrong. I shouldn't have let it happen. We both got caught up in emotions when their mother died."

"That sucks." Henry turned his attention to Frankie, losing the sentiment. Frank realized the concern was an act. "And you, little guy, get over here, on my lap, now. Let's go."

Frankie took the half-eaten sandwich out of his mouth and when it was mid-air, he looked up at his Dad. "Do I have to?"

An officer put his hands on Slater's shoulders. Henry didn't shrug it off. "I'm staying right here, Frankie." The officer nodded to Frank.

"Go ahead."

Frankie got out of his seat and hesitated before he approached his uncle. Henry lifted him onto his lap. He exhaled deeply. "Oh, man, Frank, he looks just like us. Where was your wife in this?"

"My mom looked sort of like Sam," Frankie whined. "She was killed and Sam found out who did it."

Henry compressed his lips. Again, Frank saw there was compassion behind this killer.

"So tell me again how much you love Samantha?"

Frankie looked hesitant.

"Go ahead. Say it in front of your dad."

Frankie's voice quivered. "Dad and me, we love Sam with all our hearts, and Dad's marrying her, not you." He held back tears with sniffling.

"Oh, yeah? Then what's taking him so long? So how about you come live with Sam and me—"

Henry didn't have a chance to finish. Frankie raised his fists and pummeled his uncle's chest. The officer grabbed him and lifted him up in a split second, as Frankie flailed his arms and legs, making contact with Henry's head with his foot. The officer moved away from the table with the boy in his arms. "You're not taking our Samantha away! I'm not losing a second mom!"

"Whoa!"

The officer tried to calm Frankie down. "Okay, it's okay, son. He just wants to aggravate your dad." After a hand signal from Frank, the officer handed him over to his father.

"Henry isn't taking Sam away." Frank glared at his brother. "Stop terrorizing him."

Henry smirked. Before he could respond, there was a call coming in from Sam's phone that lay on the table. "Yes. Withers."

"Abby is at the front door with an escort."

Henry disconnected. "Stay put, guys."

Frank held Frankie in his arms, consoling him. The boy whimpered, and Frank seethed.

Henry got up and went to the door, which was open to the dining room. Frank put Frankie into his seat and got up from his to stand in the doorway. Slater opened the door. John Trenton confronted him standing next to Abby. In his pinstripe gray, Armani suit, he and Slater were of the same ilk.

"Who are you?"

"Dr. John Trenton. I'm a forensic psychiatrist."

Slater looked around in amazement putting his hands out, shrugging. "How many shrinks do I need in here?"

"I'm Abby's escort. If you want her in, I come in."

"All right. You're better than another cop." Henry sneered at the ESU. "You stand right here, young lady."

Abby trembled, her shivering visible through her jeans and sweatshirt. Her straight black hair settled on her back. She pushed her bangs off her forehead and looked intimidated. She interlocked her arms in front of her against her chest. She looked way up at her uncle with fear in her eyes.

"So you're responsible for home invasions?" She nodded meekly as her complexion paled. "And you wanted to be emancipated?" She sniffled and nodded again. "Answer me."

"Yes."

"It's yes, Uncle Henry."

"Yes, Uncle Henry."

"Why?"

"He wouldn't let me do what I wanted."

Henry paused and licked his lips. "That's it?"

"Yes," she answered, quivering.

"Uh!" he said, pointing a raised finger.

"Yes, Uncle Henry."

Henry turned toward Carl. "I see you weren't tough enough in the respect department. Okay, let me ask you something, young lady. Were you ever beaten so badly that you went to school bleeding with welts on your back?"

Abby's eyes widened. "No, Uncle Henry."

Frank paid attention. He'd received one of the reasons Slater did what he did.

Henry nodded. "Did you ever go to school so hungry you'd eat four kid's lunches?"

Frank began to feel for the guy.

Tears began to flow as if she was imagining it. "No, Uncle Henry."

"Were you ever locked in a closet for hours when you misbehaved?"

Tears flowed. "No. Never."

Locked in a closet, a common trait, Frank thought.

"Were you ever made to sleep on the floor, because your parents wanted the dogs to have your bed?"

That's a new one. Frank had to ruminate on that one.

"No, never," she cried out.

"And you wanted to be emancipated because Daddy wouldn't let you do what you wanted. You're a little spoiled brat. Nothing more. You know that?"

"Yes, Uncle Henry."

Henry glared at her. "And now you're going to spend—" He turned toward John, "—how many years is she looking at?"

"Ten," John stated sternly.

"So you're telling me you want to spend ten years behind bars without your family? Without your dad and brothers?"

Abby sobbed. "No."

"You don't realize how lucky you are. To have family. My parents gave my brothers away so they could have a better life. Then they went ahead and kept me, so I'd be miserable and be treated like shit, the bastards. You are going to go in there and hug your dad and brothers for dear life. You understand me?"

"Yes, Uncle Henry." Abby looked up at her uncle and then ran past John, Frank, and the cops who remained stoic, into the dining room, screaming, "Daddy!" She fell into the seat as her dad opened his arms for her. "Daddy, I'm sorry. I'm so sorry."

Carl let the tears flow. "It's okay, baby. I'm just glad you're back." He held her in his arms and patted her head. Her brothers joined in the embrace. "Abby, I can't believe you did what you did."

"Don't talk about it, Carl," John warned.

Carl nodded.

Henry stood between Frank and John. "Now, I don't know why either one of you couldn't do that." He smirked. John put his hand up to Frank not to respond. "Let's sit."

Frank took his seat, next to Frankie, and John sat on the

boy's other side. "So what's going on, Slater? Why did you want to meet us after nine years?"

"Don't BS me. You heard every bit of conversation I had with Samantha."

"Why now? Because you know it's the end?" Frank rubbed it in.

"What's that mean?" Frankie asked innocently.

Abbie wiped her tears away. "You don't know?"

"No. What?"

"He murdered seventeen women." Frankie looked shocked and jumped into his dad's lap. "Yeah, Uncle Frank told me. I guess craziness runs in our family."

That was something Frank didn't want to acknowledge, much less hear. His stomach sank. He shot John a pitiful look.

John intervened. "You know what? We have some intense stuff to talk about. Why don't you let the kids leave, Mr. Slater?"

"I'd rather have them stay. The four of them look like they need some toughening up."

"That might be, but talking about this particular issue is way above their brain capacity."

"They stay."

"You have a lot to tell us. Correct?"

"I have a lot to tell my brothers. You're not included."

"I'll be happy to leave. With the kids. Listen. You have Detective Wright as leverage. That's enough. We want this over with, as do you."

"How do you know what I want?"

"Okay. I'll be honest. You admitted it to Detective Wright. Here's the way I see it." John flipped a spec of lint off his pants. "You're angry your parents kept you and, from what you just told Abby, you were abused pretty badly. Did you murder these innocent women to get even for something? Because most serial killers kill for revenge for what happened in their own lives. In some cases, it's more simple. In some cases, it's more complicated. I've seen it many times."

Frank knew John well enough to understand what he was doing—taking the control away from Slater. Frank shielded Frankie from the view in his arms with his son's head buried in his chest.

Slater jumped up. ESU readied with weapons drawn. Slater had a sniper rifle aimed at the back of his head.

"What did you call me? A serial killer? Get out of my house, and take the damn kids with you. Now. Go!"

Frank and Carl ushered the kids out with John behind them. He nodded to Frank. ESU still held a rifle on Slater as he sat at the dining room table. Frank and Carl came back and sat.

Slater was visibly shaken. His hands trembled. He interlocked his fingers to keep them from quivering, and placed them on the table. Frank assumed the reality of what he had become had finally sunk in. Slater raised his hands to his face and buried his head in them for a moment then he wiped his fingers over his cheeks. He slumped back in the chair and looked vacantly ahead. Blinking, he came back to the room after a few moments. "Okay, put the rifle down." The officer did. "So is that what I'm called? A serial killer?"

"That's what we call it, yes," Frank said. "You went after women with the same MO. They were all professional women. And then we have the scorpion."

Slater exhaled deeply. He interlocked his fingers again and brought them up to his mouth. "I tried to stop. I did. I swear I did. With the last one, I just couldn't help it."

"Why professional women?" Frank asked.

"Okay. Before I answer that, let me set the record straight. None of what I told Abby happened, except for the closet. It was more like neglect. At a very young age, I was doing things for myself. Cleaning my own clothes, making my own meals. I slept on an inflatable bed that my parents folded up and hid during the day, as if they didn't want to show anyone they had a child. It was weird, I didn't know why. Most of the time they weren't around. I didn't have any supervision. The only time I was happy was in school. My teachers gave me the attention I needed. Then I got resentful. I got love from strangers but not from the woman who bore me."

"So where were they? Your parents."

"Our parents, bro. Remember that. Getting into shit. Big on thefts and petty stuff. Shoplifting. When they had their crew over, for a meet, that's when I was in the closet. They didn't want me seen or heard. I never had any toys around. Not even books. Then we moved a lot."

Carl put his hands out. "Did you ever think they were protecting you from their shady deals?"

"Protecting me? No, as a child that wouldn't have crossed my mind."

Carl looked around the room. "But look at all you accomplished. How did you do all this?"

"I busted my ass. They always told me I wasn't 'good enough.'"

"Slater wasn't our birth name," Frank said.

"No. It was Hunter. I was Benjamin. I changed my name legally when I was eighteen. What was yours?"

"I was Francis Hunter. I was adopted at ten, but my adoptive parents kept my first name."

"What about you, Carl?" Henry asked.

"They placed me for adoption at birth. A few days later, actually. My given name was Carlton so my adoptive parents kept it." Carl pointed to the elegant surroundings. "So how did you accomplish all this?"

Henry sighed. "I always loved to draw. That's what I did when they locked me in the closet for hours. I moved out when I was seventeen, sold my paintings on the street, supported myself. Got an art scholarship to college. That's right. From homeless to college. Loved the business world and money was the most important thing to me because I was always told they didn't have enough money to feed me.

I have a decorating business, and I love the restaurant business. So I combined them with the casinos."

Carl looked confused. "With a life like that, why did you start killing?"

"That's the ten million dollar question, isn't it?" Henry paused. "I found out about the two of you."

CHAPTER 29

Whien did you find out about us?" Frank asked.

"Nine years ago, just about the time I founded Foods Unlimited."

Frank put his hands out. "And?"

"I went back to the old neighborhood in Brooklyn, after I got my MBA.

Which was?"

"Bensonhurst." Henry sighed. "It was their last known location. I wanted to shove my degree in my parents' face. But they moved. I was so pissed, I couldn't get even. Then I was relieved. Why in hell would I want to see them? I met someone who told me I should try to find my older brothers. I had no idea what they were talking about. I got more pissed and terrified at the same time. That night my nightmares started again."

"Henry, all this can be used in court." Carl's serious tone got his attention. "Do you want an attorney?"

"No. It's over. I've wanted it to be over for a few years. I want to talk. I need to talk. The pressure is killing me. My pounding headaches are killing me."

"You know—" Carl paused. "That won't undo what you've done, right?"

"No shit."

Frank had no empathy. "What nightmares?"

"When I was little and in the closet, I'd bang my head

against the wall. Made holes in it. Because I couldn't do anything to get even with my parents. But my childhood still haunted me. How would you feel being told all the time that you shouldn't have been born, that your mom, who's supposed to love and hold you, told you that you disgusted her? My nightmares were more intense. I always awoke with a headache. When I was older and alone, I got rubber life-size dolls and actually acted out the nightmares, the fantasies. I got such a thrill, it was orgasmic. I actually came. I've always had severe headaches since I was a kid."

Frank let out a selfish sigh of relief. *Okay, the brain injuries are from environmental causes, not genetic.* "And your fantasies?"

"You want specifics, don't you, bro?"

"Yeah."

"My fantasies were sexual, even at a young age. Our parents walked around the house nude, all the time. They even had sex when they knew I was watching. Dad played the choking game. Mom even passed out a few times."

"Did you ever tell anyone about them?" Frank asked with furrowed brows.

"Never. I wouldn't rat on my parents."

"What's with the scorpion left on the bodies?" Frank said matter-of-factly. Carl grimaced.

"The breast, bro. The breast. The breast is a symbol of nurturing, and I didn't get any so I put the scorpion there to sting them, as a punishment. Those little creatures fascinated me. Their stingers, and I'd like to sting everyone. Even in business, I'd knock down everyone I could. I'd destroy them. It's my token animal. And I'm a Scorpio. I decorated everything in the color of my astro sign. The furniture in here was all dark maroon until a week ago. Wanting to change it to this—" he said, pointing to the white couches, "—was it God telling me to stop? Hell, I didn't wash down the last body because I wanted to be caught. It wasn't supposed to happen with that Carrie woman. She used the words that set me off."

"Which were?" Frank asked.

"That she didn't want children."

That was Sam's initial assessment. Man, she's on target.

"Excuse me?" Carl said stunned. "Many women today don't want children, for whatever reason, and it's no one's privilege to tell them otherwise."

Henry clenched his fists. "Don't piss me off, bro. I'm not going there right now."

Frank felt a buzz. He had to diffuse this. "Okay, fine. We'll go slowly. What happened with Carrie?"

"I just didn't run to the room with my stash of cleaning stuff. I don't know why. Something stopped me. I actually felt a pulling from something. I knew the ending would be happening soon. Why I wasn't stopped sooner is baffling to this day."

"You traveled." Frank tried to make sense of it. "You were hard to track. Was that on purpose?"

Henry shrugged. "The business."

"What triggered the first one?"

"A nightmare. One of many. It was so violent with crazy colors going through my brain, like flashes. I was doing the choking game with one of my high school teachers. A knockout blonde. I was seventeen. She was twenty-two. She was one I would have really liked to bang. Never happened. She did pass out for a minute. She woke up and slashed me with a butcher knife. Tore me to shreds. I hate the sight of blood. I woke up with a pounding headache as if a bomb exploded in my head. I tried to wake myself up and I fell out of the bed and smacked my head against the night table. It was some bang, as you could imagine. My head swelled in four places. I was so angry. I thought the only way to get rid of the nightmares was to act it out. They did stop when I acted it out with my dolls. But that didn't last. So I did with a human. I couldn't help myself. I tried to talk to myself. I couldn't control the impulse. At the time, I had no idea what I was doing."

"Why didn't you go to a doctor?" Carl asked, confused.

"Yeah, right, and say, 'Hey, Doc, I feel like strangling women.' Know where that would have gotten me? Being confined in a small space for life does not fit my personality description."

"Tell me about the first," Frank said.

"I'll do something better." Henry started to rise.

Sergeant Crane put his hands firmly on Slater's shoulders. "Where are you going?"

"To get the briefcase in the corner over there."

"Stay put." He signaled to one of his officers who used a laser to scan it.

"Just paper, Sarg."

"Bring it over."

The officer placed the suitcase on the table with the latches facing Henry. Flipping open the case, Henry stared at the glossy black folders. Frank and Carl remained silent.

One by one, Henry placed the folders on the center of the table. "These are my full hand written confessions for the seventeen murders." He quickly closed the case.

Frank sat back in his chair having a hard time wrapping his brain around this behavior. Yes, serials wrote out confessions and many wrote books, while they were rotting in a psychiatric ward. This guy defied the profile. Could it be related to brain injury? Intense swelling verses less inflammation. He couldn't make any definitive conclusions, yet. "When did you write these out?"

"After each one," Henry responded coldly. "When you read them, you won't see any emotion, if that's what you're looking for. It's all facts. I don't feel any emotion. That all dissolved out of me when I was a kid. I never cried. I'm not good at showing love, either. But I'm sure as hell a good actor."

"Oh, yeah?" the sergeant asked. "What about those babies room you got back there? Looks like you put a lot of love into decorating them. Wait till you two see those."

"Yeah, well. I love to decorate. I love inanimate things, not people. Okay, hold on. I do love children. Look, I know

I'd be a great dad. I certainly know what not to do, now don't I?"

Frank pushed, not to become emotionally attached to this guy. Slater was making that difficult. "What else is in there?"

Henry opened the case. He took out the manila envelope with his will and turned it face down on the table next to him. "Here are seventeen stacks of hundred dollar bills, one-hundred-sixty-thousand dollars in each for my victims' families. Tell them I'm sorry." He pushed the open case to the center of the table. "Anyone want a drink?" He started to rise and the sergeant pushed him down. He sneered at Crane. "Okay, there are bottles of water in the fridge. Bring out a few."

One of the officers went into the kitchen and pulled out bottles of water.

As soon as the officer brought them back, Henry twisted off the cap and guzzled half a bottle. "Okay, now this thing," He turned over the will, and pulled the documents out from the envelope.

He turned toward Carl. "You're the oldest, so you're my Executor."

Carl leaned in. "Excuse me?"

"Hey, you're an attorney. What's so difficult to understand?"

"Aren't you jumping the gun with this?" Frank asked.

"No. Just listen. There's way more in here than I'm telling you now. I split up my assets between the kids, held in a trust, which you, Carl, will set up until they're twenty-one, but Abby gets hers when she finishes her sentence, and it's not to be used for her defense. You two have a choice, keep this building—Samantha loves this apartment, especially the babies rooms—or sell it and split it. I never took out a life insurance policy—"

Frank's mind reeled. What Sam told him in the analysis of the scorpion came back into mind.

When a scorpion is blocked in, to avoid capture, they'd sting themselves to death. Henry intends suicide.

"Because I never had—"

"Henry, do you have a weapon?"

"What are you talking about, Frank? They searched me and the entire apartment." He drank the rest of the bottle of water. "All this water made me have to go take a piss. It's right over there."

"All right, go," the sergeant replied.

Henry got up and headed to his bathroom.

Frank jumped up out of his seat. "No! Don't let him go."

"Oh, one more thing before I take a leak. Frank, you will take a visit to our parents. It's documented in there. Then the will goes into effect."

"Where are they?"

"Somewhere in Central Florida. Tell them what a monster they created. But they're not to get a dime." He headed to the bathroom, prying something from his pocket, pretended to shield a cough, and slipped it into his mouth.

Frank noticed that minute action. "Sergeant! Stop him!" He jumped up and pushed through the officers. They blocked him, holding his arms. He kicked the four of them in rapid succession, knocking three down and he jumped over the middle two who lay on the tile floor.

"Dr. Khaos!" Crane yelled. "We have to be humane. We can't deny someone physical comfort."

"He's going to end it by himself. Stop him!"

Henry entered his bathroom and slammed the door. His urinating was heard, and less than a minute later, another sound—a two-hundred-seventy-pound thud onto the tile floor with his body pushing the door open and his head landing hard. His hands grasped his neck, his pupils dilated, and his fingertips turned pink. Foam spilled from his mouth.

"Cyanide," the sergeant yelled as his team got into action to call EMS and the local precinct. "We don't have the anecdote for that with us."

One officer bent over Henry and started to pound on his chest in the CPR rhythm but did not attempt mouth-to-mouth resuscitation. "Almond odor. Cyanide confirmed."

Frank left them, yelling Sam's name. He pushed the bedroom door open and saw her awake but trembling.

"What the hell took you so long? Seesh."

He pulled the blanket off her and stared at the rope design around her body, her arms, holding her knees and arms together. He held back tears. "Oh God, Sam, always the wiseass. Where in hell do I find how to open these?"

"The shears on the night table. Henry said it was for precaution."

"He had everything planned. Down to his death. Looks like Cyanide." Frank stared at the design, not knowing where to start. He picked up a single column. It took several sawing movements to get through the rope. Her breathing was labored. So was his.

"Hold on." She lifted her head and struggled to move it forward. "He pushed the bow into here."

Frank followed her gaze to the top of her hands that lay on top of her knees. He dug in and pulled up the bow. The connections unraveled and he attempted to unwind her legs. It was awkward. He had to pause a few moments to find the correct direction to pull the rope.

When Sam was almost free—her ankles were still bound and rope dangled—but she was able to straighten out her legs, he pulled her into his arms "Oh, man, Sam, I was never so afraid of losing you. I love you."

With both arms around his neck, she broke down crying. "I love you too, Frank. But do you love me enough?"

"Yeah, I do, princess. Yes. I sure do. You should have seen Frankie stand up to Slater defending us as a family, Sam."

"A family?"

"Yeah, a family. Samantha Wright, will you marry me? And be Frankie's mom?"

She clutched him for dear life. "Yes, Frank. Oh my God, yes!"

A loud applause came from the bedroom doorway. The ESU team, Case, Lex, and Bella didn't stop applauding and whistling.

Frank covered Sam with the blanket. "Some privacy, please?"

Sergeant Crane came in. "No can do. Get the rest of the ropes off her feet and she has to get checked out. She's going to the hospital. EMS is here." He left as abruptly as he entered and closed the door.

Frank, sliced the rope all around Sam's feet, and she slipped them out of the remaining loop. Then he saw her. "Oh man, Sam. You do look cute in a diaper."

She swatted his bicep.

છગ્ચ

They kept Sam until noon the next day in the ER of the hospital that was a few blocks away from Henry Slater's building. Dehydrated and hungry, both needs were met, but she was antsy to get back to work. As much as she pleaded to the doctors, they wouldn't let her leave. They had given her tests up the wazoo—six-hours' worth, working to two a.m.—everything from blood work, EKG, a cardiac stress test, a trauma survey to test her stress level. The more the doctors pressured her, the more her stress level went up. How did they expect her not to be stressed after what she went through? Talk about inappropriate timing. She yelled at them at a decibel level that surprised even her. It got to the point the docs threatened to have her committed for a psych evaluation.

The doctors wouldn't even allow Case to interview her, and he really didn't need to immediately because he had the wire and recordings of very word and also Frank's wire. A formal debriefing she couldn't escape. And there was so much she needed to know. She heard the thud of Slater falling and Frank confirmed what she thought. However, she didn't hear their conversation in his dining room. Her obsessive-compulsive need to know everything was really put to the test.

She acted so hyper, not being able to make herself comfortable in bed last night, the docs gave her something to help her sleep. It worked. She hadn't had a good night's sleep since Carrie's murder.

She'd have to wait in one of the secluded rooms reserved for law enforcement personnel until Frank picked her up. He was due at any minute. Dressed in a fresh blouse and pair of jeans that Frank brought her last night, she still lay on the bed. She didn't have time to let her mind wander to the case.

Recognizing the two voices in the hall, she sat up, smiling. Frankie ran into the room and straight into her arms. She hugged him tightly. "I wouldn't let Uncle Henry have you, Sam."

"Did you tell him, yet?"

"Not yet. I wanted us to tell him together."

"Tell me what?"

Frank lifted his son onto his lap. "What have you wanted Sam and I to do?"

Frankie's eyes opened wide. "Get married?"

"Yes."

He bopped up and down on his dad's lap. His gaze darted between the two of them. "Are you? You are?"

"Yes we are!" Frank replied, hugging his son. "Now let's get out of here."

Frankie jumped off his dad's lap, yelling, with his arms thrown up into the air, "Yes! Yes! Yes!"

They exited the room to applause and shouts of congratulations by the hospital staff. Sam, still getting used to the idea, flushed and held onto Frank's arm. "Where are we going?"

"We have off till late this afternoon, so first stop is in Brooklyn."

❧❧❧

Sam felt overwhelmed from her first undercover assignment, and not having been debriefed yet left her with so many questions that she didn't talk to Frank until they got into his Explorer.

She felt drained. "Where are we going?"

"Just relax." He lowered the back of her seat. "I want you to close your eyes and nap." She glared at him. "Seriously, the nurse told me they had to give you something to sleep, and that it could also have a residual effect. You may be tired today and even tomorrow. You're not used to that stuff. Take advantage of the rest."

She reclined and in a few minutes, Frank heard her sleeping breath. "Frankie, you up?"

"Yes, Dad, why?"

"We're going to Sam's parents' house," he whispered. "I want to introduce you and ask her dad for Sam's hand in marriage."

"You have to ask permission?"

"They're very old fashioned. Her parents would like that. Now listen to me, champ. I heard your call to Sam. We'll talk about those tests, later. Her father called, too, and spoke with Henry. Dr. Wright got very confused, so we're not going to talk about that, okay? And I don't want you to repeat any of the conversation you heard. Especially the scary parts."

"Why?"

"It's a legal thing. We have to protect Henry's rights. And you and I will talk about it."

"What happens if he asks?"

"I'll try to tell him we'll talk about it when you're not with us. Or that it was a case and Sam was undercover. We can't talk about it too much, anyway because the case isn't closed yet and that's the truth. Understand?"

"Yes."

"I want you to be on your best, most respectful behavior. Got that?"

Frankie rolled his eyes. "

Hey! I saw that."

Frankie laughed. "Okay, Dad. I will. Chill."

Frank tried to hold back a laugh at his son's last word.

ৎৡৎ

Sam's parents sat in the den watching TV in their one-family home in the Madison section of Brooklyn. Befitting their upscale lifestyle, they renovated the entire house over the last year. Creams and some dark greens interspersed in the fabrics and wall décor. The wood paneled floors shone from a recent polishing. The doorbell rang. Her father lifted a panel in the shade behind him with his index finger.

"It's Sam!" He jumped up and hurriedly left the den to answer the bell. As soon as he opened the door, he didn't hesitate to accost her. "What in the world is going on? Where have you been?" He stared up at Frank and then down at Frankie. "We've been worried sick."

"Daddy, can we at least come in?" Sam walked into the living room, with Frank and his son following. They sat on the couch on the wall by the staircase.

"Yes, of course."

Sam's mother approached Frankie with a smile. "And who might you be as if I couldn't guess?"

Frankie giggled. "Frankie."

Sam's mother sat on the couch. "Frank, he's a miniature you."

"He sure is," Frank said proudly. "I'm told that by everyone."

"How old are you, sweetheart?"

"I'm eight."

"You're a big boy for eight!"

Frankie looked up adoringly at his father. "I'll be big like my dad."

Sam's dad sat next to his wife. Apparently, the small talk didn't interest him. "What is going on Sam? Where in the world were you when I called? And who is that man you were with?"

"Dr. Wright, please, take it easy. I'll explain as much as I legally can. Sam was working a case. We had eyes and ears on her. She wore a wire."

Sam relaxed. She figured she'd let Frank take care of it.

"Uncle Henry was a case?"

"Frankie, what did I tell you?"

The boy frowned. "I just didn't know what it was called."

"Who's Uncle Henry, sweetheart?" Sam's mother asked.

"Dad's brother. He just found out he has brothers, and I have cousins. How cool is that?"

"That's very nice," Sam's father said. Sam could guess there was more on his mind.

"Yeah and he has this great house in Manhattan."

"Oh? Okay, Frankie, I'll ask you, since my daughter is short on words today."

"Dad, don't, please." Sam stared at him with eyes wide open and her head tilted toward Frankie.

Dr. Wright hesitated. He had to understand his daughter's tone. He always did. He changed the subject. "Okay, Frankie, so what do you want to be when you grow up?"

"I wanted to be a doctor like my dad."

"That's wonderful, sweetheart. Both of us are doctors, too," Sam's mother said, already enamored with the little boy.

"Yeah, well. I changed my mind."

"When did you do that, champ?"

"Dad, don't be mad."

"I won't be mad. When did you change your mind?"

"When we were in Uncle Henry's house."

Sam cringed. "And what do you want to be, now?"

"Uncle Henry's house was so nice and he makes a lot of money in business, so I want to be an MBA like him. He told me what that means."

"Okay, go for it, champ."

Frankie smiled and bobbed his head. "I liked everything, even his deli sandwiches, except for one thing."

"What's that, sweetheart?" Sam's mother asked adoringly.

"I don't think I'll murder anyone," Frankie said matter-of-factly.

Frank scooped him up into his arms fast and carried him into the den. "What did I tell you? By talking about this, you are going against the law. Do you want to be arrested?"

Frankie whimpered. "No, Dad. I'm sorry."

Sam's parents sat stunned. Sam was ready to explode. She missed that conversation.

Sam's father and she rose at the same time.

"Sam, Dr. Wright, in the kitchen, now, Frankie you say here." He put his son back on the love seat.

"He'll stay here with me." Sam's mom moved next to him. She put her arm around Frankie who started to cry.

"I didn't mean to say anything bad."

"I know you didn't, sweetheart."

❧❧❧

Sam's father leaned against the stainless steel kitchen sink. "What kind of danger are you exposing your child to? And you're a psychiatrist!"

Frank stared sternly at the gray haired man sporting a moustache. "Hold on."

"Don't tell me to hold on. Sam, I don't like this man."

Crap. Get his permission to marry his daughter? Yeah right. Not today.

"No, you listen, sir, not meaning any disrespect, but I know what I'm doing, so does the FBI and NYPD. Sam was protected. Frankie was protected. A full team of the Emergency Service Unit in full gear was in the apartment, along with me."

Dr. Wright sat down at the table. Frank and Sam sat after him. "So what happened?"

"This guy managed to escape the authorities in fourteen states, until he came to New York. He got careless with the last kill, Sam's best friend."

"Carrie?"

Sam started to cry. "Yes, Daddy."

"They got DNA. He wasn't in the system, so they came up with me in an extended search."

"Familial DNA."

"Yes, it's ninety-nine percent accurate. I have another brother, Carl, who's an attorney.

"How was your son involved?"

"Sam was with the guy. Don't get upset, but the FBI treated her as a hostage. Henry knew who she was from the start. He wanted it to stop. He called, saying that he wanted to meet his family before he turned himself in. He wanted to see the kids, too. We negotiated for a full team to sweep the house and stay in there. That's all I can legally say right now."

Dr. Wright compressed his lips. "So how are you going to deal with your son's blurting out what he was party to?"

"We're going to be talking about it, long and hard. It's going to be rough."

"Yes. It is. Kids can't contain themselves like adults. And how are you dealing with the familial DNA?"

"It hit me hard. Especially with the genetic component. I'd be leery about having another child. After we negotiated to have the kids leave, we spoke to him in concrete terms. I can't tell you the conversation but the damage to his brain was from consistent head trauma in childhood and additional damage as an adult, from a fall. I didn't tell Sam this yet." He put his arm around Sam, "but I'm not afraid of having a baby anymore." He kissed the top of her head.

Sam became tearful and wrapped her arms around his torso.

Dr. Wright stood up tall. "Oh no, you're not! You're not even married yet!" He stormed out of the kitchen to the living room.

"We blew it," Sam said in exasperation.

Frank pulled her into his arms. "We'll make this work, princess."

Holding hands, they got up and joined her parents in the living room.

Frankie accosted them as soon as they crossed the threshold into the room. "Did you ask him?"

"No, it wasn't the right time."

Sam's father didn't disguise his angst. "Ask me what? You're the only one I can get a complete and honest answer from."

Sam and Frank slumped down into the couch. Frank smiled. Sam knew what he was thinking. Okay, he'd let his son be the bearer of the good news.

"We came over for my dad to ask your permission to marry Sam."

Sam's mother gasped. Sam followed suit.

"Yeah, and when they get married Sam will be my mom, and I can call you Grandma and Grandpa."

Sam's mother melted. "Oh, Sam." She and Sam got up and Sam embraced her.

"Mommy, I love him so much, and Frankie."

Her mother's eyes reddened as she looked up toward her husband. Tears flowed. Her husband merely nodded and plopped into a chair. He wasn't won over, yet. Frankie picked up on Dr. Wright's expression and gave his dad a quick glance. He got up and walked with intent over to him. The little guy stood between his legs.

"Dr. Wright, we love Sam." The man's expression changed to more relaxed. "And my dad is going to marry

Sam. I don't care what you say." He started to cry. "I already lost one mom, and I'm not going to lose another."

Dr. Wright embraced Frankie with all he had and broke down crying. "Oh my God, Frankie, you're something else. You know that? We're going to love being your Grandma and Grandpa."

CHAPTER 30

At six-fifteen, Sam and Frank literally ran down the hall to the war room in the Queens precinct for the Henry Slater debriefing. She called when they were stuck in traffic on the Brooklyn-Queens Expressway because of a five-car pileup but the FBI doesn't take kindly to excuses. They slowed about a foot from the door. She listened, heard the expected voices then knocked.

"Come in," Lieutenant Hicks yelled.

They entered to a full house. Her gaze traveled to Lieutenant Hicks, Detectives Withers and Richards, Dr. Trenton, the two FBI technicians who controlled the equipment in the van, and Special Agent Case. She and Frank took their seats next to John Trenton.

The lieutenant spoke first. "I want to tell you that everyone in this room listened to the full conversations on the tape so we're not repeating anything now, except for you, Sam, when you were in the bedroom. You'll catch up. I also want to say to you, Detective Wright, thank you for a job well done." Sam smiled. Lieutenant Hicks paused. "And also to the detectives in this precinct, Detectives Withers and Richards, the FBI task-force headed by Special Agent Case, and to Dr. Khaos and Dr. Trenton, as well."

Agent Case took over. "This is the status, thus far. The FBI is going to through everything. Analyzing the confessions alone could take six months. We haven't even touched the will yet. If more connections are revealed through the documents, we'll have to call on your detectives, again. His apartment is now a crime scene, so we have our investigators as well as NYPD Crime Scene on site right now. They've been there since you left the apartment and we expect to be there round the clock, a full week. Detectives Withers and Richards will be there as well for the duration. Then we'll tackle the documentation Slater provided and add to it. Waiting for forensic reports will actually save us time so we don't have to go over the paperwork again. He's prioritized, so it'll be expediently done. And now that he's neutralized, we can afford to wait and take the time. I'll tell you this guy was organized. Lucky for us. We are in possession of two million seven hundred twenty thousand dollars in hundreds that he gave us at the apartment to give to his victim's families." Sam gasped. "Yes, Detective Wright, you didn't hear this part. That's one hundred sixty thousand dollars each—"

Sam interrupted. "That's hardly enough. But I want that going to Carrie's parents, not her creep husband."

"We might not have a choice but we're far from that. So, don't get yourself crazy."

"I'm beyond crazy right now, Agent Case."

Frank pulled her close to him. "Stop," he whispered.

She folded her hands in her lap.

"Again, That money will only be distributed to the families after we fully investigate from which account and business it came from. Remember, we said, he didn't use the name Henry Slater. However, maybe he knew we were getting closer and he changed the accounts back into his name. Who knows? We're getting warrants for his Delaware registered businesses as we speak. We also don't know—and this could be a major game changer—if he had a legitimate partner who rightfully owns half of the monies. We're looking at another year, at the very least. He did say, Detective Wright, he wanted you and Dr. Khaos to live in the apartment if you kept the building. And he wants you to take the furniture in the two babies' rooms if you're not going to live there." Sam's breath hitched. "He also left the building to Dr. Khaos and his brother, Carl Glendale."

John looked at Frank and smiled. "Lucky you."

"What am I going to do with a building like that?"

"An investment," John said, puzzled.

"We're years out on that one. We found the superintendent a couple of hours ago. He was away visiting his children in Maine. The building is in his name and he maintains it. But he knows very well Henry Slater is the owner. He's being interviewed as we speak. He did lead Crime Scene to storage bins in the basement, only because he was asked specifically if Mr. Slater had any, by one of their investigators. Guess what they found in each of three bins?"

"Cash," Sam blurted out.

"Yes. It's estimated to be about two million in small denomination bills, singles, fives, and tens, in each bin. The money has not been removed yet, though it is guarded."

"Crap," spurted from Withers's mouth. "Where in hell did all this money come from? And all liquid? I can't get a couple thousand bucks if I need it, earlier than the due date without a penalty."

"Excellent question, Detective. It's only been a little over twenty-four hours, so believe me, it's a process, and our contact at the casino is dead. One more thing." Agent Case compressed his lips and a solemn expression came over his face. "When we heard you ask him, Detective Wright, how he found you, and he responded, 'want the list?' we sent a local unit to Strident. Unfortunately, they found Madame Lily deceased. Tied up and strangled. Also, with a sedation patch on her shoulder. A crime scene unit is still there as well."

"Oh no." Sam paled. "She had to be leery of him. Did he force himself into her office? Did he torture her? Why would she give us up?"

"We may never know the answers, but we will be interviewing everyone you and I saw at the club." Sam nodded.

"We're going to re-interview everyone and Mike Shef-field's family," Case continued. "I hope that, on Slater's computer, we'll find his vendors. Did he pay them or scam them? We have so many questions. Right now, all of the monies we have are being deposited into an escrow account the FBI will set up. Detective Withers, have any updates?"

"Yes, actually." Withers opened his file. "You were cor-rect, again, Detective Wright." Sam hiked her brows. "We were able to speak to five of the vic's parents. They con-firmed it. Their daughters always told them they didn't want children. We'll reach the others but the answers will probably be the same."

"Wow. Okay, so if Slater wanted children, he must have interviewed the women as he did me. That came up in our initial conversation, way before the bedroom."

"Then why did he even bother to get to the bedroom?" Withers asked.

"For one," Frank said, "his murders were premeditated. He came prepared to kill, having his supplies. Second, he was getting even with his mother—"

Sam interrupted. "But wouldn't that make him not want children?"

"Let me finish, please. To answer your question, Sam, no. He told you how much he wanted children, what a great dad he'd be. He wanted to do the opposite of his parents. He looked for highly educated women, which his mother was not, probably for the more intelligent genes. Summer told us, as did the other women we interviewed that he nev-er got violent. And he told you, Sam, that they were great for sex, but not as a life-partner."

"Okay, Frank," Bella said. "So you're telling me, at his age, he still hadn't found a woman that could be a life-partner and the mother of his children? That's trying way too hard if you ask me."

"Maybe not."

"Hold on, Frank," Withers said. "Are you thinking there might be little Henry Slater's running around out there?"

Frank paused, compressing his lips before he spoke. "Yeah. I could have many more nieces and nephews."

"Then where are they?" Agent Case said. "There was no sign of children in the apartment."

"The apartment was child proofed," Sam answered. "There was no glass in the furniture. Everything had rounded edges. He had diapers and baby wipes. I didn't have a chance to look around. They're probably with their mothers who he let live."

"If the children are safe and sound with their mothers, I'm good." Brett paused to scan his notes. "Dr. Khaos, there was a post it note on the inside of the briefcase."

"And?"

"We heard him tell you and Carl that before the will is executed, that he wanted you to deliver a rather unpleasant message to your birth parents."

"Too bad we can't," Frank said, relieved. "Detectives Withers and Richards tried to track down the Andrews Agency that handled Carl's adoption. They've been closed since the nineties, with no paper trail."

Case let out a deep breath and pulled a copy of the post-it off his notes. "Here. Your birth parents are Joshua Hunter and Camille Hunter, formerly Camille Carter. They're both sixty-one, living now in Crystal River, Florida." Frank looked at Case as if his eyes threw daggers. "Take it."

Frank shot up and left the room without looking back.

Everyone in the room looked at each other, not knowing what to do or who should respond.

Sam started to get up. "Damn, he can't get a break."

"What happened, Sam?" John asked.

"My father practically hit him over the head yesterday. The idea of us getting married made my dad's blood boil. Thanks to Frankie, my dad accepted it."

John got up, patted Sam on her shoulder. "Sit. Let me handle it."

e✧e✧

Frank meandered to the small lounge at the end of the hall. Institutional green leatherette cushioned armchairs connected into small groupings. The walls were even a more bland green, matching his mood, perfectly. He sat with his legs apart, hunched over with his hands clasped between his legs.

He looked up as John's shadow came into his view. "Hey, man."

John sat in the chair next to him. "Want to talk?"

"Nothing to talk about. This was the last thing in the world I ever wanted to do was see my birth parents. I never ever let it enter my mind. First, Carl, okay, I can deal with him, then Slater, and it's his wishes I have to carry out? Isn't there a law saying I don't have to?"

"No. Even those on death row can have their dying declaration."

"And if I don't go?"

"Simple. All the monies go to the government."

Frank emitted a sarcastic laugh.

"Look," John continued. "If all this money is legit and can be distributed, the kids can have a pretty good life. Bottom line, if you don't go, you're not the only one affected."

"Where the hell is Crystal River?"

"Don't laugh. It's not far from my parents. Has some pretty cool stuff for Frankie to see. Manatees, a wild life park that has a fifty-three-year-old hippo named Lu, springs for going tubing in, alligators, lots of alligators."

Frank stared at him, dumbstruck.

"No, seriously, you'll love it. Frankie will see cows and horses grazing in the grass alongside the roads, farms with fresh produce, oh, and no potholes or pollution."

"You know how to do the hard sell, don't you?"

"It's not only that. And you need to think long and hard about what I'm about to tell you."

"What?

"As much as Ricky's parents abused him, they gave up parental rights right before he came back to Vicki and me, freeing up the adoption. I sent them thank you letters for allowing that so he could have a better life."

"You're kidding me?"

"No, I'm not. And you might want to do that, too. I bet you'll feel cleansed."

"You want me to thank two people who created a serial killer with such craziness in the home?"

"But they didn't have a chance to do it to you and Carl. They freed the both of you. It's too late for them to be arrested, but Ricky's parents will be in prison a long time. They placed you and your brother for adoption so your adoptive parents could save your lives. Though, for you, it took a while."

"You may be right. Too bad my brain can't absorb it right now. Being in the mental health field or not, it's going to take its toll." Frank ran his hands over his head and exhaled deeply. "When can we go?"

"How about Spring break?"

"That's in April. I have Frankie's schedule memorized."

"Okay, in two and a half months. Plenty of time to arrange it. We'll all go. Though I'm just getting back, I think it'll fly so I can be your support. I'll arrange it with the captain. You can stay with us. My parents have plenty of room."

"Your brain works too fast for me, man. Yeah, okay. Thanks. Still don't know about the 'thank you,' though. And what about you?"

"What about me?"

"Didn't that doc, Charles Matthews, tell you 'no more hostage situations'?"

"Yes. And I did my due diligence. Agent Case backed me and sent a report that ESU was safeguarding the apartment before I came in. We're good."

ознഌ

It was a cold sunny day the last day in January, but luckily, for visitors, there was no snow on the ground to slow them down. Frank drove through the entry gate of the Jewish Cemetery in Nassau County and pulled into a spot by the main office. Blurry-eyed, Sam took in the beautiful landscaping—what would be beautiful come spring. Right now, the barren bushes and trees sent a message through her—that the universe still mourned for Carrie. That comforted her, at least her best friend, her sister for life, wasn't forgotten. She quivered in the passenger seat as her hands rested on the map of the grounds.

Sniffling, Sam unfolded the map and pointed. She leaned toward Frank and with her gloved finger showed him the route. She wouldn't have been able to get any words out so pointing would have to do. She took tissues out of her bag and blew her nose.

"Are you sure you're up for this, Sam?"

"How can you say that? Of course I am."

"I can say this because you've been non-stop since this case began."

"So has everyone else on board. Okay, she's all the way up at the other end. Take this road to your right, and go three streets up."

Frank pulled out and followed her directions. "Damn, these rows are narrow." The car's tires bumped over rocks in the road.

"It's meant for only one car at a time. Come on, you did it before."

"No, we came in the back entrance for the funeral. It was right there," he said pointing to the area on the map.

"Then why didn't you do that again?"

"Because, you told me to go in here and I didn't want to argue and upset you more."

"Ugh! Frank, okay, just drive. I'm sorry. Turn left, go up five streets." He waited at the first cross street to allow a car to pass then continued. "Now make a right and take it all the way up to the end." She sat back in the seat and repeatedly inhaled and exhaled deeply.

Dara, please help calm me down.

"Oh, I forgot to ask you. Did you ask Theresa to protect me when Slater had me?"

Frank did a double take. "Yes, I did."

"Well, she did when you all were having your meeting. I felt her arms around me and under the ropes to loosen them, I really felt her, Frank." She patted his hand. "She's with you."

"She's with us, princess. We're here. Ready?"

"Ready as I'll ever be. It's right over there. Collect rocks."

"Why?"

"It's tradition to put rocks around, instead of leaving flowers." Sam got out of the Explorer and walked slowly to the gravesite of Carolyn Baines, picking up rocks. Crying uncontrollably, she bent down on her knees on the mud—no grass or headstone yet, just a ground marker—and leaned back on her heels. "Hi, Carrie," she said, with the tears impeding her speech, "I'm—here." She blew her nose and tried to contain herself by first running her hand over her mouth and holding it there. "Carrie," she exhaled a deep breath, "Okay, I'm good now. Carrie, you can rest easy now." Tears started again. She coughed. "Guess I'm not so good. But we found him, Carrie. He's not going to hurt another woman again. He's dead. Exactly what he should be." Clouds passed over the sun. Sam looked up at the sky. She nodded. "Thanks for giving me the signal you heard me, Carrie."

The cloud moved past her and to the left. She brought herself up, leaning on Frank for balance. She opened her hands, held them together, and he dropped several more rocks into them, keeping a few for himself. Sniffling, Sam placed rocks all around the marker.

These are from everyone who worked on your case, Carrie. There were tons of us so I can't mention everyone but I have to do justice and tell you some. I know you'd want to know so you can thank them in your own way. First, my partner Nick Valatutti, he's the one who got the Queens precinct to listen to us. He had to leave for a couple of weeks to take care of a health issue with his wife. But he'll be back, and Thank God his wife will be okay. Detectives Lex Withers and Bella Richards knocked themselves out for you, Carrie. Bella had her strange points, but hey, don't we all? Special Agent for the FBI, Brett Case, I have to tell you, Carrie, this man knew his stuff. The way he kept eyes and ears on me to keep me safe from Slater, I'll be forever grateful. And the ESU teams, you know what they are, the Emergency Service Unit, they followed protocol to the T. Oooh, Carrie, I must tell you, Dr. John Trenton's wife, Vicki, she's teaching me how to cook. You remember all the bad meal stories we told each other, and I'm sure John had some heart-to-heart conversations with Frank. Yeah, Frank Khaos, from the Aries case who I told you at first I couldn't stand? Well, since we haven't spoken in a month, that's all turned around now, to love. Frank's been my rock, Carrie. We had our ups-and-downs and we're getting married. You're the first of our friends to know. And I have to tell you, Carrie, Frank is now my BFF, coming in second to you. I'll call your parents so they can rest easy now, but I wanted you to be the first to know. I'll always love you, Carrie Baines.

Sam rose and put more stones around the grave. She nodded to Frank that she was done. Reaching his side, she interlocked her arm in his.

As they walked to the car, Frank's cell rang. "Yeah, Khaos." He paused. "We'll be there ASAP."

Sam looked up.

"We have to go. Now."

The End

To be continued.
Book Four, Libra.
Henry Slater's children,
coming soon
From Ronnie Allen and
Black Opal Books.

About the Author

Ronnie Allen is a New York City native, born and bred in Brooklyn New York, where she was a teacher in the New York City Department of Education for thirty-three years. As a New York State licensed School Psychologist, she was given the opportunity to be one of three educators to create a unit in her school for emotionally needy students. Her various roles included classroom teacher, staff developer, crisis intervention specialist, and mentor for teachers who were struggling. Always an advocate for the child, Allen carries this through as themes in all of her novels which focus around the health and wellbeing of children.

In the early 1990s Allen began a journey into holistic healing and alternative therapies. She actually completed her PhD in Parapsychic Sciences in 2001, writing the dissertation when she was home for four months recuperating from being in a coma for twelve days. Medical science had given up on her and told her husband and son that she had less than a two-percent chance of survival. Well surprise, surprise! Here she is! Definitely the survivor. And so are her characters!

Along the way, Allen has picked up many certifications. She is a Board Certified Holistic Health Practitioner as well as a crystal therapist, Reiki practitioner, metaphysician, dream analyst and Tarot Master Instructor. She has taught workshops in New York City and in Central Florida where she now lives in all of these mediums both in person and online with the goal being to teach people how to make the mind body connection for their healing and personal growth.

Combining a love of the crime genre and her psychology background, with her alternative therapies experience, writing psychological thrillers is the perfect venue for her.

CPSIA information can be obtained
at www.ICGtesting.com
Printed in the USA
BVOW08s0850050218

507254BV00027B/1135/P